Part III of the American
Kitsune Series

Written by Brandon Varnell

Illustrated by Kirsten Moody

ISBN-10: 0692533311
ISBN-13: 978-0692533314

WORDS YOU SHOULD KNOW!

Chūnibyō: A Japanese term that roughly translates to Middle School Second Year Syndrome. People with Chūnibyō are often teens, but can also sometimes adults. They have trouble separating reality from their own delusions and tend to think they have special powers.

Tsundere: A term used to describe someone who has a cold and sometimes frosty personality at first, but generally reveals a warmer, softer side over the course of a story.

CONTENTS

DEDICATIONS

There are many people that I'd like to dedicate this book to; people who made writing this possible. They've been a big help throughout my journey to become an author, and it's been their encouragement that has given me the will to reach out and try to attain my dreams. My parents, my sister and her husband, my editor and proofreader, my illustrator and, just as importantly, my readers. All of these people have helped me in my journey to write this book. To them I will forever remain grateful. Thank you.

Chapter 1

Some Things Change, Others Stay the Same

Lilian awoke to the new day with a smile.

Sitting up in Kevin's bed, the sheets falling away from her vivacious frame, she stretched her arms high above her head, her exertions accompanied by cute noises that would have knocked Eric Corrompere out cold had he been present to hear them.

"It's a good thing Eric isn't here," Lilian said, seemingly to herself, even as she groaned from the pleasant sensation of her muscles stretching taut.

The neck of her shirt—it was actually one of Kevin's, but he had given it to her—slid off her shoulders to reveal silky smooth skin. She absently slid the neckline back up before looking out the window. It was a beautiful day outside; the sky was a clear, light blue, and the sun was shining down upon the earth with its radiant beams of light. It was the perfect day for her and Kevin to go out and do something fun.

Speaking of Kevin...

Lilian looked down at the floor to see her beloved mate—or the person who she hoped would one day become her mate. Kevin was in his sleeping bag, lying on his back. She could see his chest rising and falling at a slow, steady and reassuring pace. His breathing was deep and even, a sure sign that he was sleeping heavily.

Crawling out of bed with ninja-like stealth, Lilian made her way to Kevin's prone form until she was literally on top of him. Her body lightly straddled his; she didn't apply enough pressure to wake him, but even so, she could still feel the natural heat that his body emitted. She missed sleeping with that heat, but knew she could get it back soon. Lindsay was officially out of the running for his heart, and the only other person she had to contend with was that *tsundere* goth loli. It was no contest.

Leaning down, she pressed her lips to his forehead. Her tails also moved forward and gently poked his temples. The two fluffy appendages glowed a whitish yellow for a brief moment, before the light faded.

She leaned back and smiled. The enchantment she had cast would be enough to ensure that he continued sleeping—at least until she finished preparing everything that she needed to wow and impress him.

The kiss was not a necessary part of the enchantment. She just kissed him because she wanted to.

After getting off her chosen mate, Lilian made her way to the bathroom, where she took a very brief shower.

She would have normally taken her time getting clean. Like most kitsune, Lilian enjoyed the finer things in life, which included long hot showers and even longer baths. One of her many guilty pleasures was sitting under the spray of the shower, allowing the hot droplets to run down her body and soothe the muscles in her back—or lounging in the hot bath, letting the soothing heat soak into her body and lull her into a sense of contentment. She couldn't do that today. There were several very important things that she needed to do, and she wanted to accomplish them as quickly as possible. The sooner they were completed, the better.

The first item on her list was choosing something to wear that would catch Kevin's attention. Before now, all of the clothes she'd worn were sexy little numbers, their sole purpose being to send men into a state of aroused delirium. They were the kind of clothes that emphasized her inhumanly beautiful body and generous proportions.

It had become increasingly obvious to her that those kinds of outfits wouldn't work on Kevin. It wasn't that he didn't like seeing her in them—she had seen very convincing evidence that he did, indeed, enjoy seeing her in them—but that he simply couldn't handle her sexy outfits… yet. She was positive that would change if she gave him a few more months to accept and return her love. She just needed to be patient.

Nodding to herself, she entered their bedroom while wearing nothing but a towel and rummaged through the dresser where she kept all of her nightwear.

While she normally would have put on her daytime clothes, Lilian's purpose this morning was to get his attention, and nothing got attention better than lingerie. Even if she didn't have any intention of donning one of her more sinful garments, she still wanted to wear something eye-catching. And regular, everyday clothing just wasn't eye-catching enough in her mind.

Unless it was extraordinarily skimpy.

Reaching into the drawer, Lilian pulled out the first article of clothing that she could find. She blinked once, and then frowned. The item in her hand was a pink lingerie dress made of partially translucent material and a dark pink G-string. Definitely not something that Kevin would be able to enjoy without flipping out. Or passing out. Whichever came first.

Onto the next selection then!

The next item she grabbed was even worse: a leopard print two-piece. The bra-like top was held up by a pair of really thin black strings, and dipped into a V-cut that showed off a more than generous portion of her cleavage. Black gauze-like material with floral embroidery around the bust ensured that her nipples would barely be covered.

The bottom was even worse. It was just a rhomboidal-shaped patch of leopard print fabric connected to the top with two small metal circlets, which was barely held together by thin black strings. The fabric didn't extend to cover her butt. It was just a small string that went between her cheeks and left her small, shapely rear completely exposed.

This was definitely not something that Kevin would be able to withstand. It was almost a certainty that he would pass out from this.

Next!

Lilian grabbed another item from her drawer.

Her left eye twitched.

She shoved the article back in and grabbed another garment.

Her left eye twitched again, and it brought friends.

Her right eye began twitching, too.

After rejecting several more outfits, Lilian was at her wits end.

"They're all too sexy!" She grabbed at her hair and moaned. "How am I supposed to get Kevin's attention if he's too busy freaking out to even pay attention to me?!"

You're the one who bought those clothes.

"Quiet you!"

Hey, don't get mad at me. I didn't force you to buy those clothes. This is all your fault for not having the foresight to choose less revealing nightwear.

"!!!!"

Right. Quiet. I'm being quiet now.

Lilian huffed in anger, feeling a chill of annoyance run down her spine before turning her attention back to her current problem. She supposed that she could just wear one of her normal outfits, but she wanted to wear something that would really turn Kevin's head. It had to be something cute, something that would make him stare—if not in lust, then at least in admiration.

Why don't you just wear one of his shirts and a pair of pajama bottoms?

"I thought I told you to..." Lilian trailed off from the beginning of her angry tirade, a thoughtful expression crossing her face. She looked up at the ceiling, her eyes glazing over as she pondered the suggestion. "You know... that's not a bad idea. I suppose I should thank you..."

You're welcome.

"Don't get a big head now," Lilian mumbled as she grabbed some clothes from Kevin's drawer and laid them on the bed. After a couple minutes in which she did nothing but stare, Lilian chose what she believed to be the best combination of the bunch: A small black T-shirt with a strange-looking white helmet on the front, and black pajama bottoms with a symbol she had seen on the controller to Kevin's game system running along the fabric like polka dots.

They were perfect. They wouldn't show off a lot of skin, but the shirt was very small and would be a tight fit around her chest, the better to show off her impressive bust. That it also revealed a tantalizing glimpse of her flat stomach was just a bonus.

After putting them on, Lilian moved over to the full-body

mirror on the closet door and looked herself over.

"Hmmm…" She spun around. "It's not bad… but I think it's missing something." It took her a moment, but the answer soon came to her. "Ah-ha!" With two swift motions, Lilian used her enhanced strength to tear the bottom half of the pajama pants off. Now, instead of pajama bottoms that went all the way down to her feet, they were shorts that only covered enough so that her bottom wasn't showing—unless she bent over. "There. It's perfect."

Um, no it isn't.

Lilian narrowed her eyes. "Yes, it is."

Isn't the whole purpose of this to keep Kevin from passing out?

"Of course it is. Why else do you think I'm not wearing any of my sexy lingerie?"

But isn't ripping his pajamas like that basically putting you back to square one? You know he's going to flip out, if not because your butt is practically showing, then because you ripped his pajamas.

Lilian scoffed.

"You clearly don't understand how the male mind works. This clothing is a lot less suggestive than any of the other articles I have, but it still shows off how desirable I am." Lilian smiled at herself in the mirror. Her reflection smiled back. "Yes, the moment Kevin catches a glimpse of me, he'll lose all sense of self-restraint, throw me onto the bed, and make me scream out his name in blissful ecstasy until my throat grows hoarse and I become a quivering mess of post-orgasmic bliss."

Uh… huh… right. You clearly haven't learned anything from the previous three weeks, have you?

"Did you say something?"

Not a thing.

"Good."

Lilian stared at her reflection in the mirror for a moment longer before nodding. She looked perfect. Kevin would definitely fall in love with her once he got a glimpse of how attractive she was—and this time he wouldn't pass out from overstimulation….

… Hopefully.

With the task of selecting her outfit complete, the only tasks left were to cook breakfast and wake her mate with a kiss. Then they would enjoy a nice meal together and he would see how much she loved him, after which he would bend her over the table and have his wicked way with her. It was the perfect plan. A plan worthy of a kitsune.

With a giggle, she skipped to the kitchen.

"Ufufufu…"

***

It was early in the morning when Kevin Swift woke up and tried rousing Lilian from her slumber.

"Lilian. Wake up, Lilian."

He wasn't having much success.

"Come on, Lilian. It's time to get up."

Kevin frowned as Lilian refused to wake, as if she'd been trapped within a deep sleep—or in a coma. She didn't even wake up when he raised the volume of his voice, or when he began to incessantly shake her shoulder. The fox-girl just continued resting on her side, her red hair fanning across the bed like an extra sheet of silk.

Lilian had kicked the covers off some time ago, which gave him an unfettered glimpse of her heart-shaped buttocks, covered only by a pair of purple panties. The curve of her hips flowed into a pair of gorgeous legs, one stretched out languidly against the bed while the other bent at the knee. She wore a dopey smile, and would occasionally let out cute giggles at intermittent intervals. She was clearly experiencing a very pleasant dream.

His eyes began twitching as another giggle emerged from Lilian's gently parted Cupid's Bow lips. He decided that a bit more force might be necessary to wake the girl. Thus, he grabbed her shoulder, and shook her with a little more strength than he'd used previously.

"Lilian, you need to wake up now. I've made breakfast for you, and you don't want the breakfast I made getting cold, do you?"

Unfortunately for Kevin, the lovely fox-girl still refused to wake. She just mumbled something incoherent—he could have sworn he'd heard the word "Beloved" somewhere in there, but couldn't be sure—and snuggled deeper into her pillow.

"Lilian, if you don't get up right now, I'll—what the heck?!"

Kevin yelped when Lilian's prone form suddenly sprang into action. Before he could even contemplate what was happening the redhead jumped at him, wrapping her arms around his waist as she slammed into him with a surprising amount of force.

Unable to maintain his balance Kevin tumbled to the ground, taking Lilian with him. For a moment, his world became disoriented, his vision spinning around like a car that had been flipped in an accident. When the moment ended, Kevin's breath left him as his back smacked against the white-carpeted floor.

It took him several seconds to reorient himself, mostly because his mind was rattling around inside of his skull. Everything appeared blurry, moving in and out of focus. When he finally regained his bearings, Kevin gained a newfound appreciation for his situational altercation.

He was lying on his back. On the floor. Lilian was on top of him, still asleep somehow, her legs straddling his waist and her face nuzzling against his chest. Kevin wasn't one-hundred percent sure, but he could almost swear his housemate was purring—which he found odd, because he knew for a fact that foxes didn't purr. They lacked the proper larynx, laryngeal muscles, and neural oscillator that allowed cats to purr.

Her crotch was also rubbing against the pitched tent that had suddenly sprung forth in his pants, proving that, even if she didn't know it, her body and actions did indeed have an effect on him.

"Lilian! What do you think you're—"

Kevin couldn't finish his sentence, because Lilian giggled in her sleep… and stuck her hands underneath his shirt to begin feeling him up. It was the latter action that caused him to lose the ability to form coherent sentences.

"Oh, Beloved. I'm so glad you've realized that I'm the only one for you!"

"The only—" Kevin's face grew hot. Red hot. It blazed with the fire of a million suns. "Lilian, what are you saying?!"

Lilian just giggled. Her eyes were closed as she continued nuzzling his chest with her nose. She was quite obviously still asleep.

"Now we can get to the kissing…"

Kevin's face turned an even darker shade of crimson, like a sun that was about to go nova. It burned with a ferocious intensity that could only be matched by females found in *shōjo* manga.

Kevin could feel his masculinity points dropping by the second—good thing they weren't hit points, or his HP gauge would already be in the red.

"And the petting…"

Steam started pouring out his ears. Her words conjured all sorts of erotic images, scenes of him caressing Lilian's bountiful body; fondling her magnificent breasts, grabbing her shapely butt, and doing all sorts of other naughty and titillating things to her—things that would have made his friend Eric die from blood loss.

"And you can finally bend me over the table, rip off my clothes, and ravish me to your heart's content!"

It was her last comment that finally did Kevin in. In all honesty, he had been finished even before Lilian's last words. They were simply the final nail in the coffin for him.

Without warning, all of the blood that had not already rushed down to his male anatomy went straight to his head. Kevin Swift passed out, blood spurting from his nose like a broken fire hydrant. He was gone long before his head, jet-propelled by the massive quantities of carnelian fluid shooting from his nostrils in an almost never-ending stream, smacked against the floor.

All the while Lilian—who, surprisingly enough, didn't get any of the blood launched from Kevin's nasal passages on herself—continued giggling in her sleep, completely oblivious to the fact that she had just made him pass out via a nosebleed, one that would have put all the nosebleeds Eric ever had from his audaciously perverted antics to shame.

Too bad. She would have been rather proud of her accomplishment.

***

"W-w-what are you saying?!"

Despite the amount of blood rushing to Christine's porcelain cheeks, they felt incredibly cold, like a winter's chill back home in Alaska. It didn't take long for her to realize what that meant; she was blushing. A yuki-onna's face didn't get hot when they blushed, instead growing cold as their powers spiraled out of control, which may have also contributed to the crazy amount of mist and frost gathering in the room at that moment.

"W-w-we can't do that here! Are you crazy?!"

"Oh, but I am crazy. Crazy for you." The figure standing before her spoke in a male voice that sounded articulate and smooth. His tone was softer than silk and more honeyed than a high-class male prostitute. "But you already knew that, didn't you?"

His blue eyes stared into her own crystalline orbs, smoldering with the kind of passion that made her knees weak and her heart race to the beat of ten-thousand drums. He took a step forward. Then another. His messy blond locks swayed with each step, hovering over his eyes and creating an alluring aura of mystique that nearly froze Christine in place.

Nearly froze, because as he moved toward her with his slow and steady gait, like a predator stalking its prey, she took one involuntary step back to counter his increasing closeness. However, while she did indeed move backwards, a part of her wanted him to reach her, to capture her, to pin her in place and claim her mind, body and soul. She squashed this part with ruthless efficiency—or rather, she tried to. She didn't have much success.

"W-we shouldn't..." The pale blue dusting her cheeks, reminiscent of winter, darkened in hue, becoming deeper and spreading across the bridge of her nose. The color complemented her nearly translucent white skin. "... I-i-it's not right."

He smirked at her, and in doing so, made Christine's breathing hitch and her heart skip a beat.

"Oh, but it is right. Nothing could possibly be more right than what we're about to do."

Christine stopped moving, or rather, the wall behind her impeded her ability to move anymore. This did not stop him, and he continued moving forward until his body was practically melded to hers. A combined noise of surprised gasp and pleased moan escaped her parted lips as his masculine body pressed against her more feminine one. A most unusual heat pooled in her loins, contrasting sharply with her cool body temperature.

"No... I don't want this..." she muttered, half-heartedly trying to push him away even as her heart begged to let him take her.

"But you do," he countered, his eyes narrowing in a

combination of amusement and bishounen sensuality. Christine noted that the only thing he needed to be a picture-perfect pretty boy was an inordinate amount of sparkles surrounding him. "You would have used your powers to freeze me in place if you didn't want this."

Christine had nothing to say to that. It was true. She was just being stubborn.

"I want you, Christine."

Christine gasped, both at the way he said her name—with an intense, sensual growl that caused her panties to become damp—and the way he ground his pelvis against hers, sending tendrils of arcing ecstasy through her body, like an electric jolt, only infinitely more pleasant.

"I want you so badly, Christine," he continued, his lips hovering right next to her ear. His breath was hot on her earlobe, sending goosebumps across her skin and a delightful tingle through her core. "And if you don't want me, then you'd better push me away now, before I end up doing something you'll regret."

She looked into his eyes, their foreheads nearly touching they were so close. His blue eyes were hooded with desire, with lust, for her. He wanted her, badly. And if she was being honest with herself, Christine wanted him just as much.

Her eyes fluttered closed as she tilted her head up and parted her ice-blue lips. He wrapped his arms more tightly around her waist, pulling her closer against his solid, masculine body. She quickly wound her arms around his neck in return.

Was this it? Was this the moment she had been waiting for? The moment they would...

"Christine."

His hot breath washed over her mouth, causing her body to shudder pleasantly. She could feel her desire for this man, for this moment, burning within her. She'd never desired something so fervently before. It caused her unbearably chilly body to undergo a most pleasant combustion.

"Yes, Kevin?" Her voice was nothing more than a breathy whisper filled with longing.

"It's time for you to get up."

"What?"

***

Christine opened her eyes...

... and found herself staring at a ceiling. Her ceiling. There was an annoying beeping in her ear—her alarm clock, she realized belatedly. She blinked several times, lifting her hand to shut the infernal noise-making machine off, while also taking note of her sudden surroundings. Her body was covered in a thin layer of sweat and felt incredibly cold, even though she had the heater turned up to 95 degrees. There was a slight damp spot on her sheets underneath her bum—and along her inner thighs. Her left hand was also buried in her panties.

She blinked several more times.

Then her face became mottled with righteous anger... and shame, but mostly righteous anger.

Tsundere mode: activated.

"T-t-t-that IDIOT!" Christine roared, throwing her sheets off and jumping out of bed, her face bluer than a blueberry popsicle. Steam burst out of her ears like an eruption of Old Faithful. The walls, floor and ceiling became covered in a layer of ever-expanding hoarfrost, which moved along every surface like an alien entity threatening to invade her personal space.

Christine barely noticed what her out-of-control powers were doing to her room, busy as she was raging.

"I can't believe it! First he barges back into my life like some kind of sparkly vampire from a teenage romance novel, then he has the gall to not even remember me, and now he's invading my dreams, too?!"

Christine's mind conjured an image of Kevin, his handsome face smiling as he told her how he hoped they could become friends. Her face became a much darker shade of blue, as a combination of outrage and embarrassment swept through her body with the power and intensity of a Category 5 hurricane.

"DIE!"

Several shards of ice flew from her hands to impale the wall behind the imaginary vision of Kevin that her mind had conjured. She didn't even notice that she had just punctured several holes in her wall.

"You think you can invade my dreams like that, asshole?! I'll show you!"

More ice flew from her hands, turning the wall into Swiss cheese. Christine remained utterly oblivious to the destruction she was causing to her own house. She would have noticed in any other circumstances, but her outrage was such that the only thing on her mind was killing the illusory image of Kevin, which her subconscious had projected for her to take her frustrations out on.

"DIE! DIE! DIE! DIE!"

***

"I'm really sorry about that, Kevin," a contrite Lilian said several minutes after Kevin had nearly died of blood loss.

They were in the dining room getting ready to have breakfast. She sat down at the table while Kevin served her a plate of whole-wheat pancakes and a glass of orange juice. The beautiful two-tails actually had the decency to look mildly embarrassed, if the redness staining her cheeks was any indication.

"I had no idea why I didn't wake up in time to make breakfast for us. And I'm sorry about how I, well, you know…"

"It's fine." Kevin breathed out deeply, pushing his own embarrassment back with ease of practice. He still couldn't believe he'd suffered a nosebleed like that! He wasn't Eric! "It wasn't like I disliked it or anything…"

"Did you say something, Kevin?"

"N-no!" Kevin squeaked. He rubbed the back of his head sheepishly, giving Lilian a grin so wide that his eyes were forced shut. "I didn't say a thing! Nope! Not a thing!" He nodded effusively. "Yep, I didn't say anything!"

"Really?"

Lilian stared at him, frowning. Kevin found that he couldn't look directly at her when she did this, yet also found himself incapable of looking away; or maybe he just didn't want to look away. What an unusual and uncomfortable feeling.

"Are you feeling alright?" Lilian continued, looking at him with a concerned gaze. "You've been acting a little strange this morning."

"Strange? Why would you say that? I haven't been acting strange at all! Aha-hahahaha!"

Lilian gave Kevin a queer look, clearly not convinced by his horribly fake laugh. High-pitched and forced, there was absolutely nothing natural about it. He eventually trailed off when he realized this, and tried everything humanly possible not to squirm underneath that vivid green-eyed stare.

After several more seconds of staring, Lilian shrugged, concluding that Kevin's unusual behavior must be a human thing. He nearly sighed in relief.

"Thank you for making me breakfast. It's very good." She changed the subject easily enough, cutting a slice of pancake with her fork, spearing it and taking a bite. It was good, most certainly, but the reason she enjoyed the food so much wasn't just because of its pleasant taste, but also because Kevin was the one who cooked it for her.

"Well, it's not broiled fish with steamed rice, miso soup and pickled vegetables, but I suppose it's alright." Kevin remembered how Lilian had made them a traditional Japanese breakfast several times since their meeting almost one month ago. It had been outstanding and made Kevin feel almost like he was living in *Maison Izumo*, a boarding house in one of Eric's favorite manga. Her food had been so good that he completely ignored the oddity of a kitsune raised in Greece being capable of cooking traditional Japanese cuisine.

"It's better than alright." Lilian beamed at him. "You're a really good cook. I always enjoy eating the food you prepare."

Kevin's cheeks suffused with warmth.

"T-thank you," he mumbled, turning his head so Lilian wouldn't see him blush. He knew it was probably too late for that—Lilian was staring right at him—but that had never stopped him before, and it definitely wasn't going to stop him now.

Wanting to get off the topic of his cooking skills—he didn't deal well with praise when it wasn't about track—Kevin swiftly changed the subject.

"So, um, I was thinking we could go see a movie today."

Lilian perked up, literally. The tips of her foxy ears pointed straight towards the ceiling and her back straightened. Even her two bushy-red tails were directed upwards.

"A movie?"

Glad that he was able to direct the conversation away from his cooking, Kevin nodded. "Yeah, there are a few new movies that just came out a little while ago. I haven't had a chance to see them yet."

Since meeting Lilian and dealing with the drama that accompanied her, he hadn't been able to see any of the new movies that had come out. He hadn't even considered going until about two days ago.

"What kind of movie did you want to watch?" Lilian looked positively curious.

"There's this one movie I want to see about a group of people who are saturated with cosmic radiation and gain superpowers. It's one of those action movies about superheroes and villains and stuff."

"Humans gaining superpowers?" Lilian lips curled in amusement. "You humans have the most fantastical story ideas. I guess that's one of the reasons I've always been so fascinated by your kind. All of you possess such incredible imaginations."

Kevin's brow furrowed. "Was that an insult?"

"Not at all," Lilian shook her head, smiling, "I think you're misunderstanding what I meant—that was a compliment. Other yōkai might feel superior to humans because we have powers and you don't, but I'm not one of them. Kotohime always told me that humanity's imagination is what has led them to some of the greatest achievements in history for both human and yōkai."

"Ah, I see, Kotohime…" Kevin thoughtfully scrunched his nose. "That's your maid, right?"

"One of them. Kotohime has been my maid and bodyguard ever since I gained my second tail. Our other maid is her sister, Kirihime."

Right, he'd nearly forgotten that Lilian's family had two maids. That was so not fair. He wanted a maid, too! He could just imagine what having his own maid would be like.

A girl in a French maid outfit stood before him, her skirt barely covering her any of her thighs. It was so short that every movement she made revealed her white panties and black garters. The low-cut bodice allowed him to see titillating hints of cleavage, the short-sleeves leaving the silky skin of her arms visible. A bonnet sat atop the crown of her head, whilst beautiful red locks of hair glimmered down her back like a gentle wave. Bright green eyes smiled at him.

"Welcome home, Master. Would you like me to take your coat?"

"Yes, I would. Thank you."

"You are most welcome. Now then, Master, what would you like first? Would you like me to make you some dinner? Or maybe you would like me to draw you a hot bath? Or, perhaps you would like... me?"

"I think I'll take you, my dear. Right here. Right now."

The maid giggled. It was a beautiful thing to hear.

"Very well, Master. Would you like to take me on the bed, the couch, or the dining room table?"

"Let's do the table this time. Is that okay with you?"

"Of course." She smiled at him. "Anything for my Master."

"Kevin?"

"..."

"Hello? Lilian to Kevin?"

"..."

"Muuu, I hope you're not ignoring me."

"..."

"I'm stripping naked right now."

"Don't strip in the kitchen!" Kevin shouted, red-faced and breathing hard. He blinked several times.

Then his eyes landed on Lilian.

She was still fully clothed.

He pouted.

"That was a mean thing to do."

"Sorry, Kevin," Lilian giggled, "but you were spacing out for a second there. I had to get your attention somehow."

"Whatever," Kevin mumbled, trying not to let her words get to him. He couldn't believe he'd been daydreaming like that! And about Lilian, of all people! Lilian! In a maid outfit! A sexy maid outfit! What the hell was wrong with him?

He started eating, hoping that if he did something it would take his mind off the admittedly hot daydream he'd just had.

"Ne, Kevin?" Lilian asked into the pervasive silence.

Kevin didn't look up as he cut a slice of pancake and stuck it in his mouth.

"Yes?"

"Since you're taking me to the movies, would that make this a date?"

Unprepared for such a forward question, Kevin swallowed the food while also sucking in a gasp of air, causing the bite of pancake to become lodged inside of his airway.

"Inari-blessed! Beloved!"

He heard Lilian's shout, but couldn't say anything, as he was a little too busy choking on bits of pancake. His hands went to his throat, clawing at it in panic as he struggled to breathe.

A hand rested on his back and started rubbing it. The act felt strangely soothing, warm even, and Kevin could feel the food somehow getting dislodged from inside of his windpipe, almost as if it was dissolving.

"Are you alright?" a worried voice asked in his ear.

"I-I'm fine." Kevin coughed several more times, pounding his chest with a fist to dislodge that last bit of pancake, while also silently berating himself. He really should have learned not to eat when Lilian was about to speak by now. Nothing good ever came of it.

"Here, drink this." Lilian handed him a glass of orange juice, which Kevin drank greedily. "Better?"

Kevin continued drinking until all of the orange juice was gone, sighed, and then set the cup on the table. He cast a grateful smile in Lilian's direction.

"Much better, thanks."

"You're welcome." Lilian returned his smile with a beautiful one of her own. As she sat back down in her chair, the gorgeous two-tails resumed their previous conversation. "Now, about that date…"

"D-date?!"

"Yes, date." Lilian looked at him oddly. "That is what it's called when two people of the opposite gender go out together, isn't it?"

"Ah… w-well, yes, it is." Kevin scratched his cheek with his left hand. "B-but, I don't think… I mean, this isn't really a date, right? I mean it could be, but, uh, well, a date sort of implies that… you know… that you and I… I mean, that we…"

"You're speaking nonsense, Kevin." Lilian's lips curved into a delightful u-shape. She wasn't quite sure if Kevin was at the *Gibberish of Love* stage yet—he wasn't spouting embarrassing non sequiturs, after all—but he was definitely *Emotionally Tongue-Tied*. He even seemed to be undergoing a minor *Dere Dere* moment of denial, which was normally something only tsunderes like a certain violent yuki-onna did.

Lilian thought it was adorable.

"Right." Kevin's shoulders slumped, as if he wanted to disappear into his seat. "Sorry."

Lilian resisted the urge to pull the teen to her bosom and smother him with affection. *Keep calm, Lilian. Remember, slow and steady wins the race.* Those words gave her the strength to resist her overly enthusiastic disposition when it came to giving Kevin more love and affection than he was capable of handling.

"You don't need to apologize. I'm just happy we're going to be doing something together, just the two of us."

She placed her hands over his. Kevin looked at their hands, then up at Lilian's face, at the soft curve of her lips. His pink cheeks darkened in hue and he looked away, though he didn't jerk his hands out from under hers, which Lilian considered a small victory in her battle for Kevin's heart.

"Ah, um, me too," he mumbled, causing Lilian's smile to widen. She may not have her mate yet, but it was only a matter of time. All the signs were there.

Yes, Kevin was as good as hers.

Ufufufu...

***

Two hours after breakfast, Kevin and Lilian were riding to the mall.

As was routine, Kevin pedaled while Lilian sat behind him, her arms around his waist and her right cheek resting against his back. She could feel his heartbeat from this position, thumping in a steady, though fast-paced, rhythm. It was a reassuring sound, one that she loved hearing. It would not be inaccurate to say that she would gladly stay like this forever if she could.

Her eyes closed as she allowed the soothing beat of Kevin's heart to lull her senses. She scooted just a bit closer, pressing her body more fully into his. Maybe it was just because of the cold air hitting them as they rode down the street, but Kevin's body seemed much warmer than usual. It was so incredibly soothing. So soothing that she could just...

"Lilian?"

Lilian blinked at the sound of her name being called. It took several seconds to realize that Kevin was the person calling her. It took her several more seconds to notice that her face was pressed against his back, and longer still to realize that she had been drooling on the back of his shirt.

Whoops. Better not say anything and hope he won't notice.

"Yes, Be—Kevin?" she asked, yawning a bit. Wow, did she feel groggy. Kevin's warmth was really something.

"Everything okay back there?" he asked, his head turning to look behind him as she sat up. "You stopped talking to me about halfway to the mall."

Lilian let out another yawn as she stretched her legs out on either side of the bike. Her toes also stretched themselves out, wiggling several times for good measure. She really wished she could take her tails out and stretch those, too. It was most unfortunate that humans weren't supposed to know about the existence of yōkai, otherwise she would have.

"M'fine," she murmured as the last vestiges of sleep left her. "What were you saying?"

"Nothing important." Kevin shook his head. "Anyway, I've been trying to tell you for the last few minutes that we've arrived."

Lilian looked around and realized what he meant; they had arrived at the mall. It loomed over them like a castle to the final boss battle of a Japanese RPG. A massive, multi-story complex that was composed of several buildings connected via a series of walkways. It looked like they were on the west side, near the food court. The arcade was on the opposite side.

"Oh... that was fast."

Kevin gave her a strange look that she couldn't interpret before shaking his head.

"Come on. Let's lock the bike up and get to the theater. Since it's still early, there shouldn't be any lines."

"Right!"

The two entered the mall and strode down the large walkway, devoid of people due to the early hour. The theater was located near the food court, an expansive space marked by bright neon signs and red carpet.

Kevin and Lilian walked past several posters hanging on the walls and a number of giant support pillars, stopping in front of the ticket booth where a bored-looking woman stood behind a glass panel. The expression on her bland face was the utter definition of "I hate my job."

"Welcome to Maverick Theaters," she greeted in a tone that was every bit as dull as her face, "what movie would you like to see today?"

"Two tickets for the *Fantastic Four*."

"That'll be fourteen dollars."

Kevin pulled out his wallet and paid for the tickets, which the woman slid under the glass panel, all the while her perennially bored eyes stared at him.

"Here are your tickets. Enjoy the show," she drawled.

"Thank you."

After receiving their tickets, the pair went to the concession booth, where a peppy middle-aged woman waited for them to order. Her pleasantly smiling face was filled with good cheer, a startling contrast to the woman at the ticket booth. She appeared to be the epitome of what a proper concessionist should be.

"Lilian, do you want popcorn or candy?"

"Um." Lilian's nose scrunched up cutely as she surveyed the various treats available. "I'm not sure. I'll have whatever you're having."

Kevin nodded and turned to the woman.

"We'll have one large popcorn and two medium Diet Cokes, please."

"Actually, make that one large Diet Coke." Kevin gave Lilian a look, but she just smiled at him. "Please indulge me with this, Kevin."

A moment later, Kevin looked away, his cheeks coloring slightly.

"Fine," he mumbled, "one large Diet Coke, then, please."

The woman gave them a knowing smile, which made Kevin feel like he had worms wriggling inside his intestines. It was a most unpleasant feeling, so he tried to ignore it.

"Coming right up."

Kevin's face was a mask of embarrassment as he paid for their refreshments and they entered the theater. On the other hand, Lilian's beaming smile was bright enough to illuminate the entire room.

After the woman had brought their concessions, she had wished them a "happy date" and mentioned how "cute they looked together." While the words caused Kevin to feel nothing but self-consciousness, Lilian couldn't have been happier.

There weren't very many people in the theater—it was still early and the movie had been out for awhile. Because of this, finding those perfect seats in the exact center of the theater took little to no effort on their part.

With a bit of a sigh, Kevin set their large soda in the cup holder between them before plopping down himself. Lilian daintily seated herself right next to him, her eyes sparkling with excitement.

"This is so cool! I've never been to a movie theater before," she exclaimed. Kevin had already assumed as much, knowing what he did of her life before arriving in Phoenix. "And look at that screen! It's so big!"

An unbidden smile came to Kevin's face. While this girl said some questionable things at times, her enthusiasm when experiencing something new was astoundingly child-like. She just acted so innocent—at least in matters that didn't involve him, her, no clothing and a bed… or the dinner table. It was one of her more endearing traits.

The innocence, not the matters relating to her sexual desires and fetishes.

"There are a lot of theaters that have larger screens than this."

Lilian turned in her seat to pin him with an expression that shimmered with unrepressed excitement.

"Really?"

"Oh, yeah," Kevin nodded. "This is one of the smaller theaters. There's a much larger one in Arizona called the Capri de Grande. It's pretty far from here, though, like, all the way down in Scottsdale. Otherwise, I would have taken you there instead."

"So this Capri de Grande is the largest theater around?"

"The largest one here in Arizona, sure. There are much, much bigger ones in states like California and New York—and France has the largest theater in the world." Kevin's smile turned nostalgic as fond memories replayed in his mind. "I remember one time when my mom took me to France. It was the only time she and I spent any time together during that trip. The place was amazing. It was this gigantic skyscraper that towered over everything, and it had spotlights and viewing screens that played movie trailers all over the outside. There were a lot of small theaters in it, but the largest one was this massive room that looked like something straight out of the Renaissance period. It was incredible."

"It sounds amazing." Lilian smiled gently at her mate. "I wish I could see it one day."

"You might be able to," Kevin replied absently. "I've been to France a number of times, more than any other country I've visited. I think it's because France has one of the largest fashion industries in the world. Anyway, I'll take you to see it whenever we go to visit."

Lilian's breath hitched and her heart skipped several beats. She could practically hear her blood pounding in her ears.

"Do you mean that?" she asked in a soft voice.

"Of course," Kevin said, then paused. Several seconds passed as the words he had just spoken replayed in his mind, his face swiftly growing red as it underwent spontaneous combustion.

"Kevin?" Her questioning tone startled him into action.

"W-what I mean is… I mean that, uh, i-it's, well, we could, you know, if you, mom and I…" Kevin tried several more times to say something, anything that would explain away his words in a non-embarrassing way. He couldn't, so he did something else. "Oh, look! The show is about to start!"

Did he just make a horrible attempt at changing the subject on me?

Lilian stared at her mate in silence. Several seconds passed before she realized that, yes, he had indeed changed the subject, and yes, he had also done an awful job of it. Then again, this was Kevin she was thinking about. What else should she have expected?

Why is he getting so embarrassed, though?

His behavior had been quite odd for the past two days—ever since Lindsay had turned him down, now that she thought about it. It was almost like his behavior had reverted back to when they'd first met, though it clearly hadn't resulted in something she had done. After all, she hadn't tried to seduce him or walk around his house naked since her battle with Kiara, and those were the only times he acted this way around her. Strange.

Either way, Lilian allowed her—hopefully—future mate to have his peace of mind, and turned back to the screen.

The lights dimmed as the screen went black. Words soon appeared and, not long after that, several movie trailers came and went. As the movie began playing, Lilian became fascinated with the phenomenon that was American comics being turned into live-action movies.

As the motion picture progressed, Kevin reached out for some popcorn at the same time as Lilian. A jolt like lightning traversed his fingers, causing them to jerk back reflexively as his face flushed. He peered at his friend from the corner of his eyes. Lilian must have sensed his eyes on her for she graced him with a dazzling smile, reached into the bag, grabbed a handful of popcorn, and gave some to him.

"T-thanks," he muttered softly, his face still feeling very hot. The smile that Lilian gave him didn't help matters. Not at all.

"You're welcome."

That was not the only time the pair found themselves in such an awkward—for Kevin, at least—situation. Several times they had both leaned over to get a drink at the same time, only to nearly bump heads. Kevin eventually decided to just go without drinking for the rest of the movie.

While he sat there, watching as the heroes found themselves caught within a cosmic space storm, Kevin tried to figure out why he felt so self-conscious.

Come on! Get of a hold of yourself, Kevin! What's wrong with you? Why are you acting this way? You haven't acted like this since Lilian first barged into your life, he reprimanded himself. *Heck, you're being even worse than before! You haven't acted like this much of a fool around anyone except for...*

Kevin's eyes widened marginally as he realized several important facts about the newly developed shyness he was experiencing around Lilian.

While it was true that he had always been prone to girl-shyness around the time he'd reached sixth grade, there were different levels of how timorous he became based on his closeness to the girl in question.

Girls that he didn't know were often met with silence. Girls who tried chatting with him—for reasons that were beyond his poor male brain to comprehend—were also met with silence—and the occasional wheezing gasp. Girls that he did know might get some stuttering, and with Lindsay, it hadn't been unusual for him to say something extremely stupid or simply lose consciousness.

His current level of discomfort with Lilian was akin to the severity he'd had with Lindsay, but that should have been impossible. That issue had been taken care of. He'd already confessed to the tomboy, so why had this most vexing complication decided to crop up now, of all times?

Kevin tore his gaze from the screen to Lilian, sitting beside him, paying rapt attention to what was happening on the big screen. Or, she was, until she seemed to feel his eyes upon her. Then she looked at him.

Their eyes only met for a moment before Kevin felt his cheeks begin to burn. He quickly turned back to the movie, trying to calm his frantically beating heart.

Okay, Kevin. Calm down, just calm down! There's no reason for you to act like this. It's just Lilian. You've been living with her for almost entire month, so you shouldn't be affected by her like this.

Just because someone *shouldn't* didn't mean they *weren't*, however, and Kevin knew that. He could feel his heart pounding in his chest, like a battering ram trying to break out of his ribcage. A few beads of sweat ran down the sides of his forehead, as all of his logical thought processes and higher brain functions seemed to leave him. All because of the girl sitting next to him.

Could it be that I really...

Kevin hadn't finished his thought before a velvet-soft hand slid into his own and delicate digits laced through his fingers.

He stared at the hand now resting within his, at the unusually perfect fingers that were a stark contrast to his own calloused digits. His vision then traveled past the hand, up the arm and onto the smiling face of Lilian, who appeared to be enjoying the movie.

He looked back at their conjoined hands, then up at her. Back down to their hands. Up at Lilian again. Eventually, and with a strange sort of numbness, Kevin relaxed as the warmth from Lilian's palm and fingers spread from the point of contact to the rest of his body. His own digits soon followed Lilian's example, gently coiling around her hand and lacing through her fingers.

Kevin turned back to the movie, thereby missing Lilian's "cat that ate the canary" grin. Everything seemed to be proceeding smoothly. She was confident that, very soon, she will have gained Kevin's love.

Yes, all according to plan.

If it weren't for the fact that they were in a movie theater, this would have been the part where Lilian let out her "ufufufu..." laugh. However, since they were in public and she couldn't do that without people thinking she was weird, she laughed within the confines of her mind instead.

Soon, Kevin's love will be all mine, ufufufu...

***

"That was a really fun movie," Lilian said as they exited the theater. Her eyes sparkled with a perplexing sort of incandescence, as if they were a pair of stars twinkling during the waning twilight hours. "I absolutely loved the story. It was so exciting! The way those heroes gained their powers was really interesting. I feel sorry for the villain, though. He had been one of their friends, but because no one had been around to help him when he needed it, he turned into a bad guy."

Kevin grinned at Lilian.

"I'm glad you enjoyed the movie."

"And the romance between Reed Richards and Susan Storm was just inspiring! I wish I had a relationship like that."

Lilian peered over at Kevin with a gaze full of such longing that he needed to turn his head, the better to hide the growing stain on his cheeks.

"Ah-ah ha! W-well, I'm sure you'll get a relationship like that soon."

"Oh, I know. We'll probably be in that relationship even sooner than you think. Ufufufu..."

"Did you say something?"

"I said thank you for taking me to see the movie."

As Lilian graced him with an alluring smile that managed to

light up her face in a way the overhead lights never could, Kevin thought his heart would melt through his chest.

"You're welcome," he mumbled softly, then shook his head, forcing himself to maintain a calm facade. "What do you think we should do next?"

As if answering his question, Lilian's stomach chose that moment to be heard, gurgling like some kind of creature was living inside of it. Her cheeks became suffused with a mild shade of red. She looked so cute that Kevin also began blushing.

"Well... I am a little hungry," she said, sounding just a tad sheepish. "That popcorn wasn't very filling."

"Do you want to head over to the food court?"

Lilian thought for a moment, then shook her head.

"No, I'd like something that isn't that fast-food stuff. Could we go to an actual restaurant?"

"Sure, I don't think that will be a problem, maybe..." Kevin trailed off as his mind quickly calculated a decent estimation of how much a meal for two would cost at an actual restaurant. "... Yeah, we could do that."

That was enough for her. Without further prompting, Lilian grabbed Kevin's hand and quickly began pulling him through the mall.

"Come on, then!"

"H-hey, wait! Lilian, slow down!"

"Hurry up, Kevin! I'm starving!"

As the fox-girl dragged him off in search of a restaurant, Kevin wondered why his heart felt like it was ready to burst.

***

Kevin stood outside of a small changing stall.

He and Lilian were inside of a clothing store called Alexandria's, one of those small boutique stores that sold stylish clothing, jewelry and other expensive items. The woman working in the shop and several teenage girls were staring at him and giggling, but he did his best to ignore them.

A sudden rustling of fabric and several thumps came from inside the stall, letting him know that Lilian was still in the process of putting on some new clothes that had caught her attention.

He wasn't exactly sure how they'd ended up going from

eating at Pita Pita's to shopping for clothes. It seemed like one minute they'd been finishing lunch and the next Lilian was dragging him into a clothing store.

Fortunately for his wallet, they didn't plan on buying any clothes today. Kevin had already bought Lilian more than enough outfits to last a while. They were only in the store because his red-haired housemate had been enthralled by an outfit on display, and being the person that he was, Kevin suggested that she try it on. Who knew, maybe he could get it for her birthday or something.

Speaking of which, just when was Lilian's birthday? She had never told him, although in her defense, he had never thought to ask either.

Note to self; remember to ask Lilian when her birthday is.

The sound of rustling curtains told Kevin know Lilian had finished changing. The sound of her voice behind him emphasized this fact.

"What do you think, Kevin?"

Turning around, Kevin got a full-view of Lilian in all of her breathtaking glory. Shimmering in the light, the dress she wore was the same color as her hair and fit her like a glove. The shoulder cut revealed the incredible smoothness of her bare shoulders. It didn't have a dip in the front, thankfully, but it clung to her body in such a way that it didn't really matter.

Kevin mastered his blush quickly, closing his eyes and taking several deep breaths. He could do this. He could. It was just Lilian. He'd seen her in far less before. This was nothing.

"I really like the way you look on that!" Kevin's face turned red as he completely messed up his words. "I mean I like the way that looks in you!" The red darkened. "No! Wait! I mean you'd look really good with that off!"

Lilian wondered if Kevin knew that steam was pouring out of his ears.

"Kevin, are you okay?"

"Y-yes, I'm fine... it's just... I'm just... auu..."

Before the situation could degrade any further for poor Kevin, a new voice spoke up, sounding almost surprised.

"Kevin? Lilian?"

Two sets of eyes turned to see Lindsay standing a few feet away. With her were several other girls who Kevin vaguely recognized as belonging on the tomboy's soccer team. Her wide eyes blinked in surprise. Kevin had the distinct impression that he was the cause, and he belatedly realized that she had probably never expected to find him in a women's clothing store. He could understand. Less than a month ago, he would have never expected to find himself in a women's clothing store, either. The girls behind her were pointing at Kevin as they giggled.

It took every ounce of willpower Kevin had not to run away screaming.

Gathering whatever was left of his nearly nonexistent dignity, Kevin coughed into his hand and tried to pretend he was not in a women's clothing store making a fool of himself.

"Lindsay, what are you doing here?"

"Just picking up some items that I need, and window shopping, too, I guess." Which was her way of saying her friends wanted to look at cute clothes and dragged her along, as Lindsay didn't like shopping at girly stores. She was a tomboy through and through. "And you two? I'm kinda surprised to see you looking at more clothes. Didn't you guys do some shopping just a few days ago?"

"We did," Lilian answered for both of them. "We're just looking right now. I wanted to try this on—" she gestured to the dress she was wearing, then gave a beaming smile in Kevin's direction— "—and Kevin was kind enough to indulge me."

"Is that so?" Lindsay grinned as Kevin tried to hide his blush by sinking his face into his shirt. Behind the blond tomboy, he could hear girlish squeals and words like "how romantic" and "what a nice boyfriend" coming from the peanut gallery. He wished they would stop talking. "That's nice of him."

Lilian nodded her head effusively. "Isn't it?" Her brilliant smile was soon replaced by curiosity. "You mentioned that you were doing some shopping of your own. Are you looking for clothes?"

"Naw." Lindsay shook her head. "We're just sort of wandering around. We were actually about to grab some ice cream. Would you two like to join us?"

Kevin and Lilian looked at each other, silently conversing. A moment later, they looked back at Lindsay and nodded.

"Sure," Kevin said.

"Cool. I think this is the last store my friends plan on dragging me to. Once they finish looking around, we'll head over to the ice cream parlor."

***

Kevin and Lilian bought some ice cream with Lindsay and the rest of her soccer friends. Since they had already eaten, however, they only got a small bowl with two different flavors (chocolate and strawberry) that they ended up sharing—all Lilian's suggestion, of course. How the beautiful fox-girl had convinced him to share a bowl of ice cream with her was something Kevin would never understand.

"Is something wrong, Kevin?" Lilian asked when she noticed his spoon pause halfway to his mouth.

"No," Kevin said after a moment. He ate the spoonful of ice cream, swallowed, and then went in for another scoop. "I was just thinking about something, that's all."

"Oh?" Lilian's tone was tinged with inquisitiveness. "What were you thinking about?"

"Nothing important."

"Hmmm…" Lilian decided not to try prying the information from him. It probably wasn't that important anyway. Certainly not as important as enjoying ice cream with her mate. "If you say so." Scooping some ice cream onto her spoon, Lilian held it up near Kevin's mouth and smiled. "Here, you should try some of the strawberry ice cream as well."

Kevin looked like he wanted to turn into a *kappa,* a type of turtle yōkai, so that he could hide within his shell.

"I-I can feed myself you know. You don't have to feed me like I'm some kind of baby."

Lilian pouted at him.

"I know that. I'm not doing this because you can't feed yourself. I just want to do something nice for you."

Kevin tried not to feel too embarrassed by Lilian's words or actions. He also tried to ignore his racing heart, instead choosing to silently contemplate the fox-girl, before slowly deciding there was no harm in indulging her.

"W-well, I suppose it would be okay if you're just trying to be nice."

"Thank you. Now try some of this strawberry ice cream. It's really good. It even has cheesecake bits in it."

While he and Lilian partook in a bowl of cold, creamy goodness together, the other members of their little troupe gossiped. Quite naturally, they were the subject of said gossip. The all-girl's soccer team spoke about him and Lilian with all the subtlety of a Death Star destroying a planet.

"Oh. My. God. Aren't those two just the cutest?"

"I know, right? They look so adorable sitting there together, sharing a sundae. It's, like, totally cute."

"I'm still surprised Kevin had it in him to even speak to a girl like Lilian. I mean, just look at her! She's gorgeous!"

"I know, right? Wasn't he, like, majorly shy around girls or something?"

"Totes. The poor guy couldn't even talk to a girl a month ago. Now look at him."

"I wonder what changed?"

"I know, right?"

"Jessica... you say that way too much."

"I know, ri—I mean, sorry."

As the conversation flowed around her, Lindsay stared at the blond and the redhead. Kevin was blushing, sending furtive glances in the direction of the other girls as they talked. His cheeks would darken in hue each time, like solar flares, before his eyes skittered away again. Lilian must have heard the gossip as well, but she didn't seem to care. All of her attention was on Kevin, delighting in the act of feeding him ice cream.

Just how Lilian had convinced Kevin to let her feed him was something Lindsay would never understand. It should have been impossible—yet there she was, seeing it with her own eyes. Maybe the girl's miraculous powers of persuasion lied behind that sexy pout of hers, or perhaps it lay within those large green eyes, which held an innocent allure few men—and maybe even some women—would be unable to resist. Lindsay couldn't say for sure.

Maybe it has something to do with her boobs...

Now there was a thought. Lilian's breasts were definitely enticing, and large. They were also the subject of much conversation at school, both from guys and girls, and Lindsay had once heard that all men loved big boobs. Then again, Eric had been

the one to say that, and he was a pervert. She probably shouldn't listen to him.

Regardless of the how, seeing them like this really did strike home the point that Lilian was a much better match for Kevin than she was. Lindsay had never made a concerted effort to make Kevin hers, which she supposed was because he had already liked her, but Lindsay would be lying if she said that had been the only reason.

The truth of the matter was that she had wanted him to man up and tell her how he felt without any prompting on her part. She still didn't know if that decision had been a mistake or not, but guessed that only time would tell.

"Are you all right, Lindsay?"

Snapping out of her trance, she looked at her friend, Chelsea, who was staring at her in concern.

"Hmm? Of course. Why wouldn't I be?"

"You haven't touched your ice cream."

Lindsay looked down at her untouched bowl of vanilla ice cream, then grabbed the spoon and scooped some up.

"I'm fine. I was just thinking about something and it distracted me."

Chelsea looked unconvinced, but seemed to decide not to pry.

"If you say so."

The gathering of giggling females continued talking as Lilian and Kevin had traded positions, with a blushing Kevin now feeding an ecstatic Lilian. Lindsay remained contemplative, absentmindedly eating her ice cream while debating the merits of having not pursuing Kevin more seriously. However, all of that was about to change.

"MY TIT MAIDEN!"

It started with bestial shouting. As the loud, resounding cry of joy and lust reverberated down the hall like the roar of a perverted old man hyped up on Viagra, Kevin, Lilian, Lindsay and everyone else turned their heads to see Eric Corrompere flying towards them at Mach speed.

"Oh, my beautiful Tit Maiden, with those overgrown mammaries that I love so much!" Eric cried out, tears streaming out of his eyes in quantities so vast it was a wonder he hadn't caused the entire mall to flood. "It's always a joyous day when I get a chance to bask in those grabiliciously ginormous gazongas of yours!"

He appeared before Lilian, his hands reaching out to grab hers. None of them knew for what purpose, but it didn't matter anyway. He didn't succeed.

Quicker than a whip, Lilian snatched her hands away from his grasping appendages, the fingers of which wiggled like a perverted tentacle monster. This did not deter Eric, however, who simply began crying joyful tears that much harder.

"Please give me the chance to squeeze those giant tatas of yours!"

Lilian opened her mouth to speak—likely to let the lecher know where he could shove his request—when a fist brutally drove itself into Eric's cranium.

"DOOF!" Eric was slammed face first into the floor. He sat up, rubbing his head as a large lump formed on top, and glared at the person responsible. "What the hell was that for?!"

"That was for being an idiot." Kevin's right eye twitched violently as the vein on his forehead pulsed in time with his heartbeat.

"An idiot, am I?!" Looking like an enraged baboon, Eric jumped to his feet and menacingly shook his right fist at Kevin. "Who are you calling an idiot?!"

"You, obviously." Kevin sat back down and crossed his arms. "Seriously, Eric, can't you, for once in your life, think with something other than that thing dangling between your legs?"

"Maybe I will when you start thinking with yours!" Angry and defiant, Eric stood to his full not-inconsiderable-height and stared his best friend down with an expression reminiscent of the Hulk's —if the Hulk had looked like a human that had been crossbred with a monkey. "Maybe if you weren't such a pansy and actually acted like a man for once, I wouldn't have to act like this! Did you think about that? Well?!"

Kevin's eye twitching increased.

"What is that supposed to mean?"

"It means what it means."

"That's not an answer! And don't try to sound so cryptic! You're not a wise old man wearing a bathrobe; mysterious and vague doesn't suit you!"

As Kevin began arguing with Eric, Lindsay leaned over in her seat and whispered to Lilian, who was watching the battle of words unfold with rapt attention.

"It looks like Kevin's beginning to get a bit protective over you, huh?"

Lilian smiled.

"It does seem that way, doesn't it?"

"I don't know what you did to help Kevin get over his girl problem," Lindsay continued, "but I'm glad you did." Looking at the curvaceous redhead, Lindsay bit her bottom lip. "And please, take care of him for me."

Observing the soccer player with keen eyes that saw more than they probably should, Lilian sat silently for several seconds before her countenance softened.

"Don't worry, I will. I promise."

Lindsay gave her a grateful, if watery, smile.

"Thank you."

"You're welcome."

The two smiled at one another, sharing in a moment of camaraderie, one that they had yet to experience in the three weeks they'd known each other. It looked like this would be the beginning of a beautiful friendship—

"I'm just saying that if you stopped pussy-footing around, we wouldn't be in this mess! You'd have your girl and I'd have my Tit Maiden! Everyone would be happy!"

"No, they wouldn't! You clearly don't know what you're talking about! No one would be happy but you! And stop mentioning Tit Maidens!"

—and the deterioration of another friendship.

Chapter 2

Mall Time Troubles

Half-an-hour after leaving the ice cream parlor Lindsay and her soccer friends, along with Kevin, Lilian and Eric, met up with Justin, Alex and Andrew.

Several minutes after that, they ran into Christine.

"Let go of him! Can't you see that Kevin doesn't like you yanking on him like that?!"

"Me? Ha! You're the one who's pulling his arm off, ya damn vixen! You let go!"

"You first!"

Standing on the sidelines of what looked to be an epic argument between a certain fox-girl and a snow maiden, Eric, Lindsay, Alex, Andrew, Justin and the rest of Lindsay's soccer team all watched the ensuing conflict with their best "I have no idea how this happened" faces.

"Wow, those two really don't want each other to have Kevin," Katy, one of Lindsay's soccer teammates, said, her eyes riveted on the battle.

Lindsay watched the tug-of-war between Lilian and Christine —who had appeared a few minutes after they'd left the ice cream parlor—worrying for her friend caught in the middle of this fiendish struggle. Kevin wasn't looking too good, what with the eyes rolled up in the back of his head and the arm yanking and everything.

"Do you think we should stop them, Eric..." Lindsay trailed off, her expression deadpanning when she saw Eric viciously biting his T-shirt and glaring daggers at his best friend.

"Damn that Kevin!" he grumbled, though, because his mouth was full of shirt, it sounded more like "mam ma Feffin!" Lindsay did her best to translate the boy's unusual tirade. "Foof Af Fim, fanfing fere wif fose fomen fifing ofer him! Fuffy Bafard! Fam fu, Fefin Sfif!"

Somehow, Lindsay actually managed to translate the string of unintelligible mutterings: "look at him, standing there while those women fight over him! Lucky bastard! Damn you, Kevin Swift!" At least, that was what she thought he was saying. It wasn't like she had ever listened to someone speak while they were gnawing on their shirt.

Standing to Eric's left, Alex and Andrew were also discussing the dilemma of Kevin, whose arms looked like they might tear at the seams if they were pulled any harder.

"I am feeling this strange combination of envy and sympathy for our friend." Alex's frown expressed his conflicting feelings quite accurately. "Is that natural?"

Andrew took a good, long look at Kevin. The blond teen's limp body dangled between the two girls as they yanked with all their might. Each time one of them pulled him toward them, Kevin's head would flop around like a wet noodle, making him look more like a ragdoll than a human. Neither of the girls fighting over him seemed to notice that he was already unconscious.

"I am not sure. I certainly do not believe feeling pity and envy for one person at the same time is natural, and yet, I cannot help but share your sentiments. I am unsure as to whether I envy him or feel sorry for him."

"... Cat... fox?... cold..."

Everyone within Justin's generally vicinity stared at the boy very, very oddly.

Lindsay turned back to the tug-of-war, frowning.

"I'm still not even sure how this happened," she mused. Should she stop those two before they hurt Kevin even more? She wanted to, but...

"That," Andrew started, also turning back to the *War of the Kevin,* "Is something I believe the rest of us would like to know as well."

His words were met by several nods all around, as it seemed

everyone wanted to know the exact same thing. Lindsay tried recalling the events that had led to this moment.

***

Not long after Eric joined the group, they met up with Kevin's other friends. The twins joined their expanding party first, having met them just as they were leaving the ice cream parlor. Justin was the third person to join them after he saw the group coming out of a sweet shop with several bags of candy.

With the group having expanded, they all decided to travel to the arcade. None of the girls were big on arcade games, but that didn't mean they weren't into earning tickets to win prizes. Some of the stuffed animals at the ticket booth were just too adorable.

While on their way to the arcade, they ran into Christine. The yuki-onna dressed in gothic lolita fashion had been coming out of a store that sold, well, gothic stuff, just as the large troupe walked past her. It didn't take the girl much effort to spot Kevin within the group. It also didn't take very long for her face to turn a lovely shade of "beach-ball blue" as she remembered her dream that morning.

"YOU!"

The entire group halted in their tracks, turned, and watched as Christine stomped over to Kevin with a face that could outshine a star.

Kevin blinked several times as the snow maiden marched up to him with DOOM in her eyes, or embarrassment—no one present could be sure. With *tsunderes*, those two things tended to go hand in hand.

"Eh? Christine?"

Kevin was about to smile at his friend and give her a proper greeting when he noticed something unusual about the girl.

"Hey, are you feeling okay? Your face is all, um, blue."

"You… you… you…!"

Christine's face became, surprisingly enough, even bluer than before, shifting from an icy hue to a deeper ocean blue. The temperature around her also began dropping at an astonishing rate, causing several girls to cry out when they were suddenly struck by icy winds and hoarfrost that froze their skirts solid.

"My Gothic Hottie!"

Eric, completely oblivious to the mood, as well as Christine's embarrassment-induced rage, rushed toward the pretty girl with snow-white skin. His hands, already extended, made creepy grasping motions that had all of the girls shivering in disgust and fear, or maybe they were still shivering from the cold. Perhaps a combination of both? Kevin wasn't sure.

"Oh, how I've missed those tiny titties of yours! Please give me the honor of squeezing—guh!"

Several globules of saliva flew from Eric's mouth as Christine embedded her fist into his gut, driving the wind from his lungs in one fell swoop. As the perverted young man fell to the floor and curled up in a fetal position, gasping in agonic asphyxia, the pale-skinned girl stared down at the new target of her anger and embarrassment.

Tsundere protocols: activated.

"DIE!"

"GYYAAAA!"

"YOU DISGUSTING, LECHEROUS PIECE OF SHIT!"

"GAAAA!"

"DIE! DIE! DIE!"

"MOMMY!"

"What's this girl's malfunction?" Lindsay leaned over and cupped a hand to her mouth, whispering into Lilian's ear.

"That girl's a *tsundere*," was Lilian's very succinct answer. She didn't seem to care if Christine heard her or not.

"*Tsundere*?" Lindsay blinked, then again for good measure. "Why does that sound so familiar?"

"Um." Lilian decided to educate her new friend, pulling out her handy-dandy book, "TvTropes for Dummies," and flipping through the pages. "Let's see, there's… *yandere*, nope. *Dandere*? Nope. *Kuudere*. Uh uh. *Himedere*? Um, that's not it either…"

Lindsay watched the redhead flip through the pages of her book, then turned to look at Kevin. "What is she doing?"

"Don't worry," he reassured her, "this is just a part of her character concept."

"Her what?"

"… Never mind."

"Ah-ha! Found it!" Lilian cried out triumphantly. Coughing into her hand, the redhead adopted a lecture pose, her left arm bending at the elbow to support her right arm, the hand of which held the book up to her face. She then began to read. "The Japanese term *tsundere* refers to a character who alternates between two distinct moods: *tsun-tsun* which refers to someone who acts cold and irritable, and *dere-dere*, which is when someone acts demure and shy."

Lindsay didn't get it. "Um, what?"

"This term was first used to describe characters who had a cold and sometimes even harsh personality, but over the course of a story would reveal a soft and vulnerable side. In recent years, this character archetype has become flanderized, and now people generally associate it with characters who flip between these two emotional extremes at the slightest provocation."

"I am so lost," Lindsay muttered.

"Don't worry," Kevin reassured her again, "you'll get used to it."

For some reason, his words made Lindsay groan.

Lilian ignored them and continued. "The character's *tsun-tsun* side can range from giving their crush 'the silent treatment' to 'shoving their face in a blender while shouting obscenities and threatening with murder.' Anime enthusiasts have theorized why a *tsundere's* behavior can vary so wildly. Most generally agree that the reason has to do with the conflicting feelings of affection they have toward a love interest, and their reaction to having those feelings in the first place."

"Uh…"

"Basically—" Lilian snapped the book shut and put it back into her Extra Dimensional Storage Space— "*Tsunderes* are people who have a tendency to act really bitchy and cold, but are actually really nice people on the inside."

"I'LL KILL YOU! I'LL MURDER YOU DEAD!"

"OH, GOD NOOOOO!!"

"… Most of the time."

Lindsay looked at the gorgeous redhead for a moment longer, before deciding to ignore everything Lilian had just said. She didn't even want to consider what this girl was talking about. *Tsun-tsun? Dere-dere? Tsunderes?* Count her out. She had no interest in that Japanese stuff Kevin and his friends obsessed over.

Instead, she looked over to where Christine was laying waste to one of the boys in their group... only to wince when she saw the pale-skinned female stomp on Eric's better-left-unmentioned male anatomy. The squeal that followed, reminiscent of a pig being gutted, nearly made Lindsay reach down to protect her own non-existent gonads. That had to hurt.

Lilian adopted a thoughtful mien. Her left hand rose to cup her chin, while her right hand held her left arm aloft at the elbow and her hips cocked at an angle.

"Although, considering she's beating on Eric and not Kevin, I wonder if this girl is a true *tsundere* or just a really, really violent girl."

"Ugh, whatever," Lindsay grimaced. "A-anyway, don't you think we should stop her before she kills him?"

"I don't see why," Lilian replied, gazing at the scene with an expression of apathy. "While he did not do anything extremely perverse today, I am sure he did something to deserve this. It's probably karma."

"DIE INGRATE!"

"SOMEONE, HELP ME! JESUS? ALLAH? KAMI?"

Looking at the violence taking place several yards away, Lindsay considered the salacious teen as he screamed for help, then slowly nodded her head.

"Yeah... I think you might be right."

Lindsay had to wonder why neither she nor any of the people present were bothered by the violence being committed in front of them. It might have had something to do with the recipient of said violence.

Eric Corrompere was a well-known peeping Tom. Every girl knew of his unabashed licentiousness. They also knew that, if given the opportunity, he would peep on them without a second's hesitation. His lecherous actions were so bad that all of the older high school girls warned the freshmen about him and had even put several contingency plans in place to deal with Eric, in the event that they discovered him doing something that put their virtue in jeopardy.

Kevin Swift also watched the massacre taking place. He knew that he should feel bad for his friend, but for some reason, he didn't. It was probably because of that strange feeling he had seconds before Eric tried pouncing on Christine. He didn't really understand, but it felt like he had just barely dodged the bullet.

Justin just stared at Eric with unusually round eyes. He was not one for showing emotion often, but, when he did display something other than boredom, it was only under the most dire or perplexing of circumstances.

He turned to look at his friends, his normally half-lidded, apathetic eyes were somewhat wider than normal. "… help…?"

"OH, GOD! WHY ARE YOU DOING THIS?"

"Why? Why?! I'm doing this because you're a damn pervert! And all perverts deserve to DIE!"

"IIIYYYYAAAA!"

The twins gave Justin a look of barely masked incredulity.

"Do you really want to get in the way of that?" asked Alex.

"Because I sure don't," finished Andrew.

Justin looked down at his pervy friend, who, by this point, looked a lot like a lump of misshapen meat that had been beaten with a mallet by a psychotic butcher. His cries were also growing weaker. Everyone present was surprised that he hadn't passed out from the pain yet.

Justin looked back at his friends. Slowly, ever so slowly, he nodded at them.

"… Point…"

***

Not long after Christine finished trying to ensure that Eric would never be able to procreate, the yuki-onna decided to join them.

"I-it's not like I want to be with you or anything, idiot! It's just boring walking around by myself! Hmph!" she had said with a face that reminded Kevin of an icicle and steam pouring out of her ears.

Shortly after her entrance into the group, they made it to the arcade, at which point the two yōkai began fighting over the boy they were mutually attracted to—even if one of them was unwilling to admit it. Both wanted Kevin to play an arcade game with them. Unfortunately, not only were the games they wanted to play completely different (Lilian wanted to play "House of Haunted Horrors" while Christine had been looking forward to a game of air hockey), they also didn't want to share Kevin with the other. Hence the fighting.

"Let! Go!"

"No, you let go!"

The two continued pulling on the poor teen's arms, their teeth gritted and their eyes narrowed in fierce expressions of rivalry. Sparks flew between them, arcs of arcane energy that struck the ground like miniature lightning bolts, causing several people to skitter away in fear of being zapped. They didn't even pay attention to the way Kevin's head lolled limply back and forth each time they yanked on his arms, or the way his eyes had rolled into the back of his head. Go figure.

"I told you, Kevin's going to be playing that zombie shooting game with me!" Lilian glowered at the stupid snow-maiden who was trying to steal her Kevin.

"It's called 'House of Haunted Horrors,' idiot! And no he isn't! He's going to play air hockey with me!"

"Hey! Don't call me an idiot!"

"I'll call you whatever I damn well please! Now get your grubby paws off him, fox-skank!"

Lilian bared her fangs at the snow maiden, her grip on Kevin's arm tightening. She refused to lose to this stupid goth-loli who was trying to steal her mate.

It wasn't until several minutes after the fight began that Lilian remembered something important about this girl: she was a *tsundere*.

Lilian grinned.

"Why do you even want to play a game with him anyways?" she asked, her voice slyer than a fox. While she kept Christine occupied, she subtlety glanced in Eric's direction. The young man was stewing in jealousy and anger, a boiling pot of overflowing emotions. Yes, he would work nicely. "I thought you didn't like Kevin."

"Eh?"

The question actually brought a pause to the fighting as Christine took a moment to register the words more fully. When she did, her face became a blushing wreck.

She let go of Kevin, as if holding the boy had scalded her hands. This allowed Lilian to pull the insensate young man into her waiting bosom. Too bad the young man in question wasn't awake to enjoy it.

"I-I-I don't... I mean, i-i-it's not like I want him to... to..."

As Christine tried to come up with a proper excuse to explain why she was fighting over Kevin, her face became bluer and bluer as her yuki-onna powers started circulating through her body beyond her control.

Lilian then witnessed the activation of Christine's *tsundere* protocols, which consisted of blushing, stuttering and becoming abnormally violent. She had to admit, it amused her a lot. It was like playing a successful prank without even trying.

"Shut up!" Christine shouted, stomping on the ground like a petulant child. "Shut up, shut up, shut up! Idiot! Skank! Big-breasted cow!"

"B-big breasted cow," Lilian growled. She calmed down a second later and snorted derisively. "You shouldn't insult someone just because they have bigger boobs than you. It makes you seem petty; breast envy is such an undesirable trait."

"B-breast envy!" Christine squawked, before going on another tirade. "Y-you-you don't know what you're talking about! Ignorant! Stupid! Foolish woman! I-I-I'll kill you!"

Whether Christine would have actually gone through with her threat would never be known. The moment she let go of Kevin, Eric saw his chance to finally claim his Goth Hottie for himself. There was no way he would let this girl also go to Kevin! That prudish jerk already had his Tit Maiden! He couldn't allow that idiot to claim another girl for himself!

"My Gothic Hottie! Come to papaaaaggGGGHHH!"

"DIE!"

"UWAAAG!"

Lilian smiled. It always felt nice to see such a well-crafted plan executed without fail. While a part of her felt bad for placing that enchantment on Eric to make him act with even less intelligence than usual—oh, who was she kidding? She didn't care about that pervert. The only thing she cared about was that she had finally gotten Kevin away from that stupid *tsun-loli*.

Try and steal my mate, will you? That'll show you!

"Don't worry, Beloved." She gently stroked Kevin's blond hair, her touch loving and gentle. "I'll protect you from that violent *tsundere*... eh?"

It was only now, after the argument between her and Christine was over and done with, that Lilian finally realized her chosen mate was unconscious.

"Beloved! Oh, Inari! Beloved, are you okay?! Speak to me, Beloved!"

While Lilian began shaking Kevin in the hopes of waking him up—which was very counterproductive—and Christine continued to violently emasculate a certain pervert... again, Lindsay stood off to the side with the others, all of them watching the scene unfold with matching befuddled expressions.

None of Lindsay's friends knew what to make of the scene before them.

"This is the second time these two have started fighting each other today. I wonder why they hate each other so much?"

"I know, right?"

"Ah! You don't think they're love rivals, do you?"

"You mean that goth girl is also in love with Kevin? Really?"

"It certainly looks that way, doesn't it? I mean, why else would she fight over him like that?"

"I know, right?"

"Speaking of that girl, doesn't she look awfully familiar? I think I've seen her sitting on the bleachers during P.E."

"That's right! She's the one who never participates in class. And I have her in my literature class, too. I wonder why I never noticed her before?"

"I know, right?"

"You're doing it again, Jessica."

"I know—Oops. Sorry, my bad."

While the group chatted and observed the chaos unfolding, Lindsay could only wonder how, or maybe when, Kevin's life had become such an unholy mess.

"Mercy!" Eric screamed shrilly, his face a mask of agony. "Please! Show me some merccyyyYYYYYYYAAAAA!!"

"You don't get to beg for mercy, worm! Now hurry up and DIE!"

"Oh, god! AAEEIIIII!!!"

"Beloved? Beloved?! KEVIN!"

Yes, Lindsay really didn't envy Kevin. Not at all.

***

Kevin and Lilian sat in a small café, ignored by the crowd of patrons who'd also congregated there.

It was later in the evening and the sun was beginning to set; light gold hues containing purple streaks marred the sky. Splotches of orange and yellow disrupted its splendor, but also somehow enhanced the sunset's overall visual appeal.

The large group had split up a while ago; each of them heading back home, all except Kevin and Lilian. Since they didn't have parents waiting for them, they didn't have any set time they needed to return.

Of course, Kevin normally liked getting home early. It was Monday, which usually meant they had school the next day. Since the campus was closed until repairs could be affected, however, he figured it would be all right to indulge Lilian's desire and stay out a bit later than the norm.

Leaning back in his chair, his head tilted toward the ceiling, Kevin tried to ignore the dull ache in his body. His arms were sore from Lilian and Christine playing tug-of-war with them. They literally felt like they had been torn at the seams. He also felt extraordinarily exhausted. Dealing with two girls fighting over him for reasons that he couldn't understand was tiring.

And just what was up with those two anyway? Why had they been fighting over him? Lilian he could understand, but Christine? Why would she fight over him? She didn't even like him, as she constantly reminded him every time they saw each other.

Kevin covered his face with his hands and groaned. He really didn't want to think about this right now.

"Are you alright, Kevin?"

Lowering his head, Kevin's eyes landed on Lilian. The twin-tailed beauty was staring at him in obvious concern. It was almost enough to warm his heart. Almost, because he was simply too tired to feel much of anything at that moment.

"Yeah, I'm fine." He sighed and lowered his hands back onto the table. "I'm just not feeling too well, I guess."

Lilian's worried frown became more prominent.

"Did you not have fun today?"

"It wasn't that I didn't have any fun," Kevin replied, "I mean, this morning when we saw that movie together was nice, and it was fun when we had ice cream, but after that…"

Shaking his head, he tried putting what had transpired after visiting the ice cream parlor out of his mind. He really didn't want to remember the disastrous series of events that happened later on that day.

"Is there anything I can do to help?" Lilian asked earnestly. Kevin actually cracked a smile, even as he shook his head.

"I'm fine. A good night's rest and I'll be good as new." When he saw the concerned look remain in place, he gave Lilian a more genuine smile filled with gratitude. "Thank you for being so concerned for me, though. It means a lot to me."

"You're welcome," Lilian cheeks suffused with warmth. There was just something about having the person she loved expressing gratitude toward her that sent her heart thumping wildly against her chest.

Silence settled over them as they sat there, two small lattés in front of them. It was neither discomforting nor oppressing, this moment, just a comfortable quiet between two friends who, if Lilian had her way, would become much more than mere friends in the near future.

"Do we have any plans for tomorrow?"

Kevin opened his eyes, which he had closed sometime during the pause in conversation. Blinking, he looked at the girl for a second, then frowned.

"I hadn't really thought about tomorrow, to be honest," he admitted, "though, considering what happened today, I don't think I'm up for another trip to the mall any time soon." They had been going to the mall too much lately in his opinion, anyway. "I'm thinking of just staying home and relaxing."

"Oh."

Kevin observed Lilian as she squirmed in her seat, and couldn't help but wonder why she seemed so nervous. Was she anxious about something? Or was it... ah, that must have been it.

His lips curled upwards. "Did you want to do something tomorrow?"

Lilian looked surprised, but soon graced him with a bedazzling smile as she shook her head. "Not really. So long as I'm with you, I don't really care what we do."

Kevin couldn't keep the blush from appearing on his cheeks. He tried to cover his red face by taking a sip of his latté. He needed to calm down. This wasn't something to get embarrassed over. Lilian said stuff like this all the time. Heck, she had been saying stuff like this for as long as he'd known her. This really wasn't a big deal.

But if that's the case, then why does my heart feel like it's melting out of my feet?

"I-is that so?" he asked, trying to ignore how his heart was turning into a puddle of goo. Lilian seemed to have other ideas.

"Oh, yes."

Before Kevin could even think of removing his unused hand from the table, Lilian placed both of her hands over it. He nearly spit out his drink when he felt her warm, soft-as-silk fingers holding his larger, more calloused hand. He still ended up nearly choking when the scalding liquid went down the wrong tube.

While Kevin coughed and sputtered as the burning latté traveled down his airway, scalding his throat like liquid fire, Lilian raised his hand to her face. Kevin eventually stopped choking on his drink, and it was during this time that he noticed what the girl was doing.

His wide, frightened eyes made him look similar to a rabbit staring down the barrel of a shotgun. And, much like a terrified bunny, he was unable to pull away from Lilian's enchanting gaze as she pressed the palm of his hand to her cheek. As his calloused hand touched skin that was softer than velvet, a shiver went from his feet to the crown of his head, and then traversed his spine down to his tailbone.

"Nothing brings me greater happiness than spending time with you," Lilian told him earnestly.

In the face of such sincere, overwhelming emotion, Kevin could do nothing but stare. This girl... how could she make such embarrassing statements so easily?

"Lilian..." His throat felt dry, constricted. He couldn't speak, but still knew, in his heart, that he had to say something. To say nothing at all when Lilian spoke with such heartfelt and earnest sincerity would be an insult to her. And so, Kevin gathered his courage and tried to speak. "I..."

"I finally found you, Lilian."

"Yeah, I finally found you... wait." Kevin paused, his nose wrinkling like a candy wrapper. "What?"

While Kevin felt nothing but confusion, Lilian froze. That voice. She knew that voice. She knew it as surely as she knew her own. But how could that be? There was no way that woman could have found her!

Unable to control the instincts that took hold of her, Lilian released Kevin's hand and turned her head in the direction of the familiar feminine voice.

Standing before them was a gorgeous woman with proportions that put her own impressive figure to shame. Her long raven hair reached all the way down to her backside, swaying hypnotically in an unseen breeze. Large, almond-shaped eyes the color of dark chocolate stared at her with equal amounts of disapproval and relief.

She wore a dark red kimono made of silk, which stopped halfway down her thighs, revealing long porcelain legs. Flower motifs swirled around the entire garment. They started at the hem and traveled upwards in a tornado pattern, with the flowers becoming smaller and more sparse the further up they went, until they disappeared on her left shoulder.

It was such an odd outfit to see in America, especially Arizona, that it stood out more starkly than if Dante from *Devil May Cry* had walked into the café right then with guns blazing.

The gorgeous femme drew a lot of attention, and not just from Lilian and Kevin. Whether it was because of her incredible beauty, the fact that she was wearing a kimono in America, or because of the katana currently sheathed in a plain-looking scabbard at her side was unknown. It could have been all three.

No one except Lilian noticed the smaller blade strapped across the woman's back, partially concealed underneath her pink obi. While someone carrying a *wakizashi* (a short sword used by samurai) was not inconspicuous, even in Japan, there were far more important things to look at. Like the katana. Or the woman's breasts.

They were huge. Her breasts, that is.

Lilian felt like a small animal that had been trapped by a much larger and more ferocious predator—or a young yōkai who'd been caught by the *pedobear*, which was a feeling she hoped to never experience again. It wasn't pleasant.

In the face of the kimono-clad beauty's overwhelming

presence, all Lilian could do was stare in a combination of fear, shock and just a little consternation. There were so many emotions boiling within her it was a wonder she actually managed to speak.

"K-Kotohime!"

"Hello, Lilian-sama."

The woman smiled. Lilian shuddered. Inari-blessed, she'd forgotten what it was like to be on the receiving end of that smile. Beautiful and terrifying at the same time, it was a smile filled with unimaginable horrors, the smile of a monster hidden behind the veneer of a traditional Japanese beauty. It spoke of nothing good. It told her that she was absolutely, utterly and uncategorically screwed.

"I'm in trouble, aren't I?"

Such an obvious question should have never been asked.

"Yes." The woman's voice, lyrical and beautiful in a way that caused all the people present, regardless of gender or sexual preference, to swoon. "Yes, you are."

As a clearly befuddled Kevin watched her and the katana-wielding femme, Lilian slumped in her seat.

And this day had been going so well, too.

Chapter 3

The Maid-slash-Bodyguard, Kotohime

Kevin didn't think the situation could get any more awkward than this.

Actually, that was a lie; he could think of plenty of things that would make this situation more awkward—but, as most of those things involved whipped cream, bananas and his mother showing up at the most inopportune moment, he didn't believe they were worth mentioning.

... Anyway, the point remained that this particular predicament had quickly gone down the drain, and was getting more awkward by the second.

After Lilian's maid-slash-bodyguard, Kotohime, found them at the small café, the two kitsune plus one human had traveled back to the Swift residence.

Sitting at the table, her back straight and her bearing similar to those samurai he often saw in anime and manga, Kotohime cut a surprisingly imposing figure. Surprising, because the woman was drop-dead gorgeous, with her perfect white skin, dark raven hair, large doe-like eyes, and a bust even bigger than Lilian's. When most people thought of imposing samurai, they didn't think of a woman who looked like a pinup model.

At least her clothing helped present the image of a traditional Japanese beauty—if not a samurai—but really, who the heck wore kimonos in this day and age? And to wear one in America, of all places? Talk about weird.

Kevin thought about mentioning the woman's odd choice in clothing. He wanted to ask why she was wearing something so outdated. Two aspects of her appearance prevented him from doing so: her katana, and the strangely terrifying gleam in her eyes. Those two characteristics made Kevin feel like she would slice and dice him if he so much as opened his mouth. So he did the smart thing and kept his mouth shut.

"Let me see if I understand correctly, the series of events that led to you living here." Kotohime paused to take a sip of the tea Kevin had prepared, which he didn't even know he had until he'd searched the pantry. He didn't drink tea. Maybe Lilian had bought it. He supposed it didn't matter. They had some, and he would be forever grateful for that small miracle. Now maybe he and Lilian could get out of this situation without being skewered.

Setting the cup back down, the femme fatale took to staring at Lilian with those unfathomably dark eyes. Kevin felt for her. The redheaded kitsune was practically quaking in her seat.

"After running away from home, you hitchhiked from Tampa Bay all the way to Phoenix?"

That was another thing he had learned; Lilian's immediate family—plus two maids—had apparently been staying at one of their vacation homes in Florida when Lilian had run away. Kevin didn't know why, but he assumed the reason had something to do with family issues.

Lilian squirmed uncomfortably as she sat across from the woman, looking like a child that had been caught stealing gum from a grocery store. It was undeniably cute, but Kevin felt bad seeing her this way, even if she had sort of brought it upon herself.

"... Yes."

"And after hitchhiking across the country, you ran into an inu yōkai on the one night she lost control of her lust for battle?"

A little known fact about female inu was their susceptibility to losing control over their battle lust one night out of the entire year. Kevin thought of it as a sort of annual PMS, except that the female in question was less liable to cry and more prone to rip one's head off. He didn't say anything about that, though, because he had no desire to be gutted by this Kotohime woman's katana.

Consequently, Kevin had learned that this didn't happen to male inu. They had no annual night of battle lust, mainly because they always had a lust for battle and bloodshed. It was a 24/7 thing for them.

Lilian didn't say anything this time. After shrinking further into her seat, she simply gave the older woman a submissive nod.

"Do you know how dangerous that was?" Though her voice was still calm, still collected, Kevin couldn't help the shiver that ran down his spine. There was something dangerous lurking beneath that voice. Lilian must have sensed it as well, because her entire body shuddered from tails to ears. "Hitchhiking rides from strangers without a clue as to who they are might just be the least intelligent decision I think you have ever made. Lilian-sama, you could have easily been kidnapped, or worse. Had any of those drivers been yōkai, you would have been—"

"I know!" Lilian interrupted. Kotohime's eyes narrowed, causing the beautiful two-tails to look away. "I know it was stupid, but I…" her eyes flickered over to Kevin. It was only for a second, but Kotohime still saw it.

"I see." Kotohime regarded the two silently for a moment. She took another sip of her tea. It wasn't bad, but it was clearly packaged. These Americans knew nothing about the proper preparation of tea, it seemed. "Regardless of your reasons for traveling all this way, what you did was dangerous, reckless and selfish. Camellia-sama and Iris-sama have been worried sick."

Lilian's gut clenched.

"I didn't mean to worry them," she said softly, still not looking at Kotohime. "But I had to do this. I wanted…" her eyes flickered to Kevin again. Shaking her head, she looked back at the woman who'd had as much a hand in raising her as her own mother did, if not more. "You always used to tell me stories about the human world; how humans are free to make their own choices, how they aren't bound by outdated traditions set down several millennia ago. I wanted to experience that for myself. I wanted to see the human world for myself."

With a slight frown marring her face, Kotohime sighed.

"You have always been rather fascinated with humans and the concept of freedom, but it doesn't change the fact that what you did was dangerous. Nor does it change the fact that you were never supposed to be exposed to human society. You are an heiress to the Pnéyma clan and—"

"Don't you dare go there, Kotohime!" Lilian snarled. For the first time since this highly peculiar meeting had begun, the younger kitsune glared at the swordswoman, her eyes alight with fire. In all the time Kevin had spent with Lilian, he'd never seen her like this, never seen her with that expression of indecipherable rage. That look, it was the most inhuman thing he'd ever seen from her. "I am not some glass figurine that needs to be protected from humanity! And I'm not some commodity that the matriarch can barter favor with! I refuse to let myself be used that way!"

Several seconds of tense silence passed as Kotohime and Lilian stared at each other. The swordswoman's gaze remained placid, a sea of calm within a turbulent storm. Lilian's viciously narrowed eyes contrasted sharply with the other woman's. It was fierce and unpredictable, out of control and blazing, like a forest fire during the dry season.

Kevin watched as a strong gust of wind suddenly blew the door open and a tumbleweed flew in to roll across the kitchen floor. It made a trip around the table, then went back out the door, which closed behind it.

He blinked.

"That was weird."

Kotohime's gaze was compassionate, or at least, it seemed to be. Kevin couldn't tell, as he didn't know her very well, or at all, really. Even Lilian seemed to be having trouble determining the sincerity in Kotohime's expression.

"I understand how you feel, truly I do. However, you and I both know that you cannot continue to defy Pnévma-denka like this. If you do, then she will surely…"

"She will do nothing." Lilian's tails were a rictus of wrathful activity, waving about furiously behind her. "You and I both know that she can't afford to lose me. She won't do anything to jeopardize her precious little bartering chip."

The way she said that, so bitterly, so full of anger and frustration, startled Kevin. He couldn't help but be surprised by the sheer amount of rage and hurt in her voice. In all the time they'd known one another, he had never once heard her sound so broken up.

"You make it sound like Pnévma-denka doesn't even care for you." Kotohime's eyes were filled with sorrow as she spoke, like she couldn't help but be saddened by Lilian's words.

"Pnévma-denka..." Kevin mumbled to himself, his nose crinkling at the use of the Japanese suffix, which meant "his/her/your highness" in layman's terms. Not that the two had heard him anyway. He was more or less being ignored at the moment. It seemed the presence of one human did not matter in the face of the topic these two yōkai were conversing about.

"Does she?" Lilian's voice was filled with bitterness. "Would a person who truly cared for someone else force them to do something they didn't want to?"

Kotohime appeared untroubled by the spiteful question. Kevin didn't know if she was masking her feelings or honestly didn't care. The kimono-clad woman just calmly sipped her tea.

"If it was for the sake of her clan, then yes."

"I'm just as much a part of her clan as anyone else!" Tears were beginning to leak out of Lilian's eyes as her emotions boiled over. Kevin could almost feel the girl's inner turmoil, like a dagger knifing him through the chest. "I am just as much a part of the Pnévma clan as Daphne! Yet you don't see her being pawned off like some cheap trinket!"

"Daphne-sama is also going to become the head of the clan, and she does not have Lilian-sama's rebellious nature," Kotohime tried to reason with Lilian, as if this would somehow calm the two-tail's stormy emotions. Fat chance of that happening. Kevin was beginning to learn that kitsune were illogical creatures by nature.

Lilian's face took on a truly frightening visage as she gritted her teeth in frustration. Kevin could actually see her whiskers appearing as the control she possessed over her transformation slipped.

"Um, excuse me," he finally interrupted, trying to prevent this precarious situation from degrading any further, "but could someone please tell me what the heck is going on? What are you two talking about?"

When Kotohime's sharp gaze landed on him, Kevin's entire body froze as if he'd been violently dumped in the Arctic Circle. An indescribable feeling washed over him, chilling him to his very core. He would have called this feeling fear, but that wouldn't have done it justice. Terror would have been more accurate, but still an understatement. Being underneath that leering, predatory gaze made him feel like an insect that the woman was about to step on, something so beneath her notice that he wasn't even worth the time it would take to purposefully kill.

"Do not speak out of turn, human. While I have nothing against your kind, we are discussing clan matters, of which you have no right to know about." Kotohime scoffed, as if the very thought of her indulging his curiosity was preposterous. "Know your place."

"Do not talk to my mate like that!"

Kotohime twitched. Her gaze shifted from Kevin to Lilian. With her penetrating, dagger-like stare no longer pinning him in place, Kevin heaved a deep gasp and slumped in his seat.

"Lilian-sama, you cannot possibly mean to say that this... this boy is—"

"That is exactly what I'm saying." Once more, Lilian interrupted the woman, whose frown grew very prominent. "Kevin is my mate. I chose him of my own volition, with my own free will, and I will not allow you or anyone else to keep me from him."

"Lilian-sama, you are the heiress to one of the Thirteen Great Clans, one of the most powerful clans in our world. Someone like yourself needs a mate worthy of her stature."

"Just what are you trying to say?" Lilian's eyes flickered, her pupils shifting from their rounded shape to black slits.

"I am saying that you cannot be with a human," Kotohime replied bluntly.

Eyes narrowing dangerously, Lilian bared her canines, which Kevin noticed were very sharp. "Who are you to tell me who I can and cannot be with?"

"The matriarch—"

"The matriarch can go to hell! Do you think I care what that old hag wants? Do you really think I'll allow someone like her to use me? She doesn't care about me. She just wants someone she can train to become the perfect little doll in her power plays. I'd sooner mate with an inu than whatever pompous jerk she sets me up with!"

"You do not have a choice in the matter." Kotohime's voice grew colder than a breeze created by a yuki-onna's ice powers. Kevin shivered. Lilian did not appear to be affected. She continued glaring at the woman, her dangerously narrowed eyes and bared teeth reminding Kevin that she was not human despite her appearance.

"Very well then," the redhead said, her voice now grave. "If this is how you want to play, then you leave me with only one choice."

Lilian stood up, back straight, ears pointed toward the ceiling and her tails unwavering and still. She looked at Kotohime with a surprisingly formal gaze. Kevin wondered what she was doing.

Kotohime's eyes widened.

"You wouldn't—"

"I am Lilian Pnévma, daughter of Camellia. My Crest is that of the Lily!"

"L-Lilian-sama!" Kotohime was actually starting to look panicked. Her eyes had grown wide and round, and her voice had become slightly shrill. "Stop this at once! You don't—"

"With my Crest as my witness," Lilian continued, ignoring Kotohime completely, "and before the eyes and ears of one who serves as a vassal to my clan, and will now serve as witness and messenger to my declaration."

"Lilian-sama! Stop!"

"I declare that I am no longer—"

"All right!" Kotohime shouted, her high-pitched voice making Kevin wince. "You've made your point! Please stop!"

"Are you going to keep disrespecting my mate if I stop?" Lilian asked, her eyes narrowed and a serious frown marring her lips.

Kotohime grimaced, but shook her head.

"No. You have made your point quite clear."

"Are you going to try and take me away from him?"

"After a performance like that?" Kotohime rubbed her face, which looked haggard and worn, defeated in every way imaginable. "No, I know that such an option is no longer feasible. Not anymore. Not after you've made your intentions to me so irrevocably clear."

"Good." With that, all of Lilian's strength seemed to ebb and the young, gorgeous redhead dropped gracelessly into her seat. Her shoulders slumped and her head fell back as she closed her eyes and let out a deep breath.

Silence permeated the room once again, a stillness so

complete that Kevin feared breathing too heavily would break it and cause some irreversible catastrophe to occur.

"Um." But break it he did, because Kevin still felt utterly clueless, and his ignorance was giving him a headache. "Can someone please explain what that was all about?"

***

After the intense conversation at the kitchen table, the group adjourned to the living room, where it was much more comfortable. Kevin and Lilian sat on the couch. For reasons that were beyond him, Kotohime had opted to sit on the floor. She sat in *seiza*, the traditional Japanese way of sitting that involved kneeling on the floor with one's legs folded underneath their thighs. It looked very uncomfortable.

"How much has Lilian-sama told you about kitsune?" Kotohime didn't want to bother beating around the bush, it seemed.

"Not much," Kevin answered, his eyes squinting and nose wrinkling as he tried to remember what Lilian had told him about kitsune in general. "She mostly told me about kitsune powers, but I also know a little about her family. I know that they live in Greece, and that her family has several mansions located around the world. She mentioned the matriarch, and some of her other family members, too, like her sister and one of her aunts, but that's about it."

While Kevin spoke, Lilian quietly sat by his side. She still seemed exhausted by her actions in the kitchen, for her posture was slumped. She also had yet to chime in, which struck him as odd. Lilian was a very talkative girl... fox... girl.

"I see." Kotohime paused, considering her words. What should she tell him? How much should she tell him? Regardless of Lilian's choice, this boy was still human, and it wouldn't do for him to become too involved in kitsune affairs—not at this stage. "In that case, I believe it would be prudent for me to tell you about the Pnévma Clan first. They are one of the Thirteen Great Kitsune Clans. Known as the Great Spirit Clan, they are currently the largest and most powerful clan of Spirit Kitsune in the entire world."

"Spirit Kitsune?" Kevin's brows furrowed. He looked at

Lilian, then back at Kotohime. "But Lilian's not a Spirit Kitsune. She's a Celestial Kitsune."

"Oh? I had not realized you knew that." If Kotohime truly was surprised by this information, her face did not show it. "You are correct. Lilian-sama is a Celestial Kitsune. However, she is an anomaly within her clan. With the exception of her and her sister, every other kitsune within the Pnévma clan is a Spirit Kitsune."

"Ah," Kevin muttered, "okay."

"Now where was I?" Kotohime absently polished the blade of her katana. Kevin and Lilian both shivered. "Oh, yes! As one of the Thirteen Great Clans, the Pnévma Clan is a very important part of kitsune society. It is the Thirteen Great Clans that rule over all kitsune; they make the policies on everything from our dealings with other yōkai to policies on interacting with humans. It is the job of each Great Clan to ensure that all kitsune who fall under their jurisdiction follow the laws put in place."

So Lilian's family was a bunch of political bigwigs in the kitsune world? He should have figured it was something like that; her family did own several mansions and even had their own maids, after all. It only made sense. He actually felt kind of stupid for not figuring that out sooner.

"And what was all that... that... stuff back there about?" Kevin made a vague gesture toward the kitchen.

Kotohime had to pause before answering. When she did answer, it was slowly, as if she was carefully considering each word before speaking them. "As I have already mentioned, Lilian-sama is something of an oddity within the clan, being the only Celestial Kitsune in a clan full of Spirit Kitsune."

"The only Celestial Kitsune?" Kevin blinked. "But I thought you said her sister was also—"

"Iris-sama is not a Celestial Kitsune, but a Void Kitsune," Kotohime interrupted, "which just makes them both all the more unusual." Her eyes narrowed. "Now stop interrupting me."

Kevin flinched. "S-sorry."

Kotohime looked to be barely withholding a snort.

"As I was saying, Lilian-sama is the only Celestial Kitsune of her clan. This would normally be grounds for banishment, as the clan is not supposed to have any type of kitsune other than Spirit Kitsune. It's a part of the laws that govern the Great Clans in order to keep the balance of power. However, Lilian-sama was born with exceptionally strong celestial abilities."

There was another pause. Kotohime looked thoughtful, as if she was remembering something from long ago.

"Normally, a kitsune will not exhibit signs of their elemental affinity until they gain their third tail. Exceptionally powerful kitsune may do so some time after they gain their second. Lilian-sama and Iris-sama both showed signs of their Celestial and Void powers before they'd even gained their second tail. They possess powers that are so strong they unconsciously manifested before either of them gained a human form."

Kevin looked over at Lilian in shock and awe. Lilian noticed his expression and looked away, her cheeks surprisingly red.

"You never mentioned that."

"I didn't think it was important," Lilian admitted, though he thought there might have been another motive for her omission.

"Such a thing is generally unheard of. There was simply no way Pnéyma-denka was going to let such power go," Kotohime continued. "If she did, then the Great Celestial and Void Clans, Shénshèng and Gitsune, would have taken Lilian-sama and Iris-sama in, gaining even greater power than before and upsetting her clan's place among those two already imposing forces. Pnéyma-denka went against several generations' worth of tradition, and even broke the law to keep Lilian-sama and Iris-sama in the clan. She did this by rallying many of the lesser clans into action, perpetrating the fear they had about what would happen if Shénshèng and Gitsune gained any more power than they already had."

"She only did it to gain more political power," Lilian muttered, her voice a low-pitched growl. "She didn't care about my sister or me. She just kept us so the other two clans wouldn't gain more power through us."

Kotohime sighed sadly, but didn't say anything to dispute the girl.

"What do you mean by that?" Kevin asked. "How was that a power play?"

Before Lilian could answer—if she had any intentions of actually doing so—Kotohime spoke up again. "What Lilian-sama is speaking of are the mating arrangements that were made by

Pnéyma-denka and the leader of the Shénshèng Clan, The Bodhisattva, Shénshèng Shinkuro-dono."

Kevin's gut clenched uncomfortably as an unusual feeling welled up inside of him, one that he instinctively recognized, but couldn't identify. Whatever this feeling was, it aggravated him greatly, like an itch he couldn't scratch because it was underneath his skin, wriggling beneath layers of flesh like earthworms underneath the soil.

"What do you mean by mating arrangements?"

Beside him, Lilian clenched two fistfuls of her jean shorts, her fingers grasping the fabric with almost painful harshness.

"I mean just what I said. It is not unusual for two clans to make mating arrangements for the benefit of both clans," Kotohime answered. "Of course, generally, the mating arrangements are done between one of the Thirteen Great Clans and a lesser clan of the same type. This was the first time that arrangements had been made by two Great Clans."

Kevin still had trouble grasping the concept being presented to him, or maybe his mind simply refused to understand because of the consequences knowing would bring.

"And by mating arrangements, you mean…"

"Think of it as a human marriage contract."

Kevin sucked in a breath. He didn't really know much about marriage contracts. They had been used centuries ago—like, before America had even become America. What little he did know came from history textbooks, a couple of novels and manga he'd read, mostly ones that focused on European-esque fantasy settings, and occasionally Japan's Sengoku period.

"So then she—I mean, Lilian is…"

"Nothing is definite yet," Kotohime answered before he could finish, "Lilian-sama has not been promised to anyone, but there have been several candidates who have expressed interest in her, including Shinkuro-dono's youngest son."

Kevin frowned. The suffix "dono" meant sir or madam, but it sounded like Shinkuro held the same status as Lilian's grandmother.

Is she using a less respectful suffix because she doesn't like this Shinkuro guy?

At the mention of Shinkuro's son, Lilian's hand sought out

Kevin's. He looked down as she clutched his hand in desperation. It was shaking. Thin, feminine fingers quivered as they grasped his.

Almost without conscious thought, Kevin turned his hand over so he could return the gesture.

Kotohime saw this and frowned, but said nothing. It was not her place to mention things like propriety, not after Lilian had made her intentions toward Kevin clear.

That did not mean she would approve of this relationship, however. If Kevin was going to be Lilian's mate, he would have to prove himself first. If he did not—well, this would not be the first time a young kitsune had been left heartbroken by the loss of her mate.

***

Kevin and Lilian prepared for bed the moment Kotohime's impromptu lesson on kitsune culture ended. It was late. The sun had already sunk behind the mountain range in the distance, the stars and moon coming out to bless the night with their brilliant luster.

As he stared at his reflection in the bathroom mirror while brushing his teeth, Kevin thought about everything he had learned that day. There was a lot more to kitsune than he had initially suspected. He'd assumed that kitsune had a culture of their own, of course, but he had been expecting something similar to human culture. Everything Kotohime had told him was vastly different from what he had been expecting, and there was likely a lot more that he still didn't know; maybe more than he would ever be able to learn in his lifetime.

That thought, the realization that he knew so little about the girl who lived with him, about her people and culture, was truly humbling.

He once again went back to Lilian's situation. Her matriarch, who Kevin had learned during Kotohime's lecture was actually Lilian's grandmother on her father's side, wanted to set her up with a mate.

A Mating Arrangement. Kotohime had said that it was similar to a marriage contract. It was basically the act of two clans arranging for members of their respective clans to mate. This union would create a child, who would then become an honorary member of both clans. It was a way of tying two clans together, an alliance forged through the combining of two bloodlines.

In other words, a marriage of convenience.

And Lilian's grandmother wanted to set her up in one. Just thinking about his housemate being forced to mate with someone against her will caused a sharp pain to appear within his chest, like an icy hand wrapping around his heart and squeezing it into a fine paste. He could only imagine how Lilian must feel.

His gaze flickered to Lilian. The redhead wore a pair of yellow flannel pants and a pink spaghetti strap shirt that flattered her figure quite well—which was an oxymoron, because it implied there was some article of clothing out there that *didn't* flatter her figure. It was a preposterous notion, to be sure. Lilian was so beautiful it was almost a crime. She could probably wear mud and make it look better than a 10 million dollar gown being worn by a Playboy model.

He went back to staring at his own reflection before she could notice him looking at her.

Kevin recalled how Lilian had been unable to tell him why she was so far from home when they first met. At the time, he had assumed she was just embarrassed by her situation, but now he knew better. She had run away, all in an effort to avoid marrying some jerk she didn't even like.

After finishing their nightly ritual (brushing, flossing, and using mouthwash), the pair strolled into the hall where their progress was halted by Kotohime. The woman hadn't moved from her guard position by the door the entire time he and Lilian had been preparing for bed. She'd followed them, walking several steps behind the two like a chaperone or escort, and then stopped by the bathroom door and remained there. It was kind of creepy, but Kevin tried his best to ignore the woman.

"Lilian-sama, could I have a moment of your time?"

Lilian looked at Kotohime with an inscrutable expression. Emotions flickered within her emerald irises, flashing by before he could figure out what she was thinking. Her features, which appeared tumultuous and lost, really did not suit her.

"I suppose," Lilian turned her head to look at Kevin. "I'll be back in a bit." She smiled, but it wasn't a true smile. It didn't reach her eyes.

He smiled back, keeping up the charade. If Lilian didn't want to worry him, then he would indulge her. It was the least he could do.

"I'll just wait in our room."

Lilian's smile widened, transforming into something genuine. He wondered why, but decided not to question what made her so happy. Some things were better off remaining unknown.

***

Kotohime led Lilian onto a tiny balcony attached to the Swift residence. The older kitsune stood by the wall that acted as a railing while Lilian stood next to her, looking anywhere but at Kotohime.

A sigh was released when Kotohime realized that her charge was going to keep avoiding eye contact.

"Lilian-sama," Kotohime said, her tone resigned, "I hope you understand what you are doing. Going against Pnévma-denka's will is not something to be done lightly, or at all. Need I remind you of what happened to the last person who defied the matriarch?"

"I am not my father," Lilian snapped. She held Kotohime's gaze long enough to penetrate her maid with a fierce stare. The kimono-clad femme was unaffected. Lilian sighed and looked away.

Lilian knew next to nothing about her father, the man who had given birth to her. She didn't even know his name. Speaking about him was forbidden. Only Abercio, one of her many half-uncles and someone who seemed to have been close to her father, had the audacity to speak about him, and he'd been punished severely for doing so. Even now, after nearly a century, he wasn't allowed to enter the clan's estate in Greece.

The only thing she knew was that her father had been banished for defying the matriarch, an unforgivable offense. Lilian assumed he was dead. Kitsune with no clan didn't live very long without a benefactor, and no one would take in someone with the stigma of having been banished. Being banished meant you were a disgrace, and a disgraced kitsune wasn't someone another clan would willingly take in, lest they invoke the wrath of the clan that had done the banishing.

"True, but you are a product of his defiance," Kotohime said. "Your father had already been promised to another when he met Camellia-sama and had you and your sister. He was banished for his insolence, and the only reason Pnévma-denka accepted your mother into the clan was because of the power you and your sister possess."

"You don't have to remind me," Lilian wilted. Her ears, normally upright and perky, drooped. She did not like being reminded of their position within the clan. "I know that. Daphne always reminds me about how fortunate we are for the matriarch's mercy every chance she gets."

She didn't enjoy thinking about her extended family. Very few members of her clan actually liked her thanks to the issues surrounding her parents' union. It was that very same hatred which led Lilian and her immediate family to take up residence in the United States—well, that, and the fact that she had been a hellion for the past couple of years. Lilian assumed the matriarch had gotten sick of her attitude and decided to send them as far from the main estate as possible.

Her mother never spoke of her father. Lilian knew that the reason for this was partly due to her mom's degrading mental faculties. It was hard to talk about someone you could barely remember, and harder still to talk about someone when you had the mind of a five year old. However, Lilian also believed part of the reason was because thinking about her father hurt. The man her mother loved, and who Lilian had chosen to believe loved her back, had been a disobedient traitor who defied the matriarch. That kind of information was not something people willingly wanted to remember.

"So, that boy..." Kotohime interrupted Lilian's thought process. "Is he...?"

"Yes."

"I see." A pause. Kotohime visibly gathered her thoughts. "And does he...?"

"Of course he doesn't." Lilian shook her head. "Not that I would expect him to. He was just a child back then, a cute little boy no older than six or seven." Her smile turned bitter as she spoke. "Besides, we both know that even if his memories did extend that far back, he'd still have no recollection of me. My *family* saw to that."

The way Lilian spat out the word family, like it was poison in her mouth, made Kotohime frown.

"You should not speak ill of your family, Lilian-sama."

"Whatever," Lilian huffed. "We both know they're to blame for all of my problems. They hate me, and would like nothing better than to see me stuck in a mating arrangement with that idiot."

"You should also not speak so ill about Jiāoào-dono, Lilian-sama."

Lilian gritted her teeth, but said nothing more about her potential suitor, instead changing the subject.

"So, are you going to tell me about how foolish I am for coming here? For hoping that Kevin would remember me? That is why you dragged me out here, isn't it?"

"Do you regret coming here and discovering that he has no recollection of you?"

"No. Never."

"Then anything I could say to you won't really matter now, will it? However, speaking of your burgeoning romance, you do realize that a relationship between you and him will not last forever, correct?" Kotohime gave her ward a look of worry.

Lilian looked away. "I know that."

"And you still intend to mate with him?"

"I do."

"Even though he'll be dead less than a century from now?"

Lilian's shoulders slumped. "Do you have to make it sound so fatalistic?"

"My dear Lilian-sama, you are talking to someone who speaks from experience. I merely want you to understand what being in a relationship with a human will mean. It may seem wonderful at first, and I do not deny that humans make some of the best mates, but it does not change his mortality. It also does not change the fact that you will live at least nine centuries longer than him."

Lilian's hands clenched into fists, her knuckles turning white. "Whatever. Is there anything else you wanted to talk about, or can I go back inside?"

"Ufufufu... so eager to get back to your mate, I see. Very

well. I believe our conversation is finished."

"Good."

Lilian did not hesitate to leave the balcony. Kotohime watched her young ward walk back inside and disappear down the hallway. Her eyes remained on the spot where Lilian had vanished for a while longer, then shifted back to the sea of stars.

"Oh, Lilian-sama," she sighed, "you truly do not realize what kind of hardships await those who choose to mate with a human."

***

When Lilian entered the bedroom it was to find Kevin staring out the window, his brows furrowed deeply, making him look several years older. His sleeping bag was already set up on the floor, and she could see that Kevin had even pulled the bed's covers back for her.

She smiled softly. He really was a kind and courteous young man. Now if she could just get him to hurry up and fall in love with her, things would be kosher.

"Kevin."

Kevin's messy blond hair swayed as he jerked around, his eyes widening. Lilian wondered about what he'd been pondering to be so startled by her presence. Sure, she hadn't stomped into the room or anything, but she hadn't made an effort to be silent either.

"Oh, Lilian." Kevin smiled at her, but it appeared strained. "How was your talk with Kotohime?"

"It went about as well as could be expected, I guess," Lilian mumbled. She loved that woman like a mother, but Kotohime could be so overbearing sometimes. The depressing topic they'd discussed hadn't helped. In fact, it had pretty much killed whatever good mood she'd had from earlier that day.

Times like these made Lilian wish that she'd been born human.

"I'm sorry about how she treated you." Lilian looked at him apologetically. "She means well, and she's not prejudiced against humans, but whenever clan matters are involved, she holds to the same policies in matters of human/yōkai relationships that most kitsune do."

"What policies are those?"

"The ones that state humans and yōkai should never become

involved with each other. While it's not forbidden for a kitsune to have a relationship with a human, it is frowned upon. Kotohime doesn't agree with this policy, but she does believe that humans should stay out of kitsune affairs."

"Kind of a double standard, isn't it?" Kevin gave her a wry grin. "I mean, you kitsune pull a lot of pranks on us humans, and your own clan interacts with humans at your resort."

"The Pnévma clan doesn't actually have any interaction with humans," Lilian corrected. "Only vassals of the clan do. Members of the actual clan—those whose lineage comes directly from the matriarch—usually go their entire lives without meeting a single human. I should know," she added in a bitter half-whisper, "they tried doing the same thing to me."

"Lilian? Are you all right?" Kevin didn't like the look on Lilian's face.

"… Yes." Dispelling the resentful thoughts fluttering through her mind, Lilian focused her attention back on him. "What about you? Are you okay?"

"Oh, I'm fine, just fine." Kevin waved his hand in a dismissive gesture. "I've just got a lot on my mind right now."

"Like what?"

Kevin scratched the back of his neck with his left hand.

"I guess I'm still trying to figure out what happened back there. I'm a bit confused by those things you said back in the kitchen."

Lilian was nonplussed. "What were you confused about?"

"That stuff you were saying, about your crest and all that."

"Oh, that." Lilian's eyes shone and her mouth parted in a pretty "o" shape as she snapped her fingers. "I forgot you wouldn't know about that."

She paused for a moment, thinking about how best to explain her actions. After a second of silent contemplation, she nodded.

"Right. So, there are many customs within the clan that those words can actually be used for. Usually these customs must be recognized and witnessed by the matriarch of the clan, but because of what I was using them for, a servant such as Kotohime would suffice just fine."

That didn't explain anything, and Kevin said as much. "I'm still not sure I understand. What exactly were you hoping to accomplish? What were you trying to do?"

"I was going to banish myself from the clan."

Kevin's eyes looked ready to bulge from his sockets, such was their immense size. "E-excuse me?"

"I was going to banish myself from the clan," Lilian repeated.

"I heard you the first time." Kevin stared at the girl, his lips thinning into a tight line. "What I mean is why were you attempting to banish yourself from the clan?"

Lilian was silent.

"Lilian…"

"She wanted to take me away from you." The words were spoken so quietly that he almost missed them. Lilian looked directly into his eyes, and Kevin felt like he was drowning within the depths of her viridian gaze. Had anyone ever looked at him with so much raw, undiluted emotion before? "Kotohime wanted to take me away from you and I… I don't want that. I want to stay here with you. I want to experience life with you."

Kevin's eyes widened as Lilian's emotions poured out of her. Frustrated tears welled up in the redhead's eyes as she stared at him with a cornucopia of conflicted feelings.

"I love you! I love you so much, Kevin! I know you don't love me back. I realize that, but I… I don't care!" Lilian shook her head, her hair whipping about her face like flames caught in a breeze. "I don't want to leave you! I want to stay with you forever and ever."

While Lilian poured out her heart and soul to him, Kevin could only stare at her in abject shock. He had always known about her feelings for him—the gods knew she'd told him plenty of times already. But, until this moment, he'd not realized the extent and depths of those feelings.

Part of him had always assumed that Lilian was just enamored because he had rescued her when she was in her fox form. It had made sense at the time. He was one of the first humans that she hadn't needed to use her enchantments on, and thus, one of the only humans that she'd truly interacted with.

He knew that wasn't the case now. No one could fake emotions like that. Kevin doubted anyone, even a kitsune—a master at manipulating the emotions of others—could fake the intensity in her stare, the pure form of unadulterated emotions in her gaze. That the girl in question was one of those very kitsune wasn't lost on him.

But then, this was also Lilian, a kitsune who was surprisingly honest with her thoughts and feelings. Innocent. That's the word he was looking for. Everything that she did, from her attempts to seduce him to her love for nerd culture and sheer joy at experiencing new things was overwhelming in its purity.

A strange dichotomy, considering she wanted to screw him into a coma.

"How can you feel so strongly about me?" he asked. It was, in all honesty, the only question he could think to ask in that moment. He had several others, but for whatever reason, they refused to come to him. "We... we hardly even know each other. I know that I helped you when you were injured, but..."

The smile Lilian gave him was soft and gentle, but there was a tinge of sadness to it, like his words were slowly breaking her heart. It made him feel like the biggest prick this side of the multiverse.

"Several years ago—ten, I think it was—I met a young boy," she said.

Kevin nodded. "I think you told me about him."

"I did. Anyway, this human boy had gotten lost in the forest that separates our village from the resort. When he found me, I was very distraught. I had just overheard a conversation between the matriarch and a member of the Shénshèng Clan. The matriarch was trying to set up mating arrangements between me and a member of that clan. I was crying."

Kevin was able to conjure an image of Lilian, a little younger than she was now, lost within a forest and shedding tears of sorrow after discovering that her matriarch was trying to use her in a power play. His chest began to ache.

"You can imagine my surprise when this little boy walked up to me," Lilian continued to weave her tale, her smile soft and her eyes tinged with gentle amusement. "There are barriers put in place around the village to prevent humans from stumbling upon it. They create a very powerful illusion that makes whoever is trapped in them think they're walking around in circles. This, however, did not happen to the boy. Somehow, he managed to not only breach the barrier, which should have been impossible, but also find me."

"I suspect this was due to his age," she added when Kevin opened his mouth, correctly interpreting his question before he could ask it. "He was so young that the barrier probably couldn't detect him, allowing him to slip inside somehow."

"So what happened after that?" Kevin asked, enraptured by the story.

"He came up to me and asked why I was crying. I don't know why, maybe it was because I was so distraught, or maybe I just wasn't thinking clearly, but I told him everything. I told him about how the matriarch wanted to force me into a mating arrangement, about how I didn't want to be forced into a relationship with someone I didn't love, and how I wanted to be with someone for love and not because the matriarch told me to."

"Do you know what that little boy said to me?" When Kevin shook his head, Lilian's lips curled beautifully. "He said, 'you shouldn't care what other people want. If you don't want to mate with someone, then don't mate with them.'" Lilian's laugh was very lyrical, even if there was a hint of melancholy tinging it. "I remember telling him that I couldn't defy my matriarch. He just stared at me like I was some kind of idiot, and then asked me why I couldn't just say no."

Lilian walked over to the window to stand beside Kevin. He followed her with his eyes as she looked up at the stars. Her smile entranced him.

"And after he asked that question, I couldn't help but ask it myself. Why? Why should I mate with someone I didn't even know, much less love? Why should I follow the laws of my matriarch when it was abundantly clear that she didn't even care about me? And do you know what answer I came up with?"

"I can take a guess," Kevin said, "I imagine you decided that you shouldn't be forced to mate with someone you didn't know, right? That you wouldn't allow yourself to be... mated off?" He paused for a second, then shrugged. "Am I right?"

Lilian's nod told him that he'd hit the nail on the head.

"Yes, you're right. I decided that I wouldn't be the matriarch's pawn. That I would live my life the way I wanted to."

A moment of silence passed between them.

"So what happened to the boy?"

"The boy and I talked a bit longer. I'll admit, he kind of grew on me. I suppose you could say I felt a kinship with him. He was so adorable and earnest that a part of me wanted to take him back home. A search party the matriarch sent out eventually found us, and the boy was taken back to the resort while I was escorted home. I never saw him again."

"That's kind of depressing."

"It is," Lilian agreed. "Still, even though I never saw that boy again, I kept what he had told me close to my heart. Whenever the matriarch set me up with someone from the Shénshèng clan, I would do everything in my power to sabotage her efforts."

Memories of dozens of meetings flashed through her mind— and of how those meetings ended with the other party being thoroughly humiliated. Her lips twitched in amusement as she remembered how some of those kitsune had been ranting as they stormed out of the Pnévma compound in shame.

"The matriarch used to set me up with mating candidates every chance she got. I was forced to endure meetings with almost every male member of the Shénshèng clan, be they from the main family or a branch member, old or young. I was even forced to meet with a kitsune who was seven-hundred years older than me! Can you imagine? A young kitsune who had just gained her second tail, barely one-hundred and forty-nine years old, sitting in front of stuffy old men who were expressing an unhealthy interest in her. My breasts were still growing at the time!"

"Do you really have to mention your breasts?" Kevin asked dryly.

"I remember doing everything in my power to sabotage those meetings. I would wear the ugliest clothes imaginable. I spoke out of turn. I even did embarrassing and disgusting things in front of my potential suitors, all so they wouldn't want to mate with me."

"Embarrassing and disgusting things? Like what?"

"Never mind that," Lilian said, blushing. She quickly continued before he could question her further. "I would also play pranks. I remember one that I played very clearly. I drugged his tea, stripped him naked, covered his body in tar and feathers, snuck him out of the compound in the middle of the night, and hung him from the top of a flagpole in the middle of the human resort." Her grin was rueful and showed a side of her that Kevin had never seen before. It was surprisingly appealing. "I remember the fiasco that caused. All of the humans had to have their memories erased, and the suitor I pranked wanted nothing to do with me afterward."

"I can see why." Kevin shuddered. "You can be surprisingly vicious when you want to be."

Lilian thrust out her chest as if he'd just complimented her. "Of course I can. I am a kitsune, you know."

"I suppose that's true." Kevin paused. "So I'm guessing your antics worked?"

"For the most part. Very few of the suitors I met ever wanted to see me again. Out of all them, only one has persisted."

"Who?"

"The youngest son of Shinkiro Shénshèng, Jiāoào." Lilian scowled. "He's the heir of the Shénshèng Clan, next in line to become the Bodhisattva after his father steps down and Inari gives him the ninth tail. He's one of the most persistent jerks I've ever met. Despite everything I've done to him, he just keeps coming back."

Lilian clenched her fists at the thought about that arrogant fool. Oh, how she hated him. She hated him so much that her tails shuddered in revulsion at the mere thought of him.

"I'm still not sure I understand." Kevin's eyes still blatantly showed his confusion. "Don't get me wrong, it was a nice story, and I'm glad that you decided to take control of your life. I'm just not sure what it has to do with me."

The look Lilian gave him was so crestfallen and dejected that his heart lurched. It made Kevin regret ever opening his mouth.

"No," she said softly, her shoulders slumping and her tails dangling limply, a reflection of her despondency. "I guess you wouldn't."

Chapter 4

Meet the Runners

Kevin stepped out of the shower, an exhausted yawn escaping his lips as water dripped onto the tiled floor. With his hair matted against his face, he walked over to the sink with slumped shoulders and a staggering gait.

He hunched over, hands on the marble countertop, and stared into the mirror. His reflection stared back. It had certainly seen better days, his reflection. His eyes were slightly sunken in, with dark bags hanging underneath them. He didn't look like death warmed over or anything, but it was obvious he hadn't slept well last night.

After running a hand through his wet hair, he turned away from the mirror and walked out of the bathroom, a towel wrapped around his waist.

The hallway was mercifully clear, with no sign of Lilian or his newest guest in sight. Judging from the scent wafting in the air, one or both of them were in the kitchen. He wondered what they were cooking.

The bedroom was empty when he entered, and Kevin wondered if Lilian was the one making breakfast. A headshake dispelled those thoughts as he put on his running clothes—light blue shorts, a white shirt with blue trim and his school's mascot—a cactus—on the front, and a pair of socks.

Lilian was sitting on the couch in the living room when he entered. The shirt she wore that morning was several sizes too large and did an admirable job of covering her thighs, which he was grateful for. Kevin didn't know how much longer he would've been able to deal with her sexy panties. Her ears and tails were also out, which his eyes were inevitably drawn to.

Lilian stared at the TV, her legs tucked under her bum. Kevin couldn't see the screen from where he stood, but judging from the noise, he could tell she was watching anime. *White Out*, most likely. That was her current favorite. She seemed to have a thing for hot chicks wielding oversized butcher knives.

For just a moment, Kevin felt entranced as he stared at the beautiful fox-girl. She really was the most gorgeous example of a female he had ever met; perfectly proportioned, flaming red hair that went down to her small, shapely butt, killer legs and an amazing chest. Not to mention her ears and tails…

Kevin shook his head vigorously.

Ugh, her ears and tails? Am I really so enamored with animals that a girl with animal parts turns me on?

Damn his love for animals! Or, maybe he should blame it on his love for anime? A combination of both?

"Oh, Kevin." Lilian noticed his presence and gave him an expression so sunny he was nearly blinded. "Good morning."

"G-good morning, Lilian." Kevin coughed into his hand several times, his blush quickly receding. "I take it Kotohime is in the kitchen?"

"Yep." Lilian went back to staring at the television. "She's been in there since before I woke up, so I'm guessing breakfast will be ready soon."

"Actually, I have just finished preparing breakfast, Lilian-sama," a voice said from the kitchen. Both human and kitsune turned their heads to see the femme fatale looking at them from the kitchen entrance. Kotohime wore the same kimono as yesterday, but with one new addition: a frilly white apron.

Kevin knew he hadn't bought something like that, and wondered if this was more of that storage space stuff.

"I've made enough for the both of you." Kotohime's eyes lingered on Kevin, who felt a shiver crawl down his spine like an insipid worm. "I hope you're grateful."

"O-of course," Kevin stuttered. Why did it feel like he was staring into the face of his impending death whenever this woman looked at him?

"Stop frightening my mate, Kotohime." Lilian's voice was cold, obviously not amused by her servant's actions.

Kotohime stiffened, but quickly bowed in apology to Kevin, though the action seemed to take quite a bit of effort. "My apologies, Kevin-san. I did not mean to frighten you."

Kevin frowned at the comment, but couldn't dispute her. It was true. She did scare him, and there was no denying that. However…

"Kevin-san?" He gave Lilian a queer look, as if asking, "*what the hell?*" to the younger of the two supernatural creatures taking residence in his apartment.

Lilian giggled.

"Just go along with it," she suggested. "It'll be easier if you simply go with the flow and don't ask questions."

Kevin slowly nodded. It would probably be easier to just accept this as another kitsune quirk or something. Easier, and safer for what little sanity he'd retained since Lilian appeared in his life.

Kevin and Lilian moved over to the kitchen table. Lilian sat on Kevin's immediate right while Kotohime stood off to the side, left hand holding her sheath while her right tenderly caressed the handle of her katana. Kevin did his utmost not to gulp.

Instead of staring at the creepy yet beautiful swordswoman, he turned his attention to the breakfast.

A large drop of sweat left a glistening trail as it rolled down the side of Kevin's head. Steamed rice, miso soup, *natto* (fermented soybeans), broiled salted salmon and *umeboshi* (pickled plums) greeted his vision. The smell was divine, truly mouth-watering, but his thoughts were on something other than how appetizing the meal looked.

"This… this is a traditional Japanese breakfast…" Seriously, a traditional Japanese breakfast in America? Who did that?

"Considering I am Japanese, I felt it was appropriate," the kimono-clad woman stated with the utmost poise. If it weren't for the katana in her hand and the wakizashi hidden under her obi, she would have looked exactly like a Japanese maid. "I hope you do not have a problem with the meal that I have laboriously prepared for you."

"U-urk!" Kevin made several choking sounds. "N-no! I don't

have a problem! Of course not! I love Japanese food! Ahahahaha!"

Kotohime stared at Kevin for a bit longer, her predatory eyes watching as he laughed nervously. The laughter petered away until he grew silent, looking anywhere but at the maid-slash-bodyguard.

"I am glad to hear that, as I would be most... displeased if you didn't enjoy my cooking." Kevin's gulp caused her to smile. It was, admittedly, a very beautiful smile, but it still freaked him out. "Now then, please, enjoy the food that this humble Kotohime has prepared for you."

"R-right."

Kevin and Lilian began to eat. Or at least, Lilian did. Kevin tried to, but he'd never been very good at using chopsticks. Every time he attempted to grab some rice or salmon, the food would fall from his tenuous grip.

Lilian noticed his predicament. "Having trouble?"

"A bit." Kevin's face flushed at this shameful admittance.

"Here, let me show you how it's done." Kevin nearly shrieked when Lilian's ample chest pressed into his back after she stood up and moved behind him. She wasn't wearing a bra, and it took every ounce of willpower on his part not to flip out. "First, hold the upper chopstick like a pencil, about one-third of the way from its top. Just like that. Next, place the second chopstick against your ring finger and hold it with the base of your thumb. Move the upper chopstick with your thumb, index, and middle fingers like so. Good! Now, grab the food between the lower and upper chopsticks."

Kevin focused on Lilian's hands as she held his, so much more delicate and fair than his rougher, sun-kissed ones. Was it odd that he thought she had really pretty hands? Probably.

As he thought about Lilian's hands, an image appeared in his mind, a delusion, a fantasy the likes of which he'd only started having recently.

"Thank you for teaching me how to hold these chopsticks, Lilian," he said.

"You're welcome," Lilian smiled at him. *She was wearing a French maid outfit again.*

"However, I think I would prefer it if you fed me by hand."

Lilian blinked, but accepted his desire readily enough, her lips curving with delightful artistry.

"Very well, Master."

Acting with the grace of a pole dancer and using him as her literal pole, Lilian spun around to face him. She sat down, straddling his thighs, and grabbed the bowl of umeboshi. She plucked one of the pickled fruits and held it to his mouth, feeding him.

Before she could pull back, he gently grabbed her wrist. She looked startled, but he just smiled.

"You've got some juice on your fingers. Please, allow me to clean it for you."

She didn't get a chance to say anything before he placed her fingers in his mouth, swirling his tongue around each one to suck them clean. Her delighted gasps spurred him onwards. They were like a siren's call. Each gasp released, every moan that sounded out, made him grow stiffer than a dancer's pole and hard enough to cut diamonds. Her erotic voice drove him to continue well after he'd finished his task.

"M-Master..." Lilian whimpered as Kevin finally allowed her to withdraw her hand. She looked at her wet fingers, then back at him, her eyes hooded and her face flushed. She seemed incapable of forming coherent thoughts, but still managed to find her voice. "Would you... like me to... feed you... some more... Master?"

"Yes, I believe I would. But, I think I'm ready for the main course now."

His hands slid around her body and reached for Lilian's firm derriere, grasping her cheeks and pulling her against him like he wanted to merge with her.

"Oh! Master!" Lilian's cries of ecstasy rang throughout the house.

"Your nose is bleeding," Kotohime calmly stated. Her words snapped Kevin out of his delusion. He brought a hand to his face, blinking several times when he pulled it back and noticed that his fingers were covered in crimson liquid.

"Oh, crap!"

While Kevin wiped the blood off his face, Lilian smiled. She wasn't sure what he'd been daydreaming about, but she was positive it featured her. Just a little more time and Kevin would

accept and return her love. She just had to be patient.

"Ufufufu…"

Lilian's quiet laughter went unheard by Kevin, who had finally decided to shove two pieces of napkin up his nostrils when they wouldn't stop bleeding.

***

Kevin ran as hard as he could, his teeth gritted and his nostrils flaring in exertion. The feel of his feet hitting the track course was almost painful. His knees jarred upon every impact with the ground. The hurried *ba-dump, ba-dump* of his skyrocketing heart rate was the only thing he could hear. It pounded in his ears, a series of staccato bursts timed with his labored, raspy breathing. His entire body, the soul of his very being, was focused on this single task: beating his rival as they raced across the track.

Running beside him, nearly neck and neck, his rival Kasey Chase glared ahead, his focus on nothing but the finish line. The older teen's breathing was just as labored, maybe even worse. His face burned red with effort. His arms swung forward and backward, the overly exaggerated motions reminiscent to the pistons of an engine.

"TIME!"

The two slowed to a stop as they crossed the finish line. Kevin tried to slow his breathing, as well as his heart rate. Sweat formed on his brow, thick globules of salty liquid that ran down his face and stung his eyes. He wiped at them, droplets falling off his hair.

"Ha… ha… ha…"

Kasey Chase stood hunched over. His black hair clung to his face, sticky and coated in sweat. It ran down his back and neck, leaving a trail and soaking his clothes. His breathing was ragged and harsh. He looked like he might keel over from exhaustion.

Unlike Kevin, who was tired but not suffering any serious physical discomfort, Chase looked like he'd been running all out for several days. He had clearly expended far more energy than Kevin.

Kevin gave his rival an amused and somewhat smug smile, feeling elated. And why shouldn't he be satisfied? Even going all out, Chase still barely managed to match his time. Kevin felt positive he could increase his pace even further if he really pushed himself. This wasn't the fastest he could go.

"Tired?"

Chase glared at him.

"Not... ha... not in the... least..."

Although his words were confident, the asphyxiated sounds he made, reminiscent to that of a dying bull, told Kevin otherwise.

"Why don't you say that when you don't look ready to pass out."

"Shut up..." Chase gasped. "I could... heh... I could do this all day..."

The chuckle Kevin released was the closest he'd ever sounded to condescending. "I'm sure."

While his rival glared at him, Coach Deretaine marched over.

"Good work, Swift." He slapped Kevin on the back, causing him to stumble forward. "It's not your best time, but you still did an admirable job. Chase, you did well, but you need to work on maintaining your speed. If you hadn't slowed down at the end, you might've beaten Swift." Looking at his watch, Coach Deretaine nodded. "Take a break, you two; we'll do this again after the others get some practice in."

"Yes, Coach," the two replied in unison. As Coach Deretaine walked off to grab the one-mile runners, Kevin gave his rival another amused grin. "Looks like this is my win again."

The flames burning in Chase's eyes could have scorched the earth. "... Shut up."

***

While Kevin and his eternal rival in all things running tried to surpass each other on the track field, Lilian watched them from the bleachers. Kotohime sat beside her, having shown up late because she'd been cleaning the dishes... and because Kevin's bike was too small to seat three people.

Not that she would have ever agreed to let Kevin ferry her anywhere. The idea of being that close to the young man wasn't particularly pleasing to the older woman. It had nothing to do with the fact that he was a human. She had other reasons for keeping her distance.

"Ha!" Lilian grinned as she watched the boy she loved outrun his rival. It didn't matter that Kevin and Chase had been practically neck and neck the whole time. All she'd seen was Kevin beating his opponent. "That's showing him, Kevin! That Chasey guy can't beat you!"

"IT'S KASEY!" came a shout from across the field.

"I DON'T CARE!" Lilian cupped her hands to her mouth and shouted back. She then sat back down, huffing. "Idiot. He's just jealous because my mate's faster than him."

"NO, I'M NOT!"

"YES, YOU ARE! NOW SHUT UP!"

Kotohime stared intently at the field, and more specifically, at the young man her ward loved.

"I'll admit, he is quite fast for a human. He could probably outpace any kitsune not specifically trained in high-speed movements—provided they are not using reinforcement, of course. He also possesses impeccable reflexes and hand-to-eye coordination. However, I still do not understand what you see in him."

Lilian stopped shouting insults at Chasey-whatever-his-name-was to frown at Kotohime.

"What's that supposed to mean? Are you insulting my mate?" There was a dangerous undercurrent in her voice, as if Kotohime's next word would determine whether she lived or not.

Kotohime didn't bat an eye. They both knew who was stronger between the two of them. It wasn't Lilian.

"I mean that I simply cannot fathom what you find attractive about him." Kotohime's voice was as calm and composed as ever. "I understand that you and he share a bit of a past together, but that was many years ago, and he was just a child back then. You barely spoke for more than an hour, and he does not remember you, anyway. Any feelings you may have gained for Kevin from that encounter should have long since disappeared."

Lilian's hair swayed as she shook her head.

"My feelings have nothing to do with that. You've got things all mixed up. I don't love him because of what happened ten years ago." She paused to gather her thoughts. "I'll admit, I was... enamored back then. He helped me become the person I am today. His words, whether he knows it or not, are the words I've lived by ever since. That being said, I did not have any feelings for him back then. He was just a child, after all, and I'm not a pedophile."

"Then why…"

"Because he accepts me." Lilian glanced down at Kevin. It looked like he was having fun taunting his rival. "When I first came into his life, I sort of…" she coughed to hide her embarrassment. "Well, I may have barged into it without really taking his thoughts and feelings into consideration. I was so excited to see him again that I maybe, sorta, kinda got a little… overzealous."

"Overzealous?" Kotohime raised an eyebrow.

"I told him that he was my mate and used all those techniques you taught me to try and seduce him."

Kotohime gave Lilian a bit more of her attention. "Well, that is what kitsune do to humans, you know? We seduce them. Or we prank them. Whichever comes first, really."

Lilian knew that. Kitsune were playful, mischievous and whimsical creatures, following their instincts and desires without a second thought. They did whatever they wanted, when they wanted, and when they found something that interested them, they did everything in their power to acquire that something through any means necessary. Seduction was just one of those means.

"Yeah, well, that didn't work with Kevin," Lilian mumbled. "He's not like other males, it seems."

Kotohime needed several moments to comprehend that statement. "Are you telling me that he resisted you?"

Now that was rare. All men, regardless of species, were more or less the same: simple creatures who thought less with their heads and more with their dicks. It made them easy for kitsune to seduce. And humans were the most susceptible of all, especially those of the teenage variety.

"Well… sort of…" Lilian couldn't tell Kotohime that Kevin always passed out before she could seduce him. She thought it was cute, but her maid-slash-bodyguard wouldn't.

"I see. He must be an awfully strong-willed young man to resist you."

Lilian's ironic grin was completely lost on Kotohime.

"Yes, he certainly is."

Kevin was certainly strong-willed… just not in the way Kotohime seemed to think he was.

"Ugh, how disgusting."

Lilian glared at the snow maiden who'd intruded on their conversation. Christine had joined them not long after track practice started. She had then proceeded to sit several feet to Lilian's left and stare at Kevin, occasionally making snide remarks about him, as if doing so would convince Lilian that she didn't have feelings for him.

"Trying to seduce a man with sex is so disgraceful." Christine's delicate nose wrinkled in disgust, as if the very idea revolted her. "You foxes are all a bunch of skanky whores."

"Nobody asked for your opinion," Lilian snapped.

"It's a free country. I can say whatever I want." The challenging stare Christine issued Lilian caused the redhead's hackles to rise.

Kotohime watched the two yōkai with an amused gaze. "Ara, ara, it's so nice to see that you've managed to find yourself a friend, Lilian-sama."

Lilian and Christine switched from glaring at each other to glaring at the kimono-clad woman.

"I would never be friends with this prudish goth-loli!"

"How could I possibly be friends with this sluttish hooker?!"

The two paused, blinked, then glared at each other.

"What did you call me?!" they shouted at the same time, grinding their foreheads against each other.

Kotohime watched as the pair's argument devolved into derogatory name calling with a passive, gentle smile.

Then she started chuckling.

"Ufufufu... how nice. Those two seem to be such good friends."

***

"Ga... ha... ha..."

Kevin made for a very pitiful sight, laid out as he was on the ground like something a semi-truck had run over, his mouth gaping and his dry tongue hanging out. Frogger had nothing on him.

The muscles in his legs ached in ways they never had before. An unusual tiredness seeped into his bones, making them feel frail and brittle. Kevin didn't think he'd ever felt so exhausted in his life.

Despite all that, he felt good. Accomplished. He had just

managed to prove himself superior to his rival—and for the first time since the track meet last Wednesday (when he'd almost gotten his ass kicked by a trio of goons), it was a truly decisive victory. Finally. Finally Kevin had managed to earn enough consecutive wins over Kasey Chase that he could say, with absolute certainty, that he was the faster runner between them.

He looked to his right, his lips peeling back into a grin. "Looks like I… like I win… again… Chase…"

"Heh… heh… shut up…" Chase mumbled through his own heavy breathing. If Kevin looked pathetic, then Chase looked like death warmed over. He, too, was lying on his back on the grassy area of the track field, sucking in oxygen like a vacuum, his tongue lolling out of his gaping maw akin to a panting dog.

All around them other members of the track team practiced. Some ran down the field, while others stretched. A few were also practicing the high jump, the long jump, and even pole-vaulting.

Coach Deretaine was busy monitoring the pole-vaulters. It was a dangerous sport, and he would get in trouble if someone accidentally stabbed themselves because they weren't using the equipment properly, or because they were being stupid and trying to act macho.

Stranger things had been known to happen, especially dealing with a bunch of hormone-driven teenagers who loved getting into the my-dick-is-bigger-than-yours arguments.

"Man, you two look like crap."

Kevin lifted his head to glare at Eric as the pervy teen approached them, trailed by Alex, Andrew and Justin.

"Thanks, man. Really, I appreciate you telling me something I already know."

"Sarcasm doesn't suit you, Kevin," Eric shot back. "You don't have anywhere near enough bite to be sarcastic. You're just too nice."

"Whatever." Kevin let his head fall back onto the grass. It was cool and moist and it kind of tickled. He was really beginning to like this grass. He should do this more often. Who knows, maybe he and Lilian could go to the park and…

Don't go there, Kevin. He shook his head, dispelling the unwanted thoughts floating through his mind. The last thing he needed was to suffer a nosebleed during track practice.

Eric ran a hand through his hair. "But, seriously, you two were really going at it. What's up with you two anyway? I know you've always had it out for each other and everything, but don't you think you're going a little bit overboard?"

"Not... in the... least," Chase wheezed like a man dying from oxygen deprivation.

Kevin would have nodded in agreement, but he was too tired... and still lying on the ground. That kinda hampered his neck's range of motion. "There's no such thing as going overboard, and I needed to show Chase, once and for all, that I'm faster than he is."

"... She said..."

Everyone minus Chase and Kevin who couldn't lift their heads stared at Justin, who returned blank looks with one of his own. After several seconds of awkward silence, they decided to ignore him and looked back at the two lying on the ground.

"I don't really want to agree with Eric, but I do think you guys are taking this rivalry a little too far," Alex informed them.

Andrew nodded in agreement. "Definitely too far. You two look like you're about to drop dead any second now. I think I saw a couple of corpses lying somewhere over there that looked more alive than you two."

"Don't care." Kevin was able to sit up now that he'd gotten his second wind. He still felt pretty drained though, and knew he wouldn't be doing anymore running today.

The sound of a whistle blowing pierced the afternoon air. Coach Deretaine's hearty bellows echoed across the field moments later. "Good practice, everyone! Now get yourselves to that locker room and wash up! You smell like a bunch of unwashed jockstraps!"

With a heavy sigh that belied how tired he felt, Kevin pushed himself to his feet. His legs were a little shaky and frail, like they were made of brittle twigs, but otherwise he was fine. Chase actually needed help standing, such was his exhaustion. Hanging between Alex and Andrew, his feet dragging along the ground, Chase looked about as intimidating as a wet kitten.

"Don't think you've beaten me yet, Swift. You might be faster than me now, but I plan on getting much faster. The next track meet we have, I'm gonna whip your ass. I'll be so fast, the only thing you'll see as I fly by is my afterimage."

"Yeah. Sure. Keep telling yourself that, Chase. Whatever helps you sleep at night," Kevin retorted. "I'll beat you anytime, anywhere. You're never going to catch up to me. I'll just keep getting faster and faster until you're not even a speck on my radar."

Chase snorted as he was handed off to Coach Deretaine and dragged away.

"Kevin!"

Kevin's lips twitched as Lilian ran across the track field, a bottle of ice cold water in her right hand and a towel in her left.

Christine glared at the redhead from several yards back, trying to catch up with little success. Gothic lolita clothing and slippers were not made for running.

When Eric saw the little lolita stomping behind Lilian, he raced toward her, his hands outstretched and making creepy squeezing motions, as if he could already feel Christine's chest in his hands.

"My Gothic Hottie! Oh, how I've longed to grab those tiny little pebbles of yours! Let me—guoah!"

Everyone watched in mute silence as Eric's body made an almost graceful parabolic arc through the air. He flipped end over end like an out of control acrobat, and then crashed to the ground with a loud *thud!* several feet away.

"I'm not in the mood to deal with you today, perv!"

Christine shook her fist menacingly at Eric's pitifully moaning form, her face a startling blue as steam rose from her head like the chimney of a certain magical scarlet train.

"Ugh... urk... I regret... nothing..."

The group stared at the scene for several more seconds, then returned to what they were doing.

"Lilian," Kevin greeted, a strange warmth spreading through his chest. He did his best to ignore the butterflies that suddenly started fluttering inside his stomach, but it was very difficult.

"Here." The enchanting two-tails cheerfully held out the bottle of water and towel for Kevin.

"Thank you." Kevin reached out for the offered item. A jolt traveled through his hands as they came into contact with Lilian's, traversing his arms and sending delectable shivers in their wake.

"You did a really good job today." Lilian smiled at him, and Kevin could swear his heart skipped a beat. "You beat your rival and made it look easy."

"NO, HE DIDN'T!" Chase's familiar shout came from a distance.

Lilian gritted her teeth and began shouting back. "YES, HE DID! YOU'RE JUST JEALOUS!"

"AM NOT!"

"YES, YOU ARE!"

"NU-UH!"

"SHUT UP!"

Lilian's cheeks puffed out in anger. Everyone present stared at her. When Chase didn't yell back, she grinned and turned to Kevin.

"I think this was your best practice yet."

"Ah, ahahaha!" Kevin's embarrassed laugh was accompanied by a red stain spreading across his cheeks. "Y-you think so?"

"Of course." Lilian nodded effusively. "You were absolutely amazing, and I can tell you've been working really hard."

"T-thanks."

Kevin's eyes flickered away from her uncertainly, but soon found their way back. She stared at him, unblinking, her enchanting green eyes gazing into his with a fondness he found hard to ignore. He would have wondered how anyone could look at another with such a loving expression, but forming coherent thoughts had become a chore.

"Ahem!"

A loud cough alerted everyone to the last member of their little troupe. Several jaws dropped when they saw the person standing before them. And why wouldn't they? It wasn't everyday they met such a pristine beauty, especially one wearing a traditional Japanese kimono.

Especially one wearing a traditional Japanese kimono while also carrying a sheathed katana at her side.

They had yet to notice the *wakizashi*.

"Kevin-san." The woman's voice was so pleasantly lyrical that all the boys in her vicinity shivered, with those few who didn't having already passed out from an epic nosebleeds. "I understand that you and she are fond of each other, but I must ask that you let go of Lilian-sama's hands. You might get her pregnant."

"Get her pregnant?" Alex blinked. "Is this chick for real?"

"Did you say something?" Kotohime's eyes turned to Alex, who suddenly went paler than a ghost.

"N-no."

"That's what I thought."

Kotohime turned back to Kevin and watched as slow comprehension dawned in his eyes. He looked at the woman, then stared down at where his hands were still touching Lilian's. Kevin jerked his hands back as if they'd been burned, dropping the water bottle and towel in the process. While he bent down to pick them up and hide the inflammation in his cheeks, Lilian sent her bodyguard a venomous look. She was really beginning to despise her maid's interference in their relationship.

When Kevin stood up, items in hand, it was to see Alex and Andrew surrounding him on both sides.

"Hey, hey, Kevin." Andrew cupped a hand to his mouth so he could whisper without being overheard. "Who's the babe with the katana?"

"And why is she wearing a kimono?" Alex added, eagerly leaning in.

"That woman? That's Kotohime." Kevin looked at Kotohime. She was smiling placidly at Lilian, who looked like she wanted to tear the older kitsune's hair out and strangle her with it. "As for the kimono... it probably has something to do with her character concept."

A pause.

"Wait. What did I just say?"

"Character concept?" The twins looked at each other in confusion. They had no clue what their friend was talking about.

"Beloved!"

While none of the humans understood the words coming from Kevin's mouth, Lilian did, and she bolted toward him with a brilliant gleam in her eyes. She was so excited that she completely forgot about her decision not to call him "Beloved" anymore—

"What the—wait! Lilian—OOF!"

—and that was how Kevin found himself being reintroduced to the wonderful valley that was Lilian's cleavage. He fell on his rump as Lilian clung to him, liberally shoving his face into her chest. With the recent changes going on in his mind, he might have found this experience pleasant, if not for the fact that he couldn't breathe.

"You broke the fourth wall again! Oh, Beloved, I just knew there was a reason I loved you! You're so amazing!"

"Get off me," Kevin tried to say. However, because he was being pressed face-first into Lilian's cleavage, the words sounded more like, "Fef foff fu."

"Tee-hee," Lilian giggled. In the wake of her mate's accomplishment, she'd forgotten about her decision to give Kevin some space and earn his love naturally. "That tickles, Beloved."

"Is it just me, or are you also feeling insanely jealous of our dear friend?" Andrew twitched as he stared at Kevin.

"It's not just you." Alex was also twitching. "I just want to know how he managed to get a girl like Lilian to fall for him."

"You and me both. It's like the greatest mystery since we learned that Mei Misaki's left eye was actually fake."

"Not only Lilian, but he's also got that gothic chick after him now, too."

"I think her name is Christine."

"Right. Her. And now he's got the babe with the katana."

"Kotohime."

"Right. Damn it, I wish I had a sexy older woman like her in my life. Oh, the things I would do with those succulent—"

"You two do know that I can hear everything you're saying, correct?" Kotohime interrupted, her serene, wondrous smile still in place. Alex and Andrew felt like the *Shinigami* had just come to claim their souls.

They gulped.

"… Blue…"

The fraternal twins turned to stare at Justin like he'd sprouted a head from his ass, before realizing that their odd friend was actually talking about Kevin.

"Hey, you're right. Kevin's face does look a little blue." Alex looked at his twin. "Think we should help?"

Andrew just shrugged. "Naw, he's got this."

Several feet away, Christine had finally gotten over her shock at seeing her love-rival bowl over the boy she had mixed feelings for. When coherent thought finally returned to her, the girl did what any good tsundere in her position would do.

"W-w-w-what the hell do you think you're doing?! Get off him this instant!"

She stormed over to the twin-tailed kitsune, shouting angrily and making demands that were completely unreasonable—to Lilian at least.

"Why should I?" Lilian's eyes narrowed at the ice maiden, daring the girl to try and take Kevin from her. She unwittingly tightened her arms around him, shoving his face even further into her breasts, further smothering him. "You're just jealous because you can't do this, Ms. Tsun-Loli."

"T-Tsun-Loli?!" Christine shrieked in outrage. "Stop calling me a loli! My chest is not that flat!" A pause. "And I'm not a *tsundere* either!" Another pause. "And I am most certainly not j-jealous! W-w-why the hell would I be jealous of some cow-titted skank like you?!"

"Cow-titted?!" Lilian muttered angrily. "That's exactly something I'd expect a little girl like you to say. Your constant boob envy is very unbecoming of a young lady."

"S-sh-shut up! Shut up, shut up, shut up!" Christine stomped angrily on the ground, which began frosting as the careful control she had over her ice powers slipped. "I don't have any b-b-b-b-boob envy, you stupid, big-breasted freak! You don't know what you're talking about!"

Lilian flashed Christine a fanged grin. "Don't I? Every time I even get a little bit close to Kevin, you go off like a mutt in heat. Face it, you're jealous that Kevin likes me more than you. I don't know why, though. It's not like you two have a history together or anything. You're just some random girl that he was nice to at the arcade one day."

Christine's face turned blue as steam billowed out her ears. "Be quiet! You don't know anything!"

While Christine and Lilian continued to argue, another conversation took place several yards away.

"Do you think we should tell them that Kevin looks like he's on death's door?" Alex stared at his friend with a bit of concern. The young man had long since stopped flailing around, his arms now dangling limply at his sides. What little could be seen of his face was dark blue going on purple.

"You think he's on death's door?" Andrew had to disagree. "I wouldn't be surprised if he's already kicked the bucket."

"You may have a point there."

"… Out…"

Once again, the twins stared very oddly at their friend. Justin had been acting even more unusual than normal lately. Considering how odd he normally acted, that said a lot.

"Are you feeling alright, Justin?"

"Yeah. You've been acting even slower than usual."

"… Fine… Kevin… not fine…"

The twins felt sweat trickle down their scalp.

"Yeah, we kinda noticed that already."

Observing the group from a safe distance, Kotohime remained silent, her face stony. She did not approve of the girl's choice in mate, for many reasons, and not because she disapproved of the boy himself. There were simply too many similarities between Kevin and someone else she'd known for her to feel comfortable with him.

"Really, Lilian-sama," she sighed, "did you have to choose a human for your first mate? Such a decision is bound to cause nothing but pain." She did not receive an answer, of course, but she had not expected one either.

While everyone had their attention focused on Kevin's death-by-boob-asphyxiation, one salacious young man finally came to.

Eric groaned as his eyes fluttered open. His jaw hurt where he'd received that brutal uppercut; he could feel it beginning to swell. It would probably need to be iced. For such a tiny girl, that Christine sure could pack a punch.

"Just what I'd expect from my Gothic Hottie." Eric winced, his jaw flaring as he opened his mouth. Okay, so speaking was a bad idea. He would have to remember that.

Slowly but surely, he got off the ground. His ears were ringing and something was pounding in the back of his skull. He blinked several times, then looked around.

The scene before him was one that he'd grown kind of used to. Kevin was on the ground, dead to the world, and straddling his legs was the Tit Maiden. Her arms were wrapped tightly around Kevin's head as she shoved his face between her breasts, while the Goth Hottie angrily yelled in her face. It wouldn't be long now before the lolita girl began trying to pull Kevin out of the Tit

Maiden's chest. They'd be physically fighting over him before Eric could say eroge, he was sure.

It made him angry. Damn that Kevin! He knew one of Eric's dreams was to die in the boobs of a beautiful woman! That bastard was accomplishing one of his life goals before him!

After the moment of irrational anger passed, Eric moved on. He'd grown so used to seeing his friend's fortune that he could simply ignore it... sometimes. Instead of watching Kevin get smothered by those amazing tatas, Eric observed the track field.

It was mostly empty by now. Many of the track members had already left. The only people still present were his friends—no, wait. There was one other person present, someone he had never seen before.

His eyes zeroed in on the gorgeous femme. Her long, glossy raven hair reflected sunlight to create a halo effect around her womanly frame, as if her generous curves were a piece of the most exquisite art. Her skin was like porcelain, and the perennial blush on her cheeks made his libido skyrocket. Her large, almond-shaped eyes, full lips and pert little nose filled his mind with fantasies untold. She had a gorgeous face.

Her face was not what caught Eric's attention.

"One-hundred and six centimeters," he whispered in reverent awe. Those had to be the largest boobs he'd ever seen! They were several sizes larger than Lilian's! Those had to at least be a J-cup! How was such a thing possible?

Not that he cared about the hows. They didn't matter. Only one thing mattered right now: he wanted them. He wanted to squeeze them. To suck on them. He wanted to reenact his favorite scene from his favorite eroge, *To Heart*, on them.

And then, suddenly, a voice spoke to him. It called to him. It beckoned him, spurning him into action.

"*Grab them,*" it said.

"Where have you been all my life, you lovely, succulent bags of fun?!"

Everybody present stopped to watch as Eric raced toward Kotohime, his eyes locked firmly on those two large mountains. He planned on conquering those ginormous globes of fun. Oh yes. The jiggly times were coming. Nothing would stop him in his quest to squeeze those delightfully titanic titties.

"Come to papa—EEK!"

Silence. In the absolute stillness that now permeated the track field, Eric's heavy, frightened breathing came out several decibels louder than normal. He would have gulped as well, but doing so might cause the very sharp object caressing his jugular to slit his throat, so he refrained.

"Woah," Alex murmured.

Andrew nodded in agreement, but his thoughts were on something else. "Is that a real sword? I thought it was a prop."

"… Katana… heaven…"

The odd stares Justin kept receiving would not be ending anytime soon.

"Young man." Kotohime's voice remained serene, and that wondrous smile still adorned her face. Eric almost crapped his pants. "I must ask that you never try to grope my breasts again. Do so and my hand might slip, and you may find yourself lying face down in a ditch as your life's blood drains from your body and stains the ground. Do you understand?"

Eric lost control of his bladder. A large stain appeared on his pants, expanding quickly. Kotohime's nose wrinkled, but that was the only sign of her disgust.

"Y-yes, ma'am!" he squeaked.

"Good."

When Kotohime removed the katana, Eric's legs lost their ability to function. He fell to the ground, curled up into a fetal position, and began shuddering like a man who'd just been told he would die in seven days.

On that day, in the presence of that enchanting smile, in the face of such impossible beauty, and while staring at the largest pair of knockers he would ever see, Eric Corrompere discovered the true meaning of terror.

***

The trip back to the locker room was very awkward—for most of the people present, at least. Kotohime didn't seem bothered by it, but she was a pretty unflappable woman so that didn't mean much.

Kevin glanced at all the people walking alongside him, feeling more than just a little disconcerted. The twins weren't fighting, Eric wasn't perving, there was a suspicious-looking stain on his lecherous friend's pants, and Kotohime was humming what sounded like the Imperial March under her breath. The only person among them not acting unusual was Justin, and that was odd in and of itself because Justin was the most unusual person he knew.

Something must have happened while he was unconscious. That was the only logical explanation. The twins he could figure out easily enough, but what about Eric? He didn't think he'd ever seen the boy look so terrified before. What could have caused such a reaction?

Maybe he was better off not knowing. Wasn't there an old saying about ignorance being bliss? Besides, there were more important things to worry about anyway, such as the two girls walking on either side of him.

Christine and Lilian were certainly a lovely distraction from his friends' strange behavior. It was hard to look at either one of them for any length of time, especially Lilian. Whenever his eyes landed on the vixen, he found himself staring at something other than her face—two somethings, actually.

Whether he felt fear or arousal when he stared was something even he didn't know.

Christine also posed a Dangerous Distraction, capital on the D's. What with her lolita clothing, pale skin, delicate figure and ice-blue lips. Her fragile, almost doll-like appearance definitely turned heads, though if he was being honest, Lilian presented a much larger problem.

Of course, these two presented a much different problem than the one behind them. Turning his head just a fraction, Kevin spotted Kotohime gliding along with the grace and poise of an experienced warrior. The woman scared the crap out of him. Her presence at his back, combined with her katana already made him feel threatened. The last thing he needed was to give her a reason to use that katana on him.

Better look at something more pleasant.

He turned his head…

… and found himself staring at Lilian, or rather, staring at Lilian's boobs. Large, bouncy boobs that moved in the most enticing of ways with every step she took. Kevin didn't want to admit it, but he really was beginning to see why Eric had such a big obsession with the things.

I feel so dirty, like I've been tainted somehow.

There must have been something wrong with him. Hadn't he nearly been killed by those things minutes earlier? Why was he thinking about them so much?

I hope I'm not becoming a masochist. Damn that Eric! If his lecherous ways are contaminating me, I'm gonna hurt him.

"Something on your mind, Kevin?" Lilian asked after he looked at her for the umpteenth time in the past ten seconds. She smiled. Kevin might take more effort to ensnare than most men his age, but that didn't mean it would be impossible. She could see how her actions were wearing him down.

She could also see where he was looking.

Take that, Tsun-Loli!

Walking on Kevin's other side, Christine sneezed.

"Achoo!"

Several tiny icicles shot from her nose, impaling the ground in front of them. Lilian made a note not to step on any of those. They looked sharp.

"Gesundheit," Kevin muttered absentmindedly.

Christine cutely rubbed her nose. "Thank you."

Lilian frowned. She didn't like being ignored, especially when it was due to angry, violent tsun-lolis who thought they could get away with being, well, angry and violent, just because they were cute. Anime might work that way, but not the real world. In the real world, vicious little girls with flat chests were not able to commit acts of violence just because they were cute.

Stupid tsun-loli! You think you can steal my Kevin? I'll show you!

Christine sneezed again and several more ice shards struck the ground.

Eric stepped on one of those ice shards.

"Fucking damn it! What the hell is this?! A thorn?! Why is it so damn cold?!"

"Shut up, idiot!"

"GAOI!"

Eric's head made brutal contact with the ground when Christine proved herself capable of a flying reverse kick. Kevin was impressed. He'd have never expected such a tiny girl to be capable of jumping that high.

"Kevin?" Lilian prompted, ignoring the *tsukkomi* duo for a moment. Kevin looked at her, blinking rapidly several times.

"Um, yes? I'm sorry. I was distracted by..." he glanced over at Eric and Christine, still in the middle of their *tsukkomi* routine. Kevin was reminded of a comedy skit in Vegas. Thinking on it, these two would probably be a hit if they ever decided to travel abroad with that routine. "Well, I just got sidetracked by something." He coughed into his hand. "What were you saying?"

"I asked what you were thinking about?" Lilian walked in front of him and turned around so they could speak face-to-face. "You've been getting distracted a lot more lately. Is something wrong?"

"Ah, um, no." Kevin ran a nervous hand through his hair. "I just can't help but feel like there's something I'm not getting. Did something happen while I was..." he trailed off, trying to come up with the proper words to describe his previously unconscious state in a way that wouldn't damage his masculine pride.

"While you were knocked out cold?"

Unfortunately for him, Christine had no qualms about destroying masculine pride.

"Thank you, Christine," Kevin's slight sarcasm was missed by the yuki-onna, who appeared to think he was genuinely grateful.

"I-i-idiot!" Her cheeks flared a brilliant blue as she stuttered. "I was only being honest! W-what the hell are you thanking me for?!"

Kevin actually rolled his eyes. "I wasn't."

"Eh?'

As Christine worked out what he meant, Kevin turned back to Lilian. "So, did I miss anything?"

"Just Eric being Eric."

"Ah." So Eric had been perving on someone. That made sense, but... "How is that any different from what he always does?"

"Eric was being Eric to Kotohime."

Turning his head, Kevin caught a glimpse of Kotohime walking slightly behind and to Lilian's left, looking alert, composed and ready for anything. In her left hand was her sheathed katana.

Kevin also noticed how Eric had gone silent at the mention of Kotohime. His face paling and a cold sweat breaking out across his forehead, the most libidinous creature in existence was… staring at Christine's backside. How expected. It seemed that not even being threatened with a katana could rid the boy of his perverse nature.

Kevin turned away from his best friend with a small shake of his head. "I really want to say I'm surprised, but I'm not. I should have expected something like this would happen. Hopefully, this will teach Eric not to hit on a woman carrying a katana."

Lilian clasped her hands behind her back. "Do you really think it will be enough to stop Eric from being, uh, Eric?"

"Not at first. Maybe he'll learn his lesson after he hits on Kotohime a couple more times."

Lilian snorted.

"If Eric ever hits on Kotohime again, chances are good he'll never be able to reproduce. She's been known to castrate men who get too fresh with her."

Eric paled even more, his face turning whiter than a sheet. Kevin and the twins also paled. Heck, even Justin paled, and he was still off in his own little world.

"R-really? That's… kinda disturbing."

"Well, Kotohime can act like a pretty disturbed individual sometimes."

"I resent that, Lilian-sama." Despite saying this, Kotohime didn't appear too bothered by her ward's statement. Her tone didn't even change from its calm, soothing overtones, as if she was acknowledging the truth to Lilian's words without vocalizing it.

None of the humans felt comfortable in her presence anymore, if they ever had in the first place. Eric, in particular, seemed downright terrified—for his balls at least. He cupped them with his hands, like doing such a thing could actually protect them from Kotohime's *katana*, should she decide to use it.

"In fact, I remember this one time when someone from the—"

"I believe that is enough of that, Lilian-sama." Kotohime cut through Lilian's words decisively. "There is no need to air my dirty laundry to everyone, now, is there?"

Despite her voice ringing pleasantly in their ears, everyone felt a strange tremor run down their spines. What was this unusual fear they felt whenever the kimono-clad femme spoke? Why did it feel like the grim reaper had just come calling?

"A-ah, yes, I guess there isn't," Lilian stuttered. Kotohime may have been her bodyguard, but there were some lines that not even she could cross. This was one of them.

The rest of the trip was made in silence. When they reached the locker room, all the boys entered with Kevin being the last. He paused at the doorway, taking one last look at Lilian, whose brilliantly curled lips brightened the room by a factor of fifty, before heading inside.

"Since practice is over, I'm out." Christine turned and began walking away.

"Why did you even show up?" Lilian asked in honest curiosity. "I mean, you don't have any after school activities. School isn't even open right now, and only the track team and a few other sports teams are still meeting at school regularly. Really, why come all this way to school?"

"T-t-t-that's none of your business! Skank! Hooker! Fox-whore!"

A single, delicate eyebrow began twitching. "That was rude! I was just asking a question!"

"Whatever," Christine mumbled before walking away again. "See ya."

Lilian glared at Christine. She continued glaring even after the yuki-onna disappeared from sight.

"Tch. Stupid *tsundere*," she muttered under her breath.

"Ufufufu," Kotohime chuckled lightly. "It seems Lilian-sama has made some very interesting friends."

"You and I clearly have very different ideas on friendship," Lilian said dryly.

"Lilian?"

Upon hearing the familiar voice, Lilian turned and saw Lindsay walking toward them.

"Lindsay," she greeted congenially.

"What's up?" Lindsay brushed a few strands of hair behind her right ear and grinned. "Waiting for Kevin?"

"Yeah…" Lilian looked behind Lindsay to see the other girls on the soccer team approaching. Like the tomboy, they were all dressed in blue shorts and a white T-shirt with shorter than average sleeves. They all looked rather haggard, their skin glistening with sweat and smudged with grass stains and dirt, much like Lindsay. "Did you just get back from soccer practice?"

"Yep."

"I see," Lilian murmured, before perking up. "Listen, Lindsay, can I talk to you for a minute?"

"Eh? Um, sure." Lindsay looked a little confused, but more than willing to comply, "Just let me take a quick shower, get changed and—"

"Actually, I was hoping to talk to you right now. Kevin's getting changed and I wanted to speak with you before he comes back."

"Oh, I see. You wanna talk to me about something that you don't want Kevin accidentally overhearing." Lindsay nodded her head in a sage-like manner, though the whole "wise woman" effect was ruined when several strands of grass fell out of her hair. "I gotcha. Well, okay, I guess it'll be all right, so long as this doesn't take too long. I'm smelling pretty rank right now."

"Don't worry, this won't take long." Lilian turned her gaze to Kotohime. "I need to talk to my friend alone. I'll be back soon."

The raven-haired femme tilted her head, considering whether she should let her charge go. In the end, she nodded in assent. "Very well. I shall remain here."

Lilian led Lindsay down the hall and around a corner. She had a very important question to ask the girl and didn't want anyone interrupting them, especially Kevin.

There were some conversations that boys just weren't meant to hear.

***

Steam billowed out of the shower stall as Kevin opened the curtain. He held a wet towel in his left hand, his red boxer shorts the only article of clothing protecting his modesty. Walking out of the showers, he saw his friends were almost finished getting dressed. The other members of the track team had already left.

He also caught the tail-end of their conversation.

"… What do you guys think of Kevin's new, uh, friend?"

"I think she's the hottest piece of ass I've ever seen," Eric declared passionately, then looked around, eyes akin to a scared child's, as if he thought Kotohime might appear out of thin air to perform a rectal exam with her katana. "She also scares the shit out of me."

Alex nodded. "Agreed. I've seen a lot of pretty girls here at high school, Lilian and Christine included, but there's just something about that woman that really gets the motor running. She's one of those mature beauties. It helps that you don't see many women with a body like hers."

"She's like a super-hot anime fanservice girl from one of my eroge."

"Don't let her catch you saying that. She might chop your balls off." Kevin walked over to them.

"Meep!"

Kevin ignored the dent in his locker as he opened and pulled out his clothes.

"You guys are talking about Kotohime, right?" he asked, zipping up his pants. The four boys looked at each other, then back at Kevin. As one, they nodded.

"I don't know where the hell you found that chick, but she has to be the hottest, most bodacious, scariest woman I have ever laid eyes on." Alex and Andrew nodded at Eric's unwaveringly serious voice. Justin did, too, but Kevin was positive the young man didn't even know what they were talking about, as he was wearing headphones. "Seriously man, where did you find her?"

"It would be more accurate to say that she found us," Kevin muttered.

"Eh?"

"Nothing." Kevin dismissed his friends' confusion and threw on his shirt, a black one with a red infinity symbols decorating the front. "Still, I'm surprised you don't seem to like her." Wasn't his friend a masochist or something? Kotohime could easily be the "S" to Eric's "M."

"It has nothing to do with not liking her." Eric stood up on the nearest bench and raised a fist to his face. "She's definitely the sexiest woman I've seen outside of my eroge! And she's got the biggest breasticles I've ever laid eyes on!" Kevin facepalmed. Breasticles? Seriously? "But that doesn't change the facts! That woman is no good! I've got no desire to have my throat slit and my body dumped in a ditch somewhere!"

"Whatever." Kevin didn't really care one way or the other.

"I might be a man whose perversity knows no bounds, but even I've got standards," Eric continued, fervently remaining on his soap box.

"Get down from there, Eric." Kevin grumbled as he tried to yank his friend off the bench. "You look like an idiot."

"That's because he is an idiot," Alex pointed out.

His brother nodded in agreement. "A complete idiot."

Heedless to the people making fun of him, Eric spoke with the fervor and zeal usually seen only in crazy people wearing cardboard signs and proclaiming that the end of the world was near.

"Even I know that there are some places a man just isn't meant to go, and that chick with the katana is one of them. Like the no-man's land found in the center of the battlefield, the katana babe's tittielicious body is a place no man can get close to without suffering a horrible death. I've seen it! One cannot grasp those heavenly mountains unless they want to get dumped in a ditch and watch helplessly as their life bleeds out of their broken bodies."

"Wasn't that the threat she used on him?" Andrew whispered to his brother.

"It was indeed."

"Perverts beware! You're in for a scare!"

"Dang it, Eric! Get down from there!"

***

After rounding the corner, Lindsay turned to look at Lilian, her face the epitome of quizzical. She and Lilian had never really spoken alone before, or at all, really. Until just recently, the redhead had seemed to harbor a grudge against her, so this new situation was more than a little odd.

"So what did you want to talk about?" Odd or not, Lindsay didn't dislike the girl, and thus, was willing to lend an ear.

Lilian stared at Lindsay, her lips curling downwards as her inner conflict came to the fore. A question was on her lips, but she seemed afraid to know the answer. Lindsay waited patiently, however, knowing that the beautiful girl would eventually talk. Lilian wasn't the type to stay silent for long.

"I want to know why you turned Kevin down," she said at last.

Lindsay froze, eyes widening to the size of baseballs. It would've been comical, if not for the nature of the question.

Lindsay looked down at her feet, which suddenly seemed far

more interesting than Lilian. "I'm not sure why it matters. Aren't you happy? Now you can have Kevin all to yourself, provided that cute goth girl doesn't grab him first."

At the mention of her somewhat-rival for Kevin's affection, Lilian scoffed. "Christine has no hope of getting with Kevin. She's too *tsundere*."

"I'm still not sure what a '*tsundere*' is."

"She will never admit to liking him, much less wanting to be something more than just friends. Relationships like that never happen in real life. It would take some kind of incredibly complex and ridiculously over-the-top Plot Device to get them together."

"What's this about a Plot Device?"

"Not even The Author is stupid enough to do that."

"Who's The Author? And are you ignoring me?"

"And it's not that I'm not grateful to you," Lilian continued, making it clear that, yes, she was ignoring Lindsay. "I am. Truly. I just want to know why. Why would you let Kevin go like that?"

Despite her annoyance at being ignored, Lindsay did not lash out at Lilian like Kevin would have. She had more restraint than him, but she was also pensive. She decided to focus on the question being asked, and not the zany things Lilian kept mentioning. It was more important anyway.

"Did you know that Kevin and I used to be best friends?" The surprise that spread across Lilian's face answered her question without words needing to be spoken. "I would even go so far as to say that I was better friends with him than Eric will ever be. Back then, he and I used to do everything together—we played together, went to the park together, we even took baths together."

Lilian's right hand twitched in agitation, but she did her best to keep cool. All of this had happened long before she had re-entered Kevin's life, maybe even before they had ever met. There was no reason for her to get upset.

That did not mean it didn't bother her.

I want to take a bath with Kevin, too.

"One day, all of that stopped." Lindsay frowned. "It happened when we were in seventh grade. We were hanging out like usual, playing some kind of game, when I kissed him on the cheek."

Lilian's left hand joined the right in twitching.

"Kevin's face turned beet red, so red you'd have thought his face was trying to mimic a bonfire." Lindsay's lips twitched into a slightly amused smile. "I remember how he stared at me with these wide eyes, his mouth hanging open like one of those cartoon characters."

"Anime."

"Huh?"

"Anime characters," Lilian repeated, her stare making the tomboy uncomfortable. "Not cartoon characters. Cartoons and anime are two different things."

"Uh… right, anime characters." Lindsay shook her head and got back on track. "Anyway, after that day, Kevin seemed incapable of talking to me. Most of the times I tried talking to him, he would just blush, stutter and run away. Sometimes, he might actually talk, but it was always something stupid like 'I like your hills' or 'freshness the bestest.' One time he even started speaking in French. At least I think it was French. It sounded French-ish, sort of." Lindsay paused to collect her thoughts. "Oftentimes, though, he just spouted gibberish. I couldn't understand a single word he said. I even had the French teacher try to translate it for me once, but she couldn't make heads or tails of it."

"Is that so?"

Lilian bit her lower lip. So Kevin had been struck by *Gibberish of Love* with Lindsay? That was not something she wanted to hear, but she took consolation in the fact that he didn't seem to be affected by the tomboy anymore.

Lindsay smiled in fond remembrance. "Yeah, he was kind of a dork like that. So, anyway, after that Kevin and I stopped hanging out, and Kevin's problem seemed to expand to all girls. At first I thought he was just going through some kind of phase, and that he'd get over it if I just gave him some space." She grimaced. "I don't think I need to tell you how that turned out."

"No," Lilian agreed, "you don't."

"I more or less lost my friend after that. Kevin stopped spending time with me and we grew further and further apart. But, even then, I never gave up hope. I had hope that someday he would start talking to me again, and that maybe he would pluck up the courage and tell me that he liked me as more than just a friend."

"But he did do that, didn't he?" Lilian asked rhetorically. "That's what he wanted to talk to you at the mall, right? He told me so himself."

"Yes." Lindsay's smile became melancholic. "He did confess his feelings, but by that point, it was already too late."

Lilian scratched her head. "I don't get it."

Lindsay's morose smile spoke of her emotional state than words ever could. "Even though I haven't been able to talk to Kevin much these past few years, I've been friends with him for a long time. I know things about him that no one else does. That's how I knew I lost him the moment he confessed for me." Lindsay looked to the side, her eyes staring at nothing. "Kevin wouldn't have been able to confess that easily if he still liked me."

Lilian's eyes widened. "Oh..."

"And besides," Lindsay looked at the kitsune once more, a wide smile spreading across her face, "you're good for him. I don't know what you did to Kevin, but ever since you came into his life, he's become more confident. He's no longer shy around girls, he can talk to me like a normal person—he's really come into himself, and I know it's thanks to you."

"I... I didn't do that much." Lilian crossed her right arm under her chest to grab her left elbow, looking away from the other girl, her cheeks turning a nearly luminescent red.

"I beg to differ," Lindsay contradicted. "Because of you, I have my friend back. It may not be in the way I wanted, but I think it's better to be friends with Kevin than not be with him at all."

Lilian wondered why this girl's praise made her feel so uncomfortable. "I guess. But I still don't see why you would have turned him down. I'm not complaining," she added upon seeing Lindsay's expression. "I just know that if I had been in your position, I wouldn't have let him go."

The smile on Lindsay's face grew soft, with just the faintest trace of sadness. "And that's why you deserve to be with him more than me."

Lilian looked surprised. "You think so?"

"Yes, I don't deserve to be with Kevin, because I was willing to let him go. You're not. I guess that's one of the differences between us. Aside from that," Lindsay clasped her hands together, "I have it on good authority that he likes you."

"Really?"

Lilian perked up. She knew that she affected Kevin on, at the very least, a physical level. She knew that he found her appealing. She even knew that he liked her as a friend. What she didn't know, and what Lindsay was suggesting, was that Kevin liked her as something more.

"Definitely," Lindsay nodded, her face somehow appearing both serious and mischievous. It was impressive. Lilian would have to remember that expression for later. "Haven't you noticed that Kevin sometimes acts differently with you?"

Lilian tilted her head.

"Now that you mention it, he has been stuttering and blushing a bit more." It wasn't as bad as when they first met, but she also wasn't walking around their apartment naked these days either. "And sometimes he'll say something that doesn't make sense..." Lilian trailed off, her eyes widening. "Wait! Are you telling me that Kevin is afflicted with *Gibberish of Love* whenever he's around me?"

"Yes," Lindsay smiled, nodding. "That's exactly what I—wait." She interrupted herself. "Gibberish of what now?"

"Ha! I can't believe it!" In her joy, Lilian completely forgot about Lindsay's presence as she began jumping up and down like a crack addict on a pogo stick. "He's been struck by *Gibberish of Love* because of me!"

"Uh... Lilian?"

"Yes, yes, yes! Take that Christine! You stupid tsun-loli!"

"What's a tsun-loli?"

"This is great! I knew Kevin would fall in love with me eventually! It's only a matter of time now before he loses control of his carefully hidden lust, throws me on the bed, and makes me scream out his name in delirious ecstasy until my throat gets sore and I become a wet, quivering bundle of nerves."

Lindsay's entire face, from the roots of her hair down past her neck, turned bright red. "I-I really didn't want to hear that."

Lilian then began to laugh. "Ufufufu..."

Lindsay looked like Sadako had just walked out of her TV. "You're really starting to freak me out, Lilian."

Without warning, Lilian turned back to Lindsay and gave the girl a big hug, lifting the poor soccer player off of her feet and twirling her around, laughing like a loon. Lindsay thought she heard some bones creak ominously, but couldn't be sure. It definitely hurt, though. The redhead was stronger than she looked.

Setting the girl back down, Lilian ignored the way Lindsay's legs wobbled precariously and beamed at her.

"Thank you!"

"Um, sure. You're, uh, welcome?" Lindsay blinked several times in an attempt to uncross her eyes. She was almost certain Lilian had broken something important, like her spine, maybe.

Lilian gave Lindsay one last smile. "If you'll excuse me, I need to get back before my Be—I mean, I need to get back before Kevin notices I'm gone. Thanks again."

As the redhead trotted off with an extra bounce in her step, Lindsay watched her disappear in muted silence, her back aching and her body feeling like a pantheon of angry gods had trampled on it.

"What… what just happened?" she asked into the stillness of the hallway.

***

Kevin wasn't feeling too hot at the moment.

He would have liked to say it was because of how hard it was to pedal home after such an intense track practice, that the intense soreness devastating his legs was the reason he felt like utter crap. Unfortunately, he couldn't, because claiming that was the reason would be a lie.

That honor belonged to Kotohime, the woman traveling alongside him, though it might have been more accurate to say that she was ahead of him and slowly widening the distance between them.

She wasn't riding a bike.

She was running.

It was enough to absolutely crush his pride as a man—and a sprinter on the track team, but mostly a man.

"Damn… kitsune… and their… stupid… reinforcement…"

Holding him tightly around the waist, her front pressed against his back and her left cheek nuzzling his shirt, Lilian giggled. "Geeze, Kevin. I knew you were competitive, but I didn't realize you'd get so depressed from something like this."

Even though Kevin heard her, he didn't reply. Or, to be more exact, he couldn't reply. He was too busy pedaling to retort. He'd

106

never been more thankful than when they arrived home, less than five minutes later.

"Ha... ha... ha..."

As he wearily stared at the staircase before him, Kevin couldn't help but curse his mom for buying an apartment on the second floor.

I suppose I should just be glad this complex doesn't have a third floor.

"Ara, ara, you look a little tired, Kevin-san."

Kevin sent the maid-slash-bodyguard a fierce glare. He did not appreciate her condescending attitude, nor the look of superiority she gave him in return.

He looked back at his bike, which he would have to haul all the way up those stairs.

Ugh... so not cool.

He sighed and prepared himself for more physical torture.

"You look tired. Let me take the bike up for you."

"Eh?"

Before he could so much as blink, Lilian lifted his bike with one hand and proceeded up the stairs, carrying his bike like it weighed less than a feather.

He could feel his HP gauge dropping.

"Ugh... great," Kevin grimaced. "It seems even Lilian's having a hand in crucifying my pride today."

"Ufufufu," Kotohime's not-so-silent chuckling earned her another glare.

"Quiet you."

Grumbling to himself, Kevin slowly climbed the stairs, his legs shaking. By the time he reached the top, Lilian had already locked up his bike.

"Kevin." She stared at him in a way that he managed to properly interpret.

"Right, right," he sighed tiredly. "Hold on, just let me get my key out."

He stopped in front of the door, key in hand. He was about to put it in the lock when the door suddenly flew open without warning. He blinked several times, his mind momentarily blanking at the sight before him.

Standing in the doorway was a woman with a youthful face.

Her shoulder-length, light brown hair swayed from the remnants of displaced air. She wore a knee-length black skirt, thigh-high black stockings, a white undershirt with an unzipped red jacket over it, and a pair of golden earrings with small rubies embedded into them. Blue eyes much like his own stared back at him.

As the seconds slowly ticked by, Kevin's mind caught up with his vision.

His eyes widened.

"M-Mom?!"

"EH!? Kevin, this is your mother?!"

Lilian, for once, went ignored.

"Kevin." His mom crossed her arms, wearing her poker face.

So not good.

"Care to explain why my last credit card bill had several hundred dollars' worth of women's clothing on it?"

Chapter 5

Ms. Swift

There had been very few times in his life when Kevin wished he could crawl into a hole and hide.

This was one of those times.

Unfortunately, he wasn't a politician, so burying his head in the metaphorical sand wouldn't help him.

Man, and I thought the situation when Kotohime first arrived was awkward.

Standing in front of him was his mom, who should have been somewhere in Europe. When did she get home? And of all the times to surprise him with a visit, why did it have to be now? This was like a bad plot device in a *shōnen* manga!

Talk about inconvenient timing.

"Well, Kevin? I'm waiting. Are you going to explain yourself or not?" His mom crossed her arms and impatiently tapped her foot, pinning him with a stare that could have made a grown man faint. Kevin didn't, but only because he was too frightened to pass out.

Fortunately, someone decided to step in and save him.

"I'm, um, really sorry, uh, Ms. Swift." Lilian bowed apologetically toward the woman. "It's my fault your son spent so much money on women's clothing. When I first arrived, I didn't have many clothes to call my own, and he was kind enough to buy me some. If you want to blame anyone for the money your son spent, then please blame me."

"Lilian." Kevin stared at the young vixen in surprise.

Kevin's mom focused on Lilian. The young two-tails tried not to squirm when the woman's sharp eyes observed her. Lilian had always wanted to meet her Beloved's mother, but not like this. She hadn't even had a chance to shower yet! How was she supposed to give a good impression if she didn't look her best?

"Hmmm..." All thoughts fled when Ms. Swift moved, invading Lilian's personal space, staring her down from head to toe. The look in Ms. Swift's eyes was disconcerting, and it took everything Lilian had to remain still.

"What the...?" Lilian's eyes widened as Ms. Swift circled her.

"Mhm, mm, hmm, mhm..."

Kevin's mom studied Lilian thoroughly, making really strange humming noises in the process. She looked her up and down several times, mumbling the whole time.

"She's absolutely beautiful... would make an excellent super-model... wonder if she would like a job..."

"M-mom, what are you doing?" Kevin asked.

"Uh..." Lilian didn't know what to say, so she stuck with monosyllables. "M-Ms. Swift, um, are you—kya!"

No amount of foreknowledge could have prepared Lilian for what happened next. Kevin's mom reached out and shamelessly grabbed her boobs, feeling them up like one might study a pair of watermelons. Reactions varied.

"Oh my." Kotohime hid her smile behind the sleeve of her kimono.

"M-Mom! What do you think you're doing?!"

"B-Beloved! Ahn! I really don't—ah!—I really don't like this woman! Can I hurt her?"

"Don't hurt my mom!"

"Oh, wow! For a moment I thought these might be fake, but they're actually real." Ms. Swift seemed fascinated as she grabbed, squeezed and fondled Lilian's boobs right in front of her son. "Let's see; that's ninety-four centimeters up top, ninety-nine for the bust, and sixty-seven down below. Impressive. I didn't realize girls your age could get breasts this big, and you're so thin, too! Tell me, have you ever thought about going into the modeling business?"

"Mom! Don't go around trying to convince people to become

a model! And stop groping Lilian's breasts!"

"That's right! Let go! Kevin is the only person who can grope my breasts!"

"Would you stop saying things like that?!"

"Shouldn't you be more concerned about how your mom is stealing away my chastity?"

"Don't you think you're over-exaggerating things?"

"Over-exaggerating?! She's squeezing my boobs!"

"Ara, ara."

"I think these might be even bigger than mine."

"Iyahn!"

"Knock it off already, Mom!"

***

It took five minutes to pry Ms. Swift off Lilian's breasts, and another two before Kevin could suggest they all sit down.

Seated at the dinner table with his mom on the opposite side, Kevin wove his epically *ecchi* tale, while also trying to leave as much of the *ecchi* out as possible. Sitting on his left was the unflappable Kotohime, while Lilian had taken to standing directly behind him, using him as a human shield against his mother, whom the young vixen was glaring daggers at.

Unlike the last time, when Lilian had done most of the explaining to Kotohime, this time Kevin was the one being forced to shed light on their living situation. This was made exponentially more difficult due to the listener being his mother.

It took nearly two hours to explain the situation to his mother, and that was with Kevin omitting a good amount of incriminating information from his speech. As much as he loved his mom, he didn't think she was ready to hear that the two women living with her son weren't human. Kevin planned on keeping it that way for as long as possible—, like, until it became completely unavoidable in a "the world is going to end" kind of way. Yeah, that sounded like a great idea.

Ms. Swift was the picture of poise as she sat in her chair, a far cry from the molester she had been before. She didn't utter a single word during the entire recounting of events, not even to ask questions. A cup of tea sat in front of her, somehow still steaming despite how long ago it had been prepared.

"And after that Kotohime started living here for, um, uh…"

Kevin glanced over at Kotohime, a question in his eyes.

"I need to see if you are a suitable husband for Lilian-sama." Kotohime's smile caused chills to run down his spine. How someone with such a pretty smile could be so utterly horrifying was beyond him.

"I see," Ms. Swift said when he finished. Her face remained carefully neutral, and Kevin and Lilian shared a quick glance. She lifted the cup of tea to her mouth, blowing on the hot liquid before taking a sup. "This is very good tea."

"Thank you." Kotohime gave the woman of the house a gracious nod. "I am pleased to see you enjoy the tea I have prepared."

"Where did you find the tea leaves?"

"Oh, I just happened to have some on me," Kotohime said mysteriously, her perennial smile still in place, though now she appeared amused.

Ms. Swift looked at the woman for a second before understanding dawned in her eyes. "Extra Dimensional Storage Space?"

"Extra Dimensional Storage Space," Kotohime confirmed with a nod.

"Wait." Kevin ignored the shiver he got when his mom and Kotohime shared a smile. Those two sharing anything, much less a smile, could not bode well for him. "You know what she's talking about, Mom?"

"Of course." Ms. Swift confirmed. "All women have an Extra Dimensional Storage Space. It is one of the fundamental differences between a man and a woman—aside from the obvious, of course."

"Indeed."

While Kotohime and Lilian nodded, Kevin's mind fell into turmoil.

"Another one." His piteous moan. "And this one is my mom to boot!" Hands grasped chunks of blond hair as if desiring to rip them out. "Isn't there someone around me who can be considered normal? Is that too much to ask for?"

Ms. Swift observed her son freaking out.

"Hmm, it appears as though my son is distressed."

"It does seem that way. Ufufufu…"

"There, there, Kevin." Lilian rubbed his back. "It'll be alright."

"Don't patronize me," Kevin grumbled under his breath, "I so do not need you being condescending right now."

"You know I would never be condescending toward you, Beloved. That's Kotohime's job."

"Ugh."

"Ufufufu…"

"You stop laughing." Kevin shot the maid a glare.

"Ufufufu…"

"You too, Lilian. It's creepy enough with just one of you. I don't need both of you doing it."

Ms. Swift sipped her tea until the cup was empty, then set it down before placing her elbows on the table and steepling her fingers together. "So to sum things up: Lilian ran away from home and ended up in your care after getting seriously injured. Rather than doing the smart thing and getting her to a hospital, you took her here and bandaged her injuries to the best of your abilities. At which point, Lilian decided to marry you as a way of showing her gratitude. Is that about right?"

Kevin rubbed his forehead.

"Uh, more or less."

Even with the watered down version, Kevin hadn't been able to get around the "mating" issue, and could only replace the word "mating" with "marriage" to explain Lilian's continued presence.

"And Kotohime is Lilian's bodyguard, who only arrived here a few days ago when she discovered the location of her charge."

"Yes."

"I see," Ms. Swift said before going silent again.

Kevin flushed. Hearing his mom's summation of events made it all sound pretty unbelievable, not to mention stupid. Really, who the heck would believe a story like his? Too bad he couldn't tell his mom that Lilian had actually been a two-tailed fox at the time of her injury, and that he, fearing she might be some kind of secret government experiment, decided against taking her to a veterinarian where she might get reported to the FBI. Maybe it was just him, but he really couldn't see that going over too well.

"So listen, Mom, the truth is that Lilian was actually a fox when I found her, as in those animals that live in the wild and don't like humans. I would have taken her to the vet, but because she has two tails, I thought she might be a government experiment and didn't want her being taken away by the FBI so they could experiment on her again."

"I see."

"Mom, what are you doing?

"Calling the nearest psychiatric clinic... hello? Yes, I'd like you to take a look at my son. I think he's got Middle School Second Year Syndrome."

He shook his head. Not a good idea.

Kevin watched nervously as his mother took in everything with a completely passive gaze. It was so unlike her to not show any emotion at all. His mom was a very expressive woman. Very emotive. Anyone who spent even five seconds with her knew that. Then again, this situation was not exactly normal, was it?

How many other moms came home to discover that their son was living with two beautiful women? How many came home and learned that one of those two women had essentially proposed to their son?

None. That's how many.

"Kevin."

At the sound of his name being called, Kevin could only gulp.

"Y-yes?"

"I..."

This was it, the moment his mom passed judgement. He was so dead. His mom was going to rain divine punishment upon him like an entire pantheon of angry gods. Maybe she would ground him until he was 37, or perhaps she would take away his collection of anime and manga. She might even go so far as to burn them. Life as he knew it was officially over.

"... am so proud of you!" Ms. Swift squealed.

"Eh?" Kevin only had enough time to widen his eyes before his mother launched herself from her seat. "W-wait! Mom! Don't—mmmppphhh!"

"Oh, how I've waited for this day! The day my son finally became a man!"

"Mmmph!!! Mphmmmphhh!!!"

"I always thought you would remain a virgin for the rest of your life and die alone! Now I can finally rest easy!"

"Mmm mmph mmphmmphmm!"

"Don't worry, Kevin! I approve of your relationship with Lilian. I am surprised, though. I always expected you to end up with Lindsay, but I suppose it doesn't really matter. Just so long as you end up with a nice girl, I can know true peace."

"Mmphmphmphmmmmmphh! Mmm! Mmmmmppphhh!!"

"And you don't need to worry about me cramping your style or trying to stifle your relationship with Lilian. I'll be more than happy to sit back and not interfere while you two explore your relationship more intimately. I don't mind if you two share a bed. I know how young people are at your age. Sex is a natural part of any healthy teenage relationship."

"Mmmmmmmmmph!!!"

"Just promise me that you and Lilian will give me some grandkids eventually, okay? I'm not getting any younger, you know, and I've always wanted some grandchildren to spoil."

"Mmmpppphhhhh!'

While Kevin found himself incapable of speaking, or breathing, or much of anything, really, the other two occupants could only stare as the young man and his mom shared a mother-son bonding moment—emphasis on the bonding.

Lilian glowered as Kevin's mother smothered her son in affection—and her bosom, but mostly affection.

"This is so unfair. That woman is shoving Kevin's face into her boobs, and because she's his mom, I can't do a single thing about it." She crossed her arms and pouted. "Muu, I'm the only woman whose breasts Kevin should be using as a pillow."

"Ara, ara." Kotohime felt nothing if not amusement.

***

After several minutes of glowering at Ms. Swift liberally smothering her son with affection, Lilian decided that enough was enough. Pulling Kevin out of the excited woman's embrace, Lilian had gone back to clinging to him, much like she'd done when they first met.

Even an hour after the incident, the two-tails refused to let

Kevin go. With her left arm wound tightly around his right, she glared at Ms. Swift, who sat on one of the chairs with a serene smile. It was like she didn't even see the murderous expression on Lilian's face.

"You and Kevin make such a cute couple."

As if the words held dialectic powers, the aura of DOOM that had surrounded Lilian since the incident in the kitchen vanished entirely, and Lilian was all smiles again.

"You really think so?" She asked, her sparkling eyes eerily reminding Kevin of two stars simultaneously going super nova.

"So quick to change your tune," Kevin barked, embracing his role as the *tsukkomi.* "And I'm right here, you know? Do you really have to talk about me like I'm not even here?"

"Oh, yes," Ms. Swift's smile widened, "I don't think I've seen Kevin look so comfortable around a member of the opposite sex since seventh grade. Seeing you and him acting so intimate with each other really shows how close you two are."

"Still right here."

"Thank you!" Lilian's megawatt smile outshone the sun.

"Why are you thanking her? And stop ignoring me, dang it!"

"So tell me," Ms. Swift's smile turned positively devious. She leaned forward in her seat and fixed the beautiful redhead with the gaze of a gossip monger. "Have you two done the deed yet?"

"Don't talk about stuff like that while I'm here! Actually, don't talk about that stuff at all!"

Lilian pouted. She probably would have crossed her arms had she not been holding onto one of Kevin's. "No. We haven't done anything yet. Be—I mean, Kevin, hasn't ravished me in the entire time we've known each other. We don't even sleep in the same bed anymore. He sleeps in a sleeping bag on the floor, and refuses to get in bed with me."

"Oh, fine. I see how it is. Let's all just ignore Kevin. It's not like his opinion matters or anything."

"Ufufufu."

"And you stop laughing!" Kevin pointed an accusatory finger at Kotohime.

"I'm very disappointed in you, Kevin." Ms. Swift looked at her son with an almost pitying expression. "You have a hot girl who is more than willing to sleep with you, and you're not taking her up on it. That is not very manly."

"Don't talk to me about being manly," Kevin spat, "and aren't you supposed to be a responsible adult? You should be telling me that it's not okay to have sex before marriage! Not telling me that I should have sex to prove my manliness!"

His mother scoffed, as if she'd never heard such a preposterous notion before. "I'm not like those other moms, with their traditional and outdated ways of thinking. I'm a progressive thinker. Unlike most mothers, who don't understand their sons at all, I am perfectly aware that boys your age are hormonal individuals overflowing with lustful urges."

"What lustful urges?!"

"And sex is a very beautiful thing. It's not something that you or anyone else should feel ashamed of."

"Stop talking about sex!"

"Plus, I want some grandchildren as soon as possible, so I'm willing to waive aside the issues other people might have with it."

"I don't want children yet! I'm only fifteen!"

Sitting in the corner of the room, quietly cleaning her katana, Kotohime had the air of someone with primetime seats to their favorite entertainment. "Ara, ara. You seem to be a bit stressed, Kevin-san."

"Quiet you!"

***

Kevin sighed as he stepped into his room wearing black boxers and a plain white T-shirt. His hair was still damp from his shower, and several droplets of water trickled down his spine.

Lilian looked up from her place on Kevin's bed. She was laying on her stomach, a manga laid out in front of her. Kevin couldn't see which manga she was reading, but he had more important things on his mind.

Like how Lilian's position had exposed a significant portion of her cleavage. And how she wasn't wearing a bra. That would have been bad enough, but her gorgeous calves were kicking back and forth, causing the hem of her shirt to ride up and show off her wonderful, panty-clad bottom. Her tails, which she'd pulled out the moment she arrived in the sanctity of their room, lay on her side while her foxy ears twitched. Those two characteristics did not help Kevin's quickly awakening libido. Not one bit.

Damn his Otaku tendencies. Damn his love of furries.

"Do you really have to lay around like that?" Kevin turned his head so he wasn't looking at her. Yet even then, his eyes still flickered over to the magnificent view.

Lilian looked up from her manga and tilted her head. "Like what? Is something wrong?"

"Ah, um, n-no, nothing's wrong," Kevin mumbled. So this wasn't some attempt at seducing him? Now that was a surprise. Oh, his blush finally went down. Good. "I'm surprised you're not still with my mom. You two seemed to be getting along pretty well. I thought you two would still be talking."

When he'd gone to take a shower, his mom had still been conversing with Lilian. Before he'd left them, she had asked the redhead all kinds of questions, most of which were embarrassing. Honestly, what kind of mom asked some girl they'd just met when she planned on having children with her son?

Mine, apparently.

"I would much rather spend time with you. Don't get me wrong, I like your mom. At least, I like her when she's not groping my boobs or shoving your face into hers." Kevin and Lilian both shuddered, for completely different reasons, he was sure. "But, while your mom's alright, I'd prefer spending time with the person I love."

Her words instantly made Kevin feel guilty. Warm and happy as well, but also ashamed. He didn't know why. So far as he knew, he had nothing to feel guilty about. Or did he?

"Thank you." When Kevin looked away this time, he focused fully on the wall to his right. Looking Lilian in the face only made him feel worse. "I... I enjoy spending time with you, too."

Lilian smiled at him.

"Would you like to read this manga with me before going to bed?"

Kevin looked at the manga laying open on the bed. It was one that he had read several times already. The story was about a young man who, after failing to confess his feelings to the girl of his dreams, decided to sulk in the bathtub, only to have a naked alien girl randomly appear in the tub with him and decide they should get married after he accidentally grabbed her boobs.

For some reason, the story sounded very familiar to him, but he shrugged the thought off. It probably sounded familiar from having read it one too many times. If he remembered correctly, this particular manga was one of Eric's, which he'd borrowed and forgotten to return. It was definitely something his lecherous best friend would read.

"Sure."

Gingerly getting on the bed, Kevin laid down on his stomach and moved closer to Lilian, the fox-girl scooting over to make room for him.

The two laid side by side, their shoulders touching, reading one of the many great examples of perverted storytelling that the Japanese could come up with.

Kevin Swift would admit that, despite the *ecchi* nature of the manga they were reading, he actually enjoyed this particular story. It was one of the few that managed to combine fanservice with plot, mainly because the fanservice was the plot. He could also relate to this character, for reasons he didn't want to think about.

Denial, it is no longer just a river in Egypt.

In spite of his enjoyment of the manga, however, he couldn't really focus on the pages. Lilian's close proximity to him was intoxicating. Her natural scent invaded his nose, addling his senses and making it difficult to think. He couldn't properly describe her scent. It was an amalgam of wonderful fragrances; a mixture of strawberry, vanilla and something else, something that Kevin just couldn't place. Whatever it was only served to intoxicate his mind further.

There was also the fact that being this close gave him a perfect view of her face. From far away, Lilian was extraordinarily beautiful. From up close, her beauty was amplified to levels beyond his ability to comprehend.

He could see the gentle curve of her cute button nose. The way her lush pink mouth moved as she worried her lower lip made him wonder what it would be like to nibble on those lips himself. Her eyes, those wondrous and enchanting emerald irises, were open and full of life, more vibrant than a vermillion forest. Kevin could gaze into those eyes for all eternity and it still wouldn't be enough time to truly appreciate them.

"Kevin?"

Kevin blinked. And then he was back in the real world. It only took him a couple of seconds to realize that he'd been staring, and he quickly looked away. "Sorry."

Lilian shook her head and smiled.

"It's all right. I don't mind if you look at me." She looked back down at the manga, but her eyes were unfocused. "I want you to look at me," she whispered.

"Lilian?"

"It's nothing."

Kevin remained silent for a while. "You really shouldn't say things like that, you know," he said in a subdued tone.

Lilian's lips turned downwards. "What? Why not?"

"Because it's…" Kevin paused, trying to come up with a suitable answer. "That's not something you should say to just anyone."

"But you're not just anyone," Lilian's voice was that of someone stating a fact. "You're my mate. I love you."

The guilt came back and brought along friends. The unbelievable sense of shame he felt was almost overwhelming. He felt sick to his stomach.

"How can you say that so easily?"

His question appeared to bewilder Lilian. "What do you mean?"

Kevin grabbed a fistful of the bedsheets. "I mean, how can you tell me that you love me so easily? You toss around words like 'love' and 'mate' without a care in the world, as if those words were candy during a parade. How can you do that?"

"Because I do love you."

"But why?"

"I…" Lilian looked confused. Her eyes, the windows to her soul, stared at him, uncomprehending. She seemed incapable of fathoming why he would ask such an obvious question. "I don't understand. Why are you asking me this?"

"Never mind." Unable to stand being so close to this girl, this beautiful, incredible girl who could declare her love for him so freely and without shame, Kevin stood up, "Please forget I said anything."

"Kevin?"

"I think I'm going to go to bed," he said softly.

"Oh." Lilian's shoulders slumped and her ears drooped, reminding him of how a dog might look when their owner decided not to play with them anymore. "Have a good night, then."

"Yeah, you too."

Without another word, Kevin crawled into his sleeping bag. He lay on his side, listening to the rustling of paper as Lilian flipped through the pages of her manga. The movements seemed mechanical, however, as if she was simply going through the motions instead of actually reading.

His mind in turmoil, Kevin tried to rid himself of the immeasurable guilt gnawing at him. When that didn't work, he tried lessening the unwanted emotion by justifying why he shouldn't be feeling it.

It didn't work. No matter how hard he tried to justify his thoughts and actions, the guilt refused to leave him. There was a girl lying only a few feet away, who claimed to love him, who spoke with no hesitation and so much certainty that he was forced to believe her when she stated that she unequivocally loved him.

And he couldn't even say he loved her back.

Because the truth was that he didn't know. He didn't know if he loved her or was simply infatuated with her beauty. Kevin was uncertain of his own feelings. Of course, there was another problem as well, one far more all-encompassing and problematic, a question that plagued his mind.

Do I even deserve to be with her? Do I deserve Lilian's love?

Lilian was so pure—even if some of her actions suggested the contrary—and open with him. She'd given him her heart unconditionally, but he didn't think he could do the same. Did he deserve to be with her if he couldn't offer the same devotion and commitment?

No. The answer was no; he didn't deserve her. He would never deserve someone like Lilian. Because he was...

Don't go there, Kevin, he scolded himself. *The last thing you need to think about is that man.*

So Kevin laid there. The lights eventually went out when Lilian decided to get some sleep, and still he laid there, too restless to let slumber take him, his guilt overwhelming him.

It was going to be another long night.

Chapter 6

Arcades, Big Hair, and Disastrous Meetings

The next morning Lilian woke up bright and early.

Although the term bright and early was something of a misnomer. It was early, certainly, but definitely not bright. A glance out the window revealed that the sun had yet to even rise. Looking over at the clock confirmed the early hour as well. It read three in the morning. Definitely way too early for her to be up.

Groaning softly in discontent, Lilian rolled over and tried to go back to sleep. She might have been able to fall back into slumber, were it not for her eyes catching sight of a large lump on the floor covered by a sleeping bag.

Lilian's gaze locked onto the young man she'd fallen in love with. Despite the darkness engulfing the room, she could trace the general outline of Kevin's form. She couldn't make out his face, but Lilian could imagine how his closed eyes and partially open mouth looked as he slept peacefully.

For many minutes Lilian lay there, staring at her mate—or the young man she had chosen to be her mate. He had yet to reciprocate her feelings, so they couldn't really be called mates yet. While she stared at Kevin, a surge of emotions welled up inside of her, too many to count. However, one of them stood out the most.

Her heart constricted painfully in her chest as she thought about Kevin and all they had experienced in the month they'd known each other. They had been through a lot, more than most people experienced in years, and in that time, Kevin had actually begun to like her. That much she knew, and it filled her heart with joy to know that her mate enjoyed the time they had shared together.

And yet...

... She couldn't help but wish for more. She wanted to take their relationship to the next level, to become lovers and not simply friends. She wanted that, but she didn't know how to make it happen, she didn't know how to make him hers.

Lilian had already tried every trick she knew to make him fall in love with her; stripping naked in front of him, taking baths together, purposefully leaving the door unlocked while she was showering, wearing sexy lingerie. The only thing she hadn't done was use enchantments, which she refused to do. Despite her innumerable attempts, which would have worked on anyone else, Kevin had yet to respond to her earnest feelings. She sometimes wondered if he would ever love her the way she loved him.

But didn't Lindsay say that Kevin is falling for me?

Lilian had noticed the difference in Kevin's behavior around her; the way he would stutter, the things he could blurt out, almost as if he had reverted back to his original shyness when they'd first met. He could still speak to her. Indeed, sometimes he had no trouble talking to her at all. But, there were occasions when he couldn't, when forming words seemed to be a struggle for him.

Lilian rolled onto her back and sighed, wondering if Kevin was actually afflicted by *Gibberish of Love* for her. Did he really like her as more than just a friend, or was she simply misconstruing his feelings? Lilian couldn't tell. She had no answer, and that bothered her more than she cared to admit.

Realizing that sleep was likely out of her reach, Lilian crawled out of the bed. Her bare feet lightly padded along the soft carpet, careful not to wake Kevin. Just as she passed him, she paused.

From up close like this, it was much easier to pick out the details of his face. She gazed at his closed eyes, then at his parted lips, her own feeling suddenly dry.

Drawn to him like Pikachu to ketchup, Lilian knelt down and reached out to gently cup his face, feeling the texture of his skin. It was a bit rougher than her own skin, but this did not surprise Lilian. Kevin spent so much time in the sun, it was only natural. He also wasn't a kitsune. He didn't have a kitsune's preternatural beauty.

"Nng…"

Kevin's moan caused Lilian to snatch her hand back like it had been placed on a burning oven. The young human shifted a bit more, muttering incomprehensibly under his breath, before turning away and settling down again.

Lilian slowly rose to her feet and left the room, absently noting that Kotohime had taken a guard position by the door. Not really sure what she should do to pass the time—it was too early to even think about getting started on breakfast—Lilian decided to take a bath.

If there was one thing that was universally applicable to kitsune, it was that they all enjoyed a good bath. There was just something about the act of lounging in a tub of steaming hot water that appealed to them.

Of course, they only ever bathed in their human forms. Bathing in fox form only resulted in wet fur and an unpleasant smell. Really, the whole thing just lacked the general enjoyability that lounging in a tub in human form had.

Lilian was one of those kitsune who enjoyed bathing more than most. She loved luxuriating in the sensation of hot water soaking into her skin and cleansing her body.

She personally blamed Kotohime for this love of bathing. As someone of Japanese descent, Kotohime was a fox who believed bathing to be an art form.

The art of kitsune bathing was something that had been taught to Lilian when she was very little. Well, Kotohime called it that, but Lilian was sure it had nothing to do with kitsune, and everything to do with the traditional Japanese beauty's own thoughts on the subject.

The art followed the way of traditional Japanese bathing: cleansing the body first, then soaking in the tub after the body was clean. It was done this way so people wouldn't be relaxing in their own filth while they bathed.

Only the upper half of her face remained visible as she sat in the warm waters, her knees drawn up to her chest. Steam rose around her like a thick fog. She didn't know how long she spent in the tub, only that it must have been a while, as her skin had started to wrinkle.

Left with little choice but to get out, lest she turn into a prune, Lilian unplugged the drain and rose to her feet. Water cascaded off her body as she stepped out and reached for a towel, wrapping it around herself, then grabbing another to dry off her hair, before walking down the hall.

She stopped in front of the door to Kevin's bedroom. Kotohime still sat in seiza, her statuesque form immobile. Only her hands, which cleaned her katana (a task she did way too often) with reverent motions, let Lilian know that the woman was not actually a statue.

"Kotohime."

"Good morning, Lilian-sama."

"Have you been there all night?"

"No, I have not been here all night, just for most of the morning," the katana-cleaning woman admitted.

Lilian sighed and walked up to the door.

"You may want to move from that spot when Kevin wakes up. I'd rather you not scare him first thing in the morning."

"Ufufufu," Kotohime chuckled, which didn't reassure Lilian one bit. That chuckling boded nothing good. Was this why Kevin thought her own laugh was so creepy? "You need not worry, Lilian-sama. I shall try my best not to frighten the boy."

Lilian didn't say anything, knowing that was the biggest concession she'd get out of her maid-slash-bodyguard. Kotohime was well-known not just for her incredible beauty and skill with a blade, but also for her mischievous streak. The woman was a kitsune through and through.

Lilian entered the bedroom, closing the door behind her. After sparing another glance at the still sleeping Kevin, she walked over to the dresser.

That morning she chose to wear jean shorts that wrapped so tightly around her hips they appeared to have been painted on. Her off-the-shoulder shirt exposed a good portion of her cleavage and even more of her flat tummy. It was an earthen green color that contrasted nicely with her fiery hair and complimented her eyes. She really hoped Kevin would like it.

The clock read 4:30 am, which caused her lips to turn down as she realized her bath must have been a lot longer than she thought. Kevin would be waking up soon. If she wanted to have breakfast ready for him, she needed to start now.

Lilian ignored Kotohime as she hurried into the kitchen, hissing as she stepped on the cold tile with her bare feet.

As she opened the fridge and eyed the contents, she wondered what she should make. Most of her dishes were either Greek or Japanese due to Kotohime being her cooking instructor growing up, but this morning she wanted to make something different.

As her indecision mounted, Lilian saw Kevin's cookbook sitting off to the side. She grabbed it and started thumbing through the pages. Surely there was something in there that she could make for breakfast.

***

Kevin Swift's journey to consciousness was a slow process that day.

Not getting a good night's sleep several nights in a row would do that to a guy.

Groaning like Luffy after going an entire day without meat, he blinked several times and stared at the ceiling for a long moment. Despite how tired he was, or perhaps because of it, he could only focus on the events of the last few days, and how everything seemed to have happened so fast. Kevin wished he could just catch a break.

Kevin crawled out of his sleeping bag and clambered to his feet, groggily making his way over to the closet and selecting clothes to wear that day. As he grabbed a T-shirt, his pajamas started to slip off his frame, forcing him to pull them back up. It seemed he'd lost a bit of weight recently. He'd have to start eating more.

When he exited his room and entered the hall, Kevin was greeted with a surprise.

"Good morning, Kevin-san."

"Gya!" Shrieking like a little girl, Kevin spun around to face the source of the voice, his pupils dilating when he saw the familiar kimono-clad figure. "Don't scare me like that!"

"My apologies." Kotohime raised her left arm, no doubt hiding her smile behind the voluminous sleeve of her kimono. "I had not realized you were so easily frightened, ufufufu…"

Kevin twitched. "You know, I might actually believe you were truly sorry if you didn't laugh like that."

"Laugh like what? Ufufufu...."

"Like that." Kevin pointed at the woman, dropping his clothes in the process. "I mean seriously, what is up with that laugh? Both you and Lilian do it, and it never fails to freak me out."

"Ufufufu. Does it really bother you that much? I suppose I should not be surprised. A human such as yourself would have trouble grasping the complexities that govern us kitsune."

Kevin clicked his tongue. "I have enough trouble understanding Lilian when she says stuff like that. I don't wanna hear it coming from you."

"Ufufufu..."

"Seriously, stop that!"

"By the way, Kevin-san."

"What?" Kevin's baleful eyes stared into Kotohime's calm face.

"Your pajamas fell down."

At her words, Kevin looked down to see that, indeed, his pajamas had fallen off his legs and were pooling around his feet.

"Iyahn!" Kevin's shrill cry, like that of a girl who'd just been groped by a pervy old man on a train, echoed throughout the hall.

***

A freshly showered and dressed Kevin entered the kitchen to discover Lilian cooking breakfast.

His mind stalled as he watched the girl at work. Her hips swayed to an unseen beat as she stood in front of the stove, cooking what smelled like a delicious meal. He could see every curve of her small heart-shaped buttocks, not the least bit hidden by the jean shorts that wrapped around her hips. The glorious sight of her bare legs was something that had been engraved into his memory since their first meeting. Yet even so, seeing those magnificently crafted thighs and shapely calves never seemed to get old.

Her back was hidden by long crimson hair, which trailed down to her hips before parting to make way for the tails sticking out of a small flap in the back of her shorts. They swayed back and forth, their motions reminiscent of an inverted pendulum. Each time they moved, tantalizing hints of Lilian's silky smooth back was revealed to him.

He slapped a hand over his nose to keep the wet slickness from escaping his nasal cavity. Kevin had seen Lilian in far less, so just why the heck was his nose bleeding?

The sound of flesh smacking flesh alerted the beautiful vixen to his presence. She turned, her bare left shoulder becoming visible, as her hair swished in the opposite direction. When she saw him standing there, her face lit up, and the room somehow seemed just a little bit brighter.

"Good morning, Kevin."

"Uh…"

Kevin's brain suffered a serious malfunction. He could practically feel the organ melting into a fine ooze as it overheated.

"Kevin?" Lilian grew concerned when the boy refused to speak. "Are you all right?"

"I'm kosher!"

"Kosher?"

"I mean like a fish?"

"What does fish have to do with anything?"

"Everything!"

Lilian grew even more concerned. Using her tails to continue preparing breakfast, she strode over to Kevin, who, were it not for the mass amounts of red lighting his face on fire, would have looked like he'd been frozen in a block of ice.

"Hmmm." Lilian placed a hand on his forehead. Kevin stiffened even more, and in more ways than one, as blood rushed to two different places at the same time. "You don't seem to have a fever, but…" The hand was replaced by Lilian's forehead. Kevin's eyes crossed. "You are a little warm…"

"Li-L-L-L…"

Removing her forehead, Lilian stared into Kevin's wide, unseeing eyes. He looked like a bomb ready to detonate.

"Kevin?"

Kevin's body twitched and shuddered…

… And then was launched backwards, blood spurting out his nose like the tail of a comet. He flew out of the kitchen and across the living room, smacking his head against the wall on the opposite side of the apartment before sliding down in an unconscious heap.

"What's all the commotion about… oh my."

Kotohime walked into the living room and saw Kevin passed out on the floor.

She then began to giggle.

"Ufufufu…"

Lilian stared at the comatose Kevin, blinking, as if not quite sure what to make of the last few seconds. Oddly enough, even though she had been right in front of him when he underwent nasal combustion, her clothes and skin remained pristine. The same could not be said for the rest of the room.

Lilian blinked several more times.

And then she smiled.

"It looks like Lindsay might be right. He does seem to be suffering from a bad case of *Gibberish of Love*."

"And nosebleeds, too, apparently," Kotohime added with an amused expression.

Lilian nodded. "Right, and those."

Her lips curling in delight, Lilian went back to her cooking.

Truly, Kevin knew how to make her feel special.

***

Several minutes later, Kevin was roused from his slumber.

Lilian stood over him, and she was the one who helped him stand up, offering her hand and pulling him to his feet.

"Are you sure you're feeling okay, Kevin?" Lilian asked.

"I'm fine." Kevin found his feet quite fascinating that morning. It helped hide his neon red face. He couldn't believe he'd had a nosebleed like that! It was so embarrassing!

"If you're sure." With Kevin conscious again, Lilian went back to cooking breakfast. Her tails had already mixed all the ingredients together, and now the meal simply needed to cook. "Breakfast will be ready in a few minutes. Why don't you sit down and I'll bring it to you when it's done?"

Kevin was about to do just that, but then remembered something.

"Actually, I need to begin making some coffee."

"Coffee?" Lilian looked at him again. "But, you don't drink coffee."

"True, but my mom does. She can't get her day started without at least two cups of coffee every morning."

"Oh," Lilian looked surprised, "I didn't know that. I'm sorry. Had I known she drank coffee, I would have made some while I was cooking."

Kevin just laughed and waved her apology off. "Don't worry about it. I didn't tell you, so there's no way could have known. Besides, Mom won't wake up for a while yet."

"If you say so."

"I do say so."

Kevin and Lilian shared a quick smile before he opened a cabinet above the sink and pulled out several single servings of coffee, small red containers shaped like a cylinder, which he set on the countertop.

Kotohime gracefully swept into the kitchen while Kevin brewed up some coffee, drawn by the scent of Lilian's cooking. An open cookbook sat before the redhead as she dipped some bread into a batter-filled tray. Ingredients littered the counter.

"I see you have begun branching out into more than just Greek and Japanese cuisine. It smells wonderful, Lilian-sama," Kotohime complimented. "Your cooking has certainly improved since the last time I saw you."

"Thanks," Lilian beamed at Kotohime before glancing at Kevin. He had just finished preparing coffee the way his mom liked it, with plenty of cream and sugar. "Kevin, breakfast is almost ready now. Would you mind helping me get the plates and utensils?"

"Sure thing."

Kevin and Lilian went about setting the table, while Kotohime stood off to the side and observed them like a samurai guarding a feudal lord.

The two worked extremely efficiently together, she would admit, like a well-oiled machine. They seemed to have developed a routine where Kevin would set out the plates and glasses, while Lilian grabbed the napkins and utensils. What's more, they wove around each other with ease, working in complete synchronicity. They were also completely oblivious to their own sense of teamwork.

Kotohime did not know whether to be amused or appalled.

The table was soon set, breakfast was served, and a single serving of coffee had been prepared, situated in front of an empty seat.

It was at that very moment, just as Kevin set the cup of coffee on the table, that *she* appeared. Like some kind of undead abomination she stalked into the room, moaning in a way that reminded Kevin and Lilian of those zombies they killed in "House of Haunted Horrors." The imposing monstrosity lost her balance when bare feet touched chilly tiles, causing her to stumble. Her eyes were closed and her head tilted upwards as she sniffed the air, following the scent of coffee. Kevin, Lilian and Kotohime all watched in mute silence as she plopped into the chair like she didn't have a spine, her shoulders slumping as if the mere act of keeping them up took too much work. Slowly, oh so slowly, she grabbed the cup and brought it to her lips.

… Silence.

The cup was set back down.

"Ah… coffee…"

Kevin facepalmed.

"I know it's early in the morning and that you're used to staying up late, but do you really have to act so unsightly? It's disturbing."

Ms. Swift focused half-lidded eyes on her son. "That's a rude thing to say about your mother. You know I… I… can't do anything without my morning coffee," she said, yawning halfway through her dialogue.

"That doesn't mean you have to act like a zombie first thing in the morning," Kevin insisted.

"At least she's not moaning 'braaaaaiiinnnsss,'" Lilian said, moaning out the last word in her approximation of a zombie. Kevin gave her a grin that was readily returned.

"Whatever." Waving off her son's complaints, Ms. Swift looked at that morning's breakfast and let out a low whistle. "Oh, wow. It looks like somebody went all out this morning. Did you make this, Kevin?"

Kevin shook his head. "No, Lilian's the one who made it."

Ms. Swift gave Lilian a still-half-asleep smile. "This looks pretty good. You must be an incredible chef."

"Oh, uh, t-thank you." Lilian's cheeks heated up. She then poked her index fingers together while looking down at the table. "It—I really didn't do anything special, though, just followed the instructions."

"So it seems even Lilian can be embarrassed by praise," Kevin chuckled as he, perhaps unknowingly, put his right hand over hers. "There's no need to get shy on us now. I've told you nearly a dozen times that you're an amazing cook. I'm actually jealous of how good your cooking is."

Lilian didn't know why, but she suddenly felt this strange urge to bury her face into her shirt. Unfortunately, her shirt wasn't very large and only had enough fabric to cover her chest, so she settled for hiding her nova-class red face into her equally flaming red hair.

"T-thank you," she whispered, too softly for Kevin's human ears to pick up.

"What was that?"

"N-nothing."

"I must agree with my son. This looks delicious." Ms. Swift took several long whiffs of the fragrance wafting from the food. "Smells good, too. You, my dear, are an excellent chef. Much better than my son is."

Kevin's right eye began twitching. "This coming from a women who couldn't cook a decent meal to save her life."

"I can cook!"

Kevin stared. A lot.

Ms. Swift turned her head, her cheeks growing flushed. "D-don't give me that look. I can cook."

"The last time you tried to cook, you ended up burning water."

"It was just a little mistake."

"Burning water isn't a mistake. It takes a conscious effort to do something like that. It shouldn't even be possible to burn water. The very act of doing so goes against the laws of nature."

Lilian watched as mother and son argued. Despite the harshness of Kevin's tone, his lips twitched several times, as if he was fighting back a smile.

"Ufufufu," Kotohime giggled. "These two make a most unusual family."

"They get along so well," Lilian said with a wistful sigh. "I wish our family got along like this."

"Yeah, well, you weren't that good when you first started cooking either! So there!"

"At least I learned how to cook eventually! Everything you

make ends up looking like a level five biohazard! The army could use your food as viral weaponry!"

"Mu, why can't my family love each other as much as these two clearly do?"

"Ufufufu…"

***

After breakfast the family of two plus Lilian and Kotohime headed to the mall.

Traveling to the mall had been Ms. Swift's decision. She had told Kevin, in no uncertain terms, that she, Lilian and Kotohime were going to have a "girls' day out." Kevin had not been invited, so he'd been sent off to the arcade until Ms. Swift decided to retrieve him.

Lilian hadn't been pleased. Neither had Kevin, but of the two, Lilian seemed much more upset.

"There is no need to frown like that, Lilian-sama," Kotohime told her charge as they walked through the mall. Her eyes lingered on a few men who she caught staring. A healthy dose of her killing intent had them running away in fear. "It'll give you wrinkles."

Her words caused Lilian to frown more. "But I wanted to spend some time with Kevin today," she whined.

"You spend every day with Kevin-san," Kotohime replied dryly, "one day away from him is not going to do you any harm."

"It might," Lilian grumbled.

"Ah, cheer up, Lily." A grinning Ms. Swift wrapped an arm around the younger girl's shoulder. "Our time here will fly by, and you'll be back with Kevin before you know it. Besides, with him gone we can get you some nice clothes that are sure to catch his attention."

Lilian looked up at Kevin's mom, her eyes shining at the prospect of new clothes that could aid in her seemingly never-ending quest for Kevin's affection. "Really?"

Ms. Swift's smile was so wide it nearly split her face in half. "Really. By the time we're done shopping today, we'll have several outfits that'll knock Kevin's socks off."

"Then what are we waiting for?!" Lilian cried out as her enthusiasm got the best of her. "Let's get going!"

Ms. Swift gave Kotohime a grin and the victory sign behind

Lilian's back. The voluptuous femme fatale giggled. "Ufufufu…"

"What are you laughing about?"

"Nothing, Lilian-sama. Just something interesting that I saw in the window of a store."

Their mission goal set, the group made for their first clothing store.

"You can generally tell what a store is selling by what they're displaying in the window," Ms. Swift explained to her attentive audience as they stood in front of a clothing boutique. Lilian consumed every word the woman said like they were the gospel truth. She even had a pen and notepad out that she used to take notes. Even Kotohime paid avid attention, if for no other reason than simple curiosity.

"See these displays?" Ms. Swift pointed at the mannequin. "They're currently displaying pants and long-sleeved shirts because it's the middle of September, so you can expect that whatever good deals they have going on inside are going to be for similar items of clothing."

"Hmm," Lilian mumbled as she stared at the pants with some minor distaste, "I don't really like pants."

"Wasn't Lilian-sama wearing pants when I finally found her?" Kotohime asked idly.

"That-that's just because Kevin said it would start getting chilly soon," Lilian mumbled, "And besides, those were jeans. They're completely different than the pants on display here."

"So you're allowing Kevin-san to influence your clothing decisions? How interesting. Ufufufu…"

Ms. Swift ignored Lilian giving the kimono-clad femme the stink-eye.

"There's nothing wrong with a good pair of pants. Kevin was smart to get you those jeans when he did. Even with the deal they have going on right now, these are still very expensive." She eyed the price tags and nodded to herself. "Pants bought during the summer or even near the start of fall are cheaper than during the winter, because that's when everyone's buying them. Store owners like to jack up the price while masking it behind something like a two-for-one deal. It's an old trading tactic."

Lilian tilted her head to the side before slowly nodding. "That makes sense. My mate is so smart!"

"Mate?" Ms. Swift frowned at the young woman. "Did you just say mate?"

Lilian cursed inwardly. How could she be so stupid? Humans didn't take mates. They got married. "Ah! Oh, um, d-did I say mate? I mean, uh, um, boyfriend!"

"Boyfriend?"

"Yes." Lilian was all smiles as she nodded like a bobblehead doll. "Boyfriend."

"I see." Ms. Swift looked at Kotohime, as if to ask, *"what the hell is your charge talking about?"* The other woman just shrugged, causing the single mom's frown to deepen.

In the end, Ms. Swift simply shrugged the word off.

"Well, all right. Let's head to the next store, then, shall we?"

***

Kevin frowned as he entered the arcade by himself.

Lilian would normally be with him these days, always be his side when he went to the arcade, or anywhere else really, but not today. No, today she was out shopping with his fashion guru mom and the frighteningly beautiful woman with the katana. Even though the arcade was full of people, Kevin felt strangely alone.

Rubbing a hand against his face, he released a deep gust of breath. "Why am I thinking about her? I should be glad we're not together."

Yes, he should be appreciative towards his mom for dragging Lilian off to go shopping. This was the first chance to have some time for himself that he'd had since the fox-girl entered his life. Kevin should be ecstatic.

So why aren't I?

Deciding that dwelling on this issue wouldn't help him, Kevin marched further into the arcade. He put twenty dollars worth of credits on his card, then went over to the first game that caught his eye. It was, of course, the zombie killing first-person shooter, "House of Haunted Horrors."

Five minutes later Kevin stood in front of the screen, plastic gun in hand. His index finger pulled the trigger, killing zombies with every shot. Yet his actions were automatic, mechanical, like his body was just going through the motions while his mind was off somewhere else.

Despite this game being one of his favorites, Kevin couldn't get into it. He looked over to his left, at the other station for the second player, and his mind visualized Lilian standing there, blasting away at zombies wearing the largest grin he'd ever seen.

Dispelling the image with a shake of his head, Kevin sighed and put the gun back in its holster. His character was still alive, but he just didn't care enough to play anymore.

"Kevin!"

Eric, Alex, Andrew and Justin waved as they approached. He hadn't realized they'd also come to the arcade, though in hindsight, he probably should have, as his friends rarely did anything else. While their presence didn't make his strangely gloomy mood disappear, it was enough to bring a slight smile to his face.

"Hey, guys. What's up?"

"Not much," Alex said, "You know how this works. Same crap, different day."

"Is it strange that I'm actually getting kind of bored?" asked Andrew. "I mean, I love coming to the arcade, but this place feels like it's becoming a real snore fest."

Kevin tilted his head before shaking it. "I don't think so. It's not like we can anywhere else in the middle of September. The arcade is one of the only places that's open, and if I'm not mistaken, you and Alex have gone here pretty much every day since school shut down, so of course you'd be bored of it."

"That is true," Andrew admitted.

"We also can't go on vacation since the world hasn't stopped with us," Kevin added, "just because our school is closed doesn't mean our parents have stopped working, and since none of us have a car, or even a license, well…" Kevin trailed off and shrugged.

"… Disneyland…"

Justin got several looks.

"That's right, you've never been to Disneyland before, have you?" Alex asked.

Justin shook his head.

"California Adventures is better."

"Never mind any of that," Eric shouted before whirling on Kevin. "Where is my Tit Maiden?"

"Oh, for the love of… are you still going on about that?!"

"Of course I am! I need my Tit Maiden and my Goth Hottie!

Now tell me where you're hiding them!"

"I'm not hiding anyone." Kevin paused as a vein began throbbing angrily on his forehead. "And stop calling them that!"

***

Shopping with someone who wasn't Kevin was an interesting experience. That the person she was shopping with happened to be Kevin's mother made it even more interesting.

Then again, Lilian would admit that she didn't have enough experience with shopping to make many comparisons. The only person she had shopped with before was Kevin, and Kotohime had bought all of her clothes before then. That was what happened when your family never let you travel to any human population centers.

The first thing Lilian discovered about Ms. Swift was that she was an expert bargain hunter with a keen eye for detail. She possessed profound knowledge on all things fashion. Every store they entered, Ms. Swift would lead them around, grabbing clothes off the racks seemingly at random for Lilian to try on. She was like a whirlwind.

Ms. Swift's sense of style was also similar to that of her son's, if a bit more refined. When Lilian commented on how her son made similar remarks after she had tried on some clothes, Ms. Swift had given her a smirk.

"Who do you think my son got his sense of fashion from?"

Lilian then learned about Ms. Swift's job as a fashion journalist. The woman was quite popular in the fashion industry, one of the leading experts on fashion, in fact. She had written many articles for a variety of popular magazines, which explained why she rarely came home. Her job often took her overseas to countries like France and Italy where most of the big time fashion expos took place.

"It's a nice job, and it pays well," Ms. Swift said when Lilian asked her about her job, "I'll admit, sometimes I dislike how I'm always away from my son, but it really can't be helped, and Kevin doesn't actually need me to get by. He's very responsible for his age."

It was nice to learn more about the woman who'd given birth to the man she loved. She also got some really cute outfits out of the deal, so there was that. Lilian felt positive that Kevin would approve of her new clothes.

As they continued shopping, the group of three ran into a certain blond tomboy, who also appeared to be doing some shopping of her own.

"Lilian?" Lindsay Diane strolled over to them after noticing the kitsune's distinctive crimson hair. Lilian smiled brightly.

"Hi, Lindsay."

"Hey." Lindsay raised a hand in greeting. "I'm surprised to see you here without Kevin."

Lilian crossed her arms and pouted.

"Yeah, well, I wanted to spend the day with him, but Ms. Swift suggested we have a 'girls' day out.'"

"Oh, I see. You—wait." Lindsay finally realized what Lilian had said, and turned in shock to see Kevin's mom walking up to them, carrying several sets of clothing in her perfectly-manicured hands. "Ms. Swift, I didn't know you were back."

"Hello, Lindsay!" Ms. Swift graced the tomboy with a cheery grin. "I hope you've been doing well."

"I'm alright, I guess," Lindsay said, "I was supposed to do some shopping with one of my friends, but she ditched me to hang out with her boyfriend." She frowned. "I don't mind that my friend decided to bail on me, but I really wish she would have told me first. It would have saved me an hour of sitting around, doing nothing."

"It could have been a last minute thing," Ms. Swift suggested.

"Yeah, that's what she said." Lindsay blew out a deep breath. "I still wish she would have told me."

"I know!" Lilian's exuberant cry caused Lindsay to take a step back. She took another one when Lilian got right in her face. "You can come with us!"

"Eh? I wouldn't want to impose—"

"I think that's a splendid idea." Ms. Swift clapped her hands together and beamed at the two. "Now I have two cute girls to dress up, hehehe."

Ms. Swift rubbed her hands together, chuckling in a strangely sinister way, like a mad scientist about to start a crazy experiment. Lilian and Lindsay both backed away from the woman doing her best impersonation of Shion Sonozaki, wondering if it wasn't too late for them to run away.

"Ara, ara." Kotohime had yet to play a part in this scene, so she said that.

***

Now that his friends had joined him, Kevin felt a bit less lonely. He would even go so far as to say he'd had a good time.

He and his friends had played a few games and done the things they normally did whenever they hung out together. It was nice, he admitted, being able to do something with just the guys.

"Ha! Looks like I win again, brother!"

"That was just a lucky shot! You're going down next time."

"As if. You know I'm better than you at, well, everything. What makes you think you can beat me?"

"I will beat you! Just you watch! Next round, your ass is grass."

Kevin looked over to where Alex and Andrew were yelling at each other, and promptly felt like facepalming. He knew they didn't get along, but did they really have to start an argument in the middle of the arcade?

"You think so, huh? Well, fine! Slide your card through and start the game again. I'll be more than happy to keep humiliating you in front of everyone else."

"You say that now, but you won't be saying that for long. Not once I finish beating your avatar black and blue. I'll show you who the 'King of Fighters' really is."

"… Fight…"

"Gods, I hope not," Kevin said in response to Justin's single word sentence. "The last thing we need is to get kicked out because those two couldn't keep from trying to tear each other apart."

"… Tear… like dog… fox…"

Kevin looked over at Justin oddly, but shook off the strange comment. His friend had always been a perplexing and bizarre fellow. This was just another example.

"You know, Justin, sometimes I worry about you."

"Who cares about those two! I just want my Tit Maiden and Goth Hottie!"

"Shut up, Eric!"

***

"Just when I thought my day couldn't get any worse, I run into you."

"The feeling's mutual. What are you doing here anyway?"

"I had nothing better to do."

Ms. Swift looked at the two girls trying to kill each other with their eyes. Maybe it was her imagination, but she could swear she saw sparks shooting between them. And was it just her, or had the temperature suddenly dropped several dozen degrees?

"There they go again." Lindsay ran her fingers through her hair, sighing exasperatedly. "You think they'd stop arguing since Kevin isn't here, but nope, the moment they meet, they're at each other's throats again."

"So this happens often, then?" Ms. Swift asked.

"Every time they see each other," Lindsay confirmed.

"Hmm."

While Lindsay and Kevin's mom conversed, Kotohime remained separate from the group by a couple of feet, observing. The shopping trip so far had been a decently pleasant experience. It had been a long time since she had truly mingled with humans in this manner.

Lilian's friendship with the young human girl was another surprise, but certainly not something to be displeased about. If anything, Kotohime felt this was a good thing. Her ward had very little contact with people outside of her clan, and none of them could be considered friends. It was nice to see her charge enjoying herself for a change.

A friend wasn't the only thing she seemed to have made, though. Kotohime didn't know why the yuki-onna held such a strong dislike for Lilian, nor did she understand the nature of their relationship. Their rivalry was obvious, however.

"So what exactly are they fighting over?" Ms. Swift asked. Kotohime visibly perked up. She was, after all, curious to know the answer as well.

"I can't be too sure," Lindsay shrugged. "They seem to dislike each other out of principle. I do know that a lot of their arguments revolve around Kevin, though."

"So they're fighting over my son?"

Ms. Swift looked at the two again.

"Skank."

"Loli."

"Whore."

"Bitty titties."

"Cow muncher."

"Tsundere."

"Who's a tsundere?!"

While Ms. Swift simply stared with a raised eyebrow, Lindsay chuckled nervously. "Well, sometimes they do. Other times I almost feel like they're arguing simply for the sake of arguing."

"Meat."

"Jailbait."

"… Although, I don't know if name-calling can really be called arguing…"

"Hmmm… well, regardless, I believe we need to break this up now. There are many more stores to visit, and I still have yet to find the perfect outfit for Lilian, one that will blow my dense son's mind."

"Are you sure that's a good idea?" Lindsay asked apprehensively. "I mean, Kevin's gotten a lot better at talking to girls in the last month or so, but I don't think he's ready to see Lilian wearing something too scandalous." She looked back at the stunning redhead, and quickly added an anecdote to her concerns. "Plus, this is Lilian we're talking about. That girl already causes heads to turn. I'm not sure Kevin could handle her if she's too, um, ah…"

"Sexed up?" Ms. Swift offered when Lindsay trailed off. The girl nodded, her cheeks flushing at the woman's words.

"Uh, yeah, I guess…"

"Excuse me," Kotohime interrupted. "Are you saying that Kevin-san actually used to act even worse around women than he does now?"

"Way worse." Lindsay confirmed with a nod, then paused, her face morphing into one of befuddlement. "Wait. 'Kevin-san?'"

"Worse than even the most anti-social of social shut-ins," Ms. Swift confirmed. Lindsay pouted at being ignored. "He's like an Otaku without the hug pillows and eroge."

"I see." Kotohime grew introspective and silent. The other two stared at her for a moment longer, but, when it became obvious that she would not be speaking again, they returned to their previous conversation.

"Anyway, I'm sure my son can handle whatever clothes I buy for Lilian," Ms. Swift said dismissively. "And if he cannot, then it just means we need to work with him some more. I won't have a son who acts like a pansy around women."

"… Right."

***

"Well now, this is a surprise," said a voice with a horrible fake Spanish accent.

Kevin almost sighed. While the day had started off unpleasantly, it had steadily improved after meeting up with his friends. It had been nice to have a "guys' day out" kind of thing—though he would never call it that out loud. He didn't want his friends poking fun of him for saying something like that. Eric would have been particularly vicious with his yaoi comments.

Of course, nothing good could last forever. Kevin had learned that the hard way.

"Hello, Juan Pompadour," he greeted flatly.

"My name is not Juan Pompadour! It is Juan Martinez Villanueva Cortes!"

"Ah, right. I forgot." He actually hadn't forgotten. He just never bothered remembering in the first place. The name was simply too long, and Kevin didn't care enough to remember it.

But he wasn't going to tell Juan Pompadour that.

"It is not Juan Pompadour!!"

"Who are you talking to?"

"What are you talking about?" asked a clueless Juan.

An angry red tic mark appeared on Kevin's forehead. "Don't give me that. You were clearly talking to someone."

The look on Juan's face was that of a man staring at someone who'd just said something extraordinarily stupid. "I have no clue what you're talking about."

"Tch!"

Raising his head, Juan managed to give the appearance of a snobbish aristocrat as he looked down his nose at Kevin. "I did not expect to see you here, nor do I see my lovely *señorita* with you either."

Kevin twitched at how Juan called Lilian "his *señorita*," but didn't react otherwise.

Juan continued irritating Kevin with his voice. "Not that I am surprised, mind you. She probably got sick of your presence and decided to leave. I would, too, if I were in her position. My poor *hermosura de flor* must have finally snapped under the yoke of your *feminidad*, your girlishness."

Somewhere in one of the many stores that littered the mall, Lilian sneezed. She then began scaring the other customers by yelling at... someone—they weren't sure who—to stop calling her flour.

Kevin's right hand clenched into a fist. "For your information, Lilian is currently shopping with my mom, otherwise she would be here."

Juan's expression was infuriatingly smug. "A likely story. I bet she got sick of spending time with you and decided to find someone else to go out with. Perhaps I should go find her and... keep her company, *si*? I am sure that she would love to spend time with someone as *masculino* as myself over some weak little plebeian like you."

"Lilian," Kevin said through gritted teeth, "isn't like that."

Juan's expression was overwhelming in its condescension. "If you are saying that, then you must obviously not know women very well. They are all like that. Women are flighty creatures, prone to finding something fascinating one day and bland the next. It is just how they are. And my *cautivador le florecor* is no different."

"I may not know much about women," Kevin admitted, "but I know plenty about Lilian." He glared at the boy in the Matador outfit. "And I know that she is nothing like that. Don't compare her to other women."

"It appears you are getting awfully defensive," Juan observed with a candid smile. "Are you, perhaps, feeling jealous of me?"

"W-w-what? Jealous?! Of course not!" Kevin scoffed, looking away and glaring at something in the distance. "I have absolutely no reason to be jealous of you!"

"Oh? My mistake," Juan shrugged. "With the way you are acting, it is easy for one to assume that you are nothing but jealous swine."

"I told you I'm not jealous! Or have you already forgotten that I'm the one Lilian likes?!"

"Is that a fact?" Juan's conceited expression really pissed Kevin off. He wished he could wipe that aggravating smirk right off the pompadour boy's face. "Since you are so sure of your relationship with Lilian, then you shouldn't mind making a little wager."

Kevin narrowed his eyes.

***

After Ms. Swift stopped the argument between Christine and Lilian, they continued their shopping extravaganza. Unfortunately for Lilian, Kevin's mom found the yuki-onna to be quite adorable, and had invited her along, though perhaps "forced" would've been a more appropriate term.

"A-a-adora—th-that's—but I'm not!"

"Now, now, dear, such a cute little girl shouldn't get so angry."

"C-c-c-cute?!"

"That's right. Cute. Now come along. We must find some clothes for you."

"Wha—hey! Quit dragging me!"

"Oh, I can't wait to dress you up! It will be just like dressing up a doll!"

And so, with Christine added to their ever-growing entourage, the group resumed their activities.

It was nearly an hour later when they finally stopped for lunch. While the term "progress" may have been misleading, they had made some amazing headway in their shopping, with Ms. Swift having found two outfits for Lilian, a small trinket for Kotohime, and several items Ms. Swift decided she needed for one reason or another.

Christine hadn't gotten anything, though she had been forced to dress up in a variety of outfits, much to her embarrassment.

Of the three, Kotohime had been the only one who complained about getting something.

"I cannot accept something this expensive," Kotohime said after Ms. Swift saw her eying a very lovely, if pricy, authentic Japanese vase used for presenting flower arrangements.

It was a small hobby she had picked up in her long years of wandering, before becoming a vassal for the Pnéyma clan. None of the younger kitsune knew how someone so skilled in the art of killing had acquired an interest in an activity as mundane as flower arrangement. Only the Pnéyma clan matriarch knew the four-tails' full history, and the katana-bearing female had every intention of keeping it that way.

"You can and you will." Ms. Swift was most insistent. "You might not be able to tell because Kevin and I live in such a small apartment, but I'm actually very well off. It helps that I live below my budget," she added as an afterthought. "Buying something like this won't even put a dent in my account."

Kotohime still did not look convinced. "I do appreciate the gesture, but…"

"Look," Ms. Swift started, her friendly aura evaporating like a bucket of water that had been tossed into the sun. All the lights around her seemed to vanish as well, like they'd been sucked straight into a black hole. "You will either accept this gift as a thank you for looking after my son, or I will buy it and smash it over your head. The choice is yours."

In spite of her inherent belief that she could kill this human easily, Kotohime still felt a small thrill run down her spine. Maybe it would be better to err on the side of caution in this instance.

"Ah, well, in that case, I shall accept this gift with the utmost gratitude."

The words seemed to have a soothing effect, as the aura of death and despair Ms. Swift had been exuding vanished, and the woman was all smiles again.

"Great!"

As the group waited in line to pay for their items, Lilian leaned over to Lindsay and cupped a hand to her mouth. "Do you think that's the reason Kevin has so much trouble around girls?"

"Nah," Lindsay whispered back. "Well, maybe a little, but if that was the reason, I think he'd be terrified of women instead of just shy."

"Yeah, I guess you're right."

"What are you girls talking about back there?" Ms. Swift asked.

"Nothing," the two replied in unison, sharing mischievous grins. Behind them, Christine was nearly pouting. Nearly, because incredibly dark and broody goth girls like her did not pout. They sulked.

"How come I don't get any kind of gift?"

"I offered to buy you those clothes you tried on," Ms. Swift pointed out.

"T-those clothes looked awful on me." Christine turned her head, thereby missing Ms. Swift's pout.

This girl clearly didn't appreciate her sense of fashion.

"I thought you looked cute in them."

"C-cute?!" Christine squeaked.

Lilian grinned at her love-rival. "Yeah, cute like a little kid."

"What was that?!"

"Ara, ara, I believe that is enough fighting, you two." Kotohime stopped the fight with her words… and her katana. "You two are beginning to draw a crowd. I dislike crowds, so you won't fight anymore. Okay?"

The two took one look at the katana that had been thrust between them, gulped, and then decided to call a temporary truce.

"O-okay," Lilian mumbled warily. "We promise not to fight anymore."

"What she said," Christine muttered.

"Good. Ufufufu…"

"Does your maid always laugh like that?" Lindsay asked.

"Sometimes."

"It sounds a lot like yours."

"U-ugh." Lilian could practically feel the insult penetrating her like an arrow. "D-does my laugh really sound like that?"

"No," Christine said, "it's worse."

Lilian glared, but one look at Kotohime kept her from saying anything.

After they finished shopping, the group of five walked to the food court. Lilian headed straight for "Fat Fizoli's Pizza Parlor" and ordered a Sicilian Pizza with all the toppings.

"I see you've decided to take after my son when it comes to pizza," Ms. Swift commented after they all sat down.

Christine nearly scowled from her seat next to Lilian. Nearly. She didn't scowl, but only because her mouth was full of steak burrito. Otherwise she would have. Her scowl would've been fierce enough to send all and sundry running for the hills.

"Of course. Your son has great taste in food." As if to emphasize her point, Lilian took a large bite of her pizza and moaned in delight. "This really is some of the best food I've ever had."

"It is also not very healthy for you," Kotohime informed her ward. "I would advise against eating too much junk food like this." She took a bite of her salad. "Indulging every now and then is okay, though."

Lilian sighed in bliss as she continued eating. Even if she were inclined to get mad at her maid, the incredible burst of flavor on her tongue and the light, fluffy texture of the bread made getting irritated a chore.

"Don't worry, I won't eat more than a single slice whenever I go out, and only on rare occasions. Anymore and I'll probably get sick anyway. This stuff is really greasy."

"Very well," Kotohime relented after being reassured.

"Are you going to be alright eating just that, Kotohime?" Ms. Swift asked, glancing at her companion's sparse chicken salad.

"Yes, this is enough for me." Kotohime speared another leaf of lettuce with her fork. "I usually prefer meat to salad, but none of these fast food chains can prepare meat the way I like it. And the so-called 'Japanese restaurants' here taste less refined than garbage."

Lilian felt a large drop of sweat trail down the left side of her face. Kotohime really didn't like fast food, it seemed.

Ms. Swift shrugged. "Well, if you're sure."

"I am, but thank you for your concern."

"You're welcome."

Kotohime and Ms. Swift shared a smile, then began to discuss the finer points of fashion versus functionality.

"Don't you find it stifling in that kimono?"

"Not particularly, but that is probably because of my upbringing. Before coming into the service of Lilian-sama's family, I lived in a small village in Japan. We were a very traditional village. All the women wore kimonos, and the men preferred *hakama* and *haori* over modern clothing, so I have been wearing outfits like this my whole life."

Of course, the village Kotohime spoke of also happened to be a yōkai village, which explained its traditional setting. As a general rule of thumb, villages comprised solely of yōkai were less technologically advanced and several centuries behind the times when it came to fashion. It had to do with how long-lived yōkai were. Most lived a minimum of five-hundred years or so provided they weren't killed before then.

"Really?"

"Oh, yes. My village was extremely behind the times. Even our customs and traditions were outdated by several hundred years."

Lilian almost snorted. She didn't know much about Kotohime's past, but she did know that Kotohime was over 400 and had been serving the Pnéyma clan for more than two centuries. That meant the four-tails hadn't been living in the village she spoke of since the late 1800s at least.

"That would explain why you have the look of a *Yamato Nadeshiko*."

"I'm surprised you know that term."

"Hey now, I may not be into Japanese pop culture like my son, but I am aware of some Japanese terms. *Yamato Nadeshiko* is actually a term we use in the fashion industry." A pause. "At least, it is in Japan's fashion industry."

"Ara, how interesting."

While the adults spoke of fashion, the younger generation (discarding the fact that Lilian was 159 years old), spoke of something else: boys.

"So Christine, are there any boys you like?" Lindsay asked.

Christine was very glad she'd not been eating when that question was asked. She would have choked on her food otherwise.

"A-a b-b-b-boy—O-of course not! Why would I—it's not like—boys are nothing but perverted idiots—I mean, I could never—"

Lilian coughed into her hand. "Tsundere."

"Shut up, cow tits!"

"What about you, Lindsay?" asked a curious Lilian. She ignored the insult. Christine had used it so much by this point that any effectiveness it may have possessed had long since worn out.

"You mean are there any boys that I like?" Lindsay asked for clarification.

Lilian nodded. "Yeah."

"Well, there is one, but I'm sure you already know about that."

"Ah, right. I guess I forgot about that."

Lindsay's face became the definition of, "are you serious?"

"You forgot? Really?"

Lilian scratched at her head while looking sheepish. "Yeah, I did. Sorry."

"Forgot? Forgot what?" Christine asked.

"Nothing," Lilian dismissed the goth girl's question with a wave of her hand.

"And what about you?" Lindsay asked. "How are you and Kevin doing?"

Christine turned to spit out her Coke, creating a small puddle on the floor… which someone just happened to walk over seconds after it formed. The poor young man slipped on the spill and slammed head first onto the hard tile floor.

He didn't get back up.

"Man down! Man down! Make way!"

Christine, Lindsay and Lilian all watched as a pair of paramedics rushed up to the young man and loaded him onto a stretcher. They left soon after.

"Okay…" Lindsay's face said that she clearly had no idea what just happened. "That was weird."

Christine and Lilian nodded in agreement.

"I don't know." Lilian returned to the topic at hand. "He's always giving me mixed signals. Sometimes it seems like we're getting along really well, while others times he acts like he can barely handle being around me."

"You mean he's speaking gibberish?"

"Yeah, and while I'm sort of grateful, because I know it means he finds me attractive, I wish it would let me know how he feels about me as a person, you know?"

"Give him some time," Lindsay said soothingly. "Kevin's like every other boy when it comes to his feelings, slower than a brick wall and twice as dense. It hasn't been that long since you two met, barely a month. I'm sure he's trying to sort out his feelings right now, and that's why he keeps sending mixed signals."

"I guess." Lilian took a bite of her Sicilian pizza, but found her enjoyment of it waning. It tasted bland now.

"What makes you think Kevin even likes Lilian?" asked a scowling Christine.

Lindsay raised an eyebrow. "What do you mean? It's obvious that he likes Lilian."

"That's right," Lilian nodded decisively. "He wouldn't be afflicted by *Gibberish of Love* if he didn't like me."

"Gibberish of what now?"

Lindsay ran a hand down her face while Christine just looked confused.

Lilian shot the goth girl a sly grin. "Why do you look so displeased? Are you jealous?"

"J-j-j-j-jealous?!" Christine shrieked. Lilian and Lindsay winced at the shrill noise. "O-of course not! Why the hell would I be jealous?!"

"I don't know." Lilian recovered from the shriek and shrugged. "You tell me? I mean, it's not like you like Kevin or anything, right?"

"T-t-that's right." Christine latched onto Lilian's words like they were a life raft. "I do like him—I mean, I don't! I don't like him! I could never like that stupid, insensitive jerk! Hmph!"

Christine must have gained several levels in tsundere since their last meeting, Lilian concluded. She was acting even more belligerent than before.

"Now this is a surprise," a voice spoke up from behind the squabbling girls. "Who in their right mind would have thought you and I would bump into each other here, of all places."

Every head present snapped towards the new voice. Lilian's eyes widened, Christine scowled, Kotohime raised an eyebrow, while Lindsay and Ms. Swift merely appeared curious.

"It's you!"

Lilian shot to her feet and pointed at the intruder with a quivering finger. She could feel her breathing beginning to hitch. Phantom aches and pains appeared on her chest and legs. Her vision grew blurry as she tried not to let herself be overcome by fear.

"Hello, Lilian," Kiara greeted in a mild, polite tone of voice, as if she hadn't beaten the utter living crap out of Lilian two weeks ago.

Lilian tried scowling at the woman, but was unsuccessful. "What are you doing here?"

"Relaxing on my day off, of course," Kiara answered in a "it should be obvious" tone of voice. "I don't have any work or board meetings to attend right now, so I figured I'd wander the mall for a bit and buy a few essentials." She raised a single eyebrow at Lilian. "Is that a problem?"

Lilian worked her mouth, trying to say something, anything. However, no matter how many times she opened her mouth, nothing came out. Not a word, syllable, or even a squeak.

Kiara chuckled. "Now, now, there's no need to scared of me. I won't bite."

"I-I'm not scared of you."

"Why don't you say that after you stop shaking?"

Everyone looked to see that Lilian was, indeed, trembling. Her entire body seemed to be undergoing visible muscle spasms. She looked like a twig caught in a hurricane. All those present wondered what this woman had done to earn such a reaction from the normally cheerful and vibrant girl. Christine had a guess, but she wasn't about to draw unwanted attention to herself.

"Kiara?" Kotohime looked surprised for a moment, but then, like rays of sunlight parting the clouds, a surprisingly pleasant smile appeared. "I almost didn't recognize you. You've changed your hairstyle."

Kiara twirled a strand of her short, choppy hair between her fingers.

"I thought it was time to get rid of all that hair. It always got in the way whenever I was fighting." She glanced at Kotohime's own long, raven locks. "I don't know how you fight with such long hair."

Kotohime hid a smile behind the sleeve of her kimono. "Oh, I've learned to accommodate for it. Ufufufu…"

Kiara's grin was rife with amusement. "I'll bet you have."

"Would you care to join us for lunch?"

"Hiiii!"

"Thanks, but I think I'll pass for today." Kiara's eyes twinkled with barely concealed mirth. "I wouldn't want to frighten your charge any more than I already have."

An amused glance at Lilian revealed that the twin-tailed beauty had taken to hiding behind Christine. She peeked out from over the snow maiden's shoulder, her wide eyes reminding Kiara of a frightened child who'd just seen her first horror movie.

"Oi! Get the hell away from me, you skanky fox! Gods, you're such a fraidy cat!"

"I-I'm not a fraidy cat! Don't confuse me with some measly neko!" Lilian tried to defend herself. Considering she was hiding behind the girl she'd been arguing with awhile ago and stuttering, her words didn't hold much weight. "I just… want to eat over here instead."

Kotohime raised a single, delicate eyebrow in Lilian's direction, before turning to Kiara with a question in her eyes. "Dare I ask what you did to make Lilian-sama so frightened of you?"

"Oh, we just had a minor altercation." Kiara waved her hand as if swatting at a fly. "But don't worry, it's all been fixed now."

"You call what happened to me minor?"

Lilian didn't know whether to be displeased or relieved at being considered "minor."

"Of course. If our dispute had been more serious, you wouldn't have gotten off as lightly as you did."

"Eep!"

Lilian hid behind Christine again.

She was definitely going with relieved.

***

"Hey, Kevin, how do you know this weird pompadour kid?"

"I don't know him," Kevin scowled.

He and Juan stood in front of the basketball arcade game, both prepared to start their competition. If Juan won, Kevin would have to let the matador boy ask Lilian out on a date. If Kevin won, Juan would stop bothering him and Lilian. This wasn't something he wanted to do, making a bet like this, but he consoled himself with the knowledge that Lilian would never agree to go on a date with

Juan.

Kevin still cursed himself for allowing Juan to decide what game they played first, though. Did pompadour boy know that shooting hoops was something he was notoriously bad at? Probably, but it was too late to turn back now.

Eric and Justin stood on either side of Kevin, but the twins were still off arguing about... something. He wasn't sure if they even knew what they were arguing about anymore, but the last he saw of them, it looked like their fight would come to blows at the slightest provocation.

"If you don't know him, then why are you facing off against him?" Eric's expression was the kind people gave when they thought someone was being an idiot. "Especially in a hoop shooting competition. Everyone knows you suck at basketball."

"I know that." Kevin's scowl deepened. "I'm well aware of how bad I am at shooting hoops. You don't have to rub it in."

"Hey, don't get mad at me. I'm just saying that you shouldn't have let him sucker you into letting him pick the first game."

"... Shut up."

"Is there a problem?" Juan smirked at him, and in that moment, Kevin knew that his nemesis was perfectly aware of his lack of talent when it came to shooting baskets.

"No," Kevin lied. "There's no problem."

"Good. Then let us begin."

The buzzer went off and the gates rose, allowing the basketballs to roll towards them. The competition had begun.

It immediately became clear that neither of them was very good at basketball. However, between the two, Juan was noticeably better. For every one basket that Kevin made, Juan made at least two, sometimes even three.

By the time they reached the halfway mark, Kevin was sweating bullets. He looked at Juan as the other boy shot a basket that went in. Deciding that he needed to catch up to his rival, Kevin shot the ball in his hand, grabbed the next ball and shot that one, too. Over and over again he shot balls at the hoop, the rate at which he did so increasing in an attempt to catch up to Juan's score.

All of them missed.

Kevin glanced over at Juan, who'd made another six baskets.

The olive-skinned boy saw him looking and sent a smug grin his way that seemed to say, "you will never catch up to me." He gritted his teeth and began shooting balls even faster.

Unfortunately, his hands had become slick with sweat. One of the balls he shot slipped from his grasp and beamed some poor boy in the head, knocking him unconscious.

"Oh, my God! They killed Kenny!"

"No, he's not dead. Just unconscious."

"Oh… phew. What a relief."

By the time the buzzer went off, the score was a lopsided 42:7.

"It looks like this is my win," Juan said with a triumphant smirk. Once Kevin got over his shock at being beaten so thoroughly—though he honestly shouldn't have been that surprised—he glared at the other teen.

"This isn't over yet. Don't forget that I get to choose the next challenge."

"So you do, but it will not matter." Juan's grin made Kevin twitchy. What he wouldn't give to sock this matador costume-wearing boy in the face! "No matter the game you choose, I will win."

Kevin's eyes narrowed. "We'll see."

The next challenge was a police simulation game, one that offered several types of shooting range scenarios. The best part about the game—to Kevin—was its dual-wielding feature.

"I hope you're ready to lose," Kevin said to Juan, two plastic guns already in hand.

Juan looked at Kevin through squinted eyes. "The only one who is going to be losing this day is you."

He and Juan stared at each other, the ozone crackling as their hatred manifested on the physical planes of reality. Tendrils of lightning arced between them, striking the ground and making several people skitter away. Behind them, Eric and Justin stared.

"… Inu… pissing…"

"No kidding," Eric agreed, "I'm not sure what's more surprising; the fact that Kevin is actually getting into a fight because of a girl, or that there's someone in this world with such an atrocious sense of fashion. I mean, I'm no fashionista or whatever, but even I know that outfit just sucks."

Only after he said this, did Eric catch Justin's comment.

"Wait. What did you say?"

Justin merely tilted his head, his half-lidded eyes holding the same apathy they always did.

Eric sighed. "If I didn't know you so well, I'd think you were insane, what with all the weird, random crap you say."

"… Bad?"

"I guess not," Eric shrugged, before realizing something. "Hey, I just noticed, we're missing Alex and Andrew. Where are they?"

"… There…"

Eric followed Justin's pointing finger and nearly did a double take when he saw the large mosh pit of people fighting. Alex and Andrew were duking it out in the middle, and it was clear to him that they were fighting the hardest. Alex had a black eye and Andrew a busted lip.

"When did that happen? How did that happen? And why the hell am I just now noticing it?"

"… Snowball…"

"Ah."

Eric understood Justin's one word answer. Alex and Andrew must've started throwing punches at one another, hitting several other people in the process. This had a snowball effect, turning the entire fiasco into an all-out brawl between complete strangers.

While Eric and Justin watched more people become embroiled in the epic battle taking place several yards away, Kevin and Juan started the next challenge.

Kevin's hands came up with synchronized precision as six spheres were launched into the air. His fingers hit the trigger at a rapid fire-rate, quickly shooting down all six spheres barely two seconds after the game started.

Looking over at Juan and seeing the gaping eyes on the teen's equally shocked face, Kevin grinned. "Something wrong, Juan? You're looking a little pale."

Juan glowered at him. "There is nothing wrong."

"Good, because the next simulation is starting."

"What?!"

Juan had no time to do anything as Kevin fired off round after round, hitting the targets popping on screen with pinpoint precision. Kevin held the plastic guns in front of him, his arms crisscrossing, the weapons tilted so the butts were connected, dual-wielding like a boss.

Juan could only use one gun, putting him at a severe disadvantage. He tried using two, but soon realized it made aiming more difficult.

A little known fact about Kevin: he was ambidextrous. For as long as he could remember, he'd been using both hands equally in everything he did, regardless of what it was. It wasn't an acquired talent, but an inherent skill he'd been born with. Combine this ability with his impressive hand-to-eye coordination, gained through years of playing arcade-style shooting games, and Kevin had become practically unbeatable when it came to simulations like this.

Juan didn't stand a chance in hell of winning.

By the time the game finished, Kevin had beaten Juan handily. It might've been more accurate to say that Juan had been crushed beyond all reasonable comprehension, which explained why the pompadour boy could do nothing but gape at the screen, his jaw practically hanging to the floor as his eyes bulged like two big, round hockey pucks. The expression looked particularly ridiculous when combined with his matador outfit and stupid-looking hair.

Kevin had a hard time keeping a straight face.

"Looks like I win," Kevin declared with an air of smug satisfaction. He wasn't normally one to rub his victory in someone's face—unless their name happened to be Kasey Chase—but in this instance, he had no issue doing just that.

Juan shook himself out of his stupor and shakily glared at Kevin. "We may be tied now, but there is still one more challenge left, and I shall not allow a *campesino* like you to defeat me."

"Ha!" Kevin barked a laugh. "You can think that way if you want, but we both know who's going home the victor this day." His eyes narrowed into slits. "So, how do we decide who gets to choose the next challenge?"

Juan clenched his left hand into a fist, placing it into his opened right palm. He then brought both toward his torso like he planned to unleash a *Kamehameha Wave*. "There is only one way to decide something like this, *si*?"

"I see, so that's how it is." Kevin copied Juan's actions, hiding his hands from view. "I have to warn you, I'm an expert at this game. There's no way you can beat me."

"We shall see."

Kevin and Juan stared at each other, eyes narrowed in fierce competition. The air became thick with tension—and dust, but mostly tension. It also became surprisingly loud, but Kevin and Juan hardly noticed the shouts and yelps of pain. They were too busy staring each other down like two samurai in an old-fashioned shogun stand-off.

A tumbleweed rolled between them. They ignored that, too. This was it. The final showdown. The battle that would decide it all. Only one of them would walk away the victor.

They took a deep breath—

"Jen! Ken! Pon!"

—And exploded into action.

… Silence. Kevin and Juan looked down at their hands, both of which were scissors. They looked back at each other and their eyes narrowed further. They drew their hands back, and the process started over.

"Jen! Ken! Pon!"

"Jen! Ken! Pon!"

"Why are we saying this in Japanese?"

"Jen! Ken! Pon!"

"I don't know. Does it matter?"

"Jen! Ken! Pon!"

"I guess not."

"Jen! Ken! Pon!"

Thus continued the very intense game of rock-paper-scissors. Over and over they tried beating the other, only to come up with matching hands. It seemed neither was able to win.

This game would have continued for some time were it not for a series of extenuating and unprecedented factors that happened several seconds later.

Like Kevin and Juan being pulled into the vicious battle of Shōnen proportions that had engulfed the entire arcade. It started when someone was shoved into Juan. The boy fell on his back, which caused Kevin to start laughing.

Had he been paying attention, he might not have been caught off guard when someone's fist slammed into his face. Despite his surprise and the stinging pain in his cheek, Kevin had no issue retaliating like any normal teenager would. He hit the boy back, and thus, he and Juan became embroiled in the ever-expanding battle.

A large number of objects flew through the air: utensils, chairs, tables, a kitchen sink. As the battle continued, more and more of the surrounding property suffered from massive battle damage, until almost every arcade game, every stand and every booth became nothing more than smoking slag piles of plastic, metal and circuitry. Kevin would have wondered where the mall's security forces were, but someone punched him in the face and all thoughts on security evaporated.

Needless to say, the manager wouldn't be happy when he came back from his vacation to the Bahamas, and discovered that his beloved arcade had been demolished.

***

Kevin, Eric, Justin, Juan, the twins and everyone else who'd been present during the massive brawl—which everybody who'd been at the arcade—found themselves standing outside the now-destroyed arcade.

While the outside looked fine, the inside was a different story. Through the window, Kevin could see the massive amounts of destruction the impromptu war had caused. Arcade games were tipped over and sparking, their cables and circuits spilling out like innards. Chairs and tables lay in broken heaps. The bar looked like it had been put through a war zone. The floor had become pitted and scarred with the signs of battle. Everything was in ruins. Hanging on the automatic entrance was a large sign that read: "closed until further notice."

Eric managed to put everyone else's thoughts into words.

"Well, this sucks."

Several people nodded, Kevin included.

"It seems we shall have to postpone our duel until further notice," Juan conceded.

"Whatever," Kevin sighed. He felt tired, and old. A part of him worried about how he hardly even batted an eyelash at the sight of his favorite arcade being decimated. Another part just wanted to head home, go to sleep, and pretend this whole affair never happened.

"As we can no longer have our duel, I shall take my leave. Farwell, *mi amigos.*"

Kevin didn't bother watching Juan leave. He merely continued staring at the arcade, his eyes soulless and devoid of life.

"Kevin!"

His head snapped up at the familiar voice. A small flicker of light entered his eyes as he turned his head.

"Lilian."

He smiled as Lilian approached him, closely followed by his mom, Kotohime, Christine and Lindsay. A bizarre fluttering entered his chest, like butterflies flapping about. He did his best to ignore the feeling. Kevin really hoped he wasn't getting sick or something.

Cha-ching!

Blinking, Kevin turned to the strange noise that sounded a lot like a cash register being opened. The noise had come from Eric, whose eyes had somehow transformed into large dollar signs. Kevin would have wondered how such a thing was possible, but had no desire to deal with the headache such thoughts would bring.

Eric's expression only lasted for a moment before he was off.

"BOOBIES!"

With great agility and speed, the young pervert darted toward the group of women, his hands stretched out and grasping as he imagined grabbing onto those large mountains of flesh like a baker kneading dough.

"Come to papa, you delectable—guwog!"

Less than a second later, Eric lay face down on the ground, blood pooling underneath him from where his nose had a close encounter of the concrete kind. He was clearly unconscious.

Everyone stared at the boy lying on the ground, completely insensate, before looking at Christine, who had a large vein pulsing on her forehead like a giant tic mark. Her fist was still extended and her breathing heavy. Her arm shook with pent-up rage.

Lindsay summed up everyone's thoughts pretty well.

"Whoa, remind me never to get on your bad side."

"Don't worry," Kevin reassured her, "so long as your name isn't Eric, I think you'll be fine."

"Good to know." Lindsay seemed most reassured by Kevin's words.

***

Unbeknownst to everyone, the group of humans and yōkai were not alone. Situated on top of the mall, Professor Nabui lay on his stomach, using the scope of his personalized sniper rifle to spy on them.

He had been tracking their movements and observing their behavioral patterns for quite a while now. Ever since he'd contacted his immediate superior, in fact. It was important to learn everything he could if he wanted this mission to succeed.

Already he'd learned a number of useful pieces of information, like how that woman dressed in the kimono had very keen instincts. She could tell when her group was being watched. He'd already been forced to hide himself several times when she looked in his direction. Inagumi Takashi—Professor Nabui to his colleagues and students—didn't know who she was, or even what she was, but he knew that, whenever he decided to enact his plan, it would have to be when she was not present.

A battle against her could only end in defeat.

The rest of the group seemed oblivious to his presence, which was fine with him. From what he could see, the only other yōkai was the girl dressed in gothic lolita garb. He didn't know what she was, but had gathered through his spying that she had control over ice, or perhaps the weather. Either way, she wasn't much of a threat.

Other than her mean left hook, apparently.

He watched the group leave. It would take a bit more time to put his plan into motion, a week or two at most. He would gather more information, wait for the boy's mother to leave, and then he would strike.

"Freeze! Don't move!" a voice shouted behind him.

Inagumi Takashi froze.

"Stand up."

He stood up.

"Now put your hands in the air and turn around slowly."

He did exactly as told, making a full 180-degree turn to face someone pointing a gun at him. A cop. Two cops, to be precise.

"You're under arrest for suspected terrorist activity, carrying illegal weaponry, and trespassing on private property. We're gonna have to take you to the station."

Well, crap, this was not good. How was he going to get out of this situation?

"Put your hands behind your head and get on the ground," one of the cops ordered. "If you make any suspicious moves, I won't hesitate to shoot."

As Inagumi Takashi did what was instructed of him, a single thought passed through his mind.

I'm beginning to think I should have left my sniper rifle at home...

Chapter 7

A Wavering Heart

Ms. Swift wore a large grin as she, Kotohime, Lilian and Kevin entered the apartment. She stretched her hands above her head and arched her back. Kevin winced upon hearing it crack several times.

"He-heh, that was a lot of fun. I haven't gone shopping like that in a really long time." She looked at Lilian and her smile widened. "It helps that I had such a beautiful girl to play fashion model for me."

While Kevin somehow managed not to palm his face, Lilian put her hands on her cheeks and blushed a pretty shade of pink. "Ufufufu, thank you."

"Acting bashful doesn't suit you," Kevin mumbled, "and don't laugh like that when you're trying to appear demure."

"Ufufufu, don't be like that, Kevin."

"Seriously, stop that."

Taking her eyes off the duo as they bantered, Kotohime looked at the clock.

"Oh my, it has gotten rather late." The clock read six pm; they had been at the mall for nearly seven hours. "I suppose I should start preparing dinner."

"You don't need to worry about dinner, Kotohime," Lilian told the older kitsune. "Kevin and I will take care of dinner."

"And there you go, offering my services without even asking if I want to make dinner," Kevin said in mock irritation.

Lilian peered at him with an adorable pout. "Are you saying you don't want to help me prepare dinner?"

Looking away, Kevin scratched his cheek with his right index finger. "I didn't say that. I wouldn't mind giving you a hand in the kitchen, even though you don't really need my help."

"Maybe not, but you have to admit that it's much more fun cooking with someone else than it is cooking alone."

"Well, maybe a little."

"Try a lot."

Kotohime took a moment to study the twin-tailed kitsune she had protected for nearly 60 years. After taking a moment to observe Lilian as if seeing her for the first time, she eventually gave a nod.

"Very well, I will be interested in seeing what Lilian-sama and... the boy decide to cook."

"'The boy' she calls me," Kevin mumbled. "I get the feeling she doesn't like me very much."

"Did you say something?" Kotohime's eyes sharpened like blades.

"Not a thing." Kevin dutifully did his best to ignore the eyes boring into his skull and turned to Lilian. "Come on."

He gestured for the girl to proceed him. Lilian beamed as she went into the kitchen, Kevin trailing after her. Despite trying not to, he couldn't keep himself from admiring her small, shapely butt —and was it just him, or had Lilian added an extra sway to her hips?

While Kevin tried to find some means to pry his eyes off Lilian's rear end, Kotohime stared at him with narrowed eyes.

"Hmm..."

***

"So what are we making?" Kevin asked as he and Lilian stood in the kitchen.

"We're making *kota riganati*."

"Greek chicken?" Kevin tilted his head. "I've actually heard of that. It's a really popular dish in Greece, right? I'm surprised we haven't made it before."

"You know of it?"

"Mmm. I had it that one time I went to Greece with my mom.

I think I told you about that."

"Yeah," Lilian nodded noncommittally, "you said that you don't remember a lot of what happened back then because you were so young."

"That's right. But, while I don't remember a whole lot about that trip, there are a few things that I do remember. It's a little strange, to be honest, some memories seem sharper than others, while other memories seem like one big blur." Kevin pondered that for a moment, then shook his head. "Anyway, one of the things that I do remember was mom and I having this amazing Greek chicken during our first night there."

Kevin pulled out some chicken from the fridge and tested its firmness, frowning. This chicken wasn't fully thawed yet. Great.

"So, I don't know what ingredients we need to make Greek chicken." Kevin turned around to Lilian, chicken in hand. "What do we... Lilian?"

"Hmm?" Lilian snapped out of the fugue state she'd been in and looked at Kevin. "Yes?"

Kevin studied her with concern. "Are you feeling okay?"

"Of course. Why wouldn't I be?"

His frown deepening, Kevin set the bag of partially thawed chicken in the microwave, and used the defrosting feature to finish thawing it. He then focused his attention back on the redhead.

"I don't know. You're staring off into space like something is bothering you. Are you sure you're feeling okay?"

Lilian looked surprised for a second, but then shook her head and offered him a reassuring smile.

"I'm fine." Kevin still didn't look convinced, but Lilian didn't give him a chance to ask her anything else. "Anyway, we need half a cup of olive oil, juice from four lemons, dried oregano, garlic powder, salt and pepper, seven tablespoons of butter, and about half a cup of water. Could you get those for me?"

Kevin stared at Lilian a second longer, before nodding slowly. "Yeah, sure."

"Thank you."

Kevin went to the cupboard to gather ingredients while Lilian preheated the oven to 350 degrees, then she grabbed the non-reactive baking pan and set it on the stove.

With nothing to do but wait for the chicken to defrost, Lilian's gaze strayed to Kevin. The blond sprinter had just finished gathering all of the ingredients and was now juicing a lemon.

Watching him like this, seeing him cooking with her, made Lilian's desire to have his love soar even higher.

This... this was what she wanted; someone she could do things with, someone she could enjoy life with. She didn't want to marry some stuffy old fox who thought her similar to a prize mule. She especially didn't want to marry some brat who thought she was a toy that he could play with and discard when he was done. She wanted Kevin, a person she could do the things she enjoyed doing because he enjoyed doing them, too.

Feeling her eyes on him, Kevin looked up from his work and turned his head, their eyes meeting from across the room.

"Lilian?"

Her eyes widened and her cheeks turned a pale shade of pink when she realized that he'd caught her staring. She looked away, turning her head in an attempt to pretend she hadn't been watching him work. Her heart felt like a pantheon of gods were partying in her chest.

What... what is wrong with me?

Lilian clutched at her chest, which was pounding harder than it ever had before. She glanced at Kevin, whose mouth had opened to say something. He didn't get the chance, however, as the microwave chose that moment to beep.

"I'll get that!" Lilian announced before Kevin could speak. She hurried over to the microwave, pulling out the chicken to begin prepping it as she tried to calm her racing heart.

What is wrong with you, Lilian? Why are you getting so flustered? This isn't like you at all. You need to calm down.

When she managed to bring both her heart rate and the heat in her cheeks down to manageable levels, she turned to Kevin.

"Could you bring me those ingredients, please?"

Kevin frowned, but did as he was asked "Yeah, sure," he grabbed the ingredients and measured out the amount Lilian had requested.

It happened while he was handling the dried oregano. He had finished measuring the spice at the same time Lilian reached out to grab it. A jolt like an electric current traveled through them as their hands made contact. The feeling of electricity traversed their arms and shoulders, then made a path down their spine, sending shivers in its wake.

Lilian almost lost control of her transformation and let her ears and tails out—which would have been bad, since Kevin's mother was sitting in the living room with Kotohime. Her body shuddered from the crown of her head down to her toes.

"Kevin..."

The sound of Lilian's breathless voice made his spine stiffen and forced him to look at her. She was staring right at him with those big, beautiful emerald eyes. A moment later he noticed their hands were still touching.

"Ack! S-sorry!"

Kevin tried to jerk his hand away, but Lilian was too quick. She snatched it out of the air before he could fully retract it.

"There's nothing to apologize for." Lilian pulled his hand to her face, bringing it to rest on her right cheek. "I don't mind if you touch me. I like it when you touch me."

Kevin's mind, which should have been screaming at him to pull his hand away, had fallen strangely silent. He knew that he should remove his hand, but for whatever reason, he couldn't do it, almost as if he didn't want to remove it.

Once again, Kevin had to marvel at just how soft Lilian's skin felt. The finest silk, imported from whatever country had the best quality silk, simply couldn't compete with the unblemished and impossibly smooth perfection of Lilian's skin. From a purely physical standpoint, this girl had absolutely no faults. She was so beautiful it frightened him.

"L-Lilian?"

Lilian's eyes, which she'd closed to further enjoy Kevin's touch, fluttered open, locking him in place, freezing him like a statue made of ice. His mind went on the fritz. A strange buzzing like the sparks of an overloading circuit board filled his mind. He couldn't think, he could scarcely breathe, all he could do was focus on the vision of loveliness before him.

"Yes?"

"My hand..."

"I'm sorry. I know it's presumptuous of me to be so physical with you, especially after you told me that you only like me as a friend."

"Ah... n-no, that's not..."

"But I can't deny my desire to be with you." Her eyes bored into his, hypnotizing him with their undeniably enchanting mien. "You don't have to be with me if you don't want to. I would never try to force you to love me." She paused, considering something. "At least, I would never try forcing you to love me the way that I love you. Seducing you is an entirely different matter."

Kevin twitched, momentarily forgetting that his hand was resting against her cheek. "How is that any different?"

"It just is," Lilian insisted. Kevin would have shouted at her or something, but became mute as the feel of her impeccably soft lips brushing against his rough palm rendered him speechless. "But please, regardless of how you feel about me, will you please just let me be close to you? I want to stay by your side, even if it's just like this."

Confused and guilt-ridden, Kevin found his defenses crumbling. Despite how much experience he had when it came to dealing with Lilian, hearing that voice filled with earnest longing, seeing that open and honest expression looking at him with a love so intense it terrified him... it made resisting her impossible.

"Lilian... I..."

Lilian's eyes, half-lidded and filled with an fervent desire for intimacy, gazed at him with unfathomable depths. He could easily get lost within those orbs that seemed to reflect a never ending sea of viridian. Yet even as he stared into her vibrant irises, his gaze was invariably drawn to her soft pink lips, parted and glistening and oh so kissable. All he would have to do was...

"Yes?" Lilian's voice, nothing but a breathy whisper, caused the hairs on the back of his neck to rise. Maybe it was his imagination, but it seemed like her face was drawing closer.

His mind lost within a haze of desire, Kevin didn't even chance realize that it wasn't Lilian moving toward him, but the other way around.

Kevin tilted his head.

"Lilian..."

Lilian tilted her head up to meet his, standing on her tiptoes to help close the distance between them.

"Yes?"

"I just... wanted to..."

They were so close, close enough that Kevin could pick out the individual features of Lilian's beautiful face. Even from this distance, mere centimeters apart, her face looked perfect.

"What is it, Kevin?" Lilian's breath, warm and carrying the scent of cinnamon, caressed his lips and sent goosebumps racing across his skin.

"I think that I... that I want..."

"Go on..."

Kevin didn't say anything. He was beyond the ability of being able to form words. His body, mind and heart, it seemed, were unable to resist the hormonal compulsions controlling them. He closed his eyes and leaned even closer.

Lilian's actions mirrored Kevin's. She shut her eyes and tilted her head further. They were so close now that she could practically taste his lips and it was driving her insane. She'd always wanted Kevin, yet her desire for him had never been stronger than it was now. She didn't want him. She needed him.

Their lips were barely a centimeter from making contact. Just a little bit farther and—

"Ara, ara, you two are taking an awfully long time in here. Would you like me to help you prepare dinner?"

Like a man who'd been smacked in the face with a scorching hot frying pan, Kevin jerked away from Lilian. With his eyes wide and his cheeks looking similar to burning coals, he busied himself with measuring ingredients.

Lilian shot Kotohime the most vicious glare she could muster, but the older kitsune was unfazed. The maid-slash-bodyguard simply tilted her head and smiled innocently.

"No," Lilian ground out, practically spitting venom. "We're fine. Thank you for your concern, though."

Kotohime's knowing smile really pissed Lilian off.

"Don't mention it, Lilian-sama." The smile widened, further angering the twin-tailed beauty. "This humble Kotohime will always be there to help Lilian-sama make the best choices possible."

"Hmph!" Without giving the other woman another glance, Lilian set about helping Kevin finish dinner.

She and Kotohime were going to be having words, and soon. Her bodyguard was definitely overdue for a long, harsh conversation.

***

Kevin's mind was in turmoil as he got ready for bed that night.

Dressed in a pair of long pajama bottoms and a baggy t-shirt, he stood in front of the bathroom mirror flossing his teeth.

Kevin wasn't really sure what had happened back there in the kitchen, nor did he understand what had possessed him when he'd been making dinner. He'd almost kissed Lilian! Kissed her! What had he been thinking? Yeah, he liked the girl, but enough to actually kiss her? No... well, maybe. He honestly didn't know anymore, and that was the problem.

Even though all of Lilian's flags had been raised—and before he'd even realized it to boot—he had yet to instigate any romance between them because he didn't want to give her false hope. He still didn't know if these feelings, these desires, he had for her were because he actually loved her, or because of her body. He'd never felt this way before, not even about Lindsay. His body craved Lilian with an intensity that honestly scared him.

Another factor he needed to consider was whether he even deserved to be with Lilian. While he had never treated her poorly, he had spent a good deal of time pushing the girl away.

There was also his confession to Lindsay to consider. Sure, she had turned him down, but the fact remained that he had confessed to her, and it didn't change that his confession had hurt Lilian. Someone like him, who could confess to a girl when another girl so obviously loved him, didn't deserve a person like Lilian, did they?

He was actually grateful that Kotohime had interrupted them before he and Lilian could do something he might regret later on.

Speaking of their resident maid-slash-bodyguard, he was very impressed with her poise--terrified beyond all belief, but also impressed. Lilian had been seemingly trying to bore a hole through Kotohime's skull throughout dinner, but the kimono-clad femme had completely ignored it. That woman was colder than ice.

After dinner Kotohime had offered to clean the dishes, and Lilian had decided to help. It was obvious, even to him, that her reasons for helping Kotohime had less to do with helping, and more to do with speaking to the woman. Kevin didn't know what they were talking about, but if the hard stare Lilian had been giving the maid meant anything, he was probably better off not knowing.

Kevin looked up at the sound of approaching footsteps. By now, he'd grown so used to the way she walked that he knew it was her before the door even opened.

"Lilian," he greeted, trying not to let the heat threatening to overflow from his cheeks get past the first few layers of skin. He probably didn't succeed, but whatever.

The drop-dead gorgeous kitsune had donned a simple light blue spaghetti strap shirt and flannel pajama bottoms of the same color. The shirt outlined her figure well; he could make out hints of her bust and the small dip showed trace amounts of cleavage. And while those pants were incredibly modest—especially for Lilian—somehow, he couldn't help but think they looked adorable on her.

How can someone so beautiful also be so dang cute?

"Kevin." Lilian stopped when she saw him staring. "Do you like my outfit?"

"Um, yeah, it… it looks really good on you." This time, Kevin knew he had failed to conceal his blush. His face felt hotter than a furnace. "*Really* good."

Lilian's smile caused his heart to skip a beat. "You really think so?"

"Yes, it's, well, it looks really cute on you. And the clothing contrasts nicely with your hair. I…" Kevin coughed into his hand. "I really like it."

"I'm glad. You know, your mother said the same thing."

"Really?"

"Uh huh. You almost quoted her verbatim—except for the stuttering you did at the end there," she added with amusement. Kevin tried not to feel embarrassed.

"Ah, well, consequences of having a mom in the fashion industry, I guess."

His eyes followed Lilian as she stopped beside him and grabbed a toothbrush.

"Are you and Kotohime good now?" he asked tentatively.

"I believe so." She squeezed some toothpaste onto her toothbrush, turned on the faucet, and held the brush underneath it. "Why do you ask?"

"No reason." Feeling more than a little uncomfortable in Lilian's presence, Kevin quickly finished his nightly ritual and hurried to leave. "I'll see you in my room."

"Okay."

The last thing Kevin saw of Lilian was the fox-girl brushing her teeth. Then he closed the door behind him and leaned against the frame, his hands clenching into fists.

Why was being in Lilian's presence so difficult? He wanted to be with her, to bask in her presence, but at the same time, he also wanted to run away. He didn't understand it. It was maddening!

Why is everything so difficult?

Kevin pressed a hand to his face. He took a deep breath, held it for several seconds, then released it. After that, Kevin began making his way down the hall—

"Kevin-san."

—When a voice spoke up behind him and a hand fell on his shoulder, scaring the crap out of him.

"Holy flying butt monkeys!"

Spinning around, Kevin's wide eyes stared at Kotohime. He placed a hand to his chest, feeling his heart beating against his ribcage like the Yggdrasil Drive of a Knightmare.

"Holy crap, Kotohime! Don't do that!"

"Ara?" Kotohime tilted her head. "Don't do what?"

"That! Don't sneak up on me like that!" Kevin closed his eyes as he released a slow, shuddering breath, feeling his heart rate slowly drop back to normal levels. He opened his eyes again and focused on the katana-wielding kitsune. "Are you trying to give me a heart attack?"

"No. But, now that you mention it, I must confess, that does not sound like a bad idea. Maybe if you died of a heart attack, Lilian-sama would be willing to go back home."

"Geh!"

Not a bad idea? How could she say something like that, and with such a straight face? Did she really wish he was dead?

"But I digress," Kotohime continued as if she hadn't just told Kevin that she hoped he would drop dead. "I was actually hoping to speak with you before you retire for the night."

"Eh?" Her words startled Kevin. Why would she want to speak with him when it was clear she didn't like him? Or, maybe it was because she didn't like him that she wanted to speak with him.

He looked at the restroom door. It would be several more minutes before Lilian finished.

He turned his back to Kotohime. "I guess we could talk."

"Excellent." Kotohime clasped her hands together. "Now, if you would just follow me."

Kevin trailed after Kotohime as she led him through the small hallway, into the living room, and out the front door.

She wants this conversation to be private…

That thought worried him, especially since she still had that katana in her hand. Still, he gamely followed the woman down the stairs. She wouldn't kill him in such a public area…

… Right?

"What do you think of Lilian-sama?"

The question was so sudden that Kevin almost tripped and face-planted on the asphalt. "H-huh?"

"Do not make me repeat myself." Kotohime's hard stare reminded Kevin of a jungle predator ready to pounce. "Just answer the question."

Kevin was so frightened of Kotohime that he answered her before his mind even caught up with his mouth. "Uh… well, I really like Lilian. I mean, hanging out with her is really fun… and stuff." Even he winced at his own answer. It was certainly not the most eloquent answer he could have given. To be fair, the question had caught him by complete surprise.

Kotohime apparently didn't find his answer satisfactory, either.

"I see." Kotohime's stare was reminiscent of sharpened razors. Kevin felt like she could slice him in twine with nothing but a look. "Lilian-sama loves you. I know this, so I know that you know this as well. And yet, despite knowing about her feelings, all you can say is that you like spending time with her? Is that really the best answer you can come up with?"

"What else do you want me to say?" Kevin asked with a feeling of helpless insecurity.

"I want you to tell me how you really feel about Lilian-sama. My ward is in love with you. She loves you so much that she is willing to disown herself for your sake. Do you have any idea what that means? A kitsune who has been disowned by their clan is considered a disgrace among kitsune. It's a sign of weakness. It also means that she would no longer have the protection of her clan, which, for a kitsune like Lilian-sama, is imperative to have. However, she is willing to do this for you. She is willing to go that far because she loves you, and yet you refuse to reciprocate her feelings. Can't you see how much your indecision is hurting her?"

"I didn't know…"

Kotohime scoffed. "Of course you didn't know. I bet you didn't even think about how this would affect Lilian-sama. You're so busy caught up in your own feelings that you won't even spare a second to consider hers."

"That's not…"

"And for what? Because you're too scared to tell her how you really feel? What kind of man are you? A real man would never leave a young woman waiting for an answer after she has confessed. You're a disgrace to men everywhere!"

Oh, that did it.

"You think I don't know that?!" Kevin shouted, glaring at the four-tails. "Do you really think I don't understand what this means for Lilian? That I haven't considered her feelings? I know how Lilian feels! And I know that I'm hurting her! You think I like that I can't make up my mind? That I enjoy causing her pain? I don't! But this isn't something I can help! I don't even know how I feel about her!"

He and Kotohime glared at each other. Kotohime kept silent, surprisingly, allowing him to take a deep, shuddering breath.

"I'll admit, I like Lilian. I like her a lot. She's an amazing person, she's fun to hang out with, and I've never met a girl who shares the same likes and passions as me. Every day I spend with her brings something new and exciting. But to go from liking someone to loving them?" Now it was Kevin's turn to scoff. "Don't be ridiculous. I don't even know what love is."

Kotohime raised a single, delicate raven colored eyebrow. "But you love your mother, do you not?"

"That's completely different," Kevin snapped. "You can't compare the love someone has for their mom to the love they have for their girlfriend, or mate, or whatever. It's not the same thing. And besides, I've never even had a girlfriend before. I've only liked one girl before Lilian, and even then, I found out that I didn't

like her as much as I thought I did."

Kotohime crossed her arms under her chest, drawing attention to her katana, which she held in her left hand. "What are you trying to say, exactly?"

Kevin raked his fingers through messy locks of blond hair. "I'm saying that I don't really know if I'm in love with Lilian, or if I just like her. I'm too young to understand what love even means. I'm only fifteen! Heck, I've never even kissed a girl before Lilian."

When Kotohime raised an eyebrow, Kevin colored in embarrassment upon realizing what he'd just admitted.

"Don't ask. Anyway, my point is that I have no idea how I feel about her, and I refuse to tell Lilian I love her when I don't even what my true feelings are."

The two stared at each other, the tension rising until, quite suddenly, Kotohime relaxed. The aura of dread surrounding her vanished like mist evaporating in the summer heat, and Kevin released a breath that he didn't realize he'd been holding.

"Very well," Kotohime said at last, "You've made your point, and at the very least, I can tell that you are being sincere, which is more than I can say for most people your age."

If nothing else, she could take solace in the fact that Kevin was an earnest young man who wouldn't take advantage of Lilian's naiveté and innocence. It wasn't much, but it was still something.

"However." Her glare inexplicably sharpened, putting Kevin on edge. "Now that you've informed me about your feelings, let me tell you something. I do not know how much Lilian has told you about kitsune in general, but the people we mate with are very important to us."

Kevin was nonplussed. "What do you mean?"

"I mean just what I said. To a kitsune, there is nothing more important than their mate." Kotohime paused for a moment, thinking. "Being the long-lived supernatural creatures that we are, it is no surprise that a kitsune will have many mates throughout their lifetime. I know for a fact that Pnévma-denka is over one-thousand years old, and that she has had mated many times."

Kevin blinked as he tried to imagine a one-thousand-year-old woman with more boyfriends than Eric had eroge. He couldn't, so he did his best to put such thoughts out of his mind.

Kotohime continued. "Despite how this makes kitsune seem promiscuous to other yōkai, the truth is that a kitsune always remains loyal to our mates--past, present and future. When a kitsune takes a mate, it is a vow far deeper than anything you humans have. In human culture, marriage is a sham that's worth less than the paper it's written on. When a kitsune takes a mate, it is a commitment to cherish, care for and love that person until such a time as both agree to part ways, or the mate dies of old age if they are of a less long-lived species, like humans. Yet, even after they have parted, when a kitsune's mate is in trouble, regardless of whether they have not seen each other in months, years, decades or even centuries, he or she will drop everything they're doing and go to their mate's side to help."

Kevin tried not to squirm at the heavy topic, but it was difficult, and Kotohime wasn't making things any easier with how unruffled she appeared.

"That being said, you are even more special to Lilian-sama." Kotohime made sure Kevin was paying rapt attention before continuing. "You are the first mate she has ever had. To a kitsune, no mate is more important than their first. You are quite literally the single most important person that she will ever have in her life. No one else will ever hold the place in her heart that you do; no one else will be even half as important to her as you are. Ever. From now until the day Lilian-sama dies, every single potential mate that comes along will be judged by the standards you set."

Kevin felt as if his heart might stop. He was really that important? He meant that much to Lilian?

"I... I had no idea I meant so much to her," he mumbled, gazing at the kitsune before him, his hands shaking as they were clenched into fists. "Why? Why would she choose someone like me to be her first mate?"

"I would like to know the same thing." Kotohime's passive stare made him feel insignificant. "As far as I can tell, you have very few good qualities that would make you worthy of being her mate. You're a decent student, athletic, and you seem to be very independent, but a kitsune, especially one of Lilian-sama's stature, needs more than that. She needs someone who can stand by her side and support her as an equal. As you are right now, you're just a liability."

Kevin flinched at the insult. His mind went back to the times they had been attacked. She had saved him from Chris and ended up getting thrashed by Kiara. He hadn't been able to do anything for her either of those times. He'd been completely useless.

Is that what Kotohime is talking about?

"Unfortunately, there is very little I can do to make Lilian-sama see reason." Kotohime's eyes grew dark, and Kevin thought he saw her left one twitch. "Lilian-sama has already chosen you, so all I can do now is support her to the best of my abilities."

"You say that you're going to support her, yet all you've done so far is tell me how much you disapprove of her decision," Kevin pointed out, surprised by his own audacity. This woman had a katana for god's sake!

"That is because you are refusing to reciprocate her feelings." Kotohime's blunt statement made Kevin grimace. "Despite Lilian-sama making her intentions and feelings toward you quite clear, you have refused to accept her love and return it. That is why I do not approve of her decision to choose you as her mate."

Kevin's eyes narrowed slightly. "I already told you that I—"

"I am well aware of your feelings on the matter," Kotohime interrupted, raising a hand to forestall any defense he might put up. "You have made it clear that you lack the worldly experience necessary to make an informed decision. Truth be told, I happen to agree."

When Kevin blinked, Kotohime smiled at him; a genuine smile, not the mocking ones she'd given thus far.

"Unlike Lilian-sama, I am well aware of human culture, and I know that a fifteen-year-old boy knows little about matters of the heart. That is why I am willing to allow you the time necessary to sort out your feelings. Just be sure not to take too long in coming to a decision. The more time that passes, the longer you wait, the more your indecision will hurt Lilian-sama, and I will not stand for that. Are we clear?"

"… Yes."

"I can't hear you."

"I said yes!"

"Good."

As Kotohime walked away, Kevin clenched his eyes shut and grit his teeth, his mind plagued with conflicting emotions.

What am I supposed to do now?

***

Kevin entered the apartment, closing the door behind him, and then taking off his shoes and slouching against the doorframe.

Kotohime's words had struck him more surely than a blaster bolt. They drove home all the points that he'd been blatantly ignoring, the same points that made him unsure of his own feelings.

Lilian's love. Lilian's devotion. They were so intense and unfiltered that it made him question his own feelings, doubt his own heart. Could he offer the same fidelity that Lilian had given him? He didn't think so, especially since he was…

"Having an argument with your girlfriend's maid?" His mom's voice drifted over from the living room. Shaking his head, Kevin walked further into the apartment to see his mom sitting on the couch, left leg propped over her right knee, her posture slouched. How long had she been there?

"Lilian isn't my girlfriend," Kevin muttered.

His mom grinned. "You mean yet. You can try and deny it all you want, but I know you like her. I can't say I blame you. If I were ten years younger and had a dick, I'd tap that."

Kevin buried his red face in his hands. "Oh gods, mom! Do you always have to be so vulgar?"

"Of course. As your mother, it is my right to embarrass you."

"There's no one here for you to embarrass me in front of, so stop it."

His mom chuckled, just a bit. "All right, all right. I'll stop."

"Ha…" An annoyed sigh. "I can't believe my mom acts like such a child."

"Better than being a young man who acts like an old fart."

"Whatever."

"So, what were you and Kotohime arguing about?" his mom asked, patting the spot by her side. "Come on, sit down and tell me. I might be able to help."

After a moment's hesitation, Kevin took his mom up on her offer. He sat down and explained everything to her—minus the whole "supernatural kitsune wants to be my mate" thing.

"I'm not really sure what to do," he finished explaining. "This isn't some silly high school crush. Lilian truly loves me, like, the kind that ends in a committed relationship and not just a year or two of dating. She really wants to be with me for the rest of my— her life."

"Oh, I know that."

"You do?"

"Of course." His mom's grin was that of someone who'd just won the lottery. "I could see that she was smitten with you the moment I saw you two together. No women would ever look at someone with eyes like hers unless they truly loved that person."

"Great. Thanks for making me feel better about this whole thing, Mom. Really."

"Kevin." Ms. Swift sighed at the obvious sarcasm lacing her son's voice. "This isn't something that anyone can help you with. In the end, you need to decide if what you're feeling for Lilian is true love or simply lust. No one can possibly know what you're feeling but you."

"But how am I supposed to tell if I really love her?"

"Well, how do you feel when you're with her?"

Kevin remained silent as he thought about what he felt for Lilian, and when he started speaking, it was tentatively, with each word being carefully measured before they were voiced. "Well, I... I feel sort of like I'm on a cloud. When I'm with Lilian, I sometimes feel like I'm living in this strange dream or fantasy, and that one day I'll wake up and find out that she never existed."

"That's a start," his mom urged. "What else?"

"I, well, my heart beats really fast whenever I'm with her. Like, it sometimes feels like it's going to break my ribcage or something, and I always get this strange warmth, right here..." Kevin placed a hand over his chest and clutched the fabric of his shirt. "This is where it usually starts, but it will always spread to the rest of my body. And whenever I look at Lilian, I feel..."

"Like you could get lost in her eyes and smile?"

Kevin gave his mom an odd look. "Yes."

His mom smiled at him. "I think you already know how you feel about Lilian. All you need to do is realize it yourself."

Great, mom's being cryptic. This is just what I need after my conversation with Kotohime. Not.

Kevin resisted a sigh. "But how can I do that?"

His mom shrugged. "I'm afraid that, too, is something that you will need to figure out on your own."

Kevin rolled his eyes. "Gee, thanks for the help."

"Anytime."

"That was sarcasm, Mom. You were no help at all."

"… Meanie."

***

At the sound of the whistle going off, Kevin launched himself from his ready position into a full-on sprint. He gritted his teeth as he pushed his body to the brink. Air whistled in and out of his mouth and his heart raced like a Gundam traveling at terminal velocity during atmospheric reentry. Faster. Faster. His legs strained under the effort. 20 meters. 40 meters. 80 meters.

Finished.

"Time!" Coach Deretaine's voice rang out across the field, as Kevin and Chase passed the 100 meter mark.

Kevin hunched over as he tried to catch his breath, which was much harder than usual. Oh, dear God. He felt like someone had dropped several tons of lead onto his legs.

"Swift!"

Kevin straightened, or he tried to. His exhaustion was such that he could only straighten about halfway.

His coach marched up to him with a bit of a scowl. Oh, boy. That could not mean anything good.

"Yes… sir…"

"It seems you're having some trouble. That time was nowhere near as good as what you've been getting recently." Coach Deretaine looked down at his stopwatch and the scowl grew. "Thirteen-point-sixty-five seconds. You normally get at least twelve-point-twenty-three seconds, and you've been doing even better than that recently. This is a ridiculously slow time, especially for you."

"I'm sorry… sir…"

Coach Deretaine studied him like one might study a frog on a dissection table. Kevin blinked as his sweaty bangs fell over his eyes.

"You look tired. Is there something going on that I should know about?"

"No, sir," Kevin shook his head, straightening up. Now that he'd gotten his second wind, he felt a little better. "I just haven't been getting much sleep lately."

"Insomnia?"

"Um, I suppose."

Truth be told, he'd been up all last night thinking about his conversation with Kotohime. He still had trouble wrapping his mind around the fact that he was going to be the most important person in Lilian's life, not just right now, but ever. Being told that he was such a central figure to someone was, well, he would like to say it was overwhelming, but that felt like a gross understatement.

It didn't help that his feelings for Lilian were still conflicted. There was a part of him that wanted to accept her love and return it, but he didn't know if he could actually do that. Kotohime had said that he was the most important person Lilian would ever have in her life. Could he offer that same level of devotion?

"… Swift…"

Kevin honestly didn't know. Every time he thought about going with his feelings, he remembered Lindsay. He had thought he'd been in love with her, but when he'd confessed and been shot down, he'd barely felt a thing. The stinging pain he thought he would feel had been a mere pinprick.

"… listen… me…"

What if his feelings for Lilian were like that? He couldn't accept her feelings if his own weren't as strong as hers. That would only hurt her.

"Swift… Kev… Swift…"

Even the small conversation with his mom hadn't helped. She didn't know that Lilian wasn't human, which was part of Kevin's biggest dilemma. Unfortunately, he couldn't very well tell his mother that Lilian was a kitsune.

"Swift… listen… me…"

He could just imagine how a conversation like that would play out.

"Hey, Mom! You remember how I told you that Lilian was deeply in love with me and wanted to marry me? Well, I kind of lied. You see, Lilian is actually a kitsune. You know, those fox people from my anime and manga? So, anyway, she's a kitsune,

and she wants me to be her mate and, well, since I'm her first, that means I would be the most important person in the entire world to her. That's why I'm having such a hard time figuring out my feelings, you see?"

"… Kevin, have you been drinking cactus juice again?"

"I'm being serious here! Wait. What are you doing, Mom?"

"Calling the psychiatric ward. Hello? Yes, I'd like you to fix my son. It seems he's come down with a bad case of Chūnibyō.*"*

Kevin shook his head. Not a good idea. There was absolutely no way he could tell his mom that. He didn't want her to think he was crazy, or on drugs, or crazy and on drugs. That would just be unpleasant.

"Kevin Swift! Listen to me when I'm talking to you!"

Kevin jumped and nearly fell on his backside when someone shouted in his face. He caught himself at the last second, and looked up to see the person shouting at him.

Coach Deretaine stared down at him. Was that concern in his coach's eyes? Nah, couldn't be. It was probably constipation or something.

"You really are out of it, aren't you?" Kevin opened his mouth, but Coach Deretaine spoke before he could say anything. "Take the rest of the day off, Swift. It's clear to me that you're not at your best. Go home, get some sleep, and when you come back tomorrow, you had better be at one-hundred percent. Am I clear?"

"Yes, sir."

"Good. Now get the hell out of here."

As Coach Deretaine walked away, Kevin sighed and rubbed his eyes with his index finger and thumb. They were extremely sore.

It's because I stayed up all night.

Curse that Kotohime for exacerbating his problems even more! As if dealing with Lilian's feelings for him, while trying to figure out his feelings for her, wasn't hard enough.

"Hey, Swift!"

Kevin nearly groaned when his rival walked up to him. "What do you want, Chase?"

Chase clicked his tongue at the bored response. "The hell's wrong with you today?"

"Nothing."

The expression Chase gave him just screamed "I don't believe a damn word you just said."

"Whatever, Swift." The sarcasm in his voice was so thick that calling it sarcasm didn't do it justice. "There's obviously something bugging you. You look like someone ate you up and shit you back out."

"Gee, thanks."

"You're welcome. But seriously, you look awful. Get some rest. It's no fun running against you when I have such a blatant advantage."

"... Right..."

Too tired to even retort, Kevin ambled off the field. He tossed a wave at Alex and Andrew, who were practicing their relay—oh, no. Wait. They were fighting again. Great. Eric wasn't visible at the moment, but Kevin assumed that was just because the depraved high schooler was busy peeping on a girl or something.

"What the hell do you think you're doing Corromperre?! Stop trying to grope your fellow runners and get back to work!"

"NO! Come back my delicious grade-A ass!"

Kevin watched Coach Deretaine chase Eric across the field. Meanwhile, Eric chased one of the girls on their team across the field, his hands making those pervy grasping motions again, like he was already imagining fondling that poor girl's butt.

Must. Not. Facepalm.

"Kevin!"

Kevin looked up to see Lilian and Kotohime approaching him from the bleachers, the redhead moving at a light trot while the older kitsune languished back, taking her time.

"Lilian." Kevin did his best to ignore the mixed surge of warmth and guilt pulsing through his veins at the sight of her. He only had a marginal amount of success.

"Are you sure you're feeling okay?" Lilian's eyes shifted from joyful to concerned. "I know you said you were alright this morning, but you looked really tired out there, and you drank nearly six cups of coffee this morning. I thought you didn't drink coffee."

"I don't drink coffee, at least not usually." He tried to brush off her concerns. "Anyway, I'm fine. You really don't need to worry about me." When he saw that Lilian still looked worried, he gave her the most reassuring smile he could muster. "Thank you for being so concerned, though. I appreciate it."

Lilian scrutinized his face, but decided not to argue, accepting his words at face value. Kevin felt like he'd just stabbed himself in the heart with a knife straight from the forge.

I'm such a jerk. Here I am, lying to the girl who loves me more than anyone else, and she accepts what I'm telling her just like that. I really don't deserve her, do I?

"Well, if you're sure." Lilian perked up a second later. "Anyway, here. You look like you could use a drink."

Lilian handed Kevin a bottle of water, and he ignored the jolt that shot through him when their hands made contact.

"Thank you."

As Kevin took a quick drink, Kotohime placed a hand on Lilian's shoulder.

"You're always so thoughtful, Lilian-sama. Your mate really is lucky to have someone as amazing as you. Why, you're like every boy's dream girl; kind and caring and thoughtful and so very beautiful. I don't know a single male who wouldn't want to be your boyfriend."

While Lilian beamed at her maid-slash-bodyguard, Kevin twitched. That was totally a jab at him, wasn't it?

"Thanks," Lilian said, "but I don't really care about any other men. The only person who matters to me is Kevin."

Now it was Kotohime's turn to twitch. Her smile became fixed.

"Indeed. Your dedication and loyalty to your mate is truly inspiring, Lilian-sama."

A loud crash echoed from somewhere behind the bleachers. Lilian and Kevin looked at each other before rushing over to see what had caused such a ruckus, Kotohime trailing after them at a more sedate pace.

The scene they found was a familiar one. Eric Corrompere was laid out on the ground, his face planted into the pavement. The ground around his head was cratered, and several cracks had spread out from the center of impact. The giant baseball sized lump on his head was coated with a thin layer of ice.

"Christine," Kevin greeted the snow maiden cautiously. The

cute girl clad in gothic lolita clothing looked rather livid at the moment, and he really didn't want to get on her bad side, especially when she got like this.

"Kevin," Christine grunted, retracting the almighty fist she'd used to bash Eric's head in, "you really should keep your friend on a tighter leash."

"What do I look like, Eric's keeper? I don't have any control over what that idiot does." When Christine glared at him, Kevin nearly squealed and retracted his previous statement. "B-but I will certainly keep that in mind and do my best to stop him from bothering you." That seemed to satisfy the girl, so he relaxed. "I'm guessing Eric did something perverted again?"

"Yes," Christine growled. Kevin and Lilian took a slow step back at the sight of the girl's eyes freezing over, turning into two thick glaciers of icy blue. The air around them became cold, freezing even. Their breath came out in thick streams of mist. When they looked down, they saw the cement beginning to freeze over as hoarfrost crept along the surface, icy lines of pure white that spread out like the writhing, amorphous tentacles of Yog-Sothoth.

"Uh, Christine?" Kevin spoke up hesitantly. He almost squeaked when Christine's icy cold eyes glared at him.

"What?"

"N-nothing... it's just... your powers..."

Kevin's words seemed to have a powerful calming effect on the girl. Taking a deep breath, the yuki-onna visibly settled down. The hoarfrost receded, the temperature started to rise, and the mist stopped coming out of their mouths, which was good because it meant that they no longer looked like a trio of chain smokers.

"Okay," Christine said, breathing out a deep sigh, "I feel better now."

"Uh... huh..."

Kevin looked at her skeptically. For some reason, he didn't believe her.

"Uuuugggg..."

Eric just groaned—he wouldn't be feeling better for a long, long time.

***

Kevin, Lilian, Christine, Kotohime and a broken, bleeding Eric strode across the school grounds toward the parking lot.

"Eric, why are you following us?"

"What do you mean, why am I following you? What kind of best friend asks something like that?"

Pressing the palm of his hand against his face, Kevin had a difficult time keeping a sigh from escaping his lips.

"I might have been let out early because I'm not in the best of shape right now, but Coach Deretaine did not give you permission to leave. What do you think he's going to do when he realizes you're no longer practicing?"

When Eric didn't respond, the group turned to see the lecherous and lanky student staring off into the distance, a look of wide-eyed horror etched on his normally pervy features.

Kevin deadpanned.

"You completely forgot about track, didn't you?"

"NNNnnooo-aaahhh!!"

The three youngsters plus one kimono-clad female watched as Eric disappeared into the distance, a large cloud of dust trailing in his wake.

A strong wind blew through the clearing. Kevin could hear a few crickets chirping, and a crow in the distance was cawing in a most annoying manner.

Christine managed to sum up everyone's thoughts rather succinctly.

"What an idiot."

***

After Eric ran off, the group continued moving--unfortunately, they bumped into someone annoying before they could get too far.

"Ah! My lovely, *dulce la flor*—"

"Stop calling me flour!"

"—How are you doing this fine day?"

Kevin wondered what kind of bad karma he must have incurred to have a run-in with this idiot. Wasn't school supposed to be closed? It was, so what the heck was someone who wasn't part of the track team doing here?

"I would be doing much better if you stopped stalking me like some kind of creeper." Lilian didn't seem too thrilled about seeing the idiot, either. In fact, she looked even more annoyed than Kevin.

"Such harsh words, my beautiful *señorita*."

"If you're trying to flatter me, I'm going to tell you right now that it's not working. Now get lost."

"Denial is just another sign of attraction."

"I'm not a tsundere! And no one in their right mind would ever be attracted to you, matador boy!"

Christine stared at the young man wearing the vibrant pink matador costume with a mixture of shock and disgust. She then leaned toward Kevin and whispered in his ear. "Who the hell is this kid?"

"Just some idiot who doesn't know how to take a hint."

Christine frowned at him, but Kevin didn't pay much attention to her. He stared at Juan, gritting his teeth and clenching his fists. After a couple of seconds, the gothically dressed yuki-onna came to a startling conclusion.

"I can't believe it. You're jealous of him."

The look of disgust on her face was truly a sight to behold.

"J-jealous?" Kevin looked startled and embarrassed. He scowled seconds later, his face turning a deep shade of red. "Me? Jealous? Of him? Don't be ridiculous!"

Kevin had also taken several levels in tsundere, it seems.

"And why do I suddenly have this strange urge to strangle someone?"

"Don't ask me," Christine shrugged. "As for why you would be jealous, I honestly don't know. Maybe it's because of his infatuation with the fox skank."

"That's not jealousy," Kevin snapped. "I don't care who he's infatuated with!"

"Whatever," Christine mumbled under her breath, "It's not like I care who you're jealous of."

"I'm not jealous!"

"Come now, my enchanting little *ma bella*." Juan ignored the byplay between Kevin and Christine. "There is no need to be so distant with me. You need not be intimidated. It is just like I said; just because I am a handsome *diablo*, does not mean you need to feel *timido* in the presence of my magnificent self."

Juan slid up to Lilian and tried to wrap an arm around her, but was quickly thwarted by Kevin, who'd pushed himself between the two.

A frown crossed the matador boy's face. "Is there a reason why you are getting in my way, Sweeft?"

"It's Swift." Kevin gave the other boy a large, ear-to-ear grin that forced his eyes closed. A vein also popped out on his forehead, throbbing in time to the beat of his heart. "And I think Lilian has made it abundantly clear that you're bothering her, so why don't you just leave us alone?"

"Hmph." Juan gave him a bored look. "Sounds to me like someone is jealous."

"Who the heck would be jealous of you?!"

"Now, now, there is no need to deny it." Juan's smile was one of triumph. "I understand how you feel. I can see now that you are just jealous of the *bono*, the bond, that Lilian and I share. Understandable. It must be difficult watching the girl you're so fond of falling into the arms of another man, but really, you should learn to accept your defeat gracefully."

"Defeat?" Kevin glared as he stepped into Juan's personal space and literally ground his forehead against the other boy. Not one to be outdone, Juan pushed back as sparks flashed between them. "You must have a few screws loose if you think you've defeated me at anything!"

"That's just what I would expect someone who knows nothing of women to say!"

"I have no idea what you're talking about!"

"Ha! Of course someone like you wouldn't understand what I am speaking of! Your lack of *masculino* makes it impossible for you to understand someone as manly as myself!"

"What the heck is that supposed to mean?!"

"It means what it means, *pavo*!"

"I don't know what you just said, but it sounded pretty insulting!"

"That's because it was an insult!"

The three yōkai watched from the sidelines as the two teenage boys butted heads like a pair of bulls in a male pissing contest.

"Wow," Christine whistled, "I don't think I've ever seen Kevin get so worked up at someone before."

"Really?" Kotohime looked at Christine, who nodded. "I see..." She then went back to staring at Kevin and Juan.

"Ufufufu…"

And then she began giggling.

Christine took several steps away from the woman.

Lilian worried her lower lip. Should she feel guilty for enjoying the way Kevin appeared to be fighting over her? Maybe. Probably. But she didn't. This was the proof she needed to confirm that he did feel something for her, even if he didn't know what that something was yet.

After taking a moment to bask in Kevin's obvious jealousy, Lilian decided it was time to break the two up before their argument could come to blows. Grabbing Kevin by the arm, she gently pulled him away from the other boy.

"Come on, Kevin. You don't need to lower yourself to his level. That idiot isn't worth your time. He's just jealous because he knows you're the only person I could ever love."

Kevin blushed. Juan looked like he wanted to cry.

"Why must you always be so cruel, *ma bella flor*?"

A large vein pulsed on Lilian's forehead, though she did her best to ignore Juan something-or-other's terribly cheesy, internet-translated comments.

"And my name isn't Juan something or other! Its Juan Martinez Villanueva Cortes!"

Thankfully, Juan chose not to follow them. Most unfortunately for Lilian, Christine did.

Kevin and Lilian both stared at Christine as she attached herself to Kevin's other arm. The snow maiden who hated the cold blushed bright blue under their scrutiny but defiantly kept herself stuck to Kevin's side.

"W-what are you two staring at, huh?" she asked defensively, turning her head away from the two. "I-I'm just making sure that whore over there doesn't try anything! D-don't think I'm doing this cuz I like you, stupid Kevin!"

"What are you talking about?" Kevin proved himself to be clueless about women.

"N-nothing! Shut up! Just forget I said anything!"

While Kevin shrugged off the girl's strange behavior—he was used to it by now—Lilian glared at the girl before hugging Kevin's arm closer to her chest.

"Whatever you say, tsun-tsun-chan."

"What was that?!"

"Nothing. I didn't say anything. And I certainly didn't say anything about flat-chested little girls who act like stereotypical tsunderes. Nope. Nothing at all."

"How dare you! I am not tsundere, Titan Tits! I'm not!"

"Keep telling yourself that."

"Why you!!"

Kevin tried to ignore the two girls arguing. He also tried to ignore Kotohime, who he could just tell was staring at the back of his head. He could feel her intent, not quite killing intent but close enough, as she bore a hole through his cranium. It made him very uncomfortable.

As they continued walking to the parking lot, they ran into the Social Sciences teacher, Professor Nabui.

"Ah, Kevin, Lilian," he greeted in his heavy Japanese accent, not even the least bit Americanized despite having lived in the US for several decades already. No one knew why the man still had an accent. It was like one of life's greatest mysteries.

"The reason he still has an accent is because you're an Otaku."

U-ugh. I already told you that it's one of life's greatest mysteries, not because I'm Otaku. That's a rather harsh thing to say.

"Harsh, but true. Kotohime is right; you're a complete Otaku."

Y-you guys are so mean.

"Who the hell are you two talking to?" Christine asked.

"Yes, who are you two talking to?" Professor Nabui seconded.

Kevin didn't ask that question, mainly because he'd already asked it many times and received the same, unfulfilling response each time.

"No one," Lilian and Kotohime said in unison.

While Christine stared at the two with twitching eyebrows, Professor Nabui shook his head. Kitsune were such an odd breed.

The Japanese secret-agent-turned-professor turned to look at the statuesque bodyguard. "I do not believe we've had the pleasure of meeting. My name is Nabui Nagase. It's a pleasure to meet you, Ms..."

"Katsura," the katana-wielding beauty answer with a slight nod of her head. "Katsura Kotohime."

"You are Japanese, yes?"

"That's correct, though I have not visited my homeland for many years."

"I see. A pity," Professor Nabui said, "I often find myself missing my country. It would have been nice to hear news about what is happening there from something other than the internet."

"You have my apologies for being unable to help, Nagase-san."

"There is no need to apologize, Katsura Kotohime-san. Now, if you'll excuse me, I have some paper-work that simply must get done before the day ends." He looked at his two students, then at Christine, nodding politely at them before walking off.

Kevin and Lilian shared a look. That had been a really random chance encounter.

***

Inagumi Takashi sat behind his desk, his fingers steepled and his face carefully blank.

The meeting with Kevin and his redheaded target had been very informative, much more so than when he'd been spying on them at the mall. Being up close had allowed him to get a much better sense of who and what he was dealing with.

Who would have thought there would be another kitsune living in the area? Judging from the way she had been standing several feet behind his target, the sharp look in her eyes, and the fact that she wielded both a katana and a wakizashi, he determined that Katsura Kotohime was likely the younger kitsune's bodyguard.

That meant the girl was of some importance to the kitsune world. That was troubling, but not worrying enough to make him stop his mission.

It did mean he'd have to change his plans, however. He wasn't up for tangling with a kitsune powerful enough to be used as a bodyguard.

That was fine, though. While going after the young kitsune directly was officially out of the question, he could still go after her indirectly.

What better way to do that than by stealing away the person she cherished most?

Chapter 8

A Twisted Game of Twister

Later that day, Kotohime traveled to a complex several miles from the Swift residence. While she could have been there in minutes with some reinforcement and kitsune-style roof hopping, she wanted to enjoy the ambiance of Arizona.

Although most yōkai didn't like large cities such as Phoenix, Kotohime had no such issues. She'd spent a lengthy amount of time with the primate race before becoming a vassal for the Pnéyma clan, so she knew of humanity's worth. There was just something about the large buildings and wildlife interspersed between that she found beautiful and wondrous.

Perhaps the reason I can appreciate humanity's worth is because of him...

Kotohime's quick head-shake dispelled that particular line of thinking. It was best not to travel down that road. She'd already been there one too many times since arriving in Arizona.

That is just another reason to disapprove of Kevin-san.

Kotohime eventually arrived at her destination, one of several cookie-cutter apartments in a nice, well-maintained complex. Several people eyed her as she strolled sedately past them, but she ignored their lingering gaze as she traveled along the pavement toward one apartment in particular. She walked up the stairs and knocked on the front door.

"*Discúlpeme*! I shall be there in just a second!"

Footsteps reached her ears, proceeded by the rattling of a chain before the door swung open a moment later.

"Ah! Hello there, my lovely *señorita*. How may I be of assistance today?"

"You can be of assistance by dropping the act first," Kotohime stated flatly, "and stop using that internet translated Spanish. It's terrible. You can also drop the illusion."

"*Ma bella flor*, I do not know what you are—"

"I said drop. The. Illusion."

Juan looked at Kotohime for several seconds, then at the katana gripped tightly in her hand.

"Very well," he sighed theatrically, allowing his body to shift. His olive-colored skin turned a much darker chocolate brown, and his eyes went from light brown to pure onyx. Even his large, yellow-blond pompadour haircut disappeared, replaced by short black hair. Finally, one dark black fox-tail with a white tip sprouted from his tailbone and a pair of droopy fox ears appeared on his head..

"I hope you're satisfied. I rather like that disguise, and do not particularly enjoy being in this form," no longer speaking in his fake Spanish accent, Juan's voice had become much deeper.

"Of course you do. Only someone like you could possibly enjoy disguising yourself as an idiot." Juan pouted. Kotohime ignored it. "Now then, are you going to let me in, or should I let myself in?"

"Ah, of course. Come inside and make yourself at home." Juan smiled as he held the door open. "You know that my humble abode is always welcome to one as beautiful as yourself."

Kotohime shook her head, but didn't say anything as she entered the apartment. Juan closed the door behind her.

Surveying her new surroundings with the sharp eyes of a warrior, Kotohime found that Juan's room was just as eccentric as the young man himself. The floor was... pink. Bright, hot pink. It almost looked neon. His walls were a splash of psychedelic colors; an amalgam of reds, blues, yellows and greens that swirled together in disturbing designs. She felt dizzy just looking at them. Even his furniture looked like something a pot-smoking hippy would own.

Juan walked further into the room, but Kotohime remained where she was. He turned to face her, arms spread wide, eyes twinkling and with a grin to match.

"Do you like my abode? I got this furniture for a bargain price. I must admit, I didn't know if I would like this seventies theme, but after watching 'That 70s Show,' well, I knew that I just had to decorate my home like this."

"Yes, well, you are about forty years behind the times," Kotohime stated in carefully concealed disgust.

"That just makes it vintage."

Kotohime resisted the urge to facepalm. She would not let this... this boy know how much he irritated her.

Juan sat down on his multi-colored rainbow couch, arms resting against the head. Kotohime imagined smacking the superior look he sent her right off his face with her katana. She considered herself to be someone who was firmly in control of their emotions and behavior, but this boy really knew how to push her buttons. They'd only met a few days ago and already he bothered her.

"But you did not come here to discuss my incredible decor, did you? You wish to know something, right? You want some more intelligence. I'm fairly certain that I have already told you everything you could possibly wish to know."

"I have come here for two reasons. Firstly, I want you to stop pestering Lilian-sama."

"Oh ho? So you're here to boss me around, then, are you? I'm sorry to say this..." he paused, then smiled widely. "Actually, I'm not. I don't listen to the orders of the Thirteen Great Clans. Arizona is neutral territory." Juan raised a hand and waved it airily through the air in a dismissive gesture. "I have no reason to listen to you or any other kitsune emissary, regardless of which clan they hail from."

Dark brown eyes narrowed as Kotohime caressed the hilt of her katana with her left hand.

"You do realize that if I wished to, I could kill you faster than you could say Monstrang-dono, correct? As a kitsune hybrid, you lack the power, never mind the skill, necessary to even think of contesting me."

"It is as you say." Juan looked surprisingly calm in spite of the threat. "You could indeed kill me if you so wanted, but we both know you won't. I am too valuable, both to you and to the other yōkai who come seeking the information I possess. Yes, those other yōkai. If they came here and discovered that their most valuable resource for intelligence had been killed, well… let us just say they wouldn't be thrilled. Now, put away your sword."

"Tch!" Kotohime clicked her tongue in annoyance, but did as she was told.

"Smart move."

Juan smiled approvingly, and with a good deal of condescension. Kotohime just looked at him in disgust. This was why she hated dealing with middlemen. They always thought themselves more important than they really were. Unfortunately, she did need him alive—for now.

"I'm going to tell you right now that I will *not* stop in my pursuit of your charge. It is much too fun, but for the sake of keeping things amicable between us, I will lessen the amount of time I spend around her." Juan placed a hand on his cheek, tapping his nose several times with his middle finger.

Kotohime wasn't pleased, but knew there wasn't much she could do to stop him. "I suppose that is the best offer you will give me."

"It is."

"Fine then," Kotohime gave the kitsune-hybrid a flat stare. "I want all the information you have on Kevin Swift and the people he associates with, Valsiener… san."

"Very well." The smile on Valsiener's face disgusted her. "But that information will not come cheap. Oh, and even though this place is secure from prying eyes, I would prefer it if you called me Juan." The smile widened. "After all, that is the name I have chosen for myself, and I am rather fond of it."

***

Kevin watched Davin Monstrang count out nearly 100 bucks in cash, which was his pay for the week.

Until school was back in session, Kevin had decided to return to delivering newspapers full-time. Sure, it meant having to wake up at two a.m. every morning, but at least he made more money.

"Here you go, brat. Try not to spend it all in one place."

Kevin almost rolled his eyes. He would have, too, if this man didn't petrify him so much. Seriously, the last thing he wanted was for this guy to sumo him or something. He'd be squashed like a pancake!

"I'll try not to, sir." Kevin was just about to leave when a thought occurred to him. He looked back at his humongous boss and asked, "Have you ever had feelings for someone, but didn't know if what you felt was love or simple affection?"

"..."

Monstrang just stared at him. A lot.

Kevin felt a drop of sweat trickle down his left temple.

"... Right. Forget I asked."

***

Lilian cooked by herself that morning.

Kotohime was busy showering and Kevin was out delivering newspapers, so the task of making breakfast was up to her. She honestly didn't mind, and even enjoyed cooking—mostly because her—hopefully—future mate loved her cooking, and she loved it when he praised her.

Her tails elongated to incredible lengths, one stretching all the way to the pantry and the other heading to the fridge. They began pulling out various ingredients and setting them on the counter: bread, deli meat, cheese, condiments and lettuce. Those items weren't for breakfast, but to make sandwiches for their get-together that day.

The other day, Ms. Swift had suggested inviting their friends over for a small gathering. Having not had a get-together in a while, Kevin decided it was a good idea. Lilian, who'd never done anything like that before, also felt intrigued by the suggestion. It sounded like a lot of fun, so she was hopeful that she would enjoy herself.

A soft beeping let her know that the coffee was finished brewing. One of her tails reached out and put it on the table while the other grabbed some milk, then the sugar, and mixed a healthy dosage of both into the coffee. She retracted them both immediately after. Ms. Swift would be waking up soon, and the last thing she needed was for her—hopefully—future mother-in-law to accidentally learn about her foxy nature.

True to form, less than five minutes after the coffee was set on the table, Ms. Swift came stumbling in.

"Coffeeeeeee..." The woman moaned. Lilian almost giggled. Ms. Swift really did remind her of those zombies she and Kevin shot in those arcade games. "Coffeeeee...."

Her lips twitched. If Kevin had not confirmed that this woman was, indeed, his mother, she would have never believed it. Kevin was hard-working, an early riser and competitive. Thus far, Ms. Swift seemed to be a rather lackadaisical individual, couldn't wake up in the morning without coffee, and didn't seem to have any of the competitive streak her son had. Their closeness, however, was undeniable. The play-fighting, the way they teased each other, it was without a doubt the type of bond only a mother and son could have—and the type of bond she wished to have with her own mother.

Best not think about that, Lilian. Keep your chin up. No depressing thoughts today.

Ms. Swift plopped bonelessly into her seat. She almost knocked over the coffee when her body slumped forward. Almost. Instead of tipping it over and sending coffee everywhere, the mother of one leaned down and stuck her mouth directly over the cup, slurping it up without even lifting a hand.

A trickle of sweat rolled down Lilian's face.

What an odd way of drinking coffee.

"Ah... Coffee..."

While Ms. Swift lapped up her coffee like a dog and Lilian finished preparing breakfast, Kevin Swift entered the apartment. Gingerly taking off his shoes in the entryway, he padded through the living room and stopped just outside the kitchen entryway.

"Good morning, Kevin," Lilian greeted with near blinding radiance. She hadn't been able to say goodbye since he'd left so early this morning. "How was delivering the morning newspapers?"

"Not bad. Kinda boring though." Kevin rubbed the back of his neck, which Lilian had learned was a habit of his. "I did see some really cool wildlife, which was nice. There was a family of roadrunners crossing one of the streets. That was pretty cool, but, other than that... well, delivering newspapers is nothing but a routine."

"Coffeeeeeeee..."

Kevin and Lilian sent Ms. Swift an odd look as she suddenly moaned. They promptly sweatdropped when she started licking the inside of her cup, as if trying to eek out every last dredge of the caffeinated beverage lying therein.

"That's too bad," Lilian said before perking up. "Maybe you could take me with you next time? That way you won't be bored." Kevin's chuckle made Lilian cross her arms and pout, complete with childishly puffed-out cheeks. "Muu, don't laugh. I don't think my suggestion was that funny."

"Sorry," he apologized, his lips peeling back in a slight grin. "It's not that your suggestion was funny... well, it was, but not for the reason you're probably thinking. Anyway, I doubt I could fit you and the morning newspapers on my bike. There's a lot of newspapers, about a hundred, so they take up almost all the space."

"Oh, that's too bad..."

"Mm... Coffeeeee..."

Once again, Ms. Swift got nothing but strange looks from her son and Lilian.

Kevin shook his head. "Anyway, I'm pretty sweaty, so I'm going to take a shower."

"A shower?" Lilian blinked.

"Yep. I'll be done in a little while, so save me some food, okay? Don't let my mom eat it all."

"U-um, w-wait! Beloved!" In her surprise, Lilian used Kevin's pet name. "You don't want to go in there! Kotohime is—"

But she was too late. Lilian could only hold her breath in dreaded anticipation. A strange stillness hung in the air, stifling and thick, yet so silent that not even the crickets dared to chirp. Graveyards would've been jealous of how still the room had become.

She hurried over to the kitchen entrance, sticking her head out and peering down the hall, waiting.

She didn't have to wait long.

"A-a-a-ahh!" A startled gasp. Kevin. "Ko-K-K-Koto-Koto... eh... what?"

"How dare you!"

A loud bang rang throughout the apartment. A terrified shriek followed soon after, swiftly proceeded by more banging.

"If I had my katana with me right now, I would gut you like a dog!"

"Don't you mean gut me like a fish—EEEK!"

"I know what I said!"

Loud squeals rang throughout the house, like the cries of a dying cow.

"I should have known you were no good! You are completely unworthy of receiving Lilian-sama's affection, you lecherous fiend!"

"Hey! Don't blame me for this! You're the one who forgot to lock the door—HOLY CRAP!"

Lilian watched as Kevin ran out of the hall and into the living room. Several obviously thrown objects followed him, including but not limited to soap, shampoo bottles, hair care products, toothpaste, toothbrushes and...

"Oh, my god! Is that a kitchen sink?!"

... a kitchen sink.

"Where the heck did you get that?!"

"You don't need to know, you unworthy brat!"

As Kevin dodged randomly thrown objects ranging from small household appliances to the washing machine, Lilian sighed. This was going to cause problems. She just knew it.

Back in the kitchen, Ms. Swift finished off her coffee with a satisfied sigh. Only then did she see what was happening in her living room. She blinked. Once.

"... Is that a kitchen sink?"

***

Kevin's friends started arriving around noon.

"Alex, Andrew," Ms. Swift greeted the twins as they stepped into the apartment and took off their shoes. "It's been a long time since I've seen you two. Almost a year, if I'm not mistaken. I hope you've been well."

"We've been doing alright, Ms. Swift."

"Yeah, never better."

"Although we kinda hate your son right now, no offense."

"Too true."

"Oh, dear." Ms. Swift put her hands to her cheeks. "And what has my son done to earn such animosity?"

"Nothing," Kevin said as he walked up to the pair, "I haven't done anything. They're just being jerks."

"I think you're the jerk for keeping so many beautiful women to yourself," Alex retorted.

"That's right," Andrew nodded in agreement, "first you hide Lilian from us, and then we find out that you've got some goth girl pining after you, and don't even get me started on Kotohime. I don't understand how you could get a woman like that."

"He can't." All eyes turned to Kotohime, whose ferocious glare made them back up and caused Kevin to shiver. "I would never lower myself to even think of dating a perverted little cretin like Kevin-san. He is very lucky that Lilian-sama is so infatuated with him, or I would have castrated him by now."

Kevin audibly gulped.

"Stop threatening my ma—I mean, stop threatening Kevin, Kotohime," Lilian's voice echoed from the kitchen. Multiple heads turned to see the red-haired vixen standing in the entryway, foot tapping agitatedly on the floor. "And get back in here. I need help preparing the salad. I can't remember how to make the dressing."

Kotohime sighed, but acquiesced to her ward's command. "Very well, I shall be there in just a second, Lilian-sama." She tossed one last glare at Kevin, who broke out into a cold sweat, then made for the kitchen.

"Holy shit, Swift," Alex muttered in shock. "I thought she was going to slice your head off or something. What the hell did you do to piss that woman off so much?"

Kevin shook himself out of his fright. "You don't wanna know."

Alex and Andrew took one look at the shivering Kevin, and then both wisely decided that, yes, they were probably better off not knowing.

***

Eric stood in front of the door to his best friend's apartment. He checked himself over in the window, from which he could just barely make out his reflection. Smoothed back hair? Check. Sparkling teeth? Check. Packet of condoms in the chest pocket of his shirt? Double check. A grin spread across his face.

Today was the day. Oh, yes. This was his day to shine. Today, he would show his Tit Maiden why he was so much better than Kevin Swift. Today, he would prove to his Goth Hottie that he was the only man for her. Today, he would convince Kotohime to let him motorboat her boobie bombs.

It was all in the plan. And it was an ingenious plan, if he did say so himself.

Spraying some breath freshener into his mouth, Eric coughed several times, took a deep breath, and then knocked on the door.

The door slowly opened.

Kotohime stood in the doorway.

Eric damn near shit his pants.

Her eyes glowered with terrible lethality. They were like blades; sharp enough to cut through even steel. They sliced through Eric's soul, piercing him in ways he had never imagined being pierced. He could feel something horrible and awful and terrifying as he stared into those eyes. It pushed down on him, made him feel worthless, like dirt—no, like he was lower than dirt. He tried to look away, to turn his head, to do something, but her eyes, powerful and horrifying, held him in place. He felt like a pervert who'd been tossed into a women-only hot spring during the female *kenjutsu* practitioners bi-monthly anti-pervert meeting.

Kotohime gazed at him for several more seconds.

And then slammed the door in his face.

Eric stared at the door, his legs shaking.

"… I think I just pissed myself."

***

"Who was at the door, Kotohime?"

"No one, Lilian-sama. Just some perverted beast who doesn't know when he's not wanted."

***

Okay. You can do this, Christine. You can. All you have to do is walk up to the door and ring the doorbell. Remember to be polite, don't say anything bad, and don't let your temper get the better of you. Kevin's mom is behind those doors. You need to make a good sec—first impression on her. Don't screw this up.

Christine stood in front of the door, staring at the doorbell. Her index finger hovered over it, yet she couldn't seem to move it the rest of the way. Every time she tried closing the distance between it and her finger, her hand would freeze.

She eventually retracted her finger, and took to glaring at the doorbell. She didn't know why, but Christine almost felt like it was taunting her. Stupid doorbell.

"Christine?"

Christine nearly shrieked. She clamped her mouth shut to keep the scream from tearing its way out of her throat, and ended up biting her tongue in the process. The stinging pain seared her mind and made her curse the two newcomers.

Standing directly behind her were Kevin's friends; the boy with the funny manner of speech and the tomboyish blond. Justin and Lindsay, if she was not mistaken.

"Ah, it really is Christine. Hello." Lindsay's sunny look made Christine twitch.

"… Familiar…"

"She's the girl who became friends with Kevin recently, remember?"

"… Right…" the kid with the freaky speech impediment looked at Christine with strange eyes, "… cold…"

"Damn it, you two! Don't surprise me like that," she shouted, clutching a hand to her chest as she tried to calm her rapidly beating heart.

"Sorry." Lindsay offered the girl an apologetic and slightly chagrined grin. "I didn't mean to frighten you or anything. I was just surprised to see someone standing in front of the door. That's all."

"W-whatever," Christine turned her head and tried to ignore the uncomfortable chill spreading across her cheeks.

"So what were you doing just standing there?"

"I was… uh… I, um, that is to say… I wanted to…" Her inability to speak, coupled with the strange looks that Lindsay—and even Justin—were giving her, caused the young woman's tsundere protocols to activate. "That's none of your damn business! It's not like I even wanted to come here! I only decided to come because that idiot asked me to and I was bored!"

Lindsay looked positively flummoxed. "Uh, that wasn't really what I was asking, but okay."

Christine's blush grew brighter, spreading from her cheeks to the rest of her face, and then beginning to crawl down her neck. She could practically feel herself turning into a glacier. If something didn't happen soon, her powers would undoubtedly spiral out of control, causing the entire complex to freeze over.

Just then, the door opened.

"Christine, Lindsay, Justin, hey."

The Snow Maiden froze when she heard Kevin's voice. She turned her head ever so slowly, her ponderous movements like a rust-stained robot.

Kevin stood in the doorway wearing a welcoming smile. He wore simple clothes, blue jeans and a T-shirt with the words "Darth Vader was Framed" on the front. He looked so happy to see them, to see her, that Christine thought her face might freeze over.

"I'm glad you three could make it. Come on in. Lilian's made snacks for us. They're really good."

At the mention of her somewhat-rival, Christine felt her embarrassment turn into chilling anger. "Why the hell would I want to go in there and eat that fox-whore's food? Huh? Huh?!"

Kevin looked confused—and surprised, but mostly confused. "You don't have to eat her food if you don't want to. You could just come in and hang out with the rest of us. We're watching *White Out* right now."

"… Good series…"

"What makes you think I even want to go in there when I know that she's here? I don't wanna see that disgusting udder woman!"

"Udder woman?" Kevin and Lindsay said in unison.

"She thinks she's so hot because she's got big boobs, as if having gigantic knockers makes her more attractive than me."

"What do her boobs have to do with anything?" Kevin asked.

"I have no desire to even look at that stupid bitch!"

"You're not even listening to me, are you?"

"I have no intention of joining you people in your little 'get-together!' Have fun by yourselves! I'm outta here! Hmph!"

With one last huff, Christine walked down the stairs.

Kevin, Justin and Lindsay watched her leave.

"Um, what just happened?" asked the downright baffled Kevin.

"… Weird…"

"You of all people have no right to call someone else weird," Kevin deadpanned at Justin.

"I think I know what happened." Lindsay turned to look at the two boys. "Why don't you two head on inside? I'll talk to her."

The two boys looked at each other, then nodded. They turned back to Lindsay.

"Alright. We'll be waiting inside."

"… Luck…"

"Thanks."

***

Christine stomped down the road, making quite a bit of noise despite wearing flats, a testament to how much force she was putting into her steps.

A wall stood on her right, tall and imposing—at least when compared to her short stature. To her left, the many apartment buildings were interrupted by patches of grass and rock formations, with the occasional shrub decorating the landscape in a smattering of green. Several cardinals flitted through the large maple trees, while a number of finches sat on palos verdes and pecked at each other. A small family of quails ran out into the street just as a car passed by, almost as if they wanted to get hit.

She paid attention to none of this, however, her mind looking within, locked in a battle that she couldn't win. How could she, when the argument she was having was with herself?

Are you an idiot, Christine? Why did you do that? Nyaow *Kevin's going to think you're a total bitch, if he didn't already.*

B-but, he deserved it! That jerk knows the fox-whore and I don't get along! He shouldn't be talking about her in front of me!

It's only nyatural *that he would mention Lilian, since they live together.*

Don't remind me! The last thing I want to think about is how those are two living together!

But it's true, isn't it? Lilian lives with Kevin. Just because you don't want to think about it doesn't mean it's nyo *longer true.*

I know that…

Then you should knyow *not to let it bother you. What's Kevin going to think after you stormed out on him like that? Weren't you going to show him that you're a better choice than Lilian? I thought that was the whole point of coming out here.* Nyow *he's going to think you're just a weirdo with a temper,* nya.

U-ugh.

Christine felt like someone had punched her in the gut.

"Hey, Christine! Wait up!"

Christine turned to see Lindsay running after her. As the girl caught up, she gave the tomboy a flat, annoyed look.

"What do you want?"

Lindsay stopped and frowned at Christine's rude tone.

"I want to know why you walked out on us. Kevin was kind enough to extend an invitation for you to come over, and believe me when I tell you that he doesn't invite people to his place often. Why would you come all the way here, just to tell him off like that?"

"It's none of your business!"

"Is it because you're jealous of Lilian?"

"J-j-jeal—who's jealous?! I'm not jealous of anyone, especially not some stupid, skanky little fox who thinks she's prettier than me!"

"It's okay to feel jealous when someone else is close to the person you like," Lindsay said softly. "Believe me, I know exactly how it feels to like someone, only to find out that they no longer like you."

"R-really?" Christine asked, suddenly feeling bashful for reasons she didn't fully understand.

"Of course. You probably don't know this, but I used to have a really big crush on Kevin."

"You did?" Christine blinked, then her eyes widened. "B-but wait! If you like Kevin, then why did you turn him down when he confessed to you?"

"Turn him… were you spying on us at the mall?"

"N-no." In the face of Lindsay's flat stare, Christine could only do her best not to squirm. "W-well, maybe, but I just wanted to know what you two were talking about. I-it's not like I cared if you turned him down or not," she mumbled at the end.

"I suppose I can't blame you for being curious," Lindsay sighed, "and I also won't blame you for thinking I'm an idiot. The truth is, I was really happy when Kevin confessed to me, but I was also sad."

Christine felt nothing but confusion and a cat's curiosity. "Sad? Why?"

"Because I knew that Kevin didn't really mean it anymore. If there is one thing that I have come to understand about Kevin, it's that he has a hard time expressing his feelings, and when he does express them, he always wears his heart on his sleeve. When Kevin confessed to me, his speech felt forced, rehearsed, like he was an actor quoting lines from a script." Lindsay paused, her lips curling bitterly. "To be honest, I'm pretty sure the only reason Kevin confessed to me was because he had convinced himself that he liked me, when in truth, his feelings for me had disappeared awhile ago."

Christine remained silent while Lindsay released a gusty sigh.

"To be honest," the tomboy continued softly, "I think this was just his way of moving on, because a part of him couldn't move on if he was constantly wondering 'what if.'"

A prominent frown etched itself onto Christine's pretty face.

"And that's why you told him that you didn't like him? To let him go free?"

Lindsay shrugged. "Partly, but I also didn't want to date Kevin when his feelings for me were no longer true."

In the face of Lindsay's answer, Christine had only one thing to say.

"You're an idiot."

"Yeah." Lindsay's sardonic chuckle filled the street. "Trust me, I'm aware of how stupid that was. Now, come on. Just because Kevin likes Lilian doesn't give you an excuse to be rude to a person who wants to be friends with you."

As Christine let Lindsay pull her back toward the Swifts' apartment, a sigh escaped her lips in a breath of mist and steam.

"Friendship... right."

***

"Oh, my dear sweet babe of gothically clad proportions! You did come! I knew you would eventually see reason and let me suck on those pint-sized—GAOI!"

Everyone in the Swifts' apartment watched as Eric Corromperre sailed through the air in an almost graceful parabolic arc. When he landed on the ground in a thud of twitching limbs and pained groans, they turned to Christine, whose fist pointed toward the ceiling, her arm extended in an uppercut position.

"Shut up, ya damn pervert!"

Alex, Andrew and Justin all pulled out sheets of paper and

markers—from where, Kevin didn't know—and quickly scribbled on them, before holding them up like signs.

"10."

"10."

"5.6."

Alex and Andrew stared at Justin.

"Why a five-point-six?" Andrew asked. Justin looked at him with bored, half-lidded eyes.

"… Overdone…"

"Ah." The twins nodded as one.

"Is she always this violent?" Ms. Swift asked. Everyone else gave noncommittal nods. "Right, just checking."

After Christine knocked Eric for a loop, the group went back to their various activities, unfazed by the unmitigated violence that had just taken place. Ms. Swift was the only one who hadn't borne witness to Christine's and Eric's *tsukkomi* routine, but she seemed remarkably calm about the whole thing.

Everyone besides Eric (who was currently unconscious) sat down on the couch. Lilian, master of the remote and controller of everything they watched, pressed the play button. The once frozen figures on screen soon began to move, enacting a scene that Kevin never failed to enjoy despite how many times he'd seen it.

Lilian sat on Kevin's left, close enough to graze his thigh with her own but far enough that he wasn't uncomfortable. On his other side was Christine, and next to the Snow Maiden sat Lindsay. The tomboy stared at the screen, wondering what her friends could possibly see in this show. Cartoons were just so childish.

Alex and Andrew were not sitting down. They were standing on their feet. And shouting.

Kevin and Lilian twitched as they listened to their obnoxiously loud voices.

"Dammit! What the hell are you doing, Ichika?! You can't just give up like that!"

"That's right! Abandon your fear! Look forward! Move forward and never stop! You'll age if you pull back! You'll die if you hesitate!"

"You're quoting that all wrong! You don't sound anything like Zanbabesu!"

"I'd like to see you do it better!"

"Gladly! I'll do it a thousand times better than some illiterate idiot like you!"

"You wanna go? Bitch, I'll take you down right now!"

"There will be no fighting in my apartment." Kevin stood between Alex and Andrew before they could potentially devastate his residence.

"You mean my apartment," Ms. Swift interrupted, walking in from the kitchen, a bottle of wine in one hand and a glass in the other. "After all, I am the one who pays the bills."

"Yeah, but I'm the one who takes care of the apartment. You're almost never home," Kevin pointed out.

Ms. Swift's pout made her look several years younger, but she quickly waved her son's words off. "I hardly see how that matters. I am still the one paying for all this; the apartment, the electricity, the utilities. I even pay for that membership you have with Mad Dawg Fitness."

"I fail to see what Mad Dawg Fitness has to do with owning the apartment, and I do know that you're the only reason I can live here. And honestly, I'm not even sure why we're discussing this. I didn't mean this was my apartment when I said that. It was just a figure of speech."

"Hehe. That means this is my win."

Kevin rolled his eyes while his mom held up a hand and gave the victory sign, making a "v" shape with her index and middle finger, to everyone there. Seriously, sometimes his mom could be so childish.

As his mom walked onto the balcony, the group eventually got back to watching *White Out*, an anime about a fifteen year old girl with orange hair who became a Shinigami with a big ass sword. Kotohime brought out the snacks, setting them on the coffee table, then joined Ms. Swift on the balcony.

While the anime continued to play, Kevin glanced at his friends out of his periphery. They were an eclectic bunch. Really eclectic, and that was before taking how two of them weren't even human into account.

There was the yuki-onna who wore gothic lolita clothing and hated the cold, a pair of twins who didn't look like twins at all and acted like twins even less, a boy who had the weirdest speech impediment in the history of ever, a vivacious and vibrant beauty who, despite her propensity for committing perverted acts, was incredibly innocent and naïve. Also present was the most lecherous creature in the history of existence. Seriously. There could not be anyone more salacious than Eric Corromperre. The only person in this entire group who could be considered normal was Lindsay.

Despite how odd his friends were, Kevin wouldn't change them for the world. He turned back to the screen, and a bright smile appeared when he realized that one of his favorite scenes was about to play. Ichika was getting ready to go *Bangcock*.

"Eric! It's coming!"

Eric, who was still lying on the floor and appeared unconscious, sprang to life at his friend's words.

"Did you say cumming?"

"NO! I said coming! Now get your mind out of the gutter and come over here!"

"I'm cumming!"

"Shut up, you perverted beast!"

"*ITAI!!*"

"And don't talk in Japanese either, idiot!"

***

"Isn't it nice to see them all getting along so well?" Ms. Swift asked her current drinking companion, "I always enjoy seeing my son having fun with his friends."

Sitting on the balcony in a pair of lounge chairs, Ms. Swift and Kotohime enjoyed some early afternoon wine. Or, in the case of Kotohime, sake. Unlike Ms. Swift's somewhat slumped posture, Kotohime sat with poise and elegance, her *tabi* socks resting flat against the floor, her back straight, and her *sakazuki* resting within her left hand.

Ms. Swift was barefoot. She wiggled her toes against the cool pavement, reveling in the chilling sensation.

"It is nice to see my charge finally making friends," Kotohime admitted. "Lilian-sama has never had any friends before, unless you count her sister. However, she has never had a true friend, someone whom she met and became friends due to a shared interest and not any familial relation."

Ms. Swift hummed before putting the glass to her lips and savoring the white Zinfandel's fragrance. "And yet, you still don't approve of the affection she has for my son." It wasn't a question.

"Of course not." Kotohime took a sip of sake to hide her scowl. "Lilian-sama has given your son her love, loyalty and companionship—at great personal risk to herself, I might add. And yet, in spite of this, your son has not only not returned her feelings, but is leading her on by not telling her that he does not feel the same way. I cannot respect a man who would do that."

"I can see where you're coming from, but I think you should give my son a bit more time before handing out such a harsh assessment." Ms. Swift swirled the wine in her glass as she defended her son. "Kevin has always been a little dense when it comes to his own feelings. Right now he's confused and doesn't know how to deal with them. I know for a fact that, before Lilian came into the picture, Kevin used to have a major crush on Lindsay."

"That is the tomboyish one, if I am not mistaken."

"That's her." Ms. Swift took another sip of wine. "Anyway, he used to have a crush on Lindsay, but because he didn't know how to act around her, Kevin actively went out of his way to avoid her. Even when she tried talking to him, he would just run away." A pause. "Or pass out. He did that, too."

"Then he is a coward."

"More like a confused child who never had a father figure in his life." Ms. Swift barely withheld her grimace. "Or a very good mother, for that matter. I will admit, I am partly responsible for his inability to deal with women. Back when he was younger, I was very hard on him. I was a single mother working full-time and going to college for my bachelor's degree in journalism, and it was tough. Hiring a babysitter was expensive, so once he reached fourth grade, I stopped hiring them altogether and left Kevin to his own devices, expecting him to be capable of taking care of himself. I could've done a better job prioritizing myself; I should have given him the attention he needed, but I didn't."

Ms. Swift's eyes lost their vibrancy as she looked at something only she could see.

"I did try occasionally, of course," Ms. Swift said, her voice devoid of emotion. "I'd take him with me when I traveled, allowing him to see the world... but I was never there. Whenever we journeyed to other countries, I would leave him to do my job."

She gritted her teeth, her eyes holding tears. "I remember, every time I came back from my job, he would always be crying. I kept telling him that he needed to man up or no girl would go out with him. Pretty awful, huh?"

"Hmm…"

Ms. Swift watched as Lilian grabbed one of the sandwiches on the plate and held it out for Kevin, smiling when her son allowed the beautiful redhead to feed him.

Her smile widened when she saw the goth girl—Christine, if she wasn't mistaken—stand up and start shouting at Lilian.

"Stop acting so lovey-dovey with Kevin, boob-head!"

"Why should I listen to you? Are you Kevin? No, you're not, so why don't you just go back to watching the anime, tsun-loli. If he doesn't like what I'm doing, then he can tell me himself."

"D-don't get me involved in this argument! I don't want any part of it!"

"God damn you, Kevin Swift! How come these two tittielicious sex-bots are always fighting over you and not me?! It's not fair!"

"Shut up, Eric! And for the love of god, stop mentioning tits!"

"And don't call us sex-bots, perv!"

"Gaoi!"

Kotohime and Ms. Swift silently watched how one Eric was pummeled by Christine… again. Steam wafted from his cranium where Christine had hit him, and a large bump the size of a baseball had grown out of his hair.

"I fail to see how that justifies his behavior," Kotohime continued their previous conversation.

"Maybe it doesn't," Ms. Swift shrugged. "But I want you to understand where Kevin is coming from. He's never had a father to help him deal with the changes that boys go through, and I was never a very good parent. In fact, I'm pretty sure my version of the Birds and Bees scarred him for life. Like I said, give him some time. I'm sure he'll surprise you."

"I am giving him time. He just hasn't met any of my expectations thus far."

"That's too bad." Ms. Swift's posture slumped even further. She perked up a second later, however, and leaned forward conspiratorially.

"By the way, may I ask how you managed to store that sake in your Extra Dimensional Storage Space? I can't store anything larger than a cup in mine."

"I believe it has something to do with our comparative sizes," Kotohime admitted. "Mine is much larger than yours, you know."

Ms. Swift looked at Kotohime's boobs, which bounced and jiggled without any prompting, as if they knew they were being studied. She then looked at her own boobs, which didn't bounce.

"I don't think I like you as much as I used to," she pouted.

"Ara, ara," Kotohime's eyes gleamed with amusement. "There is no need to be like that. You are still a very youthful woman."

"Whatever." Ms. Swift's pout was that of a child who knew they were being talked down to.

Kotohime tapped her lips with her right index. "Then again, Lilian-sama is about the same size as you. However, she is also growing and, well, pardon my saying this, but hers are much more perky than yours."

"All right, all right," Ms. Swift grumbled. She should have never brought this topic up. "I get it. I'm getting older and my boobs aren't what they used to be. No need to rub it in."

"Ufufufu, I am merely saying that that could have something to do with the reason your Extra Dimensional Storage Space isn't as large as mine. However, if you are interested, I know of a great brand of cream that you can use to tighten up your chest. It works better than any surgery, and it may increase the size of your Extra Dimensional Storage Space."

"Really?"

"Ufufufu, of course."

"You know, that whole 'ufufufu' laugh of yours really doesn't fill me with much confidence in you."

***

After watching a full season of anime, the group separated. Lindsay, Christine and, for some strange reason, Justin went off to a corner and started talking. Well, Lindsay and Christine began talking. Justin just seemed to be staring off into space. The rest of them were playing video games.

"Come on! Come on! Come on, come on, come on, come on, comeoncomeoncomeon!"

Kevin gritted his teeth as he saw what Alex was doing to his controller. "Oi! What are you doing?! Stop button mashing! This isn't a fighting game, and you're going to break my controller if you keep that up."

"Take a chill pill, man. I'm not breaking anything. See? Your controller is fine. Besides, I need to be fast on the trigger finger if I want to beat all of you and—what the hell?! Damn it! Who just shot me?!"

"I did."

"Lilian?! But your player is on the other side of the map! Even a sniper rifle shouldn't have that much range!"

"Ufufufu, I'm just awesome like that."

Kevin grimaced. "Ugh, Lilian, please don't use that term ever again. It's just not you."

"Sorry, I wanted to try it out at least once."

Kevin sat on the sidelines, watching his friends play one of the many first-person shooter in his collection. He would have been playing with them, but since his system only allowed four players at any given time, they had drawn straws to see who would play the first round.

He'd drawn the short straw.

"Holy crap! Lilian just sniped me! She just shot me in the fucking head! How did she do that?"

"She shot you because you suck at this game."

"Shut up, brother! I'm good enough to kill you every time you spawn. Crap! She killed me again!"

"Ufufufu, I've got mad skills. Oh, it looks like I've racked up another kill."

"Damn it! I don't care if your tits are some of the largest I've ever seen. There's no way I'm letting—oh, for the love of—stop killing me while I'm in mid-rant!"

"Ufufufu, if you want me to stop killing you, then you're going to have to become a better shot."

Kevin wasn't surprised by Lilian's deadly skills at first person shooter games. He'd been playing video games with her ever since she started living with him. She'd been bad at first, like, really bad, but the gorgeous redhead was nothing if not tenacious. When she wasn't cooking, doing homework, trying to sex him up, watching anime or reading manga, she was playing video games.

He didn't know why Lilian loved them so much. None of the girls he knew enjoyed video games, period. Regardless, he couldn't deny that her enjoyment of video games and anime gave her a certain appeal beyond her incomparable beauty.

It made his situation that much harder.

Seeing how Lilian was having so much fun thrashing his friends like they were a bunch of newbs, Kevin decided to join the other group.

"What are you guys doing all the way over here?"

Lindsay gave Kevin an amused smile. "You know that video games were never my thing."

"Hmph." Christine crossed her arms. "Why would I want to corrode my brain by playing a game that contains nothing but mindless violence?"

"… Like…"

"Then why aren't you playing with them?" Kevin inquired, staring at his friend who merely stared back with half-lidded eyes.

"… Foxy…"

Three sets of eyes gave Justin an odd look.

"You say the strangest thing sometimes, Justin," Kevin muttered, Christine and Lindsay nodding in agreement.

***

After speaking with Lindsay and Christine… and Justin too, he supposed, Kevin concluded that it was high time they do something that could include the entire group.

The coffee table had been moved off to the side, making room for the large Twister mat, the game they had all decided to play after it won a majority vote. Kevin personally thought his male friends just wanted to use it as an excuse to perv out. No hot-blooded teenager would miss out on a chance to feel some soft, feminine flesh and pretend it was just an accident—unless his name happened to be Kevin Swift.

It was only five minutes into the game, and already, everyone playing looked like one giant pretzel. They were a tangle of limbs and torsos, all pressed together in a way that somehow looked both erotic and uncomfortable.

Eric had never been happier.

Alex and Andrew, on the other hand, were not happy.

"I can't believe we're not getting to play. This is so unfair."

"Damn it, I knew I should have chosen rock!"

"… Flexible…"

Lindsay, who also wasn't on the mat, spun the wheel for the players.

"All right, Christine, it's your turn now. Left foot on red."

"D-damn it," Christine grumbled as she looked around. "Why do I have to play this stupid game?"

"Just hurry up and make your move."

"Shut up, Speed Bumps!"

"Don't be hating just because my boobs are bigger than yours, Bee Stings."

"S-s-s-shut up!"

"Hey! No fighting, please," Kevin piped up from his place underneath Lilian. "The last thing I want is to fall on top of Eric."

"I agree with Kevin. I don't want him falling on top of me either. Now, if one of you bodaciously bodied hotties would like to fall on me, that would be an entirely different matter."

"Shut up, you stupid lecher!"

"Yeah, keep quiet, perv!"

"You two are so cruel!"

After several seconds of searching, Christine eventually found a way to put her left foot on one of the red dots.

Unfortunately, this also put her in the awkward position of being sandwiched between two men.

Christine's eyes widened as she not only felt Eric's butt pressing against her back, but also found her face only inches away from Kevin's.

Her heart thumped like a war drum in her chest. It beat even faster when he grinned at her.

"Sorry," he apologized. "This must be uncomfortable for you."

"Ah… ah…"

Christine tried to speak, but couldn't. It felt like something had been lodged in her throat. She could hardly even breathe, much less get a word out.

She didn't know why Kevin made her feel this way… actually, that was a lie. She did know why, but that shouldn't have mattered anymore. They hadn't started interacting again until last month. Granted, this wasn't for lack of trying on her part. She had tried talking to him before, but every time she thought about going up to him, her mind and body would freeze quicker than a pole in Antarctica.

Why can't I be more forward, like that stupid fox skank?

"All right, now it's Kevin's turn." Lindsay spun the wheel again. "It says right hand on blue."

"Okay, right hand on blue. Let's see. Let's see." A moment's search revealed a blue circle his hand could reach. He leaned down, stretching his arm as far as it could go, and put his hand on the blue dot.

"H-hey! W-w-w-what the hell do you think you're doing?! She said right hand on blue, not stick your face into Christine's boobs!"

"Damn you, Kevin Swift, getting to stick your face into those snuggle pups! You know that's one of my life's goals! How dare you do it before me!"

"Be quiet, Eric. You're making a fool of yourself."

"Beloved—I mean, Kevin's right. You should stop talking while you're ahead."

"That's right, ya damn pervert. Now shut the hell up!"

"Why does everyone hate me?!"

"Because you're a lech and deserve to die. And for the gods' sakes, Kevin, get your face out of my boobs!"

"Ufufufu, I'm not sure what the problem is. You don't have any boobs for him to stick his face into."

"Go to hell, you damn udder woman!"

"Udder woman? Haven't you already used that insult before? You must be losing your touch, tsun-tsun-chan."

"I'm not a tsundere!"

… The resulting silence from her statement was profound. Even Lindsay was staring at Christine, making her feel very uncomfortable.

"… I hate all of you."

The game soon continued.

"Okay, now it's Lilian's turn." Another spin of the wheel. "And it says… oh, you get a freebie. You can use whatever appendage you want, just so long as it goes on yellow."

"Okay!"

Lilian looked at all the yellow dots, trying to determine which one would be the easiest for her to reach. She lamented not being able to use her tails. Still, even without her foxy appendages, she eventually found a solution that not only worked, but would also be beneficial to her.

Ufufufu...

Kevin felt a shudder run down his spine.

Lifting her right hand off the mat, Lilian turned until her front faced the ground. She reached over Kevin and put her right hand on a yellow dot.

Her boobs were completely pressed against Kevin's back.

"L-L-Lilian!" A pitiful squeak. "Why aren't you wearing a bra?!"

"Ufufufu, I don't wear one because I don't need one."

A certain yuki-onna spontaneously combusted, steam pouring out of her ears like smoke from the windows of a house that caught fire. "W-w-w-wha—y-y-you're not—what the hell do you think you're doing?! Get your damn jugs off Kevin's back!"

"Wait. You're not wearing a bra, Lilian?" Lindsay suddenly asked.

"Nope!"

"That's incredible. How do you get your breasts to stay so uplifted and perky?"

"Um... genetics?"

"You must have some really good genetics, then." Lindsay looked down at her own breasts with a frown. "Ha... I wish I had boobs like yours."

"Why? I think you're very pretty just the way you are."

"T-thanks." Lindsay didn't know why, but for some reason, being complemented by Lilian made her cheeks flush. "Coming from someone as beautiful as you, that really means a lot."

"Tee-hee, you're welcome!"

"Hey! Stop acting like a couple of dykes and listen to me! Ms. Double-Whammies, get your damn dueling banjos off Kevin!"

"Why should I listen to you? You're not his girlfriend."

"S-s-s-so what?! You're not his girlfriend either! And I doubt Kevin likes your damn walrus tits weighing him down."

"Actually..." Kevin shifted a bit, his cheeks gaining a small sprinkling of red. "This... it's, well, it's not so bad."

"Kevin?! How could you say something like that?!"

"Yay! See, Baby Bumps? He does like my girls."

"Shut up! Shut up, both of you!"

"Damn you, Kevin Swift! Just wait until I get out of this!"

Having moved inside, Ms. Swift and Kotohime watched the group from their place on the couch.

"Look at how much fun they're having." Ms. Swift's pout was reminiscent of a child whose parents told her that she couldn't have dessert after dinner. "I wanna play Twister, too."

"Ara, ara." Kotohime held the sleeve of her kimono up to her mouth, looking nothing if not amused.

***

In the end, no one won the game of twister.

Once three o'clock hit, Christine, Lindsay and Justin went home. The twins and Eric stuck around, playing several more rounds of violent FPS goodness.

They decided to stop playing when Lilian won every single round.

Kevin returned from his trip to the bathroom to see his friends watching another anime. This one, much like *White Out*, was a mainstream anime—except it was about ninja instead of Shinigami. It was called *Shinobi Natsumo*.

"No! What the hell are you doing, Natsumo! Don't just keep using dopplegangers to overpower your enemies! That's never going to work on an opponent as powerful as Gaia!"

Kevin stifled his chuckles as Lilian shouted at the screen. He understood her frustrations. While he enjoyed the series, he really wished the main character would stop trying to run roughshod over her enemies with corporeal copies. Such strategies only remained interesting after the first couple of times. It got boring after the hundredth time. It got annoying after the thousandth time. And after the ten-thousandth time, well, it wouldn't be inaccurate to say that there were times Kevin wanted to throw his TV through a wall.

"Hey, Eric." Kevin stood next to his friend.

"What do ya want?" Eric didn't take his eyes off the screen.

"I wanted to talk to you about something."

"What? Now? Can't you see I'm busy watching sexy two-dimensional jugs bouncing around here?"

"It's important."

"Ha... fine." Eric stood up. "But make it quick, alright. We're just about to get to the best part of the entire episode."

Which Kevin took to mean they were getting to one of the parts where Natsumo found herself randomly stripped naked for no apparent reason. It happened a lot in anime—spontaneous stripping, that is.

Kevin took Eric to the spot outside where he'd conversed with Kotohime several nights ago. He didn't want anyone overhearing their conversation, least of all Lilian.

Eric crossed his arms and stared at his friend. "All right, now, what's so important that you felt the need to drag me all the way out here?"

Kevin took a deep, calming breath to center himself—

"IthinkI'minlovewithLilian!"

—and then spoke complete gibberish.

Eric stuck a pinky in his ear, pretending to clean it out. "Eh? What was that? I couldn't understand a word you just said."

Kevin grimaced and took several more deep breaths. When he finished finding his zen, he looked at Eric again. "I... I think I might be in love with Lilian."

Eric's stare made him feel like an idiot.

"Is that all you wanted to say? I could have told you that."

"Eh?"

At hearing his friend's most elegant way of expressing confusion, Eric rolled his eyes. "Look, man, it's obvious to anyone with a pair of eyes that you like Lilian."

If Kevin hadn't been startled before, then he certainly was now. "It is? Really?"

"Kevin, only an idiot wouldn't notice that you like her." Eric held out a hand and began ticking off reasons with his fingers. "You spend more time with her than anyone else—and don't give me that crap about you two living together. That doesn't stop you from avoiding her at school. You treat her with more kindness than anyone else."

Kevin opened his mouth, but wasn't given a chance to speak.

"Ah ah, don't interrupt me. I know exactly what you're going to say. 'I don't know what you're talking about,'" Eric said in an approximation of Kevin's voice, "'I don't treat Lilian any differently than I do anyone else.' Bullshit! You treat her way differently than anyone else. You might be a complete pansy when it comes to women—"

"Oi!"

"—but that doesn't mean you're weak-willed. If you didn't like Lilian, she would have never gotten away with half the crap she's done since you two met. The mere fact that you let her say the stuff she does, that you don't put much effort into stopping her when she clings to you, tells me that you like her."

To this, Kevin said nothing.

"Besides, you stare at her all the time."

"W-w-what?!" Kevin shrieked as his face turned into a neon sign. "I do not stare at her!"

Kevin looked away when Eric gave him a surprisingly deadpanned stare.

"W-what? I don't... do I?"

"Kevin." Eric's voice had never been more serious. "Just the other day, you were so busy staring at Lilian that you couldn't even run properly during track practice. Coach Deretaine actually had to curse you out like a sailor stuck in a desert just to get you to start moving."

"T-that's because..."

"And what about today," Eric continued, "the whole time we've been hanging out, you've hardly gone ten minutes without looking at her. You also let her feed you, hold your hand, and you're always smiling at her."

" What does me smiling have to do with anything?"

"Everything!" Kevin jumped in shock when Eric shouted. "Look, Kevin, most people probably think I'm just a good-for-nothing pervert, and they're one-hundred percent correct. But! I am also a pervert who happens to be your best friend. I know you; your habits and your thoughts and how you act when you're uncomfortable, so I know when you like someone. Even Lindsay never got the smiles you've been giving Lilian. Face it, you've been struck by Cupid's arrow, you've caught the love bug, the doctor of love has come knocking on your front door, you—"

"All right, all right! I get it," Kevin interrupted. He really didn't want Eric going on one of his rants. "I'm in lo-lo-love with

Lilian. But… how can I know if this is real love and not just a silly crush? What if it's not true love?"

"True love?" Eric snorted. "Kevin, there's no such thing as true love. That's a fairy tale coined by Disney in order to con money out of tween girls and their parents."

"I thought fairy tale princesses was the Disney concept?"

"They came after Disney created the idea of there being such a thing as your 'One True Love.'"

"Oh." Kevin paused. "So what should I do?"

Eric raised an eyebrow. "Are you really asking me what you should do?"

Kevin shrugged and looked down at his shoes. His black sneakers contrasted sharply with the concrete pavement. "You're my best friend. Who else am I supposed to ask? My mom? She hasn't dated since the jerkwad of a sperm donor left her. Lindsay? She's a girl." Another pause. "And now that I think about it, maybe asking her for advice is a good idea." He shook his head. "Anyway, the point is, you're my best friend. If I can't come to you for help, then who else can I go to?"

Running a hand through his hair, Eric sighed. "If you really want me to help, I do have some advice to give you. But, you're probably not going to like it."

"At this point, I am willing to take any advice you can give me under serious consideration."

"Alright then, here's my advice. You listening?" Kevin nodded. "Fuck her."

… Silence. Several crows cawed in a most annoying manner.

"I-I'm sorry, what?" Kevin looked at Eric like he'd sprouted a donkey's tail from his hindquarters.

"I said fuck her, diddle her fiddle, stick your tallywhacker in her babymaker, shove your star quarterback into her squealing cheerleader, poke your—"

"I can't do that!" Kevin exploded. Eric's blank stare would have made him uncomfortable, but Kevin was already too embarrassed to feel discomfort.

"Why not?"

"What do you mean why not? Because it's… because I… I mean… to have sex with someone that you don't even know your own feelings for… it's just wrong!" Kevin grabbed his left elbow with his right hand, looking more than a little uneasy. "Lilian, she... she really loves me. This isn't some high school crush to her; this is serious. It's the 'I wanna spend the rest of my life with you' kind of serious. If we had sex, it would be like I was declaring my intentions to marry her, and I don't... I mean, I'm not sure if my own feelings for her are that strong. What if I tell her that I love her back, and then realize later on that I don't actually love her?"

"That's the risk one takes when it comes to love." It was surprisingly sound advice coming from a pervert. "You can never know if you're going to still love someone months, years or even decades down the road. That's why so many people get divorced these days."

"But that's wrong!" Kevin exploded. "That's so, so wrong! You think I can do something like that?! That I can hurt someone like that! My mom suffered because my dad left her after I was born! Even now she refuses to talk about him!"

Kevin gritted his teeth. He didn't know his father, not even his name, but he didn't need to. His father had left his mom. She was with child, and he left her! To be born from someone like that, to have that man's blood flowing through his veins; it made him sick.

"I refuse to do that to Lilian." Kevin's eyes blazed like twin bonfires in the night. "Lilian loves me, Eric. Do you understand what that means? She loves me so much and I... I'd never forgive myself if I got her hopes up by accepting her love without being positive that I could return it with the same intensity and devotion as her."

"You make it sound like you're her soulmate or something."

Kevin looked down at his hands. They were trembling, weak. The hands of a boy born from a man who abandoned his significant other after he'd gotten her pregnant. These hands held Lilian's heart in their palms. That knowledge made him queasy.

"I might as well be."

"I'm sure you're just exaggerating." Eric rolled his eyes at Kevin's melodrama. "I know the girl is into you. Hell, everyone knows Lilian would like nothing more than for you to stick your rock hard porpoise into her moist cavernous passage—"

"Oh, for the love of—would you stop crapping out innuendos already?"

"—but that doesn't necessarily means she wants to get married, have your babies, and buy a house with a white picket fence and a flower bed."

Kevin shook his head. Eric just didn't understand. "No, she does. Trust me on this, Lilian isn't looking for a quick screw or anything. This is a lifetime commitment to her."

"Whatever. I think you're just a little too into yourself."

Kevin sighed. He wished he could tell his best friend the real reason that Lilian loved with him, but he couldn't. A conversation like that couldn't end well.

"Eric, the reason I know that Lilian isn't looking for a one-night stand is because she's actually a kitsune, and she has chosen me to be her mate. That means she'll remain by my side for the rest of my life, and because I am her first mate, I'll be the single most important person in hers."

"… Justin hasn't convinced you to do whatever has fried his brain, has he? That was the stupidest thing I've ever heard."

Kevin shook his head. Yeah. Not happening.

"Look, Kevin." Eric placed his hands on Kevin's shoulders, snapping him out of his thoughts. "Whether Lilian is looking for marriage and children or just a young man to screw doesn't have any bearing on your decision. It also doesn't change the fact that, in the end, *you* are the one who has to make this decision."

Kevin sighed. That really wasn't what he'd been hoping to hear. But then, what did he expect when asking Eric for help?

"I know you're afraid of acting on your feelings because of your old man."

Kevin's eyes widened.

"How did—"

"Oh, please." Eric rolled his eyes. "Just because I spend more time looking at tits than I do paying attention to you doesn't mean I'm ignorant."

"… I really dont't know how to take that," Kevin mumbled, "so I think I'll just ignore it."

"Whatever. The point is that I know what you're really afraid of, and I think you're being stupid. You are you and your old man is just some jerk you've never met. You're not him, and you're not the type to treat Lilian like some kind of object. You're way too nice for that."

Kevin said nothing. His eyes remained focused on Eric, who'd never sounded so... intelligent before. Was this really his perverted best friend?

"If you love Lilian, then be with her. If you want to fuck her brains out, then by all means, have at it. In matters of the heart, it is best to go with your instincts. The question you should be asking yourself isn't, 'will I end up being like my old man and leave some poor, innocent girl with a child?' The real question you should ask is, 'am I really willing to let this chance at happiness slip away because I'm too afraid to act on my feelings?'"

"That..." Kevin needed a moment to find his voice. "That was surprisingly profound coming from you."

"I have my moments." Eric clapped Kevin on the shoulder. "Now, let's go back inside. I want to finish watching *Shinobi Natsumo*."

"Sure."

"And if I missed Natsumo getting stripped naked because of you, I'm going to kick your ass."

"Eric!"

"What?" Eric shrugged. "I'm just sayin'."

Chapter 9

A Picnic Gone Wrong

The room was dark, so dark that very little could be seen. The only source of illumination came from a monitor in the corner, which allowed those present to see vague outlines of various objects arrayed around the room.

Sitting within this room were two figures. Only their silhouettes were visible, two outlines of darkness. They were seated at a small table, sitting opposite of each other.

A fist banged against the table several times.

"I now call this first meeting of the Lovely Lilian Lovers Club to order."

"Dude, there's no need to be so loud. There are only two of us here."

"Two of us? Where's our third member?"

"He said he had something important to do."

"He had something—oh. Right. I forgot I had him doing *that*."

"That? What's that?"

"Nothing. Nothing. Just a small favor I asked for. He'll be stopping by in a little bit. Let us not worry about him and start this meeting. To order!"

The fist banged again.

"Okay. Seriously dude. There's no need to do the whole fist-banging thing. There's still only two of us here. And why do we have the lights off?"

"Don't say that, man!" The first voice whined. "You're totally killing my vibe! Just pretend this is a big meeting filled with thousands of people. It's not like that day isn't far off anyway. Lilian's popularity is growing daily. Already she's being hailed as the most beautiful girl in school. It's only a matter of time before more people join our club. And it's dark in here because we're in the process of plotting our diabolical scheme. All diabolical schemes must be plotted in darkness. That's how this stuff goes."

"Uh huh... and just where did you get that?"

"From the Dungeon Master's Guide."

"Ah."

"Now then! Enough dilly-dallying and silly questions! We have a meeting to get on with." The figure leaned its left forearm against the table. "Do we have their itinerary?"

"Yes." The second silhouette held up a clipboard. "Our stalking—um, our reconnaissance has borne fruit. It seems they will be traveling to Mountain View Park today."

"Excellent! Do we know what time they're leaving?"

"No."

"That's fine. I set up a couple dozen spy cameras all around their complex. All we need to do is watch the one by their front door and we'll know exactly when they leave."

"When did you have time to do that?"

"Never mind that. Now, to the computer!"

"... Uh, right!"

***

Lilian hummed a soft tune as she waltzed about the kitchen. Her hips swung to a silent beat. If her tails had been out, they would have been swishing about as well.

Today was going to be a special day. Last night she had convinced Kevin to go on a picnic with her. Lilian's lips curled in delight. This would be their first picnic together, and one that he had promised when they'd gone shopping so long ago. She hoped it would become one of many.

This is so exciting! Kevin and I are going on a picnic!

Kotohime stood with her hands clasped behind her back, watching her charge scurry about the kitchen with a look of amusement. Lilian had always been an unusual kitsune, but it had never been more evident than now.

Very few of their kind enjoyed cooking, and even fewer enjoyed cooking for others. Most kitsune didn't even know how to cook. They had no need to learn when they could convince someone else to do it for them, and aside from that, the Pnévma Clan had several chefs who cooked for them.

Ever since that day several years ago, when Lilian had encountered a young Kevin, she'd become interested in learning how to cook. Kotohime could only assume that meeting with Kevin had been one of those defining moments in the young kitsune's life. From that moment on, Lilian had wanted to learn how to be a good mate, and apparently, good mates knew how to cook—at least according to those manga Lilian made her buy.

"There." Lilian beamed as she finished filling the picnic basket. "All finished. Now I just need to make breakfast."

Before Lilian could start something else, Kotohime placed a hand on the redhead's shoulder. "There is no need for you to prepare breakfast as well. Why don't you get ready for your picnic, while I prepare our morning meal? I believe that shower is calling your name."

Lilian pondered Kotohime's suggestion. She wanted to prepare Kevin's food, but the idea of taking a shower appealed to her greatly, and Kevin would be waking up soon. While she'd love to take a shower with him, that just wasn't in the cards right now.

"Okay. Thanks, Kotohime."

"You're most welcome, Lilian-sama." Kotohime watched Lilian walk out of the kitchen before scavenging through the fridge. "Now where did I put that hot sauce?"

***

Kevin woke up with a groan. After taking several moments to gather his bearings, he crawled out of his sleeping bag and staggered to his feet.

Moaning and groaning like a zombie from a B-budget horror flick, he stumbled out of the room and made his way into the bathroom. It wasn't long after entering that his mind went from start-up mode to high-alert. His eyes widened to epic proportions as he stared at the very beautiful and very naked girl standing in front of the mirror.

Why does she never lock the dang door? The question flitted only briefly through his mind before other thoughts consumed him.

Kevin didn't know why—actually he did, but denial kept him from admitting it—but the moment he entered the room and saw Lilian standing there naked, his eyes refused to leave her.

Slowly, ever so slowly, blue irises trailed over Lilian's body. Even now, after all this time and many instances similar to this one, Kevin couldn't get over how gorgeous this girl was. Her hair, descending like a curtain of fire, went all the way down to her small, heart-shaped derrière. Several strands lay across key points of her body, wet, shiny and erotically sticking to her skin.

While the hair covering a good portion of her breasts should have alleviated the sexual appeal, it didn't. If anything, the long locks of hair blocking the view of her nipples merely added a sensualistic allure to the already arousing sight. It didn't help that Lilian wasn't actually doing anything truly sensual. She was just being her usual self which, oddly enough, made the entire scene sexier.

After absorbing the sight of her side-boob, his gaze descended, devouring the view of her flat belly and cute belly button like a man starved, before traveling down further. He couldn't follow the curvature of her spine, but that meant little when he caught sight of her shapely butt. Her tails swished back and forth, covering and then revealing tantalizing glimpses of bare bottom. Following the compass of her tush, Lilian's gorgeous legs extended seemingly forever, ending in a pair of oddly beautiful feet. Her cute little toes wiggled on the cold tile.

By all eight-million Shinto gods, there really is something wrong with me.

This wasn't the first time he had seen Lilian naked. This wasn't even the 40th time. While Kevin hadn't bothered counting these encounters of the nude and sexy kind, it felt like the numbers had already expanded into the hundreds—a slight exaggeration, to be sure, but he wasn't one to sweat semantics.

He should have been used to this. He was used to this, and yet the sight of a naked Lilian still got to him every. Stinking. Time.

"Kevin?"

Lilian had finally noticed his presence and turned around, giving him a full frontal view of her naked body. Kevin thought his eyes might literally pop out of his skull. Heat rushed to his

cheeks… and just about every other part of his body.

If Lilian noticed how red he was becoming, she did a very good job of ignoring it.

"What are you doing in here? Did you want to take a shower with me?" At the thought of Kevin finally wanting to join her in the shower, Lilian's eyes lit up like a million-watt bulb. "I just got out, but I wouldn't mind getting back in. I could even wash your back for you."

Kevin only registered her words in an abstract sense; like a deaf person, he could see her mouth moving, but couldn't hear her words. The entirety of his being was focused solely on the vision of loveliness before him.

"Kevin?"

Worry overcame Lilian at Kevin's lack of response. She walked up to him, which invariably drew his attention to her breasts. With each step she took, they swayed, bounced and jiggled in a manner that would have made any man lose it.

Kevin felt blood rushing to his cheeks and another, far more sensitive part of his anatomy. His heart pounded in his chest like a mad drummer in a heavy metal band. He started to grow dizzy as blood fused to his face.

"Are you okay, Kevin? Your face is all red." Lilian's lovely face filled his vision. Reaching up and placing a hand behind his head, the beautiful fox-girl pulled him down until their foreheads touched. "You do feel a little hot," she murmured softly, her hot breath hitting his lips. "But you don't seem to have a fever or—eh?"

Being so close to Lilian, who looked like she'd been lovingly crafted by the hands of angels to perfectly blend enchanting innocence and deadly allure, was too much. It was way too much. The adolescent mind was not meant to be confronted with such flawless perfection, nor something so sexy. Having a body sinful enough to make Satan envious pressing against him didn't help matters either.

Lilian watched, blinking, as Kevin was launched backwards by the blood spurting from his nose like a fountain. He shot out of the bathroom, the door shattering as he slammed into it like a battering ram, and flew into the hallway. The wall cracked around his unconscious body as he struck it with the force of an armor-piercing artillery round, abrasions appearing around the center of impact.

He hung there for several seconds, and then his body slowly peeled off like the paint on a Gundam that had sustained laser damage, falling face first to the ground where he lay, unmoving, save for the occasional spastic twitch.

Lilian slowly reached up to her face, where she wiped the blood off almost absentmindedly, her eyes never leaving the still form of her (hopefully soon) beloved mate. She eventually closed her eyes and released a content sigh.

"Oh, Beloved. You always know the best way to make this lowly Lilian feel like the most important person in the world."

Naturally, Kevin did not answer.

***

"I'm really sorry about walking in on you," Kevin apologized from where he sat across from Lilian. His cheeks were still a very prominent shade of red, but at least he was speaking, and without a single stutter to boot. This remarkable showing of coherent dialect was a significant improvement from as recently as two weeks ago.

"Why are you apologizing?" Lilian tilted her head for maximum adorableness… and to express her honest curiosity. "It's not like you haven't seen me naked before. And besides, you know I don't mind you looking at me."

"I know that," Kevin muttered, looking away. "But it still doesn't feel right to walk in on a girl when she's taking a shower."

"But I had just finished my shower when you walked in," Lilian pointed out.

"That's not the point!"

"Then what is the point?"

"It's, uh, it's…" Kevin thought really hard. He could practically hear his brain farting as it tried to come up with an answer for Lilian's question. "It's just common courtesy!"

"'Common courtesy?'"

She looked over at Kotohime, who graciously explained the concept to her. "Common courtesy is defined as the simple mannerisms most humans are taught as children. Using words like 'please' and 'thank you' at appropriate times, always being respectful to your elders."

232

"So it's basically just good manners?"

"More or less."

"And not walking in on someone while they're in the shower is a part of this common courtesy thing?"

"I believe that falls more along the lines of common decency," Kotohime admitted. "In human society, there are recognized standards of propriety, good taste and modesty. Basically, people expect you to behave in a decent and proper way as defined by their social standards." Kevin squeaked like a rodent when she tossed him a glare. "Not walking in on someone while they're taking a shower is definitely one of them."

"Look, I'm sorry, okay? I didn't even know you were in there! You didn't even bother locking the door!"

"That hardly excuses your actions. It is always proper to knock before you enter a room. And in any case, you should have heard the sound of running water and known that I was in there." Kotohime set a plate of broiled fish, a bowl of rice and another bowl filled with pickled vegetables in front of her charge. "Here you are, Lilian-sama."

"Thank you."

"My pleasure."

"I was distracted, okay?" Kevin mumbled lowly.

"And is that a good enough justification for your actions?"

"... No."

"Exactly. It is not." Kotohime gave a decisive nod as Kevin shrank into his seat, his shoulders slumping. "Now, have some breakfast, Kevin-san, and be thankful that I have decided to cook something for you at all."

Kevin stared at the small bowl of rice and even smaller plate of fish. He looked over at Lilian's portion, which seemed nearly twice as large.

He sighed.

"Thank you," he murmured softly, picking up the chopsticks and using them to start eating. The food stopped halfway to his mouth, however, when a thought occurred to him. "Where did you get chopsticks?"

Kotohime finished setting all of the food on the table, then stood behind Lilian, hands clasped behind her back. "I always carry several sets of chopsticks in my Extra Dimensional Storage

Space."

Kevin used the hand still holding his chopsticks to facepalm, and consequently got rice stuck to his face and in his hair.

"Dang it," Kevin growled.

"You're making a mess of yourself." Lilian stood up and leaned over the table, brushing several grains of rice from his forehead.

"It's not my fault," Kevin muttered. When the rice was gone, the fox-girl's fingers began running her fingers through his hair, her nails gently grazing his scalp. Despite the heat threatening to burst from Kevin's cheeks, he did nothing to stop Lilian's actions. It felt really good.

"Ara, you look like you're enjoying my ward's actions, Kevin-san," Kotohime observed.

He looked at the maid-slash-bodyguard, unnerved by her neutral expression. He could never decipher her emotional state, no matter how hard she tried. Like a bank vault, the woman's thoughts and opinions were locked up and sealed tight.

At least she hasn't run me through with her katana. Sometimes, you've got to be thankful for the little things.

"Don't look too into it or anything," Kevin mumbled. "I'm only letting her do this because I've given up on trying to stop her. That's all."

"Is that so?" Kotohime raised her left hand to her face, demurely hiding her mouth with the sleeve of her kimono. "Ufufufu..."

"And stop laughing like that!"

Kotohime settled down, and Kevin and Lilian began eating. Kevin stuck the *umeboshi* into his mouth--and then promptly leapt out of his seat.

"WAAA! MY MOUTH IS ON FIRE!"

"B-BELOVED!"

Kevin ran around the room, his hands covering his mouth, which felt like it was belching fire. Lilian ran with him, trying to calm him down with little success.

"WATER! WATER!"

"Quick, Beloved! Stop, drop and roll!"

"ITS MY MOUTH ON FIRE! NOT MY BODY!"

"H-hawa!"

"DON'T GIVE ME SOME RANDOM CATCHPHRASE! HELP ME! OH, GOD! MY MOUTH! IT BURNS!!"

Kotohime watched the two panicking youngsters and placidly ate her food while standing up, her smile hidden behind her chopsticks and her eyes glittering with mischief.

Ufufufu, it's good to be a kitsune.

***

Breakfast continued after Lilian healed Kevin's mouth, and the group of three soon became four, when a half-dressed and partially asleep Ms. Swift stumbled into the kitchen. Kevin took one look at his mom, and then he sighed when he saw her state of undress.

"Geez, Mom," he mumbled, standing up and walking over to her. He deftly buttoned up her white collared shirt, which looked like it had been thrown on half-haphazardly, before fixing her collar. At least she had a skirt on this time. "You're completely useless when it comes to anything first thing in the morning. I don't know how you manage to stay alive when you travel the globe."

Seriously, his mom had no household talents whatsoever. Oh, she tried. She tried very hard to be a good mother, but the truth was that, more often than not, his mom would act like a younger sibling, forcing him to play the parent.

It should be the other way around.

"Nnnggggg... coffeeee..."

Resisting the urge to slam his face against a wall, Kevin guided the woman to her chair, which already had her breakfast and a cup of freshly brewed coffee in front of it.

The woman's tired eyes focused on the meal. Then on the coffee. The meal again. Back to the coffee.

Kevin couldn't keep himself from running a hand down his face when his mom went for the coffee, guzzling it down with much gusto.

Kotohime seemed to find some amusement in this. "Ara, ara. Swift-dono is definitely not a morning person."

"You haven't figured that out already?" Kevin asked with a hint of sarcasm. "Mom's pretty much useless in the morning. I'm honestly surprised she hasn't walked into the kitchen wearing nothing but panties and a T-shirt these past few days. She's been known to do that."

Ms. Swift had recovered enough of her mental faculties by that point to respond. "That's a mean thing to say about your mother."

"Doesn't make it any less true."

"I'm actually kind of surprised by that." Lilian's eyes were on Kevin. "You always get up so early that I sort of expected your mom to be an early bird as well."

Kevin nodded at her words. "Most people assume that, but I learned to wake up early on my own, because I knew that if I didn't, I would be going to school without breakfast... and I'd probably end up being late, since Mom normally doesn't wake up until nine or ten in the morning." He spared a glance at his mom. "I'm actually kind of surprised she woke up so early today."

"I'm up early today because I need to catch my flight back to France."

That caught the attention of everyone at the table, but none more so than Kevin. "You're leaving already?"

"Yep."

"But you've only been here for a few days."

"I technically wasn't supposed to leave France at all until Christmas break," Ms. Swift told her son. "I still have a lot of work to do. I need to interview several runway models and fashion designers for Vogue, and Elle has commissioned me for a story around Yves Saint Laurent's Fall collection."

Kevin's disappointed frown spoke volumes about his feelings. "Sounds like you're going to be busy."

"Yeah. Unfortunately, I don't know if I'll be able to make it home for Christmas this year." Ms. Swift gave her son an apologetic look. "I was only able to take time off now because I'm running ahead of schedule."

"I understand." And he did. His mom might not be much of a mother, but she always worked hard to provide for him. It was thanks to the work she did that they could afford to live so comfortably.

Ms. Swift's smile was proud, but also somewhat sad. "You always were a very mature and understanding boy. I'm very proud of you."

"M-Mom." Kevin turned his head away from everyone in the

room. He wasn't embarrassed by his mom giving him praise in front of Lilian. No. Certainly not. And the heat spreading across his cheeks was definitely not a blush either. No way.

Denial: It's a powerful defense mechanism.

***

When breakfast came to an end, Kevin carried his mom's suitcase to her car.

Ms. Swift clasped her hands behind her back, gazing at the two youngsters as they stood next to each other. Standing a respectful distance from the group, Kotohime observed the proceedings with the cool gaze of a samurai.

"Well, I suppose this is where we part ways for now."

"Yeah." Kevin shifted uncomfortably. "I guess it is."

"If I can't make it home for Christmas, I'll try to make it up to this summer, okay? Maybe we can go to Mexico or something?" Her eyes glinted at Lilian and Kotohime. "Your girlfriend and Kotohime are invited, too."

Kevin's face burned at his mother's words. "She's not my girlfriend," he muttered. Naturally, his words were ignored by all three females present.

"A trip to Mexico?" Lilian clasped her hands under her chin, her eyes visibly sparkling. "That sounds like so much fun!"

She could just imagine it; her and Kevin walking down the beach hand in hand, the water lapping at their bare feet. Lilian would eventually start a water fight with Kevin, who would retaliate by chasing her. He would catch her and pull her to the ground, which would end with her on her back and him on top. Then he would stare into her eyes, inexplicably drawn into the depths of her emerald gaze. Slowly, he would lean down to kiss her, and their kiss would be filled with passion. And that passion would soon turn into a raging bonfire as they began stripping each other of their swimsuits, which would end with her beloved ravishing her body right there on the white sandy shores, for hours on end.

Several seconds later, Lilian became a slack-jawed, drooling idiot. Kevin, Kotohime and Ms. Swift stared at the girl with matching "what the fuck?" expressions. Kevin waved a hand in front of the redhead's face, but received no response.

"Is it wrong that I am disturbed by this?" he asked. A second of silence followed his question before it was answered by Kotohime shaking her head.

"No. No, it is not."

"Good."

***

Several miles from Kevin's apartment was a large park, complete with playground, soccer field, tennis courts and a concession stand. Two Olympic-sized swimming pools were open during the summer months, though they were closed right now since it was fall. In the mild weather filled with falling leaves, it was the perfect place for Kevin's and Lilian's picnic.

Carrying a basket in one hand and a small cooler in the other, Kevin strode down a grassy hill to the soccer field. Lilian traveled by his side, and behind them, exactly six paces away, the ever-attentive Kotohime strolled with one hand resting on her katana.

"I'm so excited that we're finally going to have our picnic," Lilian beamed. She looked so ecstatic that Kevin couldn't help but smile.

"What are you getting so excited about? It's just a picnic."

Lilian's rebuttal came in the form of a very powerful pout.

"It's not 'just' a picnic. It's our first picnic together." She turned her head to fully look at him, her face emblazoned with a brilliant smile that made the world seem a lot less dreary. "That makes it special to me."

Well, geez, what could he say to something like that? And just how could this girl say something like that with such sincerity? Feeling like the world's biggest jerk for being so indecisive was bad enough. Her making comments infused with so much sweetness that he nearly choked on the fluff was like throwing gasoline on an already raging conflagration.

"A-ah... I-I see."

"Ufufufu, you're so cute when you act embarrassed like that."

... and she just butchered the entire moment with a rusty spork. Nice.

"... I really hate it when you laugh like that."

"Sorry, Kevin. It's—"

"If you mention how it's a part of your character concept, I'm going to start ignoring you."

The soccer field was quite large, about the size of two football fields, Kevin judged. Well-maintained grass lay trodden under their feet as they walked. Several dozen yards away, a group of children were running around, playing what looked like a game of tag.

They chose a shaded spot underneath a tree that had already lost most of its leaves to fall. Kevin laid a blanket down as Lilian pulled Tupperware and plates from the basket. Kotohime watched from nearby, her back against the tree and one hand casually gripping her katana.

When they finished setting everything up, Kevin couldn't keep from marveling at Lilian's spread. He picked up one of the sandwiches arranged on a disposable tray; a croquette sandwich stuffed with ground beef, sautéed mushrooms, lettuce and spinach, with some kind of light dressing.

"You really went all out today," he whistled. "This all looks amazing!"

Lilian's smile could outshine the sun, while the gentlest of blushes tainted her cheeks a lovely shade of pink. "Thank you. I had to get up a bit earlier than normal to make the bread and cook the beef, but I think it was well worth the effort."

"It looks delicious." It smelled delicious too. The scent alone was enough to almost make him drool.

Lilian leaned over in anticipation as Kevin took a bite out of the sandwich, watching with the eyes of a hawk—or a girl who'd just made her beloved a sandwich. Even Kotohime studied him with more attentiveness than normal, her expression indiscernible and scrutinizing.

"So how is it?" Lilian asked.

Kevin didn't answer at first, busy as he was savoring the flavor. When he pulled the sandwich away, it was only to stare at the food in awe.

"This… this tastes incredible. It's even better than some of the sandwiches I've eaten in France." And the French knew how to make their sandwiches.

The words were like a panacea for the redhead. Lilian's eyes shone with a brilliant luster, like gleaming twin stars. Truly, nothing made her happier than a compliment from the young man she'd chosen as her mate.

"I'm really glad you like it. I also made a potato salad." Lilian popped open the lid to a red container, spearing something that looked delicious onto a fork, which she then presented it to Kevin. "Here, try some."

"A-ah." Kevin leaned back a bit as Lilian brought the fork to his mouth. "I-I can feed myself, you know. You really don't have to do this."

"I know that, silly, but I want to do this for you." There was no pout this time, just Lilian's delightfully curled lips as she held the fork near his face. "I enjoy doing things like this for you, so please, just open up and say 'ah,' okay?"

Dang. How could he say no to that? This girl really knew how to push all the right buttons, and it didn't even look like she was trying.

"W-well," Kevin mumbled, "If you want to… then I guess it's okay."

"Thank you."

"B-be gentle please."

"Ufufufu, don't worry, I will. Are you ready? I'm putting it in."

Still leaning against her tree, Kotohime began twitching.

"You two are far too innocent," she mumbled, watching as Lilian fed Kevin. She paid careful attention to her charge. The way Lilian's eyes lit up as Kevin opened his mouth, and even went so far as to say "ah" for her, really was a sight to see. She would have found it adorable, were it not for her dislike of Kevin. The boy simply reminded her too much of another human she'd once known; a young man who'd rescued her from certain death and earned her unwavering loyalty… and her love.

It would be best not to reminisce about the past, Kotohime, the woman admonished herself.

"Would you like some food as well, Kotohime?"

The words startled her. Kotohime hadn't even realized that her charge was there until a tray of sandwiches was practically shoved under her nose.

"Thank you," Kotohime said graciously, leaning her sword against the tree and daintily grabbing one of the sandwiches. Ara. It really did taste good. She could understand Kevin's reaction a bit better now. "You really have become quite the chef," she complimented after a few more bites.

"I just followed the directions in the book," Lilian said modestly.

"You would be surprised by how many people can't follow simple directions," Kevin commented as he finished off his second sandwich. "My mom can't cook even when she's following simple instructions. The last time she tried cooking anything other than TV dinners, she nearly burned the apartment down. Heck, the last time she tried cooking a TV dinner, it exploded in the microwave."

"That's not a very nice thing to say about your mother."

"I love my mom," Kevin told Lilian, who's adorable pout made him want to squeeze her cheeks, "but I'm not going to lie and say she's a good, or even halfway decent cook. Didn't I tell you? The whole reason I learned how to cook was because I didn't want to keep eating takeout every night."

"No, you didn't tell me that, actually."

"Oh," Kevin said, right before he shrugged, "well, now you know."

"Right…"

After they finished eating, Kevin and Lilian cracked open some sodas from the cooler and enjoyed the carbonated beverage alongside the afternoon breeze.

Coach Deretaine would have a fit if he knew I was drinking soda. The thought amused Kevin, but he didn't think it for long as a voice called out to them.

"Kevin! Lilian!"

As one, Kevin and Lilian looked over to see Lindsay and what appeared to be her entire soccer team walking onto the field. The tomboy's black sport shorts wrapped snuggly around her toned hips, and the old sleeveless shirt she wore looked ready to fall apart at the lightest touch. A soccer ball was tucked under her left arm as she jogged up to them.

"Hey, Lindsay!" Lilian greeted her former rival for Kevin's affection. "I didn't expect to see you here."

"This place has the best soccer fields for a friendly scrimmage," the tomboy answered, her grin widening when she saw how close the two were. "Look at you two, getting all cozy with each other. You look like the perfect little couple."

While Kevin blushed and Lilian radiated inconceivable amounts of joy, the tomboy's attention shifted to the beautiful woman in the kimono. Kotohime struck an intimidating vision of incomprehensible loveliness, as per the usual. Her kimono that day was dark blue, and depicted a colossal wave like the kind people saw during storms.

"Good afternoon, Kotohime."

"Good afternoon, Lindsay-san."

Lindsay didn't think she would ever get used to the way Kotohime added a Japanese suffix to her name. It didn't even sound right with her American name.

"I see you're polishing your... katana."

Indeed she was. Sitting in *seiza* underneath the tree, Kotohime had removed her katana from its sheath and was laboriously, maybe even lovingly, polishing her blade with an almost tender caress.

It was all kinds of creepy.

"It is a very important process that you can never do too often," Kotohime responded, the *Uchiko Ball* in her left hand caressing the gleaming blade as if it were a lover. "The surface polish of a katana is just as important to the act of cutting as the geometry of the blade itself. It is especially important for the durability of the edge and surface friction of the blade. It would be very bad if I went into battle with a dull and unpolished katana, and my blade became stuck within the flesh, muscle and bone of the person I was gutting."

Upon finishing her explanation, Kotohime looked up from her work to see Lilian and Lindsay hiding behind a very frightened Kevin. All three of them were staring at her with wide-eyed expressions of pure terror.

Kotohime tilted her head in adorable confusion. "Ara? Was it something I said?"

***

After meeting Lilian and Kevin, Lindsay managed to somehow rope the redhead into playing a game of soccer, claiming they were one player short and needed her to play with them.

Although it was probably more accurate to say that Kevin had convinced Lilian, stating that he wanted to watch her play. Lindsay had been surprised when the beautiful girl actually blushed after Kevin's comment about how he thought she'd be really good at the sport.

Surprisingly enough, Lilian really wasn't that bad. It was obvious that she had never played soccer before, but dang if that girl couldn't kick. At least two of their goals were because of Lilian's impeccable aim and incredible kicking power. The ball had been in the net before the goalie even realized what happened.

Lindsay dribbled the ball down the soccer field, juking and weaving her way to the net on the opposing side. Other girls ran all around her, some trying to cover her and others attempting to take the ball from her.

While utilizing her unique talent for dribbling, Lindsay checked the field in her peripheral vision. Two people on her left were doing their best to keep someone from blindsiding her. Lilian was on her right, keeping pace just a few yards away.

"Lilian!"

Upon reaching the goal post, Lindsay punted the ball over to the redhead, whose pace suddenly picked up significantly. The increase in speed astounded Lindsay. It seemed almost unnatural, this sudden boost in acceleration.

Lilian leapt into the air and twisted around with an acrobat's grace, her body spinning along an axis as her foot slammed into the soccer ball, which launched it forward as if it had been fired from a cannon. It shot past the goalie and tore through the net like a rock through wet toilet paper, continuing on for several more yards before exploding against a tree in a shower of bark.

Lindsay shook her head in astonishment. Even after seeing this happen three times, it still amazed her. Who knew Lilian had so much power in those deceptively soft-looking legs?

"Lilian! That was amazing!" Lindsay ran up to the girl, her grin large enough to split her face.

Lilian's breasts swayed as she took a deep breath. "You think so?"

"Of course! I've never seen anyone kick a ball that hard before!" Lindsay's excited shout was almost drowned out by the other girls, who crowded around them to celebrate their success. Meanwhile, the other team looked like they were having a literal drop in morale. A black cloud of depression hung over their heads like a brewing thunderstorm, threatening to pour rain on them should they get any sadder.

"Well, thank you… I think."

"Anytime. Now let's keep playing!"

***

Kevin and Kotohime sat on the sidelines while Lilian played soccer.

An uneasy silence passed between them, though it might have been more on his side than Kotohime's. The maid-slash-bodyguard appeared as unflappable as always. She seemed completely unaware of the thickening tension, which grew as the indefinite silence continued.

So, naturally, Kevin tried to focus on something else.

Perhaps it was because of the mild weather that day—mild for September, at any rate—but Lilian had chosen to wear one of the outfits she'd bought with his mom. Her black skin-tight shorts appeared to have been painted on, and her tank-top stretched across her bust, revealing glorious curves that would send any man into a coma.

Yes, it was very easy to focus on nothing but that beautiful body as Lilian ran back and forth across the field.

I'm really glad Eric isn't here. God only knows what he would do if he saw Lilian like this.

As the game wore on and Lilian continued proving herself an amazing kicker, Kevin decided that he should do something nice for the girl. Every time he'd had track practice she'd always be there, keeping an ice-cold bottle of water and a towel ready for him. It was only right that he return the favor.

But what could he do for her? Maybe get her a nice gift? What about cooking a type of food that she hadn't tried?

Perhaps I could… hmm… oh, that might work.

Kevin glanced at his silent companion. Kotohime kept her attention on the game, her dark chocolate eyes locked onto Lilian as the redhead ran across the field. She seemed to be purposefully ignoring him. He tried not to let it bother him—too much.

"Hey, Kotohime?"

"Is there something you need, Kevin-san?"

"Has Lilian ever tried shaved ice?"

Kotohime broke her self-imposed attempt at ignoring Kevin, and regarded him with a curious gleam.

"Can you repeat that?"

"I asked if Lilian's ever had shaved ice?"

She pondered the question, trying to recall any time her charge might have had the human treat.

"No," she shook her head after giving the question due consideration, "I do not believe Lilian-sama has ever tried this shaved ice that you speak of."

"I thought so." Kevin stood up. "In that case, would you mind watching our stuff for a little while? I'll be back in a few minutes."

"You do not need to worry about that. I will not let anyone touch our supplies." Kotohime placed her left hand on the hilt of her katana. "And should they try to, well, no one can escape the bloody conclusion, ufufufu…"

Kevin shuddered.

"Erm… right…" By the gods, was this woman freaky. Who spoke of blood and killing so easily and laughed about it afterwards? "Well then… I… I'm going to get something real quick. Try not to kill anyone while I'm gone."

"I will do my best."

For some reason, Kotohime's words didn't inspire much confidence in him.

Kevin crested a small hill and scanned the park laid out before him, observing the various walkways surrounded by desert flora and fauna. He passed park benches sitting under shaded trees, or in the presence of giant saguaro cacti that overlooked the park like silent sentinels. The metal gates leading to the Olympic-sized swimming pools speared through the sparse foliage. Kevin remembered going there with his friends and causing a lot of trouble when he was younger.

Ah, good times.

The tiny little building beside the gates, which appeared especially minuscule sitting next to the much larger changing rooms, was Kevin's destination. He slowly ambled up to the window where an obese male with a severe acne problem and a basketball-shaped head stood. Kevin saw that he was reading a DC comic; Superman, it looked like.

"Can I get some shaved ice, please?"

"What size and what flavors?"

"Um, I'd like an extra-large with all five flavors."

Since he didn't know what Lilian would like, Kevin thought it best to let her try every flavor. Then she could tell him which one she liked best. It would be like a science experiment... only without the science part.

And perhaps he shouldn't have put the words "experiment" and "Lilian" in the same sentence. Now all he could think about was them sharing a bed and committing acts of passion and eroticism that were better left in an erotic novel... or an *ecchi* manga... or a *hentai*.

Whoa! Down boy! Kevin tried to ignore the tightening in his pants as he handed money to the guy at the register. He really hoped no one was paying attention to him. *Ugh, seriously? I'm getting turned on now of all times? Lilian isn't even present!*

It had been happening more often lately, the arousal he felt whenever he thought of Lilian. He'd never felt this way about anyone else, not even Lindsay. This desire, this craving, it was completely foreign to him. Several times he almost found himself wanting to take the redhead up on her offer of showering together. It was frightening, how badly he wanted her.

But that's not love, is it? I couldn't possibly allow us to become intimate without offering the same level of commitment she's offering me. She doesn't deserve that. And I don't deserve her.

After getting his shaved ice, Kevin was about to head back down to the soccer field. He didn't get very far, however, before three people he'd never seen before blocked his way.

They were a rather unique group of individuals. The first guy was so thin he reminded Kevin of a twig. He had wavy brown hair, and his hands and feet looked far larger on his rail-thin body than they would have on a normal person.

The second male staring Kevin down was large, the exact opposite of the skinny kid. If the first had been thinner than a toothpick, then this guy was larger than a whale. Actually, as Kevin studied the boy closer, he really did resemble a baby whale. The only person who could compete with him in the fat department was Kevin's boss.

The third was the most unusual of the group, if only due to

how normal he looked in comparison, like someone with brown hair standing beside two people with neon pink and lime green hair respectively. The only thing that appeared off about him was his height. Barely reaching up to Kevin's chest, the boy in the middle looked more like a junior high student than a high schooler.

"Can I help you three?" Kevin asked.

"You can help us by staying away from our Lilian!!" The skinny one shouted in a nasally tone.

"We don't want you hanging around our Lilian anymore!" This time it was the fat one, who spoke in what Kevin could only describe as a blubbery voice.

Kevin stared at the trio.

Blink. "Did you just say." Blink. "Your." Blink. "Lilian?" Blink. Blink.

"Are you deaf or something? Of course that's what we said! And if you know what's good for you, then you'll heed our advice and stay away from our Lilian!"

Kevin remained silent for a good three seconds, his face holding the same emotional range as a brick wall. In return, the three boys stared him down, as if they hoped glaring at him would cause Kevin to spontaneously combust.

"Right." Kevin scratched the back of his head with his free hand. "So, who are you guys exactly?"

"I'm Marcus Slim!" The skinny one introduced himself, bending his left leg while his right one remained straight, and extending his left arm. Kevin felt like he'd seen that strange pose somewhere before...

"I'm Ian Port!" The fat one mimicked Marcus' pose, only inverting it so that he was using the opposite limbs and facing the other way.

"And I'm Nick Brief!" The kid in the middle lowered his center of gravity, knees bending as he took a horse stance. He raised his arms above his head and crossed them to form a giant "x."

Kevin blinked several times as he heard the kid's surprisingly deep voice.

This kid would make a good Epic Movie Trailer Guy.

"And together we make the Lovely Lilian Lovers fanclub!" The trio shouted in eerie synchronicity, like they had rehearsed this several times before confronting him. Gaudy music reminiscent of the *Power Rangers* opening theme song started playing in the background. He looked for the source, but was unable to ascertain the source's location.

Several seconds passed. A gentle breeze blew through the clearing, and several crows cawed in a most annoying manner. Finally…

"Are you three into the *Power Rangers* or something?" Kevin asked. "It's totally cool if you are, but you might want to think about not doing that in public."

The trio, who had remained in their weird *sentai* poses until that point, tripped and fell face-first onto the hard concrete. They quickly jumped back to their feet, however, and shook three menacing fists at Kevin—at least, he thought they were supposed to look menacing. They actually looked kind of stupid.

"'Power Rangers?' 'POWER RANGERS?!'" Nick shouted. Kevin noticed that he was holding a hand to his nose. Blood leaked between his fingers. "We don't watch that crap! *Power Rangers* is just America trying to milk the success of authentic Japanese TV shows! We're fans of *Kamen Rider!*"

"You do realize we live in America, right?" Kevin was a fan of Japanese pop culture as much as the next manga-obsessed American teenager, but even he had his limits. "And it doesn't change the fact that *Kamen Rider* is a show made for children under the age of ten."

Once again, Nick growled. With his deep voice, it actually sounded kinda menacing, even though he was, like, under four feet tall.

"How dare you! Not only have you taken our Lilian from us, but you're also making fun of *Kamen Rider!*"

Kevin rolled his eyes.

"I haven't taken anyone from you. Lilian is free to do whatever she wants." It just so happened that "whatever she wants" meant spending time with him. "And don't talk about her like she's some kind of object."

"Don't think we don't know what you're trying to do! We don't know what you did to Lilian, but we know you've somehow coerced her into staying with you!"

"Yeah. Yeah. You're probably blackmailing her or

something!"

"You make me so mad!!!"

As the three began shouting at him, Kevin sighed and ran a hand down his tired face. "And they're not even listening to me."

"That does it!" Marcus screamed out in comical anger. The quivering of his red-faced jowls reminded Kevin of this filler episode to an anime he once watched, in which Wendy Marvell ended up becoming a member of the Butt Jiggle Gang. This guy's face was very reminiscent of those jiggling butts. "I'm not gonna let you get away with stealing our Lilian from us! You're going down!"

Wait. Did these three want to fight him? For real? Kevin wasn't one for violence; he'd never been in a real fight before—unless he counted the time Chris Fleischer ripped his chest open. And he didn't count that. Saying he'd gotten into a fight implied he actually fought, and he hadn't fought Chris so much as he'd nearly been killed trying to defend Lilian.

He could probably consider that time Kiara sent those three jabronis after him, but again, he hadn't really fought. It was mostly a series of coincidental events and dumb luck that kept him from having his ass handed to him on a silver platter.

Kevin was just about to try and talk his way out of this situation when something happened that shocked him speechless: the three high school boys began to transform.

Marcus became even thinner than he already was, his arms melding into his torso as his hair sunk into his head, which took on the form of an umbrella. The fat one, Ian, grew even fatter as his facial features shifted from his face to his stomach. His mouth turned into a large, gaping maw that reminded Kevin of the Saarlac pit. The last of the trio, Nick, burst into flames before his form took on a spherical shape, like a ball of noxious gas that had been lit on fire.

"You three are yōkai?" On any other occasion, Kevin would have smacked himself for asking such an obvious question. Of course they were yōkai. No human could transform like that, or at all, though he couldn't figure out what type of yōkai they were.

"That's right," Marcus said, "I'm a karakase-obake!"

"And I'm a blob!"

… Silence. Several crickets began chirping. A crow cawed

somewhere in the distance. Kevin even thought he heard a bullfrog, which he knew for a fact didn't even live in this park.

"Seriously?" Kevin's face looked as incredulous as he felt. "A blob? That's the kind of yōkai you are?"

"Don't look at me like that!" The gaping mouth on Ian's stomach flapped. By the gods, that was disturbing. "How would you like it if I made fun of you for being human!"

"I probably wouldn't care that much," Kevin shrugged. "But, seriously, a blob? I didn't even know there were yōkai like that, and I've watched *Inuyasha* and *Nurarihyon no Mago*."

"Whatever. It's not like being a blob was my choice."

"I guess not." Kevin looked at the flaming ball of... soul? He wasn't sure. Could souls even catch on fire? "So what are you? A will-o-wisp?"

"Don't compare me to those inferior yōkai!" Okay. So, apparently, the great ball of fire took offense to being called a will-o-wisp. "I'm a hi-no-tama!"

"Uh huh..." Kevin rubbed the back of his neck. "Aren't you guys supposed to, I don't know, not reveal yourselves to humans? I thought there was some kind of law against this."

"You're the only human here," Nick pointed out. Kevin blinked. He then looked around the park to note that, yes, he really was the only other person in sight.

On a side note, hearing a voice come from a ball of fire was kinda creepy. It really didn't help that Nick's deep "Movie Trailer Guy" voice had become distorted, growing even deeper and more gruff than before.

But there were more important things to worry about.

"Eh? Where did everyone go?"

Like the lack of people. Kevin knew for a fact that there had been at least six other people present when these three confronted him. Where was the family with that cute little girl walking her dog? What happened to that old fart with the cane? Even the guy behind the concession stand had disappeared! What the heck?

"Who cares?" Marcus exclaimed. "The only thing that matters is that no one's around to see us while we get rid of you!"

Oh, this was just great. He was alone with three yōkai, all of whom hated his guts and wanted to "teach him a lesson" for something that was beyond his ability to control. And because there was no one present to witness it, the trio was free to use their powers with reckless abandon. Well, except for the hi-no-tama. Kevin really hoped that one would limit the use of his powers, as he had no desire to see damage done to the surrounding wildlife.

Either way, Kevin knew that he was screwed.

He moaned piteously.

Why does crap like this always happen to me?

***

Lilian had noticed Kevin leaving mere minutes after he disappeared. She'd felt his eyes on her throughout the game until then. It was the whole reason she had kept playing. Knowing that he was watching made her feel special, like he only had eyes for her, like she was the most important person in his life, just as he was in hers.

Her desire to continue playing waned with his absence.

Much to Lindsay's chagrin, Lilian begged off playing another round, and went over to Kotohime. The kimono-clad femme looked up as she approached.

"You played a most admirable game, Lilian-sama."

"Thanks," Lilian said absentmindedly. "Where's Kevin?"

"He went out," Kotohime answered swiftly, "I believe he was going to get something called shaved ice." Lilian didn't know what shaved ice was, and the look she gave her vassal made that more than obvious. "Do not look at me. The only times I've spent in the presence of humans these past one-hundred years is when you had me go out and buy manga. I do not what know what shaved ice is either."

Lilian decided to accept her maid's words at face value. It wasn't like she cared about shaved ice either way.

"Which way did he go?"

"That way."

Lilian looked at the direction Kotohime pointed toward, and then dashed off at a quick trot. She hoped Kevin hadn't gone too far.

Muu, Lilian pouted as she crested a hill, *if he was going to go somewhere, he could have at least taken me with him.*

***

It must be a curse god, Kevin moaned. *There's a curse god after me. I bet it's a stupid little girl who wears a frilly red dress with green ribbons and likes to spin around a lot.*

It was the only logical explanation he could think of to explain his situation—never mind the illogicalness of blaming a curse god for his problems. It made sense to him. Not only was this the second time he'd been chased by yōkai in the past month, it was also the second time three people had wanted to beat him up, for one reason or another.

Speaking of those three, Kevin looked behind him—

"Holy crap!"

—and then squealed like a little girl when a nearby cactus spontaneously combusted after being struck by a fireball. He looked back to see the hi-no-tama preparing to launch another one at him. It flared brilliantly like a ball of, well, fire, almost as if the anticipation of being launched at him was exciting to it.

Except it's a ball of fire. Fire isn't sentient—unless you're a yōkai, I guess.

"Would you stop throwing those things already?! You're destroying the environment, idiot! Don't you know that various animals make their homes in those cacti and—hiii!"

Kevin quickly ducked when another ball of fire nearly smacked him in the face. The fireball missed, but ended up setting the bush it hit ablaze.

"Don't call us idiots! You're the one who's an idiot! Just stand still and die like a man!"

"You just proved my point! Who the heck would stand there and let themselves be—OH, MY GOD!"

Kevin swerved at the last second and avoided another fireball, which nearly slammed into his back. He could feel the blistering heat sear into his skin, and the back of his shirt actually began to burn since the fireball was so close. That yōkai was really trying to kill him!

Not good. This was so, so, so not good. Why did this always happen to him? He was a good person, wasn't he? He'd never done anything bad before. He never drank, never did drugs, didn't bully people, respected the elderly, and did all the things that a good, mature and responsible young man should do.

So why the hell does this keep happening to me?!

Because it's funny.

"Shut up, you idiot!"

… A pause.

"Wait. Who the heck am I talking to?! What the heck is going —oh, sweet baby Jesus!"

Kevin dodged another fireball, which slammed into a bench and exploded in a shower of fiery splinters. He yelped when several of those splinters struck his shirt and burnt straight through to his skin.

"Stop shooting those, dang it!"

"Stop moving and I will!"

"Like I would possibly believe that—EEK!"

Another fireball. He swerved right, dodging it. The ground several feet in front of him burst into flames and Kevin swore.

"Dang it. At this rate, that guy's going to set the whole park on fire."

More than a third of the park was already up in flames. The fires were slowly spreading to the rest of the park, though, so it wouldn't be long before the entire place turned into a giant cinder.

He needed to think of something, and fast.

"Holy flying—WHOA!"

The blob came out of nowhere, flying straight at him. Kevin avoided being flattened like a pancake by rolling across the ground, but it was a near thing, and it hurt. He gritted his teeth at the jarring impact, feeling his shoulder pop out of place. Whoever said shoulder rolls were easy had obviously never tried one.

I think I'm beginning to hate Link. He makes doing crap like this look easy.

While the blob bounced along the ground like a rubber ball, Kevin found the karakase-obake standing a couple yards in front of him.

Its umbrella top was spinning.

It was also spitting… water?

"Ga!"

Kevin hissed as the water hit his skin and began eating away at it. Okay. It wasn't water. Acid, then? Whatever it was, he couldn't afford to get anymore on him. That stuff burned.

He dove to the left, avoiding another fireball, which exploded against a bench. He then turned and ran off the cement path, using the cacti and trees as cover. He saw several birds, a couple of squirrels and even a poor little bunny running away from the melting, burning landscape.

He winced.

"Sorry, little woodland—desertland creatures. I really don't want you guys getting involved, but I also don't want to die." A pause. "And I doubt this small habitat will last long with these three chasing me, regardless of where I go."

Moving faster than he ever had before, faster even than when he raced against Chase, Kevin wove through the desert landscape. This didn't stop the trio of angry and jealous yōkai from chasing him, but it did slow them down, giving him some time to think.

Kevin Swift had never been one for religion. He didn't begrudge others who were religious, but he hadn't been brought up to believe in one himself. He'd never gone to church or anything of the sort, but in that moment, Kevin prayed. He prayed for a miracle to get him out of this situation.

"Oh, dear baby Jesus. Please, please, please don't let these yōkai catch me, or light me on fire, or harm me in some way. Oh! And save the animals, too. They really don't deserve having their homes burned down, especially not for a reason like this."

Yes, those were prayers. And, oddly enough, someone answered Kevin's most unusual prayers. It just wasn't answered by any god.

"What do you three think you're doing to my mate?!"

"Lilian?!"

It was, indeed, Lilian who found them. She stood some distance away, hands on her hips and a surprisingly intimidating glare marring her features. She stared daggers at the trio of yōkai chasing him. Her foxy ears had been let out, and they twitched violently as if to emphasize her displeasure. Her two white-tipped fox-tails writhed behind her like a pair of king cobras spitting venom.

"My Lilian!" The three yōkai boys cried out in unison, happy tears streaming out of their eyes as they gazed upon the object of their obsession. It didn't seem to matter that she looked ready to flambé them, or that her body was shaking in apoplectic rage. They seemed joyous merely to bask in her presence.

Kevin would have shuddered, but another fireball came close

to turning him into a pile of ash, forcing him to swerve.

"Did you just say that I was 'your Lilian?'" The redhead twitched, and the writhing of her tails became increasingly intense. Ominous shadows hid her eyes as Lilian lowered her head, long locks of crimson falling in front of her face. "You know what? I take my question back. I don't care why you're chasing my mate anymore. It doesn't matter. All that matters is that you are, and I'm going to teach you three a lesson."

Oh boy. She was serious. In all the time he'd known her, Kevin had never seen such a severe and menacing look on her face. Was this what Chris went up against after he'd passed out from blood loss? Scary.

"How could you say something like that, Lilian?" Nick seemed genuinely shocked. At least, his voice did. It was kinda hard to tell since he was a ball of fire and all. "He doesn't deserve to have someone like you in his life! He's just a human!"

Kevin winced.

"I'll be the judge of that," Lilian said as bright orangish yellow fox-fire burst into existence, hovering over the tips of her tails. "Now get lost!"

With a ferocious shout, Lilian launched the fox-fire at the trio of supernatural creatures. The first one struck the blob in the face—um, stomach—while the second one hit the umbrella, setting it alight.

"Uwa! I'm on fire! I'm on fire! Get it off! Get it off!"

"Don't you mean put it out?"

"Shut up and help me!"

"What do you want me to do? I'm a hi-no-tama. I light things on fire. I don't put them out. Do a barrel roll or something."

"UWA! Hot! Hot! HOT!"

While the blob was launched backwards and the karakase-obake began rolling along the floor—which did absolutely nothing to put out the fire consuming its umbrella head—Lilian threw a light sphere at the hi-no-tama, which didn't even flinch and continued sending fireballs at Kevin.

"Ha! Your Celestial powers may be devastating, but my elemental nature is fire. Something as simple as that won't work on me—"

"Then try this on for size!"

SMACK!

"OOOF!"

Kevin watched in mute shock as one of Lilian's tails extended and struck the hi-no-tama with incredible force. The fire-natured yōkai went sailing into air, screaming loudly. It ascended higher and higher into the sky, its form getting smaller with each passing second before it vanished in a twinkle of light.

"And now for you two! Stay away from my mate!"

An angry Lilian launched more and more light spheres at the two remaining yōkai, causing them to scurry away in fear. Kevin simply stood there like an idiot, watching Lilian thrash the three unusual beings that had given him so much trouble.

He also made a mental note never to get on Lilian's bad side. She was really scary when angry.

When the three yōkai were gone, Lilian turned to Kevin, breathing hard, as if she'd just finished running a marathon. Her eyes scanned his body, searching for what he could only guess were injuries.

"Are you okay? You're not hurt anywhere, are you?"

"Not unless you count my pride," Kevin muttered softly. Lilian's ears twitched.

"Did you say something?"

"… No," Kevin shook his head. "I didn't say anything. Thanks for the rescue."

Lilian beamed at him. "Of course. I'll always come to your rescue whenever you need it."

Kevin tried to ignore the clenching in his gut. He looked around—and promptly sweatdropped.

"Uh, Lilian?"

Lilian was all smiles. "Yes, Kevin?"

"What are we going to do about, well, all this?" Kevin gestured to the surrounding area. What trees and cacti hadn't been burned to cinders by the hi-no-tama had melted due to the karakase-obake's acid. The cement pathways were fragmented where the blob's fat and surprisingly dense body had landed. Scorch marks littered the ground, and several fires still burned brightly nearby, sending their plumes of smoke into the sky like a Moltres rising out of a volcano. It looked like a warzone.

"Uh… leave before anyone can pin the blame on us?"

Kevin deadpanned. "That's not what I was talking about."

"… Mugyu…"

"Don't go picking up random catch phrases!"

***

It was evening.

Dinner had ended a while ago. Kevin knew that, were he to turn his head, he would find Kotohime washing the dishes, humming a soft tune that sounded suspiciously like the opening theme song for *Death Note*. Lilian was probably in the restroom.

He leaned against the wall, staring at the darkening sky. The sun remained invisible, hidden behind a thick layer of dark clouds. Lightning streaked through them, flashes came and went within a split second. They perfectly reflected the stormy collection of thoughts that gathered within his mind.

On August 19th, almost one and a half months ago, Kevin had been an ordinary high school student. There had been nothing particularly special about him other than his ability to sprint short distances in seconds, his independent streak, and a severe inability to talk to girls.

Now he was living with a fox-girl who wanted to mate with him, her equally foxy maid who didn't like him, and had discovered that yōkai actually existed. He'd also been in several confrontations with various yōkai, some of which had ended with violence, and one of which ended with him befriending a violent yuki-onna. It went without saying but, for an ordinary high school student like him, it was all getting to be a tad bit overwhelming.

Man, when life throws a curveball, sometimes it really curves.

"There you are." Kevin turned his head as Lilian joined him on the balcony. Her pink pajama bottoms looked awfully cute. It contrasted well with the large T-shirt she wore, which fell off her left shoulder, leaving her unblemished and perfect skin visible. "I was wondering where you had wandered off to. What are you doing out here?"

"I was just thinking," Kevin answered, turning his head back to stare at the sky.

Lilian stopped on his left and placed her hands on the wall. "What are you thinking about?"

Kevin did his best to ignore the feeling of Lilian's eyes on him. "A lot of things. So much has happened recently, and I guess I'm having some trouble wrapping my head around it all."

"A lot has happened lately, hasn't it?" Lilian shuffled just a bit closer to Kevin. "My fight with Kiara and Chris, that stupid goth tsun-loli, and those three other yōkai we ran into today. I can see how this would be overwhelming for anyone. But you know what?"

Kevin turned his head and was struck speechless.

Bright green eyes shone with a vibrancy that even the brightest star could never hope to match. Lilian's lips had curved in an expression of tenderness and love that he'd only ever seen from her.

Were her lips always that glossy?

"I wouldn't trade it for the world, because I get to be with you. Even with everything that's happened, all I need to do is look at you to know that every hardship I've been through was worth it."

It was like a chain reaction. Kevin's heart thumped like a ticking time bomb, pumping blood straight to his face, which he already knew was boiling lobster red. Why did everything this girl say have to be so heartfelt and genuine?

He looked back at the sky, more to give himself time to master his blush than for any other reason.

"That's something I don't really understand," he said into the silence. "Why me? Out of all the guys you could possibly choose to be with, why do you want me to be your mate? I'm not that special. I'm just a jock who can run really fast."

"Because I love you," Lilian answered simply, as if it should have been obvious.

"Why though?" he pressed. "I'm nothing special. I've got no talent that makes me unique, nothing that makes me stand out. This isn't some kind of anime, where the beautiful girl falls in love with the main character just because he showed her a bit of kindness. Things like that don't happen in real life."

Lilian's answering sigh was so despondent it made Kevin feel like kicking himself in the balls.

"I wish I could give you a straight answer," she told him sadly, "but I honestly don't know what to tell you. We kitsune are ruled by our emotions, so I don't even really understand why I feel so strongly about you. I just know that I love you." Lilian shrugged. "That's enough for me."

Yeah, well, that wasn't enough for Kevin. He couldn't just go with the flow. He wanted—no, he needed to understand these feelings. Kevin couldn't afford to go with his whims, to be guided by transient desires, not if he wanted to keep from following in his old man's footsteps.

He chose his next words carefully. "I heard from Kotohime that a kitsune's first mate is a pretty big thing in your culture."

"Oh? She told you that?"

"Yes."

"Hmm, I'll have to speak with her later. I didn't want something like that coloring your perceptions."

"Why?"

"Because you're too nice." Lilian ignored the look he sent her and stared at the sky, hands clasped behind her back. "If you found out how important a kitsune's first mate is, I thought you might decide to start dating me because you felt obligated to. I don't want you to be with me because of something like that. I want you to become my mate because you love me, you know?"

Kevin was astounded by her answer. Truly, this girl's love for him was more pure than fresh snow.

He looked back at the desert landscape. "Yeah. I can understand that."

"Also, kitsune mating isn't really a cultural thing. It's just... instinct."

"Instinct?"

"Yes." Lilian's red hair swayed as she nodded. "All kitsune instinctively know what they want in a mate. It's... I guess you could say it's almost like the traits we look for in a mate is hardwired into our DNA. Something like that. I don't really understand the whole thing. I kinda fell asleep when Daphne was lecturing me on that part."

Kevin chuckled when an image of Lilian, her face planted on the desk as she snored away, entered his mind. It was, not so surprisingly, a very cute image.

"Anyway, that's more or less the gist of it. When we find someone who has the traits we desire in a mate, we seek to make them ours. It supposedly has something to do with our desire to procreate and have kits. Even kitsune like myself, who have not gone through a single mating period, have this instinct hardwired into us."

"Mating period?"

"A lesson for another time," Lilian determined. "This chapter is beginning to get a bit too long."

"Right..." Kevin felt a drop of sweat trickle down his forehead. "I guess I kinda understand what you're getting at. I mean, it's sort of the same with humans. Not the instinct thing, but how we look for people who we think are desirable and stuff. That still doesn't explain why, out of all the people on this planet, you chose me."

Lilian sighed, her shoulder slumping a bit. "If you don't remember, then I'm not going to tell you."

Kevin tilted his head. "Remember? Tell me what?"

"Nothing," Lilian muttered morosely.

Kevin gave her a strange look, and Lilian responded by shuffling closer to him. He only had a moment to be surprised before she grabbed his arm, wrapped it around her waist, and set her head on his shoulder.

"Let me stay like this for a while, okay?" she murmured softly in his ear. "All this talk of mates is making me a little depressed."

Kevin wished he could claim ignorance about the origins of Lilian's sadness, but even he wasn't that stupid. He knew why she was sad, and that knowledge made his stomach twist.

"Okay."

He ignored his own discomfort in favor of letting Lilian do as she pleased. It was the least he could do after she saved him from those yōkai today, especially since he hadn't been able to give her the shaved ice, having dropped it during the yōkai trio's initial attack.

Lilian's hair carried the scent of lilacs, reminding him of spring. Her scent didn't bring him comfort, however, but did the opposite instead. He still didn't know what to do.

Not matter what anyone said, Kevin wasn't sure he'd ever be what Lilian needed in a mate. It wasn't like he'd had many great male role models to show him what to do in a situation like this.

Kevin thought about his father, the man he'd never met, the man who abandoned his mom. Loyalty. Fealty. Those words had meant nothing to that man. He had abandoned the woman who'd sired his son, leaving her alone and stricken with grief, forcing her to work several times harder than what should have been necessary just to survive.

How could someone who had the blood of a man like that flowing through them ever be able to accept and return the love of another?

Lilian deserves better.

Standing underneath the September sky, with a beautiful vixen in his arms, Kevin's mind was consumed by dark thoughts, which the sky seemed to mirror. That night, there wasn't a single star to be seen, covered as it was by dark clouds rolling in from the west.

Chapter 10

Secret Asian Man

"And time!"

Kevin Swift slowed his all-out sprint to a jog and then to a walk after passing the finish line. Several sweaty bangs fell into his eyes, which he brushed away with some minor irritation. He really did need a haircut.

Coach Deretaine stared at his stopwatch, blinking. "Twelve-point-fifteen. Not a bad time, Swift. You've been getting better. You've surpassed your old average again."

Still trying to catch his breath, Kevin took a moment to answer. "Thanks, Coach."

"Whatever," Chase grumbled. "I could… have gotten… that time… too…"

"Say that when you aren't lying on your back, Chase."

"Bite me."

"All right," Coach Deretaine pocketed his stopwatch. "I plan on running you two through a few more sprints, but take a quick break. Hydrate yourselves and rest up."

"Yes, Coach," Kevin said while Chase mumbled incoherently.

Chase slowly clambered to his feet as Coach Deretaine started yelling at other members of the team. His breathing was hard, and his cheeks were redder than a blimp. He walked over to Kevin with a noticeable limp.

"How have… how have you gotten so fast?" he asked.

Kevin did the infamous Shaft head tilt to convey his

confusion. "What do you mean?"

"Don't play dumb," Chase spat, his demeanor suddenly turning fierce. "Last week you were barely able to make thirteen seconds, and now you're running at twelve-point-fifteen? People don't improve that quickly."

"You do remember that I wasn't feeling too hot last week, don't you?" Truth be told, he wasn't feeling too good this week either, but it wasn't due to lack of sleep. "Anyway, if you don't like how much faster I am than you, then maybe you should think about training harder."

"That's easy for you to say," Chase grumbled. "You're the one who's getting times nobody has a right to achieve. I've been working my ass off, and I still haven't gone past twelve-point-fifty-eight."

"Not my problem."

"Tch."

Kevin turned away as Chase grew silent, his mind continuing to run wild even though his body was still. It happened often lately. Whenever he wasn't occupied by strenuous physical activities, his mind became consumed by guilt. He just couldn't stop obsessing over his current situation.

Only the act of running gave him any respite, however temporary it might have been. That desire to reach the finish line, to defeat his opponent, gave him the focus needed to push aside his problems. Too bad each sprint only lasted around twelve seconds.

"I noticed Lilian isn't with you today."

"She said she had something else to do today. Last I saw, she was headed for the library."

"Really?" Chase quirked an eyebrow. "So, she finally got tired of watching you, huh? About time, if you ask me."

"Nobody asked you," Kevin snapped. "The only reason she's not here is because I asked her not to come."

"Ah, I take it there are some problems in paradise?"

Kevin sighed. He'd been doing that a lot lately. Sighing, that is. "I guess you could say that."

"You wanna talk about it?"

Kevin thought about it for a moment, before deciding he had nothing to lose. And Chase actually had experience with girls, so maybe the older boy could give him some advice.

Or maybe he'll just make fun of me.

Kevin laid out his problem for Chase, telling him of Lilian's feelings and his own confusion. It took nearly ten minutes, and by the time he finished, Chase was frowning.

"That does sound like a bit of a problem. And you're saying Lilian's serious about this? Like, seriously serious?"

"It's more than just her being serious." Kevin ran a hand through his sweaty hair. "I can't really go into details, because I honestly don't understand them myself." Half-true. For obvious reasons, Kevin couldn't give Chase the entire story. "But, suffice it to say that Lilian's not looking for a simple high school romance. She wants something more permanent. More lasting."

"I think I can kinda see where you're coming from." Chase nodded in a sagely manner. "I would be pretty annoyed if someone wanted to be in a serious relationship with me. I mean, we're in high school. Who the hell marries the person they dated in high school? Nevermind the first person they ever dated, period. That crap just doesn't happen often."

"It's not that." Sweat flew off Kevin's hair as he shook his head. "To be honest I... I don't think I would mind being in a more permanent relationship with her. I'm just not sure if I really deserve to be with her. I don't know if I can give her the same commitment that she's willing to give me. Lilian is such an amazing person. Sure, I found her annoying at first, but I think I only felt that way because I was so hung up on Lindsay that I couldn't see anyone else in that light."

"Don't forget that you couldn't even talk to girls without passing out."

Kevin grimaced. "Did you really have to bring that up?"

"Yes."

"You're a real friend," Kevin said, his voice rank with sarcasm. "You know that?"

"I try," Chase grinned when Kevin glared at him. He became serious moments later. "So why don't you think you deserve to be with her?"

That was the question, wasn't it? There were many reasons he didn't deserve someone like Lilian, a lot of which he didn't want to share with anybody, much less Chase.

He looked down at his hands. They looked so weak, so frail,

so human.

"Because I'm weak. Every time a problem comes along, Lilian's always been the one who solves it. She hasn't needed my help at all. Even if I tried to help, I'd only become a liability."

He thought about that time with Chris. Had it not been for Lilian, he would have died that day. Of course, he wouldn't have been in trouble in the first place if not for her, but that was just semantics.

It was the most recent event, however, that had solidified his uselessness. Those three yōkai who attacked him had been losers. Literally. Their human forms were pathetic and nerdy, and their yōkai forms were just as bad. Even that hi-no-tama had looked ridiculous, like a fart engulfed in flames, yet he'd been powerless against it.

"She needs someone who can stand by her side and support her as an equal. As you are right now, you're just a liability."

Kevin gritted his teeth. Kotohime was right. He was a liability. He couldn't protect Lilian. He couldn't even protect himself.

Even if I returned the love Lilian has for me, it wouldn't do any good. I'd still be a liability. His mirthless smile reflected his inner thoughts perfectly. *She's better off without me.*

He'd never been bothered by his own humanity before, but there was always a first time for everything, he supposed.

"Well, I can definitely see how that would be a problem," Chase admitted. "I mean, needing a girl to fix all your problems is pretty pathetic. You've probably lost a couple hundred man points for that."

"Oh, shut up."

"But, honestly, I think you're looking at this the wrong way." Chase looked at the track field, eyes staring at something only he could see. "All you're thinking about is how you feel. You feel like you don't deserve to be with Lilian. You're the one who feels pathetic. Did you ever stop to think that maybe Lilian doesn't think that way? That maybe the reason she chases after you so fervently is because she believes you're not pathetic, that you do deserve to be with her. That maybe, just maybe, you have something that she believes is worth chasing after?"

"I... no. I've never thought about it like that."

Chase shrugged. "Then maybe that's your problem. You're

only thinking about yourself. Try putting yourself in Lilian's shoes. There's obviously something about you that she finds worthy of her. She wouldn't still be chasing after you if she thought you weren't worth all that time and effort."

"When we find someone who has the traits we desire in a mate, we seek to make them ours."

Kevin remained silent, recalling Lilian's words.

"Maybe you're right," Kevin admitted slowly. "I've been focusing so much on how I feel that I never really took Lilian's feelings into account."

"That's because you're an idiot who has no experience with women."

"Hey!"

"On the other hand, I am an experienced and cultured young man who has already dated several girls, and therefore, have more knowledge about them than you."

"Ugh, whatever." Kevin found that he didn't have any ground to stand on in this argument, so he just dropped the subject. "At least I can run faster than you."

Chase's face turned red. "That won't always be the case! You might be having your fifteen minutes of fame right now, but just wait, I'll eventually catch up to you, and when I do, you'll be eating my dust!"

"I'll believe that when I see it."

"Chase, Swift! If you've got time to be arguing, you've got time to do some running! Get over here!"

"Yes, Coach!" They gave each other one last glare before jogging over to the starting line.

***

The library was the only place outside of the locker rooms that remained open while the gym was undergoing repairs.

A large cylindrical building made of brick, grass and steel, the library looked like a giant rectangle with a single spire jutting out of the ground from its hindquarters.

Bookshelves lined the walls and created numerous aisles for people to walk down. A small section near the cylindrical spire was dedicated to computer stations, while the center contained tables and chairs for people to read or do their homework at.

Lilian Pnéyma sat at one of the tables reading a *shōjo* manga, a love story, and one that she hadn't read yet. Perhaps it was a little odd for a girl, but she'd always been a bigger fan of *shōnen* than *shōjo*. She just preferred stories with more action.

Lilian wasn't reading this manga for the sheer enjoyment of it, however. Oh no. She was researching. Her eyes scanned each page, studying everything within them in great detail. Only after she had memorized the entire page would she move onto the next.

As she continued reading, a scowl crossed her face.

"Why doesn't this thing have any useful information?!"

"Shhh!"

Lilian ignored the strange shushing noises coming from all around her. She also ignored the glares she could feel at her back. They weren't important. "Doesn't this stupid thing have anything I can use in it?!"

"SSHHH!!"

"Lilian?"

Looking up from her manga, Lilian saw Lindsay standing before her holding what looked like a soccer manual.

"Hello, Lindsay," Lilian said morosely. She went back to studying her manga.

"Everything okay? You seem a little down."

"Yeah... I'm fine," she mumbled.

"Uh huh..." Lindsay's tone conveyed skepticism, but she didn't inquire any further. "So what are you doing here?"

"Researching."

"Researching?" Lindsay sat down opposite of Lilian. "What are you researching exactly?"

Lilian sighed, but stopped paying attention to her manga. It wasn't helping anyway. "I've been trying to research ways to help me get closer to Kevin."

Lindsay looked bemused. "And you're doing that by reading manga?"

"Kevin had this manga in his collection, so he must like it. I thought there would be something in here that I could use to bring us closer together. It's also a surprisingly good story," she admitted. "Though it hasn't given me any helpful ideas."

Lindsay slowly shook her head. "I don't think I'll ever understand your enjoyment of manga. Kevin, I get. He's a guy.

267

They like comics and stuff—"

"Manga," Lilian interrupted.

"Excuse me?"

"It's called manga, not comics. Comics are made in America. Manga are from Japan."

"Same difference." Lilian's resulting frown made Lindsay feel like she'd stepped on a bed of spikes. "A-anyway, it doesn't really change my point. Guys like that kind of stuff. They enjoy stories with explosions and superpowers and whatnot. But you're a girl, so I don't know why you'd enjoy reading something like that."

"You just don't understand because you've never read a manga before," Lilian insisted. "These aren't just stories filled with cool battles. A lot of manga are actually really complex, and can cover everything from life-lessons to differences in moral philosophies and how there's no such thing as good or evil, just shades of gray. There's a lot of intriguing concepts in here, and the artwork is beautiful. Besides, not all manga are action stories."

Lilian held up the manga she'd been reading.

"This one is, for example, is a romance. It's about a girl with jet-black hair, a sinister smile and a silent demeanor. Because of this, she's often mistaken for a horror movie character called Sadako. However, behind her scary demeanor is a misunderstood teenager. All she wants to do is make friends, but she's just too shy to fit in. When a popular boy from her school befriends her, she makes more than just friends—she makes enemies, too. It's a very sweet romance, and it won the best *Shōjo* Manga award several years ago."

"Okay, I'll admit, that does sound kind of interesting." Lilian smiled in triumph, but Lindsay soon burst her bubble. "However, I don't see how this manga will have anything that you can use. You're hardly the shy, misunderstood heroine."

"I was actually putting Kevin in place of the shy, misunderstood heroine."

At that very moment on the track field, Kevin Swift felt an inexplicable sense of shame and self-loathing, along with a major drop in his HP gauge. This caused him to trip over his own two feet as he raced down the track, which subsequently caused him to face-plant into the hard polyurethane.

Lindsay snorted. "I doubt he'd appreciate that. And I still

don't think you'd find anything useful. He might not be the most outgoing person I know, but he's not one of the shy, unpopular types either."

"I know." Lilian slumped in her seat. "I was just hoping I would be able to find something useful in here. None of my H-series have helped me, so I wanted to try something different."

"H-series? What is... no. You know what? Never mind. I don't want to know." A pause. "Anyway, I thought I told you not to worry and just let things go at their own pace. Kevin likes you, that much is obvious to anyone who's seen you two together. You just need to give him some time to figure this out."

"I don't want to wait for him to figure this out!" Lilian growled and stood up before slamming her hands on the table, just because she could. "I want to be with him now! My heart is aching for him and my body yearns for his touch." She slammed her hands on the table... again. "I'm sick and tired of waiting! I want him to profess his love, then bend me over this table and ravish me until I've screamed myself hoarse!"

By the end of her rant, Lilian was shouting. Loudly. Very loudly. Nearly everyone in the library had heard her thunderous, ear-piercing rant, and they all stared at her, eyes wide and jaws dropped. The librarian looked absolutely scandalized.

"Uh..." Lindsay blushed as she stared at her friend. Heavily. Her nose was also bleeding, and she discreetly wiped it off with her sleeve before anyone could notice. "Lilian... you... did you really have to..."

"What?"

"N-nothing. Never mind."

Lilian frowned at the tomboy. She opened her mouth, but didn't get a chance to speak.

"Lilian Pnéyma!" A loud shout reverberated throughout the room. Lilian groaned as she turned to see Ms. Vis stomping up to them, her expression marred by RIGHTEOUS ANGER™—and indignation, but mostly RIGHTEOUS ANGER™. "How dare you—in all my years—why, I've never. How could you say something so shameless? And in a library of all places!"

Lilian grimaced. She so did not need this.

Ms. Vis clearly didn't care what she needed, and continued ranting. "I do not know how your parents raised you, but they clearly did not do a very good job. You cannot shout in a library, and you should never say something so… so scandalous in public, or anywhere for that matter. It appears that someone must educate you on proper, lady-like behavior. I believe it is time that you and I had a very long heart-to-heart conversation, young woman."

"Um, no."

Lilian stared at the pasty-looking vampire-esque teacher, enforcing her will upon the older woman through the use of an enchantment. She watched, satisfied when she saw the lights in the older woman's eyes dim.

"You and I don't need to have a conversation," Lilian said, waving her hand through the air.

"We don't need to have a conversation…" Ms. Vis droned.

"We have already spoken at great length about this, and have come to an understanding." Another hand wave.

"We have already spoken at great length and come to an understanding…."

"Now, you are going to go out, buy several gallons of rubbing alcohol and take a bath in it." One last hand wave.

"I need to buy several gallons of rubbing alcohol and take a bath…"

As Ms. Vis walked out of the library, Lilian sat back down, looking satisfied.

Lindsay stared. "W-what just happened?"

"Hm?" Lilian tilted her head, before she realized what Lindsay was asking about. "Oh, that? Don't worry." She waved a hand dismissively. "That was just me using my Jedi mind trick to make Ms. Vis leave us alone."

Lindsay blinked, the time it took for her to compute Lilian's sentence. Ever so slowly, she nodded.

"Okay. Right. I understand. Every girl needs her secrets."

Lilian smiled and winked at the tomboy. "I'm glad you understand."

"By the way, where's your, um, bodyguard?"

"Don't know. Don't care. I'm busy."

"… Right…"

***

Kotohime watched the woman scan her groceries, her dark gaze sharper than razor blades. The store employee—Susan, her name tag said—looked like she wanted to piss herself, quivering as she was under the swordwoman's piercing stare.

Suddenly, Kotohime sneezed.

"Bless you."

"Thank you." Kotohime wiggled her nose cutely, and then went back to staring.

***

"That was some fall you took," Alex said, "I can't believe you biffed it like that. Seriously, that was some funny crap."

Lying on the bench, a bottle of melted and no longer cold water pressed against his face, Kevin groaned. "Glad to know I amused you so much." The sarcasm in his voice was thick enough to stab with a pitchfork.

Alex dismissed his sarcastic tone. "So, how are you feeling? Everything okay?"

"Of course he's not okay, idiot! Just look at him. It looks like someone decided to play Frogger on his face."

"Not helping…" Kevin mumbled.

"Oi! Don't call me an idiot! I was asking out of concern!"

"Your concern isn't needed!"

"Seriously guys. Not helping."

Kevin went ignored as Alex and Andrew broke out into a fight.

"HA! Serves you right, jerk! This is what you get for stealing both my Tit Maiden and my Gothic Hottie!"

Kevin twitched. He would have said something, but his face hurt too much, so he just ignored his idiotic best friend. Why were they even friends again? He was having a hard time remembering.

"… Talking…"

"I thought stuff like that only happened in anime," Eric said, somehow managing to understand what Justin had said.

"… Real…"

Kevin wished his friends would all just shut up. Couldn't they see that he had a headache? His face felt like roadkill, and he felt emasculated for reasons he couldn't understand. He wanted them to stop talking.

Fortunately for Kevin's eroding patience, Coach Deretaine

blew his whistle and then began yelling. "Hey! You four! Stop dicking around! If you've got time to fuck off, then you've got time to run drills! Now get over here!"

Kevin couldn't contain his sigh of relief. Finally. Peace and quiet.

"You look like shit."

Or not.

Kevin cracked his one good eye open to see a figure standing over him. Even though her face was cast in shadow, he recognized her instantly.

"Christine. Is there something you wanted? Or did you come all the way over here just to tell me about how awful I look?"

Christine crossed her arms. Kevin imagined she was scowling. "Is that what you say to the person who's going to help your face feel better? If that's how you're going to be, then maybe I shouldn't have come over here at all."

"I'm sorry," Kevin groaned. "I'm not in the best of moods, and my face really hurts." He looked at her again. "How can you help me, though? Unless..."

"That's right."

Christine looked around for a second, as if checking to make sure the coast was clear, and then knelt by Kevin's side. She took the bottle off his face, eliciting a hiss from him as the air stung his raw skin.

"Hold still," she said, placing her hands over his injury. The moment she did, a soothing cold swept across his face. Kevin sighed in relief.

"Thank you."

"Hmph! Y-you should be thankful. It's not often that I consciously use my powers, and I've used them for you three times now."

"I know, and I'm very—wait." If his eyes weren't covered by Christine's hands, he would have blinked. "Three times? I only remember two."

Christine squeaked. "D-did I say three times? I meant two!"

"No, I'm pretty sure you said three."

"I said two! TWO, DAMN IT!"

"Ow, ow, ow! You're grinding my eyes into dust!"

"Meep! S-sorry!"

Christine stopped grinding her palms into Kevin's eyes, and the soothing chill returned. Kevin sighed in relief.

I should really learn to keep my mouth shut.

When Christine removed her hands, Kevin looked up to see the girl scrunching her face in a mask of concentration. It looked awfully cute from up close. Yet for whatever reason, his heart didn't skyrocket like it did when he was around Lilian.

Christine finished seconds later, and Kevin felt much better, which wasn't to say he actually felt good, just that couldn't feel anything on the left side of his face. It was completely numb. That was still better than pain, however, and for that he was grateful.

He sat up, moving over so Christine could sit on the bench.

"Gods, I hate the cold," Christine mumbled, shivering as she rubbed her hands to help circulate her blood.

"You know, I've been wondering about this for a while now, but why do you hate the cold so much?"

Christine remained silent. Kevin thought she would refuse to speak, but the girl only appeared to be gathering her thoughts.

"What do you know about yuki-onna?"

"Not much." Kevin scratched his chin. He couldn't even feel it. Huh. "I know that you control the cold. You can create snow and have powers over ice, but nothing else."

"That's more than most."

"I read a lot of manga."

Christine stared at Kevin very oddly.

"I'm not even going to ask." She shook her head, as if amazed by the stupidity of his statement. "The first thing you should know about yuki-onna is that there are no men. Our race is composed entirely of women. In fact, it's considered a rite of passage for young yuki-onna to go out into the human world and bring back a man to... to... to..."

Christine's face took on a darkly vibrant shade of blue.

Steam also began pouring out of her ears.

"I think I get what you're saying," Kevin said. He, too, was blushing. "Is that what you're doing here? Trying to... find a man?"

"D-d-d-d-don't be stupid!" Christine's fist launched out and punched Kevin in the face, sending him sprawling off the bench. "T-t-t-that-s not—there's no way I would be here for something like that!"

"Okay, okay, I got it." Kevin winced as he sat back down and rubbed his jaw. Thankfully, his face was still numb, so he hadn't felt the hit. Just the fall. "Now I know how Eric feels."

"Oh, shut up." Christine glared. "I didn't hit you that hard."

"The bruise on my face says otherwise."

"W-whatever!" Christine looked away. "Anyway, the reason I'm here isn't for, well, it's not for that, so get any perverted thoughts you have of me out of your mind right now."

Kevin almost said, "*I don't have any perverted thoughts about you,*" but had the inkling that wouldn't go over very well. "Then what are you doing in Arizona?"

Christine perked up at the change of subject. "I'm here because of my heritage and the circumstances of my birth. There is a law among yuki-onna that we must all abide by. Yuki-onna are only allowed to mate with humans. Yuki-onna do this because any child born from the union between a human and a yuki-onna will always be one hundred percent yuki-onna."

Kevin listened silently, wondering if there might be some kind of scientific reason to explain why children born from humans and yuki-onna were always yuki-onna. Maybe they had really powerful DNA.

On a side note, Kevin had never heard anyone say "yuki-onna" so many times in a single statement.

"I wasn't born from a human and a yuki-onna," Christine continued. "In fact, my mother committed what is considered a taboo amongst our kind. She mated with a bakeneko."

"That's a type of nekomata, right? A cat yōkai."

Bakeneko were one of three types of cat yōkai, along with nekomata and kasha. Kevin didn't know much about bakeneko, as they weren't as prominently featured in anime and manga as nekomata were. He guessed it was because they only had one tail.

"That's right. The literal translation of their name means Fire Cart, which is odd, because they have nothing to do with carts or any other form of transportation. Regardless, bakeneko, while not as powerful as nekomata or kasha, still have a strong affinity for fire.

"Mating with any type of yōkai is considered taboo among our kind. Mating with a yōkai that has powers over fire is grounds for banishment. Because of this, the clan my mom belonged to banished her."

Kevin winced. "That's kinda harsh."

Christine's uncaring shrug said more about her state of mind than words ever could. "Life's harsh, in case you haven't noticed."

"I guess." Kevin didn't argue. After all the crap he'd been through, he agreed. "So where's your mother? Does she live with you?"

"My mother's dead."

Kevin closed his eyes as guilt slammed into him like a hailstorm of gunfire. "I'm sorry."

"It's fine. She died soon after giving birth to me, so it's not like I ever knew her. I grew up in an orphanage. Occasionally, a family would adopt me, but they would always give me back because I couldn't control my powers. It wasn't until I met my benefactor that I left the orphanage for good."

"Who's your benefactor?"

"Just some guy. He's a yōkai, or at least I think he is. I've never met him in person before. He always contacts me through intermediaries to give me a monthly stipend."

Listening to Christine made Kevin realize just how lucky he was. Yes, his mom was never at home, and yes, she certainly wouldn't be winning any "Mother of the Year" awards, but at least he had a mom. He might not know his dad—and he honestly didn't want to know—but he knew his mom, and he knew that she loved him.

Lilian and Christine had lived much harder lives than him. One had her own family trying to force her into a mating arrangement for some political crap, and the other didn't even have a family to rely on. Compared to what these two had gone through, his own problems seemed insignificant.

"You're a really amazing person." Kevin smiled at the gothic-clad female. "Really, I haven't met many people who are as strong-willed and determined as you."

Christine's face turned into a raging storm normally only seen in the frozen tundra. "Wh-wh-wh-what the hell are you saying?! IDIOT!"

"GOOOF!"

"Jerk! Imbecile! Jackass! You don't just—you can't just say

things like that to a girl, you moron!"

"Guh," Kevin lay on the ground in the fetal position, arms curled around his stomach where Christine had punched him. As the yuki-onna continued to rant, he groaned. "What did I do to deserve that?"

Christine didn't answer him. She just continued yelling.

***

Track practice ended, though Kevin hadn't been allowed to run for the last third of it. Coach Deretaine had insisted he rest, not wanting him to exacerbate his facial injury any further. Christine had left before then, huffing and stomping away like an angry rhinoceros.

Kevin would have wondered why, but he honestly didn't care anymore. Trying to understand women was a pain. Trying to understand Christine was like trying to learn the meaning of life by playing eroge. He'd likely corrode his brain just making an attempt.

"I'm telling you, the new series that just came out is fucking awesome. It's the only show in the world about trains that I can actually get on board with."

"That's just because it's a complete T and A anime. I know what anime you're talking about, and the only thing you'd find exciting about it are the massive boobs every chick in that series is sporting."

"So? You say that like boobs are a bad thing. Have you no pride as a man?"

"I have plenty of pride as a man," Kevin snapped as they walked into the school proper. "I just prefer anime with good stories as opposed to 'Massive Plot.'"

"Whatever," Eric grumbled. "You just don't know a good show when you see it."

"It's not like Kevin needs to watch shows like that anyway," Alex said.

"Yeah. If he wants 'Massive Plot,' then he's got both Lilian and that Kotohime chick to look at."

"Not to mention Christine. I think she's got the hots for him, too, though her breasts are pretty tiny."

Somewhere within the school campus, a certain yuki-onna

sneezed. She then began raging uncontrollably as the powerful urge to freeze someone's dick off consumed her.

"Do you guys have to bring my love life into this?"

"Yes."

"Definitely."

"Indubitably."

"... Love..."

"W-whatever," Kevin huffed. "And why bother mentioning Christine anyway? She doesn't like me. I mean, have you seen how angry she gets whenever I open my mouth? It's like she's hardwired toward violent responses to everything I say."

Kevin's four friends stared at him.

"Kevin." Eric placed a hand on his friend's shoulder. "You're an idiot."

"A big idiot," Alex agreed.

"A massive idiot."

".... Stupid..."

A large vein pulsed on Kevin's forehead. "Oh yeah? And why is that?"

"No reason. You just are."

The pulsing vein gained company in the form of Kevin's twitching right eye.

They continued strolling to the makeshift locker room in the main office building. Kevin didn't know how Coach Deretaine managed to convince the principal to let them use the main office building as a locker room. Perhaps Eric had a hand in convincing his father to let them change there, he theorized to himself.

While they were walking, a teacher walked up to them.

"Ah, Mr. Swift. I was hoping to see you," Professor Nabui's accent was thicker than usual that day. Kevin had a hard time understanding him.

"Um, did you need me for something?" Kevin asked.

"Indeed. I wished to discuss your last test score. If you could come with me?"

Kevin was confused. Couldn't his teacher just speak with him here? He didn't protest, however, since this was a teacher, and Professor Nabui had always been unusual.

Really, what could go wrong?

***

Lilian was worried.

After parting ways with Lindsay, she'd gone searching for Kevin, first heading to the track field and then to the gym. After remembering that the gym—and subsequently the school locker rooms—were closed until further notice, she'd traveled to the main office building.

She'd passed Christine on the way. The girl looked angry, but that was nothing new. They spent a few moments arguing before they both stalked away in a huff.

She eventually reached the office, a square building that sat next to the library. Lined with windows and painted in the school colors, Lilian could easily see inside.

She was about to walk in when someone walked out first and, upon seeing her, brightened like a million watt bulb.

A very perverted million watt bulb.

"My Tit Maiden!" Eric ran toward her, drool leaking from his mouth and blood from his nose. His hands were outstretched and his eyes were locked on her chest.

Lilian swiftly clotheslined him the moment he was within reach. She was not in the mood right now.

"Do you guys know where Kevin is?" she asked, staring at Alex. The young man gulped. He didn't know why, but that stare really scared the crap out of him.

"Kevin? He's, um, he's, oh, blast it! Why can't I remember?!"

Fear will do that to a man.

"… Japanese…"

"Oh, right!" Andrew snapped his fingers. "Professor Nabui said he wanted to speak with him, so they went off to his classroom, I think."

Lilian's stared hardened. "You think?"

"I'm sure that's where they are. I mean, where else would a teacher take a student that he wants to speak with?"

"I see. Thanks."

Lilian left soon after. Eric was still choking on the ground, his hands clasped around his throat. She didn't wait for him to recover, which also meant she missed the waterworks his personal storm cloud made when it returned with a vengeance.

On a side note, Alex and Andrew were not pleased when their clothes got sopping wet.

Lilian didn't bother knocking on Professor Nabui's door, instead going straight for the handle. It was locked. A sense of apprehension washed over her. After glaring at the handle for several seconds, Lilian looked around to confirm she was alone before releasing her "foxy parts" and channeling youki through her body and into her arms.

The door dented, bent, and then yielded to her fist, before flying off its hinges and crashing to the ground. Lilian retracted her tails and ears, transforming back into a fully human form, and walked inside.

Kevin wasn't there.

Neither was Professor Nabui, for that matter.

The room was empty.

Lilian walked further into the room. Nothing seemed to be out of place. Everything was exactly as she had last seen it.

As she continued searching, something on the professor's desk grabbed her attention. Lilian crept over and saw a single sheet of paper lying on top, a small paperweight pinning it to the surface. She grabbed the paper and held it up to her face. It read:

that your mate, Kevin Swift, has been kidnapped. If you want him back unharmed, all you have to do is hand yourself over. I shall be waiting at the All 4 Anime store on 19th Avenue and Dunlap Road. I suggest you come alone, otherwise, I cannot guarantee Kevin's safety.

Lilian stared at the sheet of paper in her hands, uncomprehending. She could barely concentrate on the words written therein, and only one phrase within the entire letter penetrated the stormy haze brewing within her mind.

"Kevin Swift has been kidnapped."

"Has been kidnapped…"

"Has been…"

"Has… has… has…"

Lilian frowned. That wasn't right.

"Been kidnapped..."

"Kidnapped... kidnapped... kidnapped..."

That was better.

Her body began to shake.

Her lips trembled before they peeled back into a feral snarl.

The sound of paper crinkling was surprisingly loud as Lilian clenched her hands into fists. Her control over her transformation slipped, ears quickly sprouting crimson fur, elongating, and moving closer to the crown of her head. Her tails sprouted from between a flap in her shorts, writhing in a rictus of furious activity. While her face remained mostly unchanged, six whiskers did appear around her nose.

Lilian didn't even bother to consider how the professor knew she was a kitsune, nor did she think about the ramifications that came with someone knowing about her origins. All her thoughts were focused on the building mass of rage coiling around the center of her stomach.

Someone had kidnapped her mate. Some pretentious little fool had taken her mate! They had stolen him from her! And now she was going to find them and Kick! Their! Ass!

Shōnen style!

"Now isn't the time for that, idiot!" Lilian's enraged voice filled the empty room.

... Sorry, my bad.

Chapter 11

Not Human

"I'm telling you! I saw Lilian with animal ears and two tails! And she destroyed Professor Nabui's door with a single punch!"

"I'm sure you're just imagining things."

"But I'm not!"

Christine sighed in exasperation. After stomping out on Kevin (something she was starting to regret), she'd found herself wandering the school campus. She hadn't felt like going home. After a brief run-in with Lilian, she'd gone to the main office building to see if she could find Kevin and apologize—w-well, maybe not *apologize* apologize, but, well, make up somehow.

Then she'd run into Lindsay. The girl had been freaking out. Apparently, someone had decided to reveal their yōkai form in public.

Really, Lilian, you just had to transform in broad daylight where everyone could see you? You couldn't, I don't know, wait until you got home to do that?

Gotta give the girl credit. She's got balls. Nyahaha!

Quiet you!

There was a reason that yōkai didn't reveal themselves to humans anymore, beyond the sheer stupidity of doing so in this day and age. While the many yōkai races were in a state of cold war with each other, they had established a common set of rules, which all yōkai were required to adhere to. The first and most important of these laws was to never reveal your identity as a yōkai to humans.

Sometime in the mid-1800s, humanity's technological

capabilities had skyrocketed. While this normally wouldn't have been a problem, it became a serious issue for one simple reason: the advancement of human weaponry.

Centuries before the invention of the musket, yōkai had been the pinnacle of power on earth, and humans were but their playthings. Only the *Miko* and Shinto Priestesses, along with a few powerful humans possessing unusual abilities, were capable of combating them. Yet those remarkable humans had eventually died out, having been hunted down to the last bloodline during the *Meiji* era in Japan.

However, all that had changed within the past century. With the invention of firearms, high-yield explosives, chemical warfare, intelligent missiles and, of course, the nuclear warhead, humanity had risen to power and now stood at the top of the food chain. Meanwhile, yōkai, the very creatures who had once oppressed humans, were forced into hiding.

Christine thought it was the ultimate example of poetic justice.

"I swear, everything I'm telling you is true!"

Christine shook her head to refute Lindsay's claim. Regardless of her feelings toward Lilian, she couldn't let a human know what the redhead was; a creature beyond the understanding of humanity.

"Look, Lindsay. I'm sure you think you saw something, but that's not—"

Christine gasped when Lindsay grabbed her shoulders and slammed her back against a wall. Hard. Her surprise was such that she almost bit her tongue.

"What the hell, Lindsay?!" She glared at the tomboy. "What was—"

"Shh!" Lindsay pressed a finger to Christine's lips, causing her to blush at the feel of someone else's skin on her mouth. "Don't speak so loudly. Lilian just walked by."

Lindsay removed her finger and peered around the corner to spy on the redhead. After a moment's hesitation, Christine followed suit, crouching underneath the tomboy and poking her head out from behind the wall. She imagined they made for a comical sight, like something out of a bad spy movie.

They watched as Lilian stormed across a sidewalk with all the grace of an angry bull seeing red.

"She looks angry," Lindsay murmured worriedly. "I wonder

why?"

"No," Christine shook her head. "She doesn't look angry. Angry is 'I can't find my damn keys' or 'where the hell is my lunchbox?' Lilian... she's not angry. She pissed."

Christine's description was, indeed, far more apt than Lindsay's. Angry did not do Lilian justice. Her lips were peeled back in a fierce snarl, and her canines looked strangely sharp, far sharper than usual. Further accentuating her boiling rage were her eyes, which glowed like two emerald moons reflected off the surface of a murky green lake. Her hands were clenched into fists. They shook violently, and the knuckles had turned a deathly white. Crimson trails of liquid ran down her hands as sharp nails dug into the flesh of her palms.

Lilian didn't even seem to notice.

"I don't think I've ever seen her look so angry before," Lindsay whispered. She sounded frightened. Christine couldn't blame her. An enraged yōkai was not something a human would ever want to see, advanced weaponry or not.

"Neither have I."

"Where do you think Kevin is? Do you think he's the reason she's so angry?"

"Possibly."

"What do you think we should do? Follow her?"

Christine knew that she should tell Lindsay to forget what she just saw and go about her business. However, her own curiosity overrode her common sense. She, too, wanted to know what had made Lilian so livid.

She nodded.

"Follow her."

***

When most people thought of Eric Corrompere, they usually thought of a person so lecherous, so perverted, that he couldn't possibly be human. And for the most part, they would be right. Eric was a pervert. He peeped on women every chance he got, he played eroge imported directly from Japan, and he had an extensive stash of hentai on his hard drive. Yes, few people in the world were more salacious than him.

However, that didn't mean he was an idiot. When Eric wanted

to, he could actually be quite intelligent. After all, it took cunning and skill to secretly install several spy cameras in the girls' locker room and have no one notice for months—the fact that they were always found eventually and he got the crap beaten out of him by a horde of vicious, angry teenage girls afterward notwithstanding.

… Right.

Regardless, Eric wasn't the idiot that everyone made him out to be. He had a good head on his shoulders. He was smart, cunning, and more than capable of making intelligent and well thought out decisions.

So, when he saw Lindsay and his Goth Hottie following his Tit Maiden, he did the most logical and well thought out thing he could.

"Hehehe… I wonder where you sexy little creatures of mammarific proportions are heading off to."

He followed them.

Okay. So maybe Eric Corrompere wasn't that smart after all.

***

Lilian had a newfound respect for Kevin.

She'd never realized how difficult riding a bike could be. Her first attempt at trying to ride Kevin's bike ended with her crashing into the school fence. After emitting some surprisingly foul expletives from her pretty mouth, she hopped back on the bike and tried again.

She ended up crashing into a cactus.

It was a very irritated kitsune who arrived at the Swift's residence. Her clothes were a mess, her hair had twigs in it, her body was covered in scratches, and her mate wasn't with her. She could deal with the first three issues, but that last one really set her off. No one messed with her mate.

Lilian didn't bother taking off her sandals when she entered the apartment. She only planned on staying long enough to look up the location of the Just 4 Anime store on Kevin's laptop. It shamed her to admit it, but she'd been so angry about Kevin's kidnapping that she hadn't realized she had no clue where the store was until well after leaving school.

"Lilian-sama." Kotohime walked out from the kitchen, startling her. "Welcome home. I am glad to see that you have arrived safely."

"Right, safely," Lilian grumbled.

"Is something the matter, Lilian-sama?"

"Nothing. Anyway, I'm going to get something, and then I need to head out again."

"I see," Kotohime paused. "I notice that Kevin-san isn't with you. Have the two of you gotten into some kind of altercation?"

Lilian did not like the way Kotohime's face twisted into an expression of mild satisfaction. Not at all.

"No, we haven't gotten into an argument. We're just... I'm just..." Quick, Lilian! Think fast! "Shut up! I'm thinking as fast as I can!"

"Lilian-sama, please do not antagonize Author-san. And please answer my question."

Lilian grumbled incoherently.

"What was that?"

"I said Kevin asked me to get something for him."

"Really?"

Lilian's nod was very emphatic. "Yes. He asked me to grab his, uh, his backpack!"

"I see. His backpack, is it?"

"That's right." Lilian nodded some more. "Kevin is working on something right now, but he doesn't have all the materials he needs, so he asked me to go back home and get his backpack for him."

"Uh huh." Lilian tried not to squirm as Kotohime stared at her with eyes that were harder than steel. "And why, may I ask, did he not come all the way over here himself?"

"Um, uh... that's a good question..." Lilian's mind traveled a hundred miles a second. "It's because he's... he's just so busy!"

"Busy?"

Kotohime's flat look made Lilian most uncomfortable. She didn't let onto this fact, and crossed her arms under her bust. "Yes! Busy! He is very busy with, um, stuff. So! When he said he needed to get some supplies from home, I offered to get them for him."

A single, delicate eyebrow rose in response to her words. "I thought you said he asked you to get them for him?"

"He did! It's just that, well, it's just..." *Oh great. Come on, Lilian. Think. Think!* "Ah! Right. Upon hearing that he needed supplies, I offered to get them first, and then he asked me to get them."

"I see."

Kotohime stared at Lilian. She stared hard. Lilian broke out into a cold sweat, her eyes looking anywhere but at her maid.

"Very well." Lilian sighed in relief when Kotohime dropped the subject and went back into the kitchen. "Though you and Kevin-san shouldn't stay out much later. Dinner will be ready in about an hour, so be sure to come back by then."

"Okay."

Lilian could not move fast enough. She rushed into her bedroom, printed out a map that showed her where Just 4 Anime was, grabbed Kevin's backpack (she had to keep up appearances), and flew out of the house.

She never noticed Kotohime's eyes following her.

"Hmm…"

***

Three people watched as Lilian flew down the stairs, hopped onto Kevin's bike, and took off down the road.

"Where do you think she's going?" Lindsay turned to look at the other two people hiding with her behind a black Ford truck. "Do you think she's going to find Kevin?"

"Who cares about Kevin?" Eric said loudly, having joined the two girls while they were spying on Lilian. He slid over to Christine until their shoulders were touching. "So, Goth Hottie, now that we're alone, hows about you and me—GUF!"

"Idiot!" Christine hissed like an angry viper. "Don't say such stupid things!"

"Yeah." Lindsay crossed her arms and pouted. "And besides, you two aren't alone. I'm still here, in case you've forgotten."

"Quick! Let's follow the boob head before she gets too far away."

"Right. Wait." A pause. Lindsay stared at the lolita. "Boob head?"

"N-n-never mind that! Just hurry!"

"All right. All right. Let's go."

The two females took off, rushing down the street at a quick trot while also trying not to be seen by Lilian.

Back where they'd been hiding, Eric Corrompere groaned and held his cranium, which had a large, frost-covered lump the size of Texas on it. "W-wait for me... ugh... I think something inside of my head just broke..."

***

Kevin Swift woke up with a splitting headache. His tongue felt dry, his mind was filled with static, and there was an annoying ringing in his ears.

Groaning, he opened his eyes and saw nothing but a white blur. Even after his vision sharpened, white remained the only visible color.

Turning his head, Kevin surveyed his surroundings. There wasn't much to the room. He saw a drab gray door several yards away, next to a glass window that he couldn't see through. It was probably one of those one-sided windows, the kind he'd seen in police movies. What were they called again? He couldn't remember.

He tried to assess his situation, to ascertain his whereabouts and figure out how he ended up... wherever he was, but that proved immensely difficult. His thoughts kept slipping away like wet, slimy eels. Electric eels. Just trying to remember induced what felt like several thousand volts of electricity running through his brain.

Still, he continued to think. He pushed through the pain, and eventually recalled bits and pieces of what had happened; track practice, following Professor Nabui into his classroom and then... nothing. Everything went blank after that.

Strange...

The opening of the door forced Kevin out of his thoughts. His eyes widened in recognition when a familiar man entered with a calm, confident gait.

"P-Professor Nabui?" Kevin stared at the Social Studies professor in shock. The teacher looked a lot different than he remembered. "What's going on? Where am I? How did I get here?" A pause. "And just why the heck are you dressed in black spandex?"

"First, my name is not Professor Nabui," Kevin's teacher said. "My real name is Inagumi Takashi. As to your other questions: you are currently within our base. I brought you here because I need you as a hostage."

"I see." Kevin paused. "And the spandex?"

An uncomfortable silence passed between them. Professor Nabui, or "Inagumi whatever," looked mildly embarrassed.

"We… ahem, our original idea was to create an armored suit similar to Solid Snake's, but we, well, we lacked the necessary funding for such an endeavor." The man's face twitched as he turned his head and grumbled. "Really, it's all Heather's fault. Damn that woman and her love of eroge."

At this point, Kevin wondered if he should feel frightened or not.

"Right." What a weird guy. And who was this Heather person that he spoke of? "So, why do you need me as a hostage?"

"We need to use you as a hostage in order to capture Lilian."

Kevin felt like someone had dropped a lead ball on his stomach. Suddenly, the situation didn't seem so ridiculous anymore.

"Why do you want Lilian?"

"Don't play dumb. We want her because she's a kitsune, of course." The ball of lead grew larger, threatening to crush his intestines. "Do you know how difficult it is to capture a kitsune? They are one of the most elusive yōkai in the entire world. We've been able to acquire inu, yuki-onna, neko and all manner of other supernatural creatures, but kitsune, we've never been able to even find one, much less capture one."

Kevin's breathing picked up. His heart rate accelerated until it felt like the pistons of a Formula One race car were slamming into his chest.

"Why? Why do you want Lilian? What are you going to do to her?"

"We're going to study her, of course," Professor—no, Inagumi Takashi—said as if it was the most obvious thing in the world. "Despite no longer being at the top of the food chain, yōkai still pose a significant threat to humanity. Surely you've realized this by now. Your encounter with Chris Fleischer should have been enough to show you how dangerous these creatures are."

Kevin's hands clenched into fists. The worry he felt for Lilian made him see white, overwhelming him to the point where he felt like he might explode. This man wanted to capture Lilian, the girl who meant so much to him, and was using him to do it.

He wanted to throw up.

I'm so pathetic.

"There is much we can gain from capturing and studying yōkai. Many of our technological advancements in viral weaponry have actually come from splicing the genetic codes of various supernal beings with viruses. The common cold plus the DNA of a kappa creates a deadly virus that causes the blood vessels to swell up with water, clogging the veins and arteries. Combining the genes of a nekomata with several strands of the flu creates a virus that causes deadly inflammation in the lungs. Even now, after many decades of research and advancement, we're still coming up with more ways to use yōkai DNA to further develop humanity."

The more Kevin listened to this man, the more he felt like vomiting—and punching Takashi in the face. Too bad his hands were tied.

Not like I could do anything anyways. This man's obviously trained in combat. I wouldn't stand a chance against him in a fight.

"Of course, we've also had many medical advancements as well. An inu's genes are part of what gives them such sturdy bodies. By injecting the genes of an inu into a human, we've given people suffering from muscle atrophy and disease the chance to walk. We've been able to create replacement eyes for people who have gone blind by cloning nekomata eyes, and manipulating their genetic structure to become compatible with a human's body. There is so much we've been able to do, so much we've been able to learn."

The more this man spoke, the more Kevin wanted to escape. To warn Lilian. To beat this man for using him like this. But he couldn't do anything. He was helpless.

It's because I'm weak. If I was stronger, then maybe I wouldn't be in this situation.

"That is why we need Lilian. A kitsune is the one specimen we don't have. I would like to thank you for your involvement, boy. Without you, none of this would have been possible."

Kevin gritted his teeth. Inagumi Takashi was too busy standing on his soapbox to notice Kevin's increasing distress, seemingly reveling in the sound of his own voice.

I can't believe this is really happening.

"Well, I think I've spoken enough." His former teacher came down from his impassioned speech. "I really only came in to let you know that we have no intention of harming you. We understand that you've been tricked by this kitsune into letting her live with you. Do not worry, though, once we get rid of her, your life will return to normal."

Kevin watched Inagumi Takashi leave. As the door closed behind his former professor, frustrated, angry tears spilled from his eyes and ran down his cheeks.

Alone in his cell, with nothing but the walls, floor and ceiling to keep him company, Kevin lamented his helplessness.

If only I wasn't so weak...

***

The trip to All 4 Anime had taken Lilian much longer than she thought it would. It was nearly twilight when she arrived. The faint yellowish glow of parking lights were all that lit the small store, which was nestled in a tiny strip mall.

Lilian didn't understand why some evil person would use an anime store as their base of operations, but she figured they were just trying to be genre savvy or something.

She stood several dozen yards away from the store, hiding behind another building and peeking around it. The front appeared deserted, but a glint of light from the roof caught her eye. A man stood at the top, dressed in black spandex. His gun, which reflected moonbeams off its surface, swept back and forth across the parking lot. He was obviously searching for her.

Okay. So, she definitely wasn't going through the front door. That meant she would have to get creative.

After taking a deep, calming breath, Lilian released a trickle of youki, dispelling the transformation that kept her tails and ears hidden. She then took another breath and started weaving an incredibly complex illusion.

"Celestial Art: Chameleon Masquerade."

The light around her body began to bend and distort. Photons wavered as they were manipulated. Had Lilian been looking in a mirror, she knew that her body would have slowly vanished from sight, fading like a ghostly mirage.

"Kitsune Art: Silence."

Knowing that just being invisible probably wouldn't fool them, Lilian silenced not just her footsteps, but her entire self. The illusion she wove was one that covered her entire body in a thin layer of youki, masking every sound she could make. No sense in letting Kevin's attackers see or hear her approach. She wanted to take these people out nice and quick.

Once she finished weaving her illusions, Lilian proceeded to go around the back.

***

Lindsay, Christine and Eric watched Lilian from a bank across the street.

"Did you see that?" Lindsay whispered harshly into the ears of an annoyed Christine, her voice shaking. "You saw that, didn't you? See? I told you that Lilian had tails and ears."

Christine twitched. "All right, all right. I believe you."

Damn it, Lilian. What the hell are you thinking?

"What do you think's going on? Where did Lilian go? How did she disappear like that?"

Christine sighed. There really was no point in hiding it anymore. Damn that stupid fox for not being careful enough!

"Lilian's a kitsune."

Christine blinked. Lindsay blinked, too, for good measure.

Slowly, like droids whose gears hadn't been oiled in decades, the two young ladies turned to look at Eric.

"P-pardon?" Lindsay's eyes fluttered rapidly, as if she was trying—and failing—to make sense of the unfamiliar word.

"Lilian is a kitsune, a supernatural shapeshifting fox." With his arms crossed over his chest, Eric had never looked more serious. "That actually explains a lot."

Lindsay tilted her head. "It does? Really? What does it explain?"

"It explains why her boobs are so big."

"Pervert!"

"Duaoh!"

Cracking her knuckles, Christine turned her attention away from the twitching pile of flesh once known as Eric to look at

Lindsay. "The pervert's right. Lilian is a kitsune, a fox yōkai. She probably used an illusion to become invisible. Illusions are a kitsune's specialty."

"And how do you know this?"

"Because Christine's a yōkai, too."

Once again, Eric, who had miraculously recovered from getting his face punched in, received nothing but stares from his two companions.

"How the hell did you know that?"

"I watch a lot of anime and read manga."

Christine facepalmed. Meanwhile, Lindsay just looked confused. What did anime and manga have to do with anything?

"Ara? What do we have here?"

The three teenagers froze.

Stepping out from the shadows of the bank, her graceful form more imposing than anything they'd ever seen, Kotohime stalked toward them with deceptively feminine footsteps. Her four fox tails swayed as she moved, back and forth, their pendulous motions hypnotic and dangerous. Predatory. Two fox ears twitched on her head, blacker than raven's feathers and seeming to absorb all light in the area.

The three of them felt an inexplicable fear wash over them, like a rupturing tide crashing against the shore. The woman stared them down, her eyes sharper than the katana she carried in her left hand.

"You are friends of Lilian-sama and Kevin-san, if I am not mistaken." Kotohime placed her right hand on her cheek and tapped her index finger, wearing a curious expression that somehow looked both cute and petrifying. "Now what could you three be doing out here at this time of night, I wonder?"

Christine, Eric and Lindsay gulped.

***

When Lilian traveled to the back alley of the store, she found another man guarding the back entrance. Like the one on the roof, he too was dressed in black spandex. Were the situation not so serious, she would have shaken her head.

Spandex? Seriously?

Walking up to the man, Lilian's youki enhanced eyes picked

out several more aspects of his physical appearance that she had not noticed before. Aside from his black spandex bodysuit and the machine gun strapped around his shoulder, he also wore night-vision goggles, combat boots and a handgun holstered at his left hip.

Better not give him a chance to use any of those.

She stopped behind him, swiftly, silently, and poked him in the back of the head with a single tail. The man crumbled like a marionette that just had its strings cut. He would have hit the ground, but that might've alerted the person on the roof, so Lilian caught him with her tails and gently lowered him to the pavement.

"Kitsune Art: Illusory Sleep."

Lilian frowned.

"Why am I saying the name of my techniques out loud?"

Because all *shōnen* characters say the name of their techniques out loud. It's standard procedure.

"It was a rhetorical question."

Oh… sorry.

"Ha… whatever." Lilian looked from the comatose body to the roof. "Now what should I do? Take out the guard on the roof? Or should I just sneak right in?" She deliberated for a moment. "Guard on the roof it is. I'll need them out of the picture if I want to escape with Kevin."

Enhancing her muscles with youki, Lilian leapt onto the roof, landing silently thanks to her **Silence** illusion.

The person guarding the front entrance stood on the opposite side, still sweeping the barrel of their gun back and forth across the parking lot. No doubt he was searching for her.

Lilian took him out in the same way as the guard down below. After lowering him onto his back, she leapt back down to ground level.

Even with the guard taken care of, using the front entrance was a dumb idea. In every manga she'd ever read, those who took the front door always alerted the bad guys to their presence. She wouldn't be stupid enough to do that.

Fortunately, all stores also had a backdoor. This one was locked, but Lilian used the key she'd gotten off the guard she'd first knocked out to open it.

"And Kevin told me the 'Dungeon Master's Guide' and

'Player's Handbook' were useless in real life situations."

The store's interior looked like a regular shop that sold anime. Paraphernalia littered the shelves, stands were situated all over the place. She could see swords and cosplay hanging on the wall behind the register. There were DVDs, manga, posters, all sorts of stuff. It almost made her wonder.

How come Kevin had never taken her here? This place was awesome.

Note to self: convince Kevin to take me to a store like this after I rescue him and we're safely at home.

Lilian observed her surroundings as she creeped around several displays. She eventually uncovered a somewhat hidden hallway off to the side where a single guard stood. She took him out quickly and quietly, then opened the door to reveal a well-lit staircase.

"Huh? I'm kinda surprised the stairs aren't darker and more ominous, but I guess these people want to avoid clichés."

Indeed they do.

"Be quiet."

You're so mean…

"!!"

Quiet! I'm being quiet.

Lilian huffed and walked down the stairs, staying alert for any potential surprises.

The stairs led to a door, which in turn led to another hallway. Lit with iridescent bulbs and covered in sterile white tiles, the hallway looked more like a research lab than a basement underneath an anime store.

It didn't take long for Lilian to realize how much bigger this basement was than her initial assumptions. She'd assumed it wouldn't be too large, maybe a bit bigger than the store it was under, but as she traversed several hallways, she began to realize…

… This place was like a maze.

Lilian took another turn, which led to a door. Opening it revealed what looked like a holding cell. It was empty, save for the many claw and teeth marks riddling the walls, floor and ceiling. Closing the door, she started moving again.

The further Lilian got the more patrolling guards she ran into. Her illusions kept them from noticing her, but being so close to them still made her nervous. Anxious. Her heart pounded in her chest. Several times she actually feared one of the patrols might have heard the rapidly beating organ.

Coming upon another door, Lilian slowly opened it a crack and peered inside. This one actually had a guard, which meant someone was being held there. Was it Kevin?

"What the hell?" The young woman decked out in black spandex stared at the door opening and closing, seemingly on its own, the illusions doing their job and keeping the female from seeing or hearing Lilian.

Before the guard could respond to this seemingly strange phenomenon, Lilian touched the tip of one of her tails to the woman's temple.

"Kitsune Art: Illusory Sleep."

The woman crumpled to the floor. Lilian stared down at the unconscious figure, then looked around the room.

It looked practically identical to the other room, with its only distinguishing feature being the large window spanning the entire wall opposite the door. Lilian walked up to the window... and gasped when she saw a familiar figure lying on the floor.

"Kevin!"

Her technique dropping as she lost control of her emotions, Lilian rushed inside and knelt down upon reaching her beloved. The young man was lying on his back, his arms on his chest and bound at the wrists. His eyes were closed and his breathing even. He appeared to be unconscious.

"Kevin! Kevin!"

Blue eyes cracked open.

"Lilian?" Kevin blinked several times. Then his eyes widened. "Lilian! What are you doing here?"

"What kind of question is that? I'm here to rescue you, of course."

Lilian sliced through his restraints with a youki-infused tail.

"You shouldn't have come here," Kevin moaned. "These people aren't after me. They're after you."

"You can't honestly expect to just ignore when my mate's in trouble, do you?"

"I sort of wished you would." Kevin sat up and rubbed his wrists to get some circulation back into them. "These people want to experiment on you."

"They can study me all they want when I break my foot off in their ass." Lilian's expression darkened. "Nobody harms my mate."

"Lilian?" Kevin stared at Lilian in surprise. In return, she smiled at him and placed a hand on his cheek.

"Haven't I been telling you? I love you, Kevin. I have for years, and nothing on this *Kami*-blessed earth is ever going to change that."

"Lilian," Kevin whispered, "I—wait." A pause. Kevin blinked. "Years?"

"D-did I say years? I meant ever since we first met."

"But I could have sworn you just said years."

"You must be hearing things."

"No, I'm pretty sure you said—"

"Hearing things."

Kevin stared at Lilian, who was all smiles. Finally, he sighed. "Right. I must be hearing things."

"I'm glad you understand."

Kevin shook his head and chuckled.

"I don't deserve you," he said honestly. "Here you are, risking your neck for me, and I can't do anything for you."

"Kevin?" Lilian became worried when frustrated tears welled up in Kevin's eyes. The young man clenched his fists and gritted his teeth.

"Ever since we've met, you've always been the one protecting me. I couldn't do anything when Chris attacked us. I was even more useless when Kiara attacked you. I couldn't even protect myself from those three pathetic yōkai the other day. I... I'm just so useless, so weak."

"Oh, Kevin," Lilian's hands cupped his face, tenderly thumbing the few tears that had managed to escape his eyes. "You are not useless. Maybe you don't realize this, but I was terrified when Chris attacked us. If you hadn't pushed me out of the way and taken that initial attack, I would be dead right now. You saved me, and not just back then either. Had it not been for you, I would've bled out back when you found me in my fox form."

"Lilian." Kevin placed his hands over Lilian's, his eyes more expressive than she had ever seen them.

"You say that you're useless, but that's just not true. You call yourself weak, but no one expects you to be capable of fighting yōkai right off the bat. Few humans ever can. You say that you don't deserve to be with me, but that's not your decision to make. It's mine, and believe me when I tell you that no one is more deserving of my love than you. I love you, and that is the only thing that matters."

"I..." Kevin swallowed heavily, his Adam's apple bobbing. He started again, paused, then gave her a self-deprecating smile. "I really am an idiot, aren't I?"

Lilian's eyes twinkled as she smiled at him. "I wouldn't say you're an idiot, just dense."

As she knelt before Kevin, her left hand on his cheek and his right one over hers, Lilian felt the urge to kiss him. She resisted, however, as they weren't out of the woods quite yet. Kisses could come later, once they were safe.

"Come on," she said softly, "let's get out of here."

"I'm afraid I can't let you do that."

Lilian's and Kevin's eyes widened. Two small needles suddenly pierced her back, seconds before her body erupted in pain, as what felt like thousands of volts of electricity coursed through her nervous system. Her muscles spasmed, contracting and twisting in torment. She twitched and jerked, her body weakening before she slumped into the startled Kevin's arms.

Darkness engulfed her.

***

Kevin stared in horror as Lilian collapsed on top of him, her body going limp. Smoke rose from her back, and he could see exposed flesh where her clothes had been burnt. The skin was red, raw, as if the flesh had been overcooked in an oven. Two small, dart-like electrodes had impaled her skin, a small trail of blood leaking from the puncture wounds. Attached to them was a cord.

His eyes followed the cord to a man holding a stun gun in his left hand. A very familiar man.

"You!" Kevin shouted, sagging under Lilian's dead weight.

Inagumi Takashi was the picture of calm. His face remained impassive, eyes colder than Kiritsugu Emiya's and twice as dead. Yet there was a strange twist to his lips, a glimpse of triumph on his otherwise bland face.

"It's rather amazing, how supernatural creatures can be so affected by our modern technology. Take this gun for instance. It's just a military-grade stun gun, nothing particularly special. Yet against a kitsune, it works just as well as it would on a normal human."

Kevin gritted his teeth. As he sat there, a limp Lilian lying against his chest, anger like nothing he'd ever felt before surged through him. He wanted nothing more than to rush up and pound his fists against Inagumi's face. He hated this man. He hated this man so much that it was only due to Lilian's soft body pinning him down that he didn't try ripping his former teacher apart.

"You talk too much."

"You think so? Then perhaps I should stop talking and finish things up." Inagumi pulled another stun gun from behind his back and aimed it at Kevin. "Do not worry. When you wake up, you'll be back in your home, and all of this will seem like it had just been a bad dream."

Before he could pull the trigger, something wrapped around his legs. Two somethings. He looked down.

"What the...?"

"Don't... underestimate... me!"

The Japanese agent suddenly found himself flying off his feet, Lilian's two tails yanking him around like he was a Barbie doll. She launched him upwards into the granite ceiling, cracks spreading from the point of impact like a spider's web. Kevin could have sworn he heard the man's bones break. Lilian then brought Inagumi back down, where he struck the floor with such force that his body bounced off the concrete.

"Lilian!" Kevin clutched the fox-girl tightly in his arms, looking down to see half-lidded pools of green staring back. "You're okay!"

"O-of course... I am..." Lilian's smile was a mixture of pain and reassurance. "Did you really... think that... that would be enough... to put me down...?"

Kevin laughed in relief. He lifted Lilian as he stood up, wrapping an arm around her waist, and then slinging one of her arms over his shoulder, allowing Lilian to lean against him for support. The redhead sagged in his grip, forcing him to adjust his stance in order to compensate for the increased weight.

"Let's get out here," he said. Lilian nodded, closing her eyes as her facial muscles twitched as if undergoing muscle spasms.

"... Okay."

They walked over to their former teacher, who appeared to be out cold. His eyes were rolled up into the back of his head, mouth wide open in an agonized scream. He looked like he'd been run over by a herd of elephants. Lying several feet away was the unused stun gun.

"Lilian?"

"Got it." One of Lilian's tails lengthened and grabbed the stun gun before retracting and offering it to Kevin. "Here."

"Thanks." Kevin checked the weapon over. It looked almost like a standard gun, except for the ends where the electric nodes were launched.

"Do you know how to use that?"

"I've never used a real gun before," Kevin admitted, "but it looks similar to the ones from *House of Haunted Horrors*. I'm sure it won't be too hard... I hope."

Lilian didn't say anything to that.

They exited the room and stepped into the hall, which appeared deserted. With Lilian directing him, Kevin ran off as quickly as he could, half-carrying the redhead whose muscles didn't seem to feel like cooperating.

He tried to run silently. Unfortunately, he was literally half-dragging Lilian with him, which made being silent impossible.

He froze after turning a corner and running directly into a passing patrol. The two sides stared at each other for all of two seconds, and then all hell broke lose.

"It's the prisoner and the fox! They're trying to escape!"

"Get 'em!"

"Crap!"

Kevin spun on his heel and ran down another hallway. The sounds of booted feet hitting pavement echoed behind them.

"After them!"

"Don't let them escape!"

He gritted his teeth, his leg muscles working overtime. He couldn't see them, but he could certainly hear the patrol as they closed the distance.

"Stop right this instant or we'll open fire!"

"Crap! Crap! Crap! Crap!"

Kevin turned his head and promptly wished he hadn't. The two guards they'd run into were gaining on them, rifles aimed at him and Lilian.

"Don't worry... Kevin..." Lilian mumbled, her voice slurred. "I won't... let them hurt you..."

Before he could question the twin-tailed kitsune, Lilian's tails shot out. The first one smacked against the left guard's face, hard. That guard was sent flying backwards, his body flipping through the air like a ragdoll before slamming against the ground head first.

The second guard was even more unlucky. He got hit in the balls.

"SQQUUUEEEEEEE!"

Kevin winced as the man squealed like a gutted pig, the sound piercing his eardrums with its shrillness. He could only imagine what Lilian must be going through. Foxes had more acute hearing than humans.

They continued to run, though Kevin had no idea where he was going, and Lilian was having trouble remembering which turns she had taken. A glance out of his peripheral vision revealed that she was slipping in and out of consciousness. Her head bobbed and lolled, then snapped back up. Her eyes lost and regained focus, struggling against their desire to close.

She must have a concussion.

Kevin felt determination surge through his body, giving him strength and a renewed sense of purpose. Every time he'd been in trouble, Lilian had been the one to save him. Now she needed his help, and he would be damned if he didn't help her.

"Freeze, you two!"

"Who let the prisoner escape?!"

"Stop them!"

Several more guards found them, but Kevin didn't allow that to slow him down. With adrenaline surging through his veins, he lifted Lilian into his arms and carried her.

He threw himself around a corner and increased his pace. Booted feet echoed loudly behind him. As he ran past a glass case with a large canister inside, Kevin lashed out with a powerful kick, shattering it. He then spun around and hooked his left foot into the top valve, pulling it down before jumping backwards, narrowly avoiding a burst of gunfire.

Several bullets perforated the canister, and fumes soon filled the hall. Kevin's leg muscles bunched as he launched the canister at the guards and took off again, ignoring the coughing that echoed behind him.

"W-what the hell is this stuff?!"

"Fuck! It's that… it's that new fire extinguishing agent!"

"I can't… can't breathe…"

"Lilian?" Kevin asked.

"We're… I think we're almost there," Lilian slurred. Kevin nodded and tried to focus on reaching the exit. After several more turns, they finally found it, though the exit was being guarded by a person carrying what looked like an AK-47 assault rifle.

"Hold it, you two! Don't make me—gyaaaaa!!!"

The spandex-clad soldier jerked and twitched, his body lighting up like a Christmas tree as Kevin shot him in the neck with the stun gun. Steam and smoke wafted from his convulsing body, which soon jerked backwards and went into a series of muscle spasms. The guard twitched several times, and then went still.

"Um. Wow. This thing packs quite the punch."

"Trust me… I am… well aware… of that…"

Kevin looked down at Lilian. He'd started to grow tired and needed to set her down again, though he still shouldered most of her weight.

"Are you gonna be okay, Lilian?"

"I'll be fine…" Lilian mumbled against his neck. "That shock really hurt… but my Celestial powers will ensure that I heal soon enough. I just need some rest."

"You can rest all you want once we get out of here."

"Mmm."

They made their way upstairs, finding no one in the anime store except for the unconscious guard lying slumped against the wall.

Kevin raised an eyebrow at the redhead, who turned her head and looked away.

"What? I had to take him out or he would've alerted his friends."

Kevin only shook his head.

Together, the two made it outside—

"All right, that's as far as you go!"

—And found themselves surrounded.

Kevin swiveled his head left and right. Men and women carrying all forms of weaponry blocked their path, along with a number of military vehicles, hummers and tanks, forming a semi-circle in the parking lot.

Standing in front of the group was a woman. Short blond hair hung about her head in a bob, and from the way she filled out her... black spandex, the woman clearly took good care of her body, though he couldn't determine her age.

"I hope you two realize how much trouble you've given me," she stated. "I had to stop playing *Fate/Hollow Ataraxia* just to come out here and get you!"

Kevin and Lilian were nonplussed.

"Um, what?"

"Now stop wasting my time and give up. If you don't, then I'll have no choice but to shoot you both."

Kevin tried to think of a way out of this mess, but couldn't. There was nothing he could do. Their situation was hopeless.

And yet...

"Kevin..." Lilian moaned, causing him to look down. The redhead looked so weak, so frail. Her body was slumped against his, and only his arm around her waist kept her from falling to the ground. "Let me go. It's me they're after, not you..."

"No."

"Kevin..."

"No." Kevin shook his head. "I can't... I won't let you give yourself up for me. I refuse."

"Kevin, you don't really have much of a choice..."

"There's always a choice. It's just that sometimes the right choice happen to also be the hardest choice to make." Kevin ignored his fear, pushing it aside in order to smile at the beautiful girl in his arms. "I'm not the kind of person who would leave someone I... someone that... well, someone who's important to me while she's in danger, especially when she's in danger because of me. I won't leave you."

"You won't?"

"No."

"Then you'll... you'll stay with me?"

Kevin instantly knew they were no longer talking about their current predicament. "If you'll have me."

"And you'll let me stay with you?"

"For as long as you want."

Lilian smiled. Despite how tired she felt, how much her body ached, and the danger they were in, she smiled at him. It was the most beautiful thing Kevin had ever seen.

"Hey! Are you kids listening to me? I said get down on your knees, put your hands in the air, and give up peacefully! I want to play my eroge, damn it!"

Kevin and Lilian looked at the woman. She appeared annoyed, probably because they'd been ignoring her. Even in the dark, they could see the angry red vein throbbing on her forehead. It was luminescent.

"Um, ma'am. You didn't say that," one of her people said.

The woman blinked. "I didn't?"

"No, ma'am. You just told them to give up or you'd have us open fire."

"Oh. Well, I'm saying it now. Hey! Brats! Get down on your knees, stick your hands in the air, and give up!"

Kevin took a deep breath, gathered his courage...

... and then began shouting.

"Shut up, lady! Just who the hell do you think I am?! I'm going to tell you something right now, so you'd better dig the wax out of your ears and listen up! I'm not an intimidating or impressive guy. I don't have any combat training or superpowers. But even so—" Kevin clenched his left hand into a fist "—even so, I'm not the kind of guy who would just hand over the woman he loves to a bunch of Power Ranger villain rejects like you!"

The blond gaped. The people around her gaped. Everyone was pretty much gaping by this point.

Except Lilian, who simply deadpanned.

"You totally stole those lines from an anime," she accused.

Kevin looked away, mostly to hide his blush. "T-that's not really important right now, is it?"

Lilian's weak giggle was like music to his ears.

"No, I guess not." She used what little strength she had left to lean up and kiss him on the cheek. "It was actually kind of cool."

"I agree."

She appeared before them without warning, her body flickering into existence like an evanescent breeze. Her dark kimono clung to her curvaceous frame, and her raven locks of hair gleamed yellow under the lamp posts.

With her back to the company of infantry and military vehicles, Kotohime faced Kevin and Lilian wearing an odd smile. She seemed... satisfied? Yes. Satisfied. Her curled lips were dazzling, and her dark eyes held a gleam of the utmost satisfaction.

"I am most pleased to see that you have decided to finally stop hesitating and make a choice, Kevin-sama."

"Eh?" Kevin stared at her with a stupid look on his face.

"For that, you have my gratitude, respect and acceptance. However—" her eyes suddenly narrowed "—I do not want you think this means I will be going easy on you. There is much that you must learn if you are to stand by Lilian-sama's side."

"Wha-what?"

Kevin stared at the woman in confusion. Lilian was blushing. The spandex wearing soldiers? Well...

"Hey! Who the hell are you?!" The blond shouted at Kotohime. She did not look the least bit pleased at being ignored... again.

Kotohime turned to the woman, her eyes wide in mild surprise. Kevin knew almost instantly that it was fake.

This woman... she really is dangerous.

"Oh, dear. I seem to have forgotten to introduce myself. How rude of me." The bodyguard bowed low. "My name is Katsura Kotohime."

Her ears shifted as she straightened, transforming into triangular fox ears covered in midnight fur. Four fluffy black tails with white tips shot out from underneath her kimono as well. Her smile was pleasant and her disposition amiable, and yet, all of the soldiers quaked in their boots as she stared at them.

Her left hand came to rest on the hilt of her katana.

"And I shall be your opponent tonight."

No one saw Kotohime move. One second she was standing before them, and the next she was gone. While the others looked around, Kevin gawked at the place she had been, wondering if she

had used some kind of instantaneous movement technique. Did this woman know the Flash Step or something?

"W-where did that woman go?!"

"Sh-she just vanished!"

"What kind of monster is she?!"

"Calm down, men!" the blond woman barked. "She's probably just using an illusion to try and scare us."

"I wouldn't be so sure of that," a voice said from behind the group of soldiers.

Everyone turned to look at Kotohime, now standing in front of one of the Hummers, her katana slowly sliding into its sheathe with a sibilant hissing of steel. No one had seen her even take it out.

Click.

The sound of Kotohime's katana being fully sheathed was like a prelude. The Hummer immediately behind her suddenly split apart like a ripe fruit that had been sliced by a cleaver, the two halves falling away and clattering to the pavement.

For one second, there was silence. No one blinked. No one breathed. They could only stare at the scene before them, their minds' refusing to believe what their eyes had just seen.

"That... that was really cool," Kevin mumbled.

Lilian grinned. "I know, right?"

The blond woman's eyes bugged out as she realized how much danger they were in. "Holy—Fire! Open fire!"

The infantry, goaded into action by the blonde's shouting, raised their weapons and prepared to fire on the four-tailed kitsune.

They never got the chance.

Kotohime gripped her katana and took a stance. Legs spread wide, feet planted firmly on the ground, the femme fatale brought the katana down to her side.

"Ikken Hissatsu."

Kotohime's sword became an indistinct blur, moving so fast that Kevin could only see the glint of polished steel reflected by the lamps' yellow light. Loud sonic booms shattered the air. Soldiers were sent flying, some hitting the ground, their bodies unmoving. Others crashed into vehicles, leaving dents in their wake. Lampposts were bent as humans crashed into them with unimaginable force, the bulbs shattering as they struck the ground.

"What the... what's going on?"

"That's one of Kotohime's special blade techniques," Lilian answered Kevin's question, "She uses reinforcement to increase the speed and strength of her swings and thrusting motions in order to generate shockwaves."

"I hadn't realized such a thing was possible." He paused, as if realizing something. "But, with everything else I've seen so far, I suppose I really should have."

When Kotohime finished, every soldier lay unconscious, and the military vehicles had been perforated with numerous holes, as if a drill had punched through them. Kotohime stood in the center of this devastation with what could almost be deemed rapture. Nodding several times to herself, she turned about and strolled over to the teens calmly, placidly, as if she hadn't just destroyed an entire infantry company and several military vehicles with a single attack.

Kevin felt a cold sweat break out on his forehead.

Note to self: never get on this woman's bad side.

"Well," she said, her pleasant demeanor greatly disturbing Kevin, "shall we head home now?"

Kevin couldn't find his voice to respond, so Lilian took the liberty of speaking for the both of them. "That sounds like a fantastic idea."

Kotohime clapped her hands together. "Excellent. However, before that..." She stuck two fingers into her mouth and whistled. Three figures walked out from behind a building and over to their decimated part of the parking lot. Kevin and Lilian recognized them immediately.

"Lindsay! Christine! Eric!" Kevin and Lilian said at the same time, their faces wearing identical expressions of shock.

"H-hey, Kevin. What's up?" Lindsay gave them an unsure wave, keeping her distance from the katana-wielding femme. Kevin couldn't blame her.

"Tit Maiden!" Eric charged the epically proportioned fox-girl. "I am so pleased to see you're unharmed! Now you can let me stick my face between those—FFUUUGYYAAA!"

Everyone stared in shock as Eric crumpled to the ground, clutching his balls. They warily eyed the foot which had struck the young pervert, and then followed the appendage to the person it was attached to.

"What?" Kevin couldn't quite hide his blush. "He wanted to grope Lilian."

Lilian smiled at her mate. "Thank you, Kevin."

The redness on Kevin's cheeks spread across his face. He couldn't help it. That smile was just too cute.

"Ah, um, you're welcome."

"I found these three following Lilian-sama," Kotohime began, gesturing to the sheepish trio, though Christine seemed more upset than anything. Eric just groaned. "It appears that Lindsay saw you transforming into your hybrid state." The elder kitsune gave her charge a reproachful glance. "You really must be more cautious, Lilian-sama."

"I couldn't help it," Lilian mumbled, her cheeks red. "I was angry. They took Kevin from me."

Kevin tightened his arm around the redhead's waist, causing her to glance at him. The world around them vanished as they stared into each other's eyes, those windows through which all emotions became visible. Within each other's gaze, they found everything they needed. It was—

"Oh, for fuck's sake! Stop making googly eyes at each other!"

Lilian scowled, her ire turning on Christine.

"How about you just keep that tsun-tsun trap of yours shut?! You're ruining the moment!"

"There's nothing to ruin! The only thing I see is a whorish little fox who thinks stripping someone with her eyes is romantic!"

"I was not stripping Kevin with my eyes! You're just jealous!"

"J-J-Jea—shut up! Shut up, shut up, shut up! Why would I be jealous of you, boob head?"

Kevin sighed and firmly planted a hand into his face. Why did this crap always happen when he was around?

"Don't hate me just because I have bigger boobs than you, teensy tits!"

"Shut up, thunderjugs!"

"Ant bites!"

"Udder woman!"

"Bitty bumps!"

While Kevin watched the two yōkai argue, Lindsay saddled up to him.

"Rough night, huh?"

"Yeah..." Kevin turned away from the arguing supernatural creatures to look at his longtime friend with curiosity. "So, how did you and Eric get involved in all this?"

"Franken jugs!"

"Cherry bombs!"

"It's a really long story," the tomboy sighed.

Kevin eyed Lindsay before slowly nodding in understanding. "I'll take your word for it."

"Mumbo Jumbos!"

"Mini lumps!"

"Are they going to stop anytime soon?" she asked, eying Christine and Lilian warily.

"God, I hope so."

"Ufufufu..."

"Oh, for all that is good and holy! Would you stop laughing like that?!"

Chapter 12

Returned Feelings

An awkward tension hung in the air between the five youngsters, although Kevin felt that term was something of an euphemism, seeing how Lilian was actually over 100 years old. Still, by kitsune standards, she was quite young, so Kevin felt the term applied just fine.

"So…" Kevin decided to address the large pink elephant stomping alongside them. "How did you three get mixed up in all this?"

Christine, Eric and Lindsay all shared a look. For once, Eric did not look at Christine with lustful intentions. Kevin didn't have time to be surprised, as the trio of high schoolers launched into a brief summary of the events that led to them ending up under Kotohime's tender mercy.

By the end of the whole story, Kevin could only sigh and palm his face with his free hand. "Really, Lindsay… I can't believe you would do something like that…"

Lindsay frowned. "What's that supposed to mean? Are you saying that I should have ignored the fact that Lilian had extra appendages humans aren't supposed to have?"

"Yes," Kevin's answer was swift and sure. "Yes, you should have. It would have been much easier on you and Eric had you never found out about Lilian's and Christine's secret. It's illegal for humans to know about the existence of yōkai, and humans that do discover it are often dealt with, usually by having their memories erased."

Lindsay and Eric paled.

"Speaking of," Lilian turned to her maid-slash-bodyguard, "just why haven't their memories been erased?"

Kotohime didn't hesitate to answer. "Because neither myself nor Lilian-sama have any skill at erasing memories. I am a combat-oriented kitsune. All my techniques are related to killing people. Erasing memories is a very subtle art that requires a finesse which I lack. And Lilian-sama is, of course, too young and not skilled enough at controlling her youki to learn such a technique."

"Muu, do have to put it like that?" Lilian, still leaning against Kevin for support, pouted at her bodyguard. "You make it sound like I don't have any talent."

"I never said that. Among all the kitsune Lilian-sama's age, Lilian-sama is definitely one of the most talented that I have seen. However, Lilian-sama is still young and lacks the control for many of the finer kitsune illusions and enchantments. Erasing memories requires at least three tails' worth of power, and the control that can only come with age."

"Hey, speaking of age, just how old are you two—GUAG!"

Everyone watched mutely as two tails, one red and one black, pounded Eric into the ground with enough force to leave a small indent on the pavement in the shape of his body.

"Ufufufu, don't you know that you should never ask a woman her age?"

"Gu... right... my bad..."

***

"Hey. You remember those people you ordered me to monitor? You were right, it seems. They went against orders to simply watch the yōkai attending Desert Cactus High School and tried capturing one. It's caused quite the mess. I imagine the news will be reporting about numerous unexplained explosions and chaos tomorrow."

"..."

"Oh? So you're going to dispatch people to get rid of the evidence. Good to know, though you may want them to get here soon. Otherwise, it'll be too late."

"..."

"No. They went after your son, not the yuki-onna."

"..."

"Yes. They were using him as bait to lure a kitsune into a trap. You'll remember from my previous report that she's been living with Kevin Swift since sometime in August. Unfortunately for them, I don't think they anticipated such heavy resistance. That four-tails was really something. She gave them a major thrashing, though I don't think she killed anyone outright. Probably didn't want her charge to witness such violence. And speaking of resistance, I take it those who made the order to capture the kitsune on your end have been dealt with?"

"…"

"All right. All right. I won't ask anymore questions about that. I know when something is outside of my jurisdiction." A pause. "Though I do have another question, and not about the group who decided to go against orders." Another pause. "I was just wondering if you wanted me to do anything about the kitsune. She's become awfully close to your son, you know."

"…"

"What a cold father you are. No wonder you left them. You're really not the sentimental type, are you?"

"…"

"Yes. Yes. Your dedication toward keeping the world safe from the yōkai menace is very admirable. I was simply saying that it's awfully frigid for a father not to be concerned for the safety of his son, especially when that son has become involved with one of the very yōkai he's claiming to protect the world from."

"…"

"No son of yours, huh? Man, you really are heartless, aren't you? But whatever. It's not like I care about that. I'll do as you ordered and keep an eye on the kitsune and her bodyguard for you. I doubt I could take that swordswoman on anyway. She managed to defeat over three dozen men without using a single kitsune technique, though she did use a wicked sword technique."

"…"

"Don't worry. I won't reveal myself to anyone. I've been doing this for nearly two years and haven't been caught yet, have I?"

"…"

"I know. All right. Out."

Dark eyes hidden under a curtain of equally dark hair stared at the cellphone in his hand. With a smile, he put the cellphone on its charging station.

Some very interesting things had been happening lately, and given how things were playing out, it was guaranteed that life would become even more interesting soon enough.

"Kevin Swift and Lilian Pnéyma. I wonder what will become of you two in the future?"

Knocking came to his door. "Justin? Justin, are you still up?"

Justin opened the door to reveal his "mother" standing on the other side. She looked nothing like him, of course, as they weren't actually related. Still, for the past two years she had been his mother, treating him just like she would her own son, and he'd played the part of son quite well, if he did say so himself.

She had been selected by the Sons and Daughters of Humanity to be his "mother" because she and her husband were unable to have kids.

Müllerian agenesi is a congenital malformation caused by a failure of the Müllerian duct to develop, which results in a missing uterus and various degrees of vagnical hypoplasia.

Justin didn't know the specifics of this disease, other than what he'd been told. He knew that women could undergo a uterus transplant to solve the problem, but that was far too expensive for an average family.

"… Wrong…?"

"No, no, nothing's wrong. I just saw that your lights were still on, and thought you'd forgotten to turn them off. I was coming up to your room when I thought I heard voices." His mom looked around the bedroom and, not seeing anyone, looked back at her son with clear worry. "You weren't talking to one of your imaginary friends again, were you?"

"No…" Justin shook his head. "… Notes…"

"I see." His mother looked relieved that her son's autism wasn't showing signs of further degradation. "Well, in either case, please be sure to turn off the lights. It's quite late, you know, and even though the school has been closed down, it's good to keep in the habit of going to bed early."

"… Kay…"

The door closed and Justin frowned. He really did like his mother, even though she only thought they were related due to a combination of brainwashing and drugs. He sometimes felt guilty about that, but guessed that was the price one paid for being a spy.

Turning off the lights, Justin crawled into bed and fell into a deep and instant sleep.

***

Lilian, Kevin and Kotohime ate a cold dinner upon their return home. It didn't taste nearly as good as it would have fresh out of the oven, but one glare from Kotohime put a clamp on any complaints they might have expressed.

"Maybe this will make you think twice about trusting a person whom you know so very little about," Kotohime said as they stared at the cold meal on the table.

Kevin would have argued, stating that, as a teacher, Inagumi should have been trustworthy, but he didn't want to be on the receiving end of her glare again.

When dinner ended, Kevin had led Lilian to the restroom so she could clean up. She'd had several twigs in her hair, dirt smudging her body, and a number of cuts that he knew didn't come from her rescue attempt. When he asked her about them, Lilian had flushed a deep shade of scarlet and mumbled something about bikes. She had then promptly changed the subject.

He had turned down her offer to shower together and walked back into the living room. That had been fifteen minutes ago.

Lilian, now clean, dry, and dressed in a large T-shirt and panties, walked into the kitchen where she found Kotohime washing the dishes.

"Kotohime."

"Something on your mind, Lilian-sama?"

"Yes, there is, actually. I know that your intentions were good, and I'm grateful that you're willing to go so far for me." Lilian paused, her expression growing dark. "However, the next time you manipulate my mate, you and I are going to have problems."

Kotohime finished drying the pot she'd used to make miso in and turned to Lilian. She smiled demurely at the younger kitsune.

"Why, whatever do you mean, Lilian-sama? Surely you are not suggesting that I manipulated Kevin-san into growing a spine and confessing his feelings for you by purposely goading him with rude and spiteful comments?" Her eyes glittered with mischief as she raised her left hand, masking her smile behind the sleeve of her kimono. "What could possibly make you think I would do such a thing?"

Lilian's snort was very unladylike. "Right. I'm sure you have no knowledge of what I'm talking about. Regardless, don't do it again. My mate is off-limits from any sort of manipulation. I refuse to manipulate him like that, so I won't let others play with his emotions either."

"Very well," Kotohime bowed in acknowledgment. "However, I do not believe Lilian-sama will need to worry about this humble maid or anyone else manipulating him anymore. Now then," she smiled benevolently at the twin-tailed beauty, "why don't you go see to your mate? He has been moping around on that balcony ever since you entered the shower."

"You know what? I think I'll do just that."

Lilian left Kotohime to continue her cleaning, traversing the living room to join Kevin outside.

She paused upon reaching the balcony to study the boy she loved. He had his back to her and was looking up at the night sky. She couldn't see his face, but she could imagine the way his brows were furrowed in contemplation.

"There you are," Lilian said as she closed the sliding door behind her. Kevin turned his head and her lips curled into a small "u" as she walked up to him. "The shower is available if you would like to take one. After everything you've been through, I'm sure a nice hot shower will help."

"Yeah…"

When Kevin went back to staring at the stars, Lilian frowned. "What's wrong?"

The blond teen sighed and ran a hand through his hair. "Nothing… I'm just… I've got a lot on my mind, I guess."

"Like what?"

"A lot of things." Kevin's eyes appeared vacant, staring at something only he could see. "So much has happened to me… it's kind of hard to believe that it hasn't even been two months since I met you and discovered that yōkai are real. I'm feeling kind of overwhelmed."

"I see." Lilian studied his pursed lips and conflicted eyes. "There's something else on your mind, though."

Kevin scratched the back of his neck and looked sheepish. "Am I that easy to read?"

Lilian's smile was that of a woman keeping a secret. "It's not that you're easy to read. It's just that I know you so well I can tell when something's bothering you." She grabbed his hand and was pleased when he didn't pull away. "Come on, tell me. What's on your mind?"

"Last week, before Kotohime arrived, you mentioned meeting a little boy near your home." Lilian stiffened when his blue eyes gazed into hers. "That boy... it was me, wasn't it?"

"How did you...?"

"It wasn't that hard to figure out." Kevin's smile was soft and gentle and contained just a hint of wryness. "It was nine years ago, right?"

"Y-yes..."

"Nine years ago my mom had just gotten her first big gig, which took her to Greece. She couldn't find a babysitter on such short notice and brought me along. The resort we went to was on a small island in the Pagasetic Gulf. Despite that being the first time I've traveled outside of the US, I can barely remember anything that happened. I know I was young, but I wasn't that young. You'd think something that exciting would have been more memorable."

Kevin's eyes were sharper than she'd ever seen them. Focused and cunning, they kept her rooted to the spot, freezing her where she stood. It was actually kind of hot.

"It didn't occur to me that the reason I don't remember what happened back then was because my memory had been erased. Humans aren't allowed to know about yōkai. It would only make sense for my memories to be erased if I, let's say, wandered past a barrier and ran into a kitsune crying in the forest, right?"

"Y-yes. That is correct." An uncomfortable chill ran down Lilian's spine now that Kevin was aware of the transgressions committed by her clan. "Kevin, listen, I am so—"

"Please don't apologize." Surprising Lilian, and perhaps even himself, Kevin placed a finger against her lips. He blushed a bit, but quickly hurried on before it could overcome his face. "I'm not upset, not with you at least. You never wished for my memories to be erased, and I doubt you were pleased when you found out."

She shook her head, emphasizing that she wasn't.

"See? Not your fault." He took his finger away, his gaze shifting to an inquiring one. "I do have one question, though. How did you know I lived in Arizona?"

"I didn't," Lilian admitted, smiling when he became nonplussed. "I had no idea that you lived here. I just... when I ran away from home, I didn't really care where I went. I just wanted to get as far away from my family's sphere of influence as possible. I had no idea I would run into you, or that you lived in Arizona. However..."

Lilian paused and brought Kevin's right hand up to her face, gently pressing his palm against her cheek. His hands were calloused and slightly rough, but she loved the way it felt against her skin. She loved its warmth and texture. This hand belonged to her mate.

"... I am very glad that we did meet again. When I first saw you, I'll admit that I was a little wary. It had been so long that I didn't know it was you. But, the moment you began to scratch behind my ears, I knew who you were. You won't remember this, but back when we first met, you had a strong fascination with my ears."

"I did?"

"Mmhmm. You were intent on touching them as much as possible. And my tails. You liked those as well."

"Huh, I didn't know that." Kevin raised an eyebrow. "I wonder if that's where my love of animals came from."

Lilian shrugged. "Maybe."

They stood in silence. Kevin slowly ran his thumb over her cheek, savoring the sensation of silk underneath his skin. Lilian almost moaned at the sensation. Although his actions held no sexual connotations, the tender intimacy of his touch was positively electric, like a gentle current pulsing through her body, leaving a pleasant tingle in its wake.

Before she could lose herself in his touch, Lilian forcefully broke the trance she'd nearly been placed in. There was something she had to know.

"Kevin, back when we were surrounded, did you really mean what you said? That you'll let me stay with you no matter what?"

Kevin flushed a bit, but still answered her. "I... Yes, I meant that. For as long as you want me to stay with you, I'll remain by your side." He scratched his left cheek with his free hand. "I don't really know what you see in me, but I suppose that, in the end, all that matters is that you see something and I..."

"Yes?"

"Well I... I think I might..."

Lilian watched as Kevin's face became luminescent.

"You think you might what?"

"It's... hard to explain. These feelings, I mean." Kevin gulped, his mouth strangely dry. "What I mean is, when I'm with you, I feel... feel..."

"Like you can take on the world?" When Kevin just stared at her in surprise, Lilian allowed herself to feel a tiny ray of hope. "Like nothing else matters so long as you're with me? Like all of your problems just vanish as if they had never existed?"

"Yes..." Kevin whispered, his eyes wide. "How did you..."

Lilian's lips curved upwards as she rested her arms on his shoulders. "I know because that is exactly how I feel every time I am with you."

Moments later, she and Kevin were kissing. Lilian didn't know who made the first move. It could have been her, but she liked to think it was Kevin. It didn't matter in the end. All she cared about was the rising tide of joy that threatened to overwhelm her, the contentment in her heart, and the sweet, blessed relief surging through her soul.

Lilian's body relaxed into Kevin's. He kissed her tentatively, shyly, more of an ephemeral caress than an actual kiss. She waited, patiently, and was soon rewarded when the blond teen became bolder.

A pair of sinuous arms wrapped around her body, pulling her close. Lilian responded to this desire for closeness eagerly, her arms around his neck tightening, her body leaning further into his. She wanted as much physical contact as possible. She didn't want even a sheet of paper to be capable of traveling between their bodies.

When they broke apart, both were breathing heavily, their faces flushed and a mild sheen of sweat glistening in the moonlight.

"Oh... um, wow," Kevin looked a little dazed. Lilian giggled, feeling giddy. "That was... that was..."

"Amazing? Incredible? Awesome?"

"All three."

They smiled at each other, mirror images of satisfaction and happiness.

"So... can I kiss you again?"

Lilian gave Kevin a surprisingly flat look. "Are you really asking me that?"

The bright red blush that lit Kevin's face made her smile. She raised a hand to his head, threading her fingers through his hair before pulling him down until their foreheads were touching.

Brilliant emerald met bright azure.

"Of course you can," she whispered, right before kissing him again.

And while they shared in their second kiss, which soon led to a third and then a fourth, Lilian felt all of her worry, anxiety, and fears slowly fade away. All that remained was a sense of pure, unadulterated joy.

Nothing could possibly ruin this moment.

Because Lilian finally had her mate.

***

Kotohime giggled to herself.

It was late at night—well, early in the morning, but still dark outside. Kevin and Lilian were fast asleep, and everything had finally fallen into place.

She had to admit, Kevin had really surprised her. While she had been expecting him to eventually accept Lilian's love and become her mate, the manner in which he had done so truly astounded her. That speech of his had been quite inspiring—corny and completely ripping off a certain anime of pure epicness, but still inspiring.

Kotohime wandered out onto the balcony, sliding the door closed behind her. She took several delicate feminine steps until she stood in front of the guardrail.

She gazed out at the landscape, admiring the velvety sky and stars overhead. The moment ended soon, though, as Kotohime gathered her youki and channeled them through her tails.

A small being coalesced into existence. It's pearly, elongated body hovered in the air, wraith-like and ethereal. It bobbed up and down on an unseen current, staring at the one who summoned it.

"Kudagitsune."

A minor fox-spirit with a long pipe-like body, these small supernal creatures acted as familiars for kitsune. While they were lacking in power, they were blessed with an ethereal form that allowed them to remain invisible to anyone but those they wished to become visible to.

"I would like you to deliver a message to Camellia-sama."

The fox familiar's tail slowly wrapped around the scroll produced from within Kotohime's voluminous sleeve. Upon being touched it, too, became ethereal like the kudagitsune.

The creature made to fly off, but before it could get too far, Kotohime remembered something. "Be sure to take your time. There are some things I must accomplish before Camellia-sama and Iris-sama come here for a visit. I believe a few weeks should be enough time."

The creature paused as if considering the request, and then bobbed in understanding, before floating away at a much slower pace than before.

Kotohime smiled as she walked back inside.

As she knelt down on the floor and closed her eyes to get some rest, she couldn't help but have one last thought.

I wonder how Iris-sama will feel about her sister having a mate?

Lying on his bed, with Lilian snuggled into his side, Kevin Swift shuddered in his sleep.

ABOUT THE AUTHOR

Brandon Varnell is a writer... the end.

... Just kidding.

Brandon Varnell is the writer of the American Kitsune series. He has absolutely no skill at anything aside from writing and looking half-baked. He used to play guitar, but due to laziness, he never went anywhere with it. He also used to play a lot of video games, but after suffering this terrible affliction called book addiction, he only plays occasionally these days. Brandon lives mostly within his own imagination, but he can occasionally be found in Phoenix, Arizona.

CPSIA information can be obtained
at www.ICGtesting.com
Printed in the USA
LVOW10s1926281117

557886LV00013B/1161/P